Divine Names

A novel by
Luay Abdul-Ilah

Translated by Judy Cumberbatch

Mira Publishing House CIC.
481a Otley Rd. Leeds LS16 7NR - GB
www.MiraPublishing.com

Divine Names
By: Luay Abdul-Ilah
ISBN: 978-1-908509-11-6
First published in Great Britain 2016 by Mira Publishing House CIC.
Printed and bound by Clays.co.uk

Mira Intelligent Read
www.MiraIntelligentRead.com

Contents

In memory of Layla Shamash

Introduction

Muhyiddin Ibn Arabi has a theory about possibilities. He believes that, before the world was created, its elements existed as latent possible things in the complete darkness, where they were separated from the Essence by the barzakh or isthmus of the Divine Names. In that eternal inertia, the Possibilities of Existing longed to be free of the darkness of non-being and to clothe themselves in the attributes of existence. The Divine Names, for their part, yearned to see their specific influences realised in the Possibilities of Existing.

The Great Master gives us an allegorical account of an encounter between the Divine Names and the Possible Things, and the discussions which took place between the active names about the first act of creation. But before I recount that tale, let me tell you about a story which came to me while I was busy reading the Master's famous book The Meccan Illuminations. I ignored it for ages, but its details went on multiplying, and demanded to be made visible in the same way as the Possibilities of Existing demanded to cross over from non-existence to necessary existence.

Part One
Coloured Buttons I

Whenever Abdel drove across Regent's Park, he was assailed by an indefinable sense of longing, a feeling of disquiet, which made his chest tighten slightly, as he breathed; perhaps I would be exaggerating if I said that the image, which immediately formed in his mind was that of a lapdog accompanied by a plump woman, wearing a summer dress, hanging down neatly below her knees, with a straw hat on her head, tilted slightly to the left; from afar, she resembled a painting of Renoir's as she walked beside the pond, her head held slightly aloft, as she bestowed her smiles on passers-by who admired her pretty dog.

Abdel had been taken aback when he first saw her, amazed by the blonde hair which draped her neck, the natural straw-coloured dress with the Japanese pattern embroidered along its hem, the purple painted toe nails peeping through her white summer sandals and last but not least the gold chain, looped round the neck of a dog which ran persistently along behind her in its effort to keep up with its elegant mistress.

Before he left the park that day, he had had a sudden fancy to go to the open air café and it was there that he had first come across Joanna in all her beauty. She was sitting on her own at a rain splashed table on which she had placed her glass of juice; Pip sat beside her, half asleep. From time to time, rays of sunlight slipped shyly through the white clouds. Abdel did not have to do much beyond making his way to her table and asking: "May I sit down?" to which she had replied "Of course."

Whenever Abdel thought of his father, the image that always came to his mind was of a face that sneered and frowned at him, simultaneously. Maybe it was his feelings of frustration at his first born son that made him look like that or rather the feelings he had subsequently transferred to the mother whom he held genetically responsible for the seeds of his son's corruption. After all, hadn't her uncle spent five years in prison for having embezzled money from the state?

Abdel was unable to remember the incident which had so set his father against him, although it had been mentioned in his hearing hundreds of times, and was frequently recounted by older members of the family either as a joke or as evidence of the brutal judgment against him.

Abdel was not yet five years old when the incident occurred. At the time, his full name was Abdel Wahhab (Servant of the Giving). His father had only chosen the name after having recourse to the Holy Qur'an; on opening the book, his eye had fallen on the Divine Name: 'al-Wahhab'

Some of his father's friends, who would visit the house, began to complain that they were missing buttons from their jackets, after they had taken them off before going into the salon. The truth only emerged by chance, when Abdel's father who was searching for his spectacles, which he thought one of his children had hidden in a drawer, opened a disused box that Abdel was seen occasionally holding, and came across a handful of coloured buttons. Overcome by a totally unjustifiable mixture of fury and intense shame, he asked his son why he had stolen them; Abdel replied truthfully in that endearing childish way of his: "To sell them."

What would Abdel's fate have been if his father had treated him with a touch of levity instead? Or had spotted the latent powers in his son, which this innocent theft revealed? However, he exploded with fury; venting his anger at Abdel's mother and pouring forth a stream of fiery words, he swore to change his son's name and to call him 'Abdel Nahāb', Servant of the Looter, the very opposite of Servant of the Giving.

When he calmed down the following morning, his father recognised that he had made a mistake, in taking that oath so precipitously. Wouldn't his action completely ruin his son's future and make him a laughing stock for ever more? But an oath was an oath. Many of his relatives intervened and tried to stop him carrying out the oath but to no avail, though he did finally agree to seek guidance from the imam of the local mosque, following a tearful entreaty by his wife, and a solution was found that satisfied everyone: namely that he would continue to call his son by the first part of his name but in his heart add any name he wished after Abdel.

* * *

Abdel soon put his reservations about Joanna aside, when he heard her speaking. Her voice was loud and childishly effusive and she said whatever came into her mind. No sooner had Abdel said something admiring about her dog than she plunged headlong into a description of Pip's good manners as if he were some kind of wunderkind rather than a dog. She told Abdel about the tricks Pip played on her to get her to let him stay on her bed each night and the extraordinary way he was able to distinguish between her friends. For a long time, Joanna had relied on her dog's discerning nature when it came to deciding whether to welcome or turn away strangers. Pip obviously liked Abdel, and his continuously and happily wagging tail emboldened his mistress to be friendlier than he had expected.

It would not be an exaggeration to say that Abdel decided to marry Joanna at that very first meeting since he glimpsed a profound sense of loneliness in her despite the many stories she told him about her numerous friends, for her lack of what may be called social skills made her an object of pity or derision to those around her. In a country such as England, someone who acts in an unrestrained manner is ultimately regarded as crazy and described as 'eccentric'. I wouldn't be surprised if Joanna was labelled in such a way even by those people whom she considered to be her closest friends.

At that first meeting, Abdel found out a lot about Joanna. He learnt about her childhood, her work, her family and her hobbies. He didn't have to do much except appear to pay attention. She took out a slim notebook from her pocket and opened it very carefully: "Look… This is Sean Connery's signature and this is Ringo Starr's… Can you believe that I saw them close up…? Don't you think I'm very lucky? Imagine… The original James Bond saying thank you to me."

* * *

When I examine Abdel and Joanna's faces, I am reminded of a famous saying by Sophocles. "Personality is fate." The only thing I might add is that fate is preceded by an incident. In the case of Abdel, it was the theft of some clothes buttons when he was still a young child, which he thought would make his father happy. When it came to Joanna, it was a different matter altogether. It had taken a number of years for Joanna's mother to realise that her daughter was going deaf. She had to be sent to Switzerland where she was placed in a private boarding school high up in the Alps. As the doctor had predicted, the high altitude had allowed Joanna to regain her hearing and she had returned to London three years later. It should be said that she learned a number of skills in the Alps which enabled her to find a job in one of the smarter nurseries: a little French, a knowledge of drawing and the ability to play the piano in a manner suited to children's demands. The only thing which she had missed out on as a result of the delay in diagnosing her disability was an ability to integrate into the world around her, since she had failed to acquire the social codes which exist in every society and which define the means whereby its members communicate with each other automatically. Perhaps this failure of hers to integrate socially communicated itself unconsciously to her moods. These swung between manic high spirits and acute depression. She would lock herself away in her room for days on end, and then pursue other people over-enthusiastically in a manner, which was incompatible with the spirit of reserve and refinement that distinguishes members of the English middle class.

Joanna was unable to determine the nature and interests of the person she was talking to when she struck up a conversation with them. Everyone seemed to resemble everyone else and she was unable to differentiate between them. She was swept along, alternating between tears and hysterical laughter and moving from one subject to another and one emotion to another with the same fervour and intensity.

Perhaps she found something out of the ordinary in Abdel's attentiveness and the way he listened and asked questions which seemed to reveal his interest in her stories; this allowed her to regain a large measure of self-confidence. For the first time, Joanna felt herself to have an importance outside her role at work. She spent hours talking to Abdel about the toddlers in her charge and their singular abilities as well as the more troublesome among the parents who were forever demanding that their children be taught to read and write even though they were less than three years old.

* * *

Abdel's first meeting with Joanna had taken place two days before his visa was due to expire. However, he decided to remain illegally in Britain, though at the same time, was careful to avoid communicating his sense of unease to her. Despite his success in attracting her attention, he failed to ring her.

He did not have long to wait. Two days after their last meeting, she was on the phone, her voice brimming over with childish joy. He invited her to a restaurant on the Thames where they played live jazz. It was a truly enchanting atmosphere suited to the dreamy mood which often enveloped Joanna. Buoyed up by two glasses of red wine, she ran nimbly onto the dance floor; as Abdel ran his fingers over her hips, he touched places, which had remained neglected by

12

men for reasons that had nothing to do with the real enjoyment of the senses; after a quiet interlude, the band struck up the samba and his companion threw herself into the music, somewhat losing her self-control. As Joanna danced unrestrainedly in the middle of the floor, the other dancers withdrew one by one, frightened perhaps of bumping into her and stood still gazing at her, with expressions of pity and mockery etched on their faces. Sweat poured down her face, making the different colours of her make up run into each other; Abdel ignored the people around and instead concentrated on making her feel, as if there were just the two of them in the dimly lit dance hall and that the band was playing just for them. As they walked along the path which ran beside the river, Joanna had whispered, choking over the words: "What do you think about finishing the evening off at my place?"

* * *

From his early years, Abdel had possessed two attributes which not only marked him out from his brothers but from the rest of his relatives as well: first was his ability to plan ahead and in secret to achieve his goals and secondly was his ability to make money. As his father would leave nothing after his death but a tiny pension and the house he had inherited from his forefathers, Abdel had started hoarding money when he was ten years old. The first thing he did, when he was no longer a child, was put all his toys in a basket and lay them out for sale near the mosque. This initiative caused his father a great deal of anguish since he had no respect for any form of work outside the civil service; however as time passed, he became convinced that his first born son was a penance from on high, visited upon him as a result of crimes committed by one or other of his ancestors. Perhaps it was this conviction that made him willing to accept the strange devilish deeds that were connected with Abdel. Was not the incident of the coloured buttons a clear message from the Invisible One about the way his son would eventually turn out? However, his father secretly believed that changing the name of his son had had an effect on his character as well. Hadn't he been the one who had insisted on carrying out his vow for fear of incurring the wrath of God, and at the same time, the one who had repudiated the Lord's gift which had allowed his son to be named Abdel-Wahhab, after the divine name, "al-Wahhab"?

*   *   *

This early discovery that he had the power to transform things into money made Abdel feel that he was profoundly different from other people; he was only really happy during the short periods he was able to steal away from his family, and secretly finger the notes that were stuffed into a cardboard box that was hidden away in a permanently locked drawer.

Shortly after he had sold his toys, the summer holidays arrived and instead of throwing himself into games with other young boys in the neighbourhood, Abdel told his father that he wished to work for their neighbour who was a carpenter. The man welcomed the father's request especially as he would not have to pay his friend's son any money, on the condition that Abdel work for a week on a trial basis. At the end of the week, the carpenter told his father that he was very satisfied with Abdel's work. In fact he commented on his remarkable ability to learn quickly. "Your son is talented… If only my sons had a quarter of his ability…"

Abdel's sudden wish to learn about carpentry was prompted by a desire for cheap table tennis bats among some of his fellow pupils. Immediately the new school year began, Abdel made a neat bundle of bats out of scraps of timber the carpenter had discarded and then varnished them. But the students wanted other things as well and he was soon urging them to buy boxes, amplifiers, and little tables.

Even at an early age, it was not difficult to glimpse the strong will that lay concealed inside Abdel's slight frame; the hard work to which he had devoted himself up till then, had given him a strength and resilience when he reached adolescence, which many of his fellow pupils envied. The bad names they gave him, such as Abdel Shaitan (Servant of the Devil) and Abdel-Mal (Servant of Money), which stuck to him for a long time afterwards, were probably prompted by jealousy. However Abdel was not particularly bothered by this since he remained fixated on thinking up new ways of making money for himself. Besides, he felt superior to his fellow pupils and deep down despised them: weren't they the ones who were paying him, rather than the other way round? It was as if superiority and distinction were determined by the direction in which the money moved.

Once, his mother had complained about the way Abdel was exploiting his younger brothers: she told her husband he was forcing them to work all hours of the day, sanding down pieces of wood, in exchange for a small piece of cake. Despite receiving a harsh scolding from his father, he did not retreat from his position: "I am teaching them a craft," he argued. "It's better than wasting their time doing something useless."

*　*　*

I very much doubt that the feelings which crept into Abdel's heart as he passed by Regent's Park were truly loving, particularly as Joanna still lived nearby with little change to the pattern of her life. Despite the break-up which had occurred after the divorce, she would certainly have been happy to see Abdel if he had surprised her with a phone call and invited her out to a café. For his part however, he would have taken to his heels immediately if she had suddenly appeared in front of him. It would be truer to say that the sense of attachment he felt at such times arose out of the sparkle which he still associated with certain moments of his life with Joanna, in particular, the instance of their first meeting which had been so magical. It was as if he were trying to hold on to the picture of the past which still lived on in his memory, by avoiding her.

Or maybe this sense of yearning was occasioned by a feeling of regret: regret that he hadn't stayed with her longer. From time to time, he thought back to the first night he had spent with Joanna after returning from the jazz restaurant. When they arrived at her house, an odd silence had fallen between them. She had contented herself with lighting candles and putting on a record of Chopin's Nocturnes as soothing but distant background music. Joanna was drenched in quietness, shot through with a transparent sadness which was in marked contrast to the hysterical abandonment that had filled her in the restaurant.

His breathing quickened now when he recalled Joanna's bedroom with its purple walls and dark red velvet curtains. He had laid the palm of his hand over her large right breast and a current of electricity had coursed through her body, making her tremble involuntarily. Her hands moved blindly over his hair and face and ears. Joanna's eyes were closed, her lips slightly parted in a daft smile, which made him frightened to go on, but the pull of her strong arms made it impossible for him to draw away. Abdel saw himself reflected in the long mirror on the wardrobe, his body flailing like a weak fish caught in the tentacles of a giant octopus. Joanna was laughing hysterically and sobbing loudly at one and the same time, torn between depression and self-absorption. When Abdel was close to penetration, her rounded legs began to push him away from her but just as he drew away, they brought him back and he felt himself suffocating. In the mirror, Abdel caught a fleeting glimpse of her legs intertwined determinedly around his back, and then a wave of desire took hold of him, and drove him into her embrace.

At dawn, the twittering of birds mingling with the mournful music of a piano brought him slowly to his senses. In the sitting room, he saw Joanna sitting at the piano playing Rachmaninov's Second Concerto which she knew off by heart. He sat down slowly on a seat near the window and watched her in amazement. She appeared to have nothing in common with the woman he had spent the previous evening with. She must have woken up early. She had managed to have a bath and comb her hair into a single plait before he awoke. Pip, the dog, was sitting on a chair excitedly following his mistress's playing. When she finished, he bounded up at her enthusiastically.

* * *

The captivating scene, which Abdel witnessed that morning, did not in fact leave much of an impression on him beyond strengthening his belief that Joanna wanted to marry him. Maybe he was the first man to have taken her seriously as a woman and shown himself to be genuinely attracted to her.

As the memory of those minutes flashed through his mind now, he started to think about the other step he had to take. But then he remembered what Joanna had said to him before they made love for the first time. Speaking with the vehemence of a child, she had told him how she loved to play the piano before sunset and how the passers-by would slow down when they walked by the window so as to catch a glimpse of this princess immersed in the strains of the Rachmaninov Concerto. It was rather as if they were watching a scene from a film, lit up by candlelight.

Perhaps the profound sense of loneliness, which Joanna was unable to put into words, lay behind the feverish struggle to perform which governed all her actions. Without her realising it, this unconscious behaviour of hers made the people who knew her more likely to reject her than give her the acceptance she longed for.

While her mother was still alive, Joanna had regarded herself as something of a phenomenon; she was a child after all, who had successfully overcome her deafness and all she had to do to regain her sense of wonder at herself was look into her mother's eyes. Inevitably, living with her mother had deepened her spirit of childish recalcitrance and sulkiness and made her certain that the situation would last forever.

Joanna first met Abdel more than five years after her mother had died, but she had changed little in the house she had inherited, except refurbish the room which looked out on to Regent's Park so that it could be rented out to a foreign student.

*   *   *

Abdel had only decided to come to London after overhearing a conversation between two friends in a café. One of the men lived in Britain. When his friend asked him what life was like over there, the traveller told him about the social security benefits you could get when you were unemployed: they pay your rent, you get a weekly wage and free healthcare, so he said.

Before leaving the café, Abdel had come to a decision. He would travel to London as soon as possible. It was as if he imagined that there was treasure lying on the streets, which anyone could pick up if they wanted; if he hesitated a minute longer, it would all be gone.

When I consider the whim that prompted Abdel to set off on his travels and the manner in which he planned for the future, I am struck by the following idea: people fall into three categories of intelligence: those who respond to the present, those who respond to the future and those, in the third category who respond to the past. It does not appear to be possible to possess more than one form of intelligence. Which category does Abdel belong to? He obviously belongs to the second category. This group of people may go through the present but only experience it as a springboard for the future. The ant with its untiring labours best illustrates this group and is closest to them. The first category is made up of many kinds of people and includes the lustful; those who are lost in the present dwell in the third category for they only possess sufficient intelligence to recognise the past. Can we put novelists in this category? Does not their profession make them gravitate towards the past in the same way as moths are drawn to the light?

Abdel's sudden decision to leave had produced a paroxysm of fury in his father and made his blood pressure rise to such a dangerous level that he was forced to remain in bed for a week. Not surprisingly, the incident of the coloured buttons reared its ugly head once more after lying dormant for a long period of time. This was even more the case as Abdel had appeared strangely obedient during the previous months, which had in turn made his father question whether he was right to feel so concerned and worried about him. How happy he had been when his young son had agreed to become engaged to Baida. It was as if he saw the marriage as a way of renewing the ties of friendship which had joined him to Baida's father since childhood. Despite the long distance that now separated them, they continued to meet at least once a year. When they were younger, they had met more frequently, spending a number of days at each other's houses during the school holidays, accompanied by their families.

Abdel's marriage to Baida would definitely provide them with the chance to see more of each other: they would finally be part of the same family, as they had pledged each other they would be when they were younger, but that blasted son of his had ruined everything at the last minute, with his decision to go away, although he insisted that he would get married to Baida when he had completed his university studies in Britain.

*　*　*

Although Abdel lived with Joanna for more than four years, he continued to think of her as green-eyed and blonde. It's true that he scarcely ever accompanied her to the beauty parlour but the way her hair shone when she came home gave the lie to the colour being natural. Nevertheless it is not possible to exclude the fact that Abdel was so self-absorbed that he was incapable of observing the changes in Joanna. In fact, he remained oblivious to the marks of age which were clearly visible on her face each morning, once her make-up had been removed, and he seemed unsurprised when he was confronted by the faded reality which emerged after she had a bath and which was so different to the beautiful memory he had of her when he had first seen her.

When Abdel thought of her now, it was as a Jayne Mansfield look-alike, and his heart lightened whenever he passed

Regent's Park. It was as if he had wiped his memory clean of all the times he had spent listening to her droning on about her problems at work or the times when night fell and he had to drink half a bottle of whisky before going to bed and forcing himself to have sex with her. Pip had frequently come to his rescue; how often had he escaped her clinginess by offering to take the dog out to the park!

When his British passport arrived in the post, Abdel didn't tell Joanna. Instead, that night he went to a night club in Soho with a prostitute and for the first time in his life, perhaps, spent his money lavishly and did not keep a tight hold on the purse strings.

On his way home, his plan to rid himself of Joanna took clear shape in his mind.

* * *

Once the divorce came through, Abdel barely hesitated before deciding to go ahead with his marriage to Baida. One of the reasons behind his decision was a deeply rooted subconscious wish to prove his father wrong in the negative idea he had of him. Aligned with this was the soporific effect the image of Baida induced in his limbs whenever he pictured her. Despite the lack of any physical contact between them, the thought of her aroused an intense feeling of possessiveness in him, brought on maybe by the memory of her extreme shyness, her slim bearing, or her dimples which reminded him of a rosy apple. He had conjured up pictures of Baida in the tedious moments he spent with Joanna, substituting her face for that of his wife as he got ready to climax in the dark while Joanna screamed out hysterically.

The wedding in Baghdad did not take long. Abdel expected to make up for the physical pleasure he had missed out on after they arrived in London. There, far away from her family, he would initiate Baida into the secrets of sex that he had learnt from Joanna and rather than remaining close would give his body the freedom to squeeze every drop of pleasure out of her succulent young body. The exorbitant price he would pay for enrolling her in a language school would be recouped in full by the pleasures he exacted from her in their daily love making. Before he left for Baghdad, Abdel had made a careful study of the way in which he should bring Baida to London to make it look as if their marriage was the fruit of a normal friendship, which they had formed after she had come to study there.

* * *

When they went to the town hall for the marriage ceremony, they took Scheherazade and Saleh as witnesses. Baida was newly pregnant, and had been forced to plaster makeup on her face to hide her pallor from her cousin. On the way to the town hall, she was stirred by a strange sense of nostalgia brought on by the British autumn, and began to cry silently; when Abdel turned to find out what the matter was, she choked back her tears, wiping them away with the hem of her blouse. She gestured towards a tree wrapped about with radiant colours and said with a laugh: "It looks like a bride."

By holding a second wedding in London, Abdel hoped

to remove any suspicions about his previous schemes and make it easier to obtain a permanent residence permit for Baida in Britain. Anyhow, in the months leading up to the visit to the town hall, Abdel had persuaded himself that they were friends who were living together without being married. This fantasy certainly enhanced his appetite for Baida, though she would doubtless have been paralysed if she had read what was going through his mind for she did everything to obey his whims out of a conviction that she was playing the role of an exemplary wife.

Abdel noticed that Baida washed her hands repeatedly each time they met Scheherazade and Saleh, but when he asked her to explain, she denied that she was doing such a thing. When she arrived in London, Baida had been very keen to meet up with her cousin. When they first visited her home, they were immensely impressed by the décor and paintings on the wall. Baida was particularly affected. Until then, she had only ever come into contact with the furniture in the family home or in the houses of friends. She felt she was in a museum and had to be careful how she moved around. In the light of such feelings, her cousin appeared to have nothing in common with the young joyous girl, who had left Iraq two decades before. Scheherazade told her: "My husband chose the furniture... He was an artist." When she saw the curious look in Baida's eyes, she added: "Stephen died years ago."

On their second visit, they met Saleh. Although he didn't say much, Baida noticed that he was eager to please Scheherazade; she observed the way he helped prepare supper and later did the washing up. When it grew late, Abdel looked at the clock on the wall and asked if the others would mind if they left for home. They only had a quarter of an hour to catch the last tube, since they had all been engrossed in a noisy discussion about Iraq and the situation there. Scheherazade appeared interested in what the others were saying and wanted to hear more. She said insistently: "Why don't you stay the night here? Helen's room is empty."

Towards the end of the night, Baida was awakened by a sporadic noise which sounded like the mewing of a cat, and which was coming through the wall beside her; when she listened more closely, she made out the intermittent moaning of a woman, the sort of sound made by two bodies making love to each other. For an instant, she pictured Scheherazade and her friend, but then resolutely banished the image from her mind. Up till then, she had done no more than form the impression from Saleh's face and movements that he was a trustworthy person; when he appeared absent-minded, she had been reminded of a child who had been forcibly removed from his mother, and had felt a sense of motherliness towards him in the same way as she felt maternal towards her younger brothers.

At first Baida thought that Saleh had come to Scheherazade's house to fix the heating or the electricity, but when he stayed on to supper, she thought he must be one of her patients; however when she realised that he was staying the night, she thought that perhaps he was Scheherazade's fiancé although neither of them were wearing an engagement ring. Baida felt sure that Saleh was sleeping in the sitting room and she relaxed. As Abdel snored rhythmically, sleep overcame her.

She awoke to hear voices and laughter coming from the sitting room. The hands of the alarm clock pointed to past ten o'clock. She expected to find everyone sitting at the dining table waiting for her to arrive and felt embarrassed. She hurriedly got up and went to join them. But she only found her cousin and Abdel there. Scheherazade was wearing a pair of glossy pink pyjamas and a black elasticated head band round her forehead. Baida thought that Saleh had already left the house but when she went to the bathroom, she saw him leaving Scheherazade's room.

Part Two
Taming the Clouds

It was years since Scheherazade had used her camera or looked through her photo album. When Baida first visited her in London with Abdel, she had given her a varnished wooden box with the lion of Babel engraved on the lid. "It's a present from Baba," her cousin had told her.

Inside the box there was nothing but a handful of old photographs, which her uncle had taken of her with members of the family, at various times in her childhood and adolescence. She could make out various dates, scrawled on the margins, some of which went back to the fifties. The photos that most surprised her were those that had been taken at her school. When she tried to remember who had taken them, her memory shrank even more, so that she was left with a puzzle that refused to be solved.

Without thinking what she was doing Scheherazade took the photos out and pushed them between the pages of the large album, which she then returned to its place in the wardrobe, where it lay out of sight, hidden behind piles of old documents and letters.

As well as the photos, her uncle had also sent her a small notebook whose outer leaves were made of black cardboard. She was surprised at how wide its pages were and wondered what it was doing in the wooden box with the photos. Did it contain a message from her uncle? What most perplexed her about the book was its age. The dark black cover had faded in places and turned pale grey and there was a smell about it that was both familiar and strange and which reminded her of the old yellow books in her grandfather's house. Even though the details of the past had been expunged from her mind, this smell still had the power to evoke memories. Occasionally it would rise up from some unknown part of her soul and leave her feeling slightly dizzy.

She put the book, unopened, among a pile of records on a shelf in the sitting room. She would read it another time. But in the middle of the night, she was awoken by a sense of unease and found herself moving towards it like someone in a dream. At first, she didn't understand what she was looking at. Only when she was fully awake did she realise it was an autograph book. Many of the pages had photographs of young girls stuck to them, surrounded by flowery hearts, underneath which were several lines of writing.

Her attention was drawn by one of the entries. "To my dearest friend, remember me when time tugs at your heart strings and I will remember you when I hear its echo in mine." On another page, she was confronted by a picture of a beautiful girl whose long hair fell down on either side of her round face. "May we meet in the distant future. I will remember you always."

Now and then she turned over another page, in an attempt to jog her memory, but she came up with nothing but an extraordinary emptiness. She paused at a sentence written in an elegant hand: "Memory is but a sweet sound that echoes through the vast caverns of life." At the bottom of the page, someone had written the date: 15th August 1957. Were these pictures of girls she had been at school with at the convent? Did the notebook with its gilded casing date from then? Perhaps there had been a craze for such things in

Baghdad at the time and her uncle had bought it for her as a present. Instead of chasing after celebrities (who were few in number at the time), students pursued their classmates and teachers and got them to leave mementoes of themselves in autograph books imported from England. "What is memory but a bell that rings above the darkness of oblivion…?"

Where had her classmates got those resonant phrases from? There must have been a special book which they passed round among themselves and used to embellish their style, in the belief that what they were writing would last forever.

Names and faces of friends, whose very existence she had completely forgotten until then, began to come back to her as she leafed through the pages, though she was unable to recall a single detail of her life with them.

How had her uncle got hold of it? After the coup, he must have gone to their house before it was confiscated and picked it up along with the other valuables. She had heard from her mother at the time that they were greatly indebted to her brother. Thanks to him they had recovered sufficient gold jewellery and money to enable them to stay in London until her father found a job.

The autograph book was the one thing her uncle had forgotten to send on. Now after so much water had passed under the bridge, he had remembered it.

And now it lay on the table in front of her. She started turning the pages again, pausing at a pair of smiling eyes that stared at her unwaveringly, urging her not to forget, and she was stricken by a sense of guilt at having abandoned them. She gently touched the smooth cheeks and carefully ordered hair with her finger tips, as if the sense of touch would help

31

awaken a moment from the past, which remained out of reach, though it seemed so close.

*   *   *

Scheherazade had bought Pink Floyd's latest album, Wish You Were Here the previous week, but hadn't had enough time to listen to it until now.

Years ago she had come to the conclusion that there was an essential difference between comfort and happiness. She categorised the material things she enjoyed such as her elegant home near Highgate Wood, her new car and her high salary as comforts. She reserved the word happiness for those rare occasions when she could forget her surroundings entirely and become absorbed by the moment.

She listened to the first track, Shine On You Crazy Diamond again and again. Richard, who was her closest friend among the people she had got to know through Stephen, had told her on the phone: "It's a lovely tribute to a friend."

The cosmic sound of the music lit up a scene in her memory. She was wandering along a road in Soho with Stephen. It was drizzling. The fine rain trickled down from a grey sky that seemed close enough to touch. She could hear All You Need is Love, the latest Beatles song coming from one of the pubs. Their bodies draw closer together. In the Partisan Café, they met up with a group of friends and acquaintances. There was sawdust on the floor and hanging on the wall was a notice board covered with various pieces of paper. When Stephen became involved in a conversation, she took advantage of his preoccupation and sauntered over to look at them. There were posters advertising a couple of forthcoming demonstrations, one protesting the war in Vietnam and the other calling for the legalisation of pot. On the wall above were announcements about various concerts and poetry evenings and lectures on a host of esoteric subjects, which included one, she remembered now, claiming to prove the existence of flying saucers.

"Remember when you were young, you shone like the sun. Shine on you crazy diamond.

Now there's a look in your eye, like black holes in the sky."

Attachment is a particularly feminine quality. Even when they were no longer holding hands, she was always aware of him as if an invisible bridge, like an octopus' tentacle reached out from her body to his, and joined her to him. The scent of his body overwhelmed her, and filled her with longing. With mounting passion, her eyes pursued him constantly as she watched the ever changing expression on his face while her finger tips devoured the rosy pinkness of his palm. When she closed her eyes, she could see him in front of her, more sharply, more beautifully defined. Maybe he was aware of what was passing through her mind for he quoted a phrase of Mellors, the hero of Lady Chatterley's Lover, adapting it slightly. "After our intensive fucking, my love, we should now be chaste." She nudged him with her elbow and pretended to glance at him angrily, while all the time exploding with laughter inside.

Wish you were here, sounded the words of the title song as if in reply. Wish you were here, and she replayed the track again.

How I wish, how I wish you were here

We're just two lost souls swimming in a fish bowl
Year after year
Running after the same old ground, what have we found?
The same old fears.

Stephen had chosen to leave their own private world even before he departed for good. "I need more air, I don't deserve you," he would say, avoiding looking at her directly.

* * *

Richard had told her a story about his mother who was suffering from Alzheimer's. She had caught the nurses off guard at the old people's home, where she stayed, and walked out into the road. Instead of making her way to the house she had lived in for the last forty years of her life and which Richard now occupied, she had gone elsewhere. When the owner of the house opened the door, he found a hard-faced old woman standing in front of him. "Can I help you?" he asked politely. "Help me?" she demanded sarcastically. "You can begin by telling me what you are doing in my house?"

"Do you know where my mother had gone?" Richard asked when he saw the startled look on her face. "Back to the house she lived in as a child. She was absolutely convinced that she had gone out an hour ago." She was heartbroken at losing her house and cried and cried when she was taken back to the home, until thankfully she forgot all about it again.

Richard's account of his mother struck a strange chord with her. When she dreamed about the past, she often saw herself in the old house her family had lived in when she was a child, before they moved to a more modern one outside the walls of old Baghdad.

She had been about seven when she left the house for good but it hadn't lost its fine shape in her mind, and though the details changed in every dream, the overall picture remained the same. She was walking along the long winding corridor (majaz) that connected the old wooden door to the spacious inner courtyard with its paving of yellow tiles. As she safely emerged from the total darkness of the tunnel into daylight she felt a sense of relief. Light streamed down from the square of sky overhead. As she wandered through the rooms, she was surprised by the objets d'art which seem to have come from all over the world; there were davenports and tables of ebony inlaid with ivory, while marble statues, gold and jewellery and rare china porcelain. She seemed oblivious to them. She was looking for something in particular, a purse maybe, or a handbag, or a special gown.

The search always took her to the first floor. Sometimes it happened when she was in one of the rooms, other times when she was standing at the top of the stairs leading down to the courtyard. Night suddenly fell upon her and she was engulfed in pitch black darkness. Her breath came in frightened gasps. How am I going to get out? The whispering around her grew louder and she began to panic.

She had been planning to go to Baghdad when she received a telegram out of the blue from her father, which read, ' We are all coming to spend the summer with you,' and forced her to cancel her trip. Her father was only coming as part of his work. The King would be visiting London in the middle of July and he had to come ahead to organise his reception and stay in the country.

It was nine months since she had last seen her family. She had missed them terribly in those first weeks after leaving Baghdad as it was the first time in her life that she had spent longer than a day away from them. In her boarding school, as the hours and minutes ticked slowly by, she counted off the days on her coloured 1958 calendar. She still had a long time to go before sitting the university entry exam. Now as she thought back, she remembered the ritual she had practiced every night before going to sleep. She would take down the framed photos of her family from where they were grouped on the bedside cabinet and gaze at them one by one.

She had only been able to meet up with them once after they arrived. The exams were almost on top of her and if she failed, she would lose her grant from the government. "Only two more weeks," her father told her reassuringly, "then they'll be over for good." On her calendar, she circled July 17th in red. It was the last day of her examinations. Underneath she had written Liberation Day.

Because of this, she was only aware of what happened on the fourteenth, four days after it happened.

As she travelled to London, her thoughts were still in a whirl. Through the window, she could see green lawns and electricity pylons passing by. Apart from an occasional ever changing patch of blue, the sky was covered in white cloud. From time to time, a shaft of sunlight escaped for a second and lit up a sudden gleam of green in the scene in front of her. Had she really finished her exams? Her father had told her that she would be accompanying Princess Fadhila during her fiancé, King Feisal II's visit to London. The latter should have arrived by now. He had been due to leave Baghdad on the eighth of July.

When she got to the suite of rooms in the hotel, especially reserved for her family, she was met with a strange silence. Instead of a welcome reception, her mother appeared in black, her eyes red from weeping, while her youngest brother jittered all over the place as if he didn't know what was happening to him.

Finally her mother said, holding back the tears. "There's been a military coup in Baghdad."

"The king's here, isn't he?" she had asked, expecting a reply in the affirmative, but instead her mother had shaken her head.

* * *

She had only gone along with Stephen to the conference on the 'Dialectics of Liberation' out of curiosity. It was taking place in the Round House again but the venue appeared cleaner and better organised that the last time she had been there. At the entrance, people handed out differently coloured leaflets. A yellow notice announcing the setting up of an Alternative University of London took her fancy. In capital letters under the list of supervisors, it read NO FORMAL REQUIREMENTS.

She had put Agatha Christie's latest novel, Endless Night into her shoulder bag, she now recalled. From time to time, she would cautiously sneak it out and return to the story, which took her far away from the sound of the lecturer's voice.

Stephen criticised her whenever he saw her reading one of Agatha Christie's books. "You're addicted to them," he told her. "Doctors and murderers obviously have something in common."

One of the speakers, Stokely Carmichael, had made an impression on her. The increasing dissatisfaction she glimpsed on the audience's faces as his tone became more sharply critical might have had something to do with it. She was amazed by his poise. He was like an actor playing a part. "Us and them.. black versus white… third world versus the west…Pythagoras did not give you geometry. It was the Egyptians who gave it to you….Alexander the Greek wept because there was no one else to kill…No white liberal can give me anything. The only thing a white liberal can do for me is help civilise other whites because they need to be civilised."

In the end is my beginning: the first words of Endless Night. She repeated them to herself as some people left in protest, while others grumbled among themselves in an attempt to stop the speaker. They had come to the conference to learn about self-liberation. Instead they found themselves being accused by an extremely severe prosecuting counsel.

Stokely Carmichael must have been quoting a contemporary revolutionary leader when he talked about the importance of hatred in the struggle against the enemy. Was it Che Guevara? How come she could still remember his words nine years later?

"Hatred as an element of the struggle, relentless hatred of the enemy that impels us over and beyond the natural limitations of man, and transforms us into effective, violent, selected and cold killing machines." Was this the kind of bitter hatred that impelled the Abbasids to treat the Umayyads the way they did after they had subjugated them? Not content with enslaving the living among them, they had also attacked the bodies of their dead. She remembered a torn photograph, which had been smuggled out of Baghdad. It showed the remains of a corpse, suspended from the ceiling by a rope and surrounded by a sea of cheering people. Her mother had stammered in horror, when she saw it, "They say that's the Prince Regent, 'Abd al-llāh."

When she had arrived at the hotel, her father had been busy in the bedroom. She was about to go into the room, when she heard her mother cry out in alarm. "Don't open the door. He'll be angry."

For the next two days, as her mother talked incessantly about what had happened on the morning of that fateful day, she could occasionally hear the sound of her father's voice chanting consoling verses from the Qur'an in the background. "Say, nothing will happen to us except what Allah has decreed for us."

"It's all the fault of the peacocks, they brought to the Rahab Palace two months ago," her mother said. "Their ugly voices were an evil omen."

When her father finally emerged, he appeared to have shrunk in size, while the wrinkles on his forehead had doubled in number. He turned away from her and his red-rimmed eyed refused to meet her own. Was he ashamed? Ashamed of what had happened or ashamed of appearing in his pyjamas, stripped bare of his former status. Or maybe he was ashamed at the collapse of dreams which he had endlessly repeated to anyone who would listen to him. "We will shortly be bringing back into cultivation all the land that has been lying unused since the Mongols laid waste to it." Or "Iraq will become the Paradise of the Middle East when work on the network of dams is completed. Babylon, Ur and Nineveh will awake from their slumbers and Baghdad will regain its former glory."

Now another phrase started to appear on his lips instead, one made popular by the leaders of the new government, 'the Bygone Era.'

He suddenly turned on her. "We're seen as belonging to the stone age. We've left no trace or reputation. We're just an illusion."

* * *

Prompted by an urgent sense of unease, she pulled out the bloated photograph album. It was ages since she had taken it out and there was now a thin layer of dust on the red cardboard cover which must have got in through the wardrobe door. How did people establish the facts of their past before photography was invented? There were two kinds of photographs in the album, those that were stuck to the thick paper and arranged chronologically and others which she had crammed in at random. In the middle of four pages devoted to photographs of Helen, there was a large faded picture of King Feisal II, lying on its side. He had signed it in black ink in the left hand corner and added the date underneath: 2nd May 1953. On the back, her father had written Coronation Day.

It had been decided that the young king would leave for London, a week before the coup took place. But the Finance Minister had asked him to delay his departure for a couple of days. There were two important laws concerning the Hashemite Union (between Iraq and Jordan) which were about to be passed and which required his signature.

Under the picture of the dead king, lay a picture of Stephen and other members of his band. There was nothing to indicate when it had been taken, though it must have been shortly after she had first seen them on the stage in the University of London theatre. Her eyes were drawn to the leather shoes and Mao Tse Tong style jackets that were much more stridently coloured than any the Chinese Leader had worn. She'd forgotten how many times the band had changed its name before finally settling on one. When she first met Stephen, they had called themselves, The Path Seekers. When they found that another group with the same name already existed, they had dropped the 'Seekers' and called themselves The Path. Before a week had gone by, two others groups with the same name had emerged. So they went back to using the second part of the name The Seekers, only to have history repeat itself again, at which point they had settled on the antithesis of the first name, and called themselves The Lost which they adopted as their official name.

On another page, there was a handful of photographs. Here was one of her family after they had recovered their fortunes and settled in Abu Dhabi. On the back her father had written in his fine, elegant hand, 'To our beloved daughter, we are looking forward to your coming.'

After losing everything her father had been forced to start at the bottom again, translating commercial contracts for British companies doing business in the Arab world. Then one of his wealthy clients who operated out of the Emirates had suggested he could play a role in setting up the new institutions of state in the country. She still had part of the first enthusiastic letter he had sent her from Abu Dhabi. "The situation here reminds me of what it was like in the twenties in Iraq, when I was still a young man and we were starting to build the state, but there are none of the intrigues and hatred we had then. Can you believe that I feel as energetic as I did then and I have the same implicit trust in the future? I won't hide from you though that I still feel tormented by the situation in Iraq as I watch the unending coups and massacres. Is it an eternal curse?'

Here was another photograph of her, this time surrounded by a crowd of demonstrators. It must have been taken in Trafalgar Square. She looked like a tourist amid the serious faces around her. People were holding banners aloft with slogans that read Stop the Bomb, Make Love Not War and Victory to the Vietcong.

Once the peace treaty had been signed, a strange quiet had fallen on Saturdays. She sometimes wondered as she strolled through the places they had once gathered in, where the thousands of protestors against the Vietnam War had gone to? How tirelessly they had worked over the years. She had once gone with Stephen to help arrange a sit-in which was being organised by the Committee for Solidarity with Vietnam. It must have been at the home of one the organisers in Hackney; she had been astonished by the way everyone co-

42

operated with each other. The young participants were like a hive of bees in the way they divided up the tasks. She later learnt that they were from various militant left-wing organisations such as the anarchists, Trotskyists, Moscovites, trade unionists and followers of Gramsci.

She remembered one of them counting the cardboard signs fixed to the end of thin wooden poles. Her eyes had been caught by an odd slogan against napalm, written on one of them. 'Pour a gallon of petrol on your child and leave him to burn.' The faint sound of Bob Dylan had come from another room mingling with the soft laugh of a woman.

On the way home, she had expressed her surprise at the orderly manner in which the Anarchists had worked. Stephen had replied in a studiedly neutral tone, "It's creative chaos, darling."

* * *

Her initial meeting with Stephen had only come about through a series of strange coincidences. These in turn had made her cling to him continuously as if there was a power out there which had played a role in setting them in train, a mysterious loving power which was dedicated to extracting her from the future which had been so carefully designed for her. All she had to do was close her eyes and let it lead her.

Easter 1964 had been grey and exceptionally cold. Outside, the rain fell persistently, heavily. The constant drumming on the window panes heightened the impression that it would never stop. She pulled out a photograph, taken at the time which showed her with another doctor and a couple of nurses, and seemed to reveal the particular awfulness of the British weather and the feeling it evoked. Despite the overhead neon lights, the advent of Easter Sunday and the artificial smiles for the camera, the total resignation and despair at ever seeing the sun again was clearly reflected in their faces.

Maybe, at the time, she had been slightly regretting the fact that she had agreed to stand in for her Irish colleague. Only two days before Good Friday, Mary had asked her to cover for her over Easter. Her boyfriend had finally agreed to visit her family during the Easter holiday. She had said with a laugh, "I must seize the opportunity before he changes his mind." She would have to leave for Dublin on the Thursday evening in order to spend a suitable amount of time with her family.

But if the truth be told, she was really regretting missing out on her chance to go to Abu Dhabi and was haunted by an image of herself sitting on the balcony overlooking the Gulf under a clear blue sky with the sun shining in all its glory.

It had been decided that she would finalise her engagement to a doctor during the visit. He was coming to the end of his studies in Britain, after which he hoped to obtain a lucrative work contract in Abu Dhabi.

When her father told her in his last letter that Samir had asked if he could marry her, she couldn't think of a reason to refuse. Since she had only met him a few times when she was over visiting her family, her feelings were neutral. The only times they had talked was in the presence of her family and the conversation was confined to her studies or his work. He had told her once that he wanted to settle in England once he had saved enough money in Abu Dhabi. This might mean working there for ten more years.

After re-arranging her shifts with two of her colleagues and getting permission from the hospital administration to leave, she had received an urgent telegram from her father, which forced her to cancel her trip. Her engagement had been postponed. Samir's grandfather had died the day before.

Instead, the two families decided to spend the summer holiday in London, once the period of mourning was over. The engagement and marriage ceremonies would take place simultaneously and she would go to Abu Dhabi when she had completed her medical internship.

Her fingers moved over one of the photos Baida had brought her. She was sitting on a short flight of steps leading down from the school building to the garden, alongside four other girls. They must have been her closest friends. She was surprised at the way they all turned their heads towards the camera, their dreamy sorrowful gaze, mirrored by the expression in their eyes. What were they thinking about? What had they talked about before they sat down on the steps and submitted themselves to the camera's lens? She had a strange thought. It was like being aboard a one way express train. Every moment was like a snapshot which moved further and further away from her.

Stephen loomed up in front of her in another photo. Where had she taken it? Most probably in Regent's Park. She could tell it was summer from the clothes, he was wearing, the artificial silk shirt with a short collar and the wide bottomed Charleston trousers.

When she entered the ward, she hadn't noticed him immediately. She was completely taken up in examining the four patients facing him which no doubt gave him sufficient time to have a careful look at her face.

When she stopped beside Stephen's bed, she didn't glance up from his medical notes, even when the nurse greeted him in a friendly manner. "Happy Easter. You look much better today."

How could she find the words now to describe what had gone through her mind when she raised her head and looked in his direction? It was his voice that first attracted her. It sounded like a breath of warm air completely at odds with the depressing morning she could see on the other side of the window, and the groans of the elderly patients behind her. She felt a tremor run through her body, the moment their eyes met which made her clutch the clipboard tightly against her in an attempt to mask what was happening.

While she was measuring his blood pressure, Stephen asked: "When can I leave hospital?" She avoided looking at him directly as she held his left wrist in her right hand and said only: "Tomorrow if you like."

Before leaving, her eyes fell on the cabinet beside his bed, where there was a drawing pad and a hardback book. She was curious to know what it was about and could scarcely believe her eyes when she found out that it was a copy of The Arabian Nights For a moment, she was aware of the chain of coincidences which had led up to this meeting. The Arabian Nights? Was this the last link in the chain or the beginning of another?

"In the beginning is my end."

She asked him casually as if not expecting an answer: "Where have you got up to?" After a short silence, he said, "I've just started the story of Aladdin and come to the bit when he stumbles across the magic lamp."

The nurse had mentioned her name when they arrived at his bed and he reminded her now that he had not forgotten it. "What will happen to Aladdin at the hands of the Moroccan sorcerer?"

*　*　*

Even when there had been no more doubt about what had happened in Baghdad, her mother persisted in preparing meals on time and taking assiduous care of any visitors who came to see them.

Was she really ignorant of the fact that they were no longer able to return to Baghdad and had lost everything they owned there? Or was it more a question of being completely resigned to her fate, something she had absorbed since she was a child? Loving hands had carried her through life, always taking her on to something better. It was impossible that they would let her down now.

'Say we are afflicted only with what God has written for us,' she murmured. How often did this verse from the Qur'an appear on her tongue at the time after it was said repeatedly by the visitors? She couldn't remember when her father had actually exploded with rage. Her mother had probably been taking a small tray of food to him. She had stopped in front of the locked bedroom door and knocked on it insistently. In the dining room, Scheherazade heard the sound of plates and spoons crashing to the floor, then her father's tones raised in anger, speaking in a way she had never heard before. His voice rasped in his throat and he sounded completely defeated. "Don't you understand who the people of the bygone era are? We're the culprits. They want to obliterate us completely, make people forget that we ever existed."

Her father had attempted to organise a commemorative service for the victims of the coup in Regent's Park Mosque, but the directors had turned down his request and when he was finally able to reserve a modest hall on the outskirts of London, he was taken aback by the small number of people who attended.

On his return to the hotel, he had said sarcastically: "Where were all those hundreds of student delegates who used to regularly attend the parties at the embassy?"

But she had gone with him to another commemorative service which had taken place in a church.

This time the modest hall was full of mourners, so much so that a crowd of people were forced to stand near the door. She was particularly surprised by the large number of people using walking sticks as they made their way laboriously towards their seats. With their aristocratic manner and grand clothes they seemed to have come from a world that was fast disappearing, an empire on which the sun would never set.

The few Iraqis who attended the service were lost among the huge crowd of former British officials. Her father was able to pick out some who had worked in Iraq after the monarchy had been established, even though it was many years since they had returned to Britain. She wondered whether it was a yearning for an age that had been extinguished that she could see on his face, as he pointed out a thin and pale old man who still bore himself erect. "That's Colonel Pierce Jones," her father said. "Have I told you about him? He was one of those, along with Lawrence, who fought on the side of King Feisal I and Nuri Sa'ied, against the Ottomans and later played a role in training the Iraqi army."

The atmosphere in the hall despite its reserve was not oppressive. Perhaps this was due to a characteristic which was particularly English: an ability to make ugly facts disappear as if by magic by pretending they never existed.

The speakers had some link or other with at least one of the three "traitors" whom the putschists had been so keen to kill simultaneously. Instead of talking about the terror of the final day of their lives, they recalled moments when they had all been together in happier times. Perhaps they wished to paint a joint portrait of themselves, which would brand them with that human characteristic which many English people thought was their most distinguishing feature, their sense of humour.

For an instant she had the vague impression that the victims were British and had nothing to do with Iraq.

The speeches seemed to her to provide some sort of pleasure, or rather comfort to the people who were there, assuaging their common grief. Language somewhat restores the dead to life: the ethereal particles of sound can on a certain day beautify their lives and keep them present.

Did it occur to her as she looked at the sea of faces on leaving the hall where the service had taken place that in a few years' time, most of the people who had attended would no longer be alive?

A thin woman came towards them accompanied by one of the organisers of the service. With her stick and hat she looked like a character from a past which had only ever existed in a novel by Jane Austen. Her frail body was shaken by the tremors of advancing years. "This is Lady Richmond," said the man who was with her, as he introduced the woman to her father. "Gertrude Bell's sister."

* * *

When she arrived at the hospital the following morning, she had been desperate to get going on her ward rounds but had kept on putting off the moment. Something had disturbed the course of her life and she needed to put a stop to it before it got out of control. She hadn't slept much the night before, only dozing intermittently as she listened to the rain tapping rhythmically on her window.

How could she rationalise this sudden transformation in herself? How many times had she leafed through Stephen's medical file? Reasons for admittance to hospital: Severe abdominal pains; diagnosis: acute inflammation of the appendix; treatment: immediate surgical intervention; age: twenty-one years, two years younger than she was; job: musician.

Just as she had anticipated, he wasn't there when she arrived at the ward. His bed was empty and made up, ready for the next patient. Nevertheless, and contrary to what she expected, she was filled with a particular kind of disappointment. Disappointment that what she expected to happen had come true.

How would she have reacted if he had been waiting for her to arrive? At most, it would have quenched that crazy sense of longing she had never experienced before.

When she returned to the clinic, she had found a large envelope on her desk, on which someone had scrawled her name in full.

It contained a bizarre portrait of herself done in charcoal. She was wearing clothes and jewellery from a bygone age and looked like the original Scheherazade. Perhaps the man with the avuncular face, sitting on a high bed was meant to be Shahriar. She was holding Aladdin's famous lamp, which was much larger in the drawing than in the original story. In front of her stood a genie enveloped in a cloud. As happened in comic books, his words were printed in a bubble nearby: Abracadabra ...I am yours to command.

On the back of the picture, Stephen had written a few words along with a telephone number: "It would be lovely to meet for a coffee."

But their meeting had not ended with a coffee.

Another London opened up in front of her, when she was with him. She responded to it with a part of herself that up to then had remained dormant inside her, awaiting a suitable opportunity to launch itself against the hitherto straightforward course of her life.

Stephen had taken her to places she had never dreamed existed in the real world.

Places such as the UFO Club.

She had followed him down the steps to the giant cellar under the Tottenham Court Road. As she grew more hesitant, the further down she got, Stephen put out a reassuring hand and drew her after him.

Her heart starting to thump in time to the pounding music as she entered the room. She felt as if she was miles underground rather than separated from the public thoroughfare by a mere ten steps.

In rare moments of lucidity, she could still smell the pungent aroma of hashish smoke which filled the room and which seemed to pervade every place she went to with Stephen.

She was surprised at how many people were there. They were everywhere, sitting on the wooden floor, grouped around tables and gyrating on the small dance floor. She remembered a glitter ball, suspended overhead in which rays of coloured light were reflected, which flashed out intermittently across the audience, illuminating their clothes and faces and moving arms. After an intermission, the DJ excitedly revealed that the next act would be The Crazy World of Arthur Brown.

The announcement sparked off a ripple of excitement among the spectators. People who had been sitting on the stairs leading up to the street, hoping to catch a breath of fresh air, rushed back inside when they heard the singer scream, "I am the God of hellfire and I bring you fire," before proceeding with a song, whose steady beat sounded like the pulsing of the heart. He jerked his painted face rapidly in time to the music, moving like a robot, first right then left as his arms swung in opposite directions.

She was afraid for the singer as she watched real flames

shoot up from his head. He was wearing a metal helmet, in the shape of a crown with horns on either side that made him look like a medieval painting of Satan surrounded by fire. But these were imitation flames conceived by ingenious lighting engineers along with the fake smoke that floated over the wooden stage.

The people around her roared out the chorus, whenever Arthur Brown returned to it. "Fire, I'll take you to burn... Fire, I'll take you to learn... I'll see you burn." Some of them were so swept away that their bodies began to writhe in the dark place next to the stage as they jumped up and down in time to the music like machines. From where she was standing, they appeared like shadowy images against a backdrop that seemed to warn that the hour of judgement was near.

When Stephen asked her what she thought about the performance, she had merely nodded her head. "It was nice." He must have read the negative reaction on her face, which made him defend the song without trying to foist his opinion on her: "Some people regard it as a satirical attack on capitalism and its one-dimensional people who are slaves to their jobs and consumerism." But he added immediately: "At the end of the day, it's just a song."

Stephen had showed her another type of consumerism.

On their Saturday walks, he had taken her to second hand markets instead of the posh shops in Oxford Street.

Two photos stuck on one page of the album made her realise the huge changes that had taken place in the fashion in hair, clothes, jewellery, shoes and makeup since then. Everything had to give the impression of being simple and ephemeral rather than grandiose and permanent as was the case with manufactured products.

Women wore their hair shoulder length and favoured a natural look, instead of the short permed styles, which required the insertion of rollers every night to keep the waves in place. Long skirts made of soft expensive materials gave way to narrow extremely short skirts made of rough denim cloth.

The jeans she was wearing in one of the photos might have been the first pair she had worn in her life. Stephen had taught her how to make them they fit perfectly, by wearing them in a bath of water, until they shrunk to size. He had also taught her how to rid them of that superficial perfection which capitalism demanded in its commodities, by ripping holes in places that could be seen and then sewing them up again.

The objective in all this was to abolish distinctions, or rather to make things distinctive by pretending the opposite.

However Stephen and his friends had not considered LSD a capitalist commodity produced in response to an artificially created need but rather a means to get to a special kind of paradise. Andrew, the first guitar player in Stephen's band, described this paradise as the temporary death of the self since the drug eliminated the boundaries between the self and the outside world. Stephen for his part said that LSD would bring about the downfall of the capitalist system, since it would help mankind become aware of its chains.

She had accompanied him to visit a friend, whose wealthy parents had gone to spend Christmas in Italy and left him their posh flat in Chelsea. She saw a number of Stephen's friends there.

In the huge sitting room, people were divided into three groups. In one of them a number of men sat on their own in a corner. They appeared to be in a hypnotic trance as they watched open mouthed as a large fly crawled across the ceiling without falling off.

She could still recall the song that had blared out from the speakers hidden in the wall. The cry of the sea gulls aroused conflicting emotions in her and she was both attracted and secretly repelled by the music. Despite its strangeness, she was able to make out John Lennon's voice. He seemed to be coming through the walls and addressing the people who were at that very moment slipping into an LSD induced unconsciousness ."Turn off your mind, relax and float downstream, it is not dying, it is not dying."

A girl appeared from somewhere, followed by a boy. They seemed relaxed or perhaps they were embarrassed by what happened to them when they returned to the sitting room. How else could she explain the way they folded their arms so tightly across their chests? When the girl drew near the big sofa, one of the women, who was sitting there, asked: "How was the orgasm?" She put out her right hand and waved it this way and that like a bird whose wings had been clipped, then said in heavily accented French: "comme çi, comme ça."

She had most probably come across Wilhem Reich's name for the first time in this flat. She saw a copy of his book The Function of Orgasm lying on one of the tables. In the Partisan Café, she noticed his name a second time on a poster, announcing a lecture on Orgone Energy to mark the tenth anniversary of the inventor's death.

The hall had been packed. It was only later that she realised that the lecture was taking place in the same church in which she had attended the memorial service for the victims of the 14th July coup. It seemed smaller than she remembered it, more modern and lighter. How distant it all seemed as she looked about her. What would have happened to those old men if they had seen these young girls in their trousers or mini-skirts? Doubtless half of them would have suffered an immediate heart attack.

She was surprised to see that the man giving the lecture was wearing a smart suit and blue necktie.

He looked more like a corporate businessman than an academic.

"Orgone: The word is derived from orgasm: the moment of sexual climax. The engorged penis releases an amount of libido, which Reich measured in the thirties and found to be charged with electricity, which he subsequently called orgone energy.

"Look around you. In the furthest reaches of the universe, some galaxy is being born, thanks to the accumulation of giant currents of this energy. All you have to do to find out about the way in which orgone currents interact, is observe the movement of spiral galaxies or watch how cyclones develop.

"Orgone energy is behind every creative action in the universe, since it underlies all forms of organic and inorganic life."

But the lecturer went one step further: "Copulation is the fundamental expression of a function which superimposes this energy on organic nature; two separate currents of orgone energy come together then overlap at the moment of orgasm. After that, they are set free outside the bodies, simultaneously releasing an intense amount of emotion.

"Similarly this energy enables us to control the clouds according to how much rain we require.

"Reich created a device for cloud busting."

The lecturer pointed at a picture projected on to the wall. "This is the cloud before the apparatus was brought to bear on it and this is the empty space it left behind it after it was dispersed."

"What about those countries which need rain?" asked a member of the audience. "Did Reich think about them?"

"Of course, he did," said the lecturer. "I forgot to mention that he also invented a machine that can move clouds from one place to another."

* * *

She pulled out another photograph from where it had been stuffed in the middle of the album. It showed Baida, Abdel and her at the entrance to the town hall in King's Cross. Saleh must have taken it immediately after they left the registry office. Abdel had said enthusiastically as he handed him the camera: "I'll send a copy to Baida's family. It's a family photo."

The moment she entered the building, she had been visited by a strange sensation. Was it a mixture of sadness and regret? She didn't tell the bride and groom that the last time she had been here was with Stephen many years before. The place hadn't changed much since then. It still had the same yellow seats and artificial roses.

"Apart from the fluorescent lights, it looks just like a funeral parlour," Stephen had said sardonically. "This is as far as the English go in expressing their happiness."

His friends had brought along a brass band. After they finished the wedding ceremony, it had played in front of the town hall near to the spot where the photograph had been taken.

A couple of policemen had come over, she remembered. Most of the people there were used to the police occasionally carrying out drug raids on their homes. But this time, the men were content to smile broadly and shake hands with them as long as the impromptu concert ended quickly and the crowd of well-wishers cleared the street as fast as possible.

She had never stopped being amazed by the sight of policemen who accompanied the demonstrations in London. It was as if both the demonstrators and the police had agreed beforehand that the march would take place in an orderly and peaceful manner so that at the end of the day, they could go back to what they were doing before.

She had only ever seen one confrontation with the police. It had occurred when a group of demonstrators attempted to occupy the United States embassy to show solidarity with the Vietcong. She was standing with Stephen and Richard towards the back of the march, but was still able to see the terrifying number of policemen surrounding the building. She couldn't believe her eyes when some of them charged into the crowd on horseback. It wasn't long before a convoy of ambulances appeared.

That night she had been filled with a sense of unease. Old images from Baghdad flickered through her dreams: abandoned streets littered with small stones that the demonstrators had used against the police; smashed glass frontages; severed electricity wires and burnt cars.

She was even more surprised the following morning to find that everything in the area where she lived seemed perfectly normal, while the Sunday papers only dedicated one page to the demonstration. She couldn't recall a single newspaper carrying the picture that later became famous, the one of a girl, with her smart skirt slipped up to expose her stockings, suspenders and panties as she struggled to escape from the arms of two policemen who were carting her away.

The government hadn't fallen as usually happened in Iraq after a demonstration; martial law had not been declared and no one had been killed.

Instead, a large number of people had expressed their sympathy for the horses that had come under attack during the confrontation with the demonstrators. A couple of days later, Stephen said that the police had received hundreds of letters asking how they were.

Her father had remained severely depressed for a couple of months after the coup. From time to time, news reached them of the trials of senior state officials. They heard that they had become comic book heroes that people passionately followed on television.

"Their real objective," said her father, "is to make them forget an entire period of time."

But she was surprised to hear him say one day, "Miss Bell was wrong to bring Feisal I from the Hijaz and impose him on Iraq." He had sighed regretfully: "It would have been different if she had let a strong Iraqi become king... Talib al-Naqib for example... All our misfortunes today stem from her infatuation with him."

*   *   *

She had been filled with a sense of misgiving when she turned to Stephen immediately after the DJ suddenly announced that Brian Epstein was dead.

They were attending a concert by Jimi Hendrix at the Saville Theatre. She had no idea who the dead person was nor why members of the audience groaned in unison at the news until Stephen whispered in her ear: "He's the man behind the Beatles phenomenon."

She subsequently read that he had died from "taking a drug overdose," a euphemistic phrase which was often used at that time.

Was it an overdose of amphetamines? LSD? Sleeping pills? The coroner had also attributed Gertrude Bell's death to an overdose of sleeping pills called Dial.

"She died in Baghdad in 1926," her father told her, "only two days before her fifty-eighth birthday." Perhaps she took the decision late at night. How else can you explain the fact that she asked her maid Mary to wake her at six o'clock?

Stephen said: "Epstein transformed the Beatles from a group of unknowns to the most famous band on earth."

She took out a photo her father had given her. Feisal I, the moment he was appointed king, surrounded by three senior British officers. Her father had pointed to a tall, thin man in his sixties, dressed smartly and fashionably and said: "That is Percy Cox, head of the British Commission to Iraq." Her eyes wandered to Feisal I.

Perhaps the young king was wondering at that very moment what it was that had prompted the Oriental Secretary to intervene so fiercely on his behalf and persuade the British officials responsible for the occupation to appoint him as king over a country which he had never seen before, not even in his dreams.

Maybe he was searching the spectators for her face, hoping to gain a degree of reassurance from her in the midst of this alien world. There she was exchanging a smile with him and a nod of the head: "I am here with you," she seemed to say." Don't worry about anything. I've done it all for you. I've laid out the country bit by bit, drawn its borders and put it on the map of the world. It belongs to you now, Prince of My Dreams."

But the new king, little by little, had started to feel irritated by his maker. As had the Beatles.

After Gertrude Bell had finished writing the constitution for his adopted kingdom, forming the council of deputies, installing a government and designing a special flag, she had been surplus to requirements.

The same thing had happened to Epstein, who had ended up doing nothing but look after the finances of the greatest thing he had invented, The Beatles.

She often wondered why Miss Bell hadn't return to England after King Feisal I was crowned, but instead had accepted the post of first director of the Museum of Iraq which she herself had built out of the artefacts she had unearthed.

A guardian of antiquities instead of a maker of kings.

Miss Bell had written to her father, a few months after the coronation. "You can rely on one thing: I will never engage in creating kings again. It's too great a strain."

She loathed one word in particular and that was retirement.

What could people do after they had moulded the destinies of generations who had not yet even been born? Tend their flowers? Knit? Tell stories to children?

Were they pleased with their new vocation as retired gods?

She had discovered that things she used to do every day without thinking could now make her happy, such as the time she spent examining her patients. Her only objective was to conquer pain and take it away from people who were completely unknown to her.

Was it true to say that the hospital was the only world in which she truly belonged?

In her will Gertrude Bell had bequeathed everything she possessed to the establishment of an institute specialising in Iraqi archaeology; should she also donate her modest wealth to the hospital?

* * *

Her eye fell on a photograph, which was not in the album. She must have put it on the television then forgotten about it. It showed Baida with an enormous belly that was out of all proportion to the rest of her figure. Abdel had laughed: "This is the only photograph of her when she was pregnant. You know she's always been against being photographed up

62

to now?"

Before they first visited her, she had been unable to recall any images of her cousin as a child. But when she saw her she became aware of something strange which seemed to create an invisible bond between them. Baida looked so like Scheherazade's mother that she was startled by the resemblance. It showed in her eyes, her hair, and the round shape of her face, in the colour of her skin, and the tone of her voice and in the indecisive and gentle way she behaved. Her mother used to tell her proudly from time to time: "You're just like your father." But she hadn't told Baida of her discovery. Nor had she told her how fond she had become of her.

Stephen always complained: "You never put your feelings into words. How can I tell if you're pleased or angry with me?"

Maybe over the years she had convinced herself that she could not translate her feelings into words, especially when she was not speaking her mother tongue; as the latter withered away, silence became the best container for them.

Or perhaps this feeling could be traced back further to a view she had held even before leaving Baghdad that language served as a graveyard for the emotions. Putting something into words killed it stone dead.

Her mother would tell her: "You've been obstinate ever since you were a child. Although you never complained about anything, you were very stubborn. If you said no, it meant no."

For years, her mother had shuttled back and forth between Los Angeles and Abu Dhabi looking after her son and his father. Her brother had settled in America once he had completed university. Meanwhile her sister had moved to Frankfurt with her husband, the doctor.

They met less and less. When her sister spoke now, she would say: "We're German." And when her daughter Helen met her two cousins, she found they no longer had a language in common.

But they remained determined to keep in touch with each other. They sent greeting cards for birthdays and the New Year and repeated the readymade formulas: Happy New Year; Happy Christmas; Our happiness will be complete when we see you.

Baida's sudden appearance had awoken a strange feeling in her of belonging to a particular part of the world. In Baghdad, her relations had continued to be born, and grow old, to marry and give birth, to become ill and die. In the photographs which Baida brought with her, she was able to see what had happened to the people, she had left behind. She asked the name of a child who appeared in a photograph and how he was related to her. In another photograph, he appeared as a man.

Abdel had given her some cassettes of songs she hadn't heard before. She could only make out the country dialect with help from him or Baida or Saleh.

They looked at each other in astonishment when she asked what had happened to Nadhim al-Ghazali, a young singer who had been famous when she was in Baghdad. Abdel laughed: "He died years ago." "And what about that handsome singer who was always on television... Hamdan al-Sahir?" Saleh said: "He disappeared along with a group of other musicians after the fourteenth of July."

She had only known Saleh for a short time. She had met him two months before Baida arrived in London.

When Mary invited her over to dinner, she hadn't told her anything about the other guests except to say that a relative of hers was coming who worked as a teacher in a technical institute.

But she was only telling half the truth.

Mary liked playing charming jokes on her friends to see how they would react. She looked on innocently even as she saw them fall into a trap of her own making.

Her relative had told her about a young Iraqi man who worked with her.

"What's he like?" "Nice." "OK, bring him with you but don't tell him anything about Scheherazade."

Mary had doubtless kept a close eye on them after she introduced them to each other.

Perhaps she was curious to know how her trick would play out and what new path her victims would follow.

Part Three
Coloured Buttons II

Abdel did not change his eldest son's name even when the reality of the situation became clear. He had only recently heard of his father's death, when Baida went into prolonged labour, and at most had formed a vague decision in his mind to name his child after him, if it turned out to be a boy.

Selim was six weeks old when Abdel received a letter from the hospital asking him to bring the mother and baby in for an urgent meeting with the specialist. At the hospital, the consultant gave him the stark news, without beating around the bush. After taking a careful look at the naked child lying on the examination table, the doctor said. "I regret to tell you that the concerns expressed by the health visitor are correct… Your child is suffering from Down's Syndrome." Although he didn't understand the technical term, Abdel asked: "But it's just an illness, isn't it? It can be cured?" As if he had been waiting for just such an answer, the doctor launched into an explanation of what caused the phenomenon. He put out the lights and a projector lit up a series of drop down pictures on the wall. "The problem is caused by the failure of Chromosome No 21 to separate properly, which can happen in the egg or the sperm. When the sperm and the egg fuse, the new cell contains three halves of that chromosome instead of two." The doctor turned to one of the three students who were present: "Examine him and tell us what you see."

As Abdel listened to them discussing his son's appearance, his blood began to boil: "Eyes close to the nose… flattened face… narrow opening to the mouth…wider than normal tongue…"

His scream was so loud that it brought the conversation to an abrupt halt. The total silence that followed was broken by the weak cries of the child who was trembling with fright. Abdel turned to Baida and ordered her to pick up her son, and then directed a stream of abuse at the doctors who did not understand a word he was saying.

On the way home, Abdel didn't say a word. He could hear a faint whimpering sound coming from the back seat, mingled with the soft tap of rain on the windscreen. He turned his eyes away from the sight of Baida and the baby that he could see reflected in the mirror.

* * *

Abdel felt a mix of emotions, when his youngest brother called to let him know that his father had died. He was convinced that the time had come for his father to die as he had suffered a series of illnesses and been in and out of hospital for a long time. However he was also troubled by a faint sense of remorse, which expressed itself in various ways: in his dreams; in the irritable sound of his father's voice which he could still hear echoing in his ears and in the conversations he occasionally found himself having with him, in which he defended himself for not having invited him to London.

Even before he left the country, his father had begun to mellow. He had changed from being a fiery tempered man who tyrannised his family to someone more amiable who merely meddled in the minor problems of the household, though for the most part his intervention only made things more complicated. This shift in his behaviour had happened after he retired as he gradually retreated in to his house and stopped going to the cafe or to visit friends who were in a similar position to himself. Bit by bit, he forgot the names of those who had worked under him, as he saw them less and less.

From the moment he arrived in London, Abdel had written to his father once a month. He always started and finished his short letters in the same way: "My dear father" at the beginning and "May God keep you as a loving father to us," at the end. This regular correspondence arose out of his father's eagerness to keep in touch with his emigrant son. He wrote extensive letters which were so long that Abdel was forced to disregard whole sections as he looked for the essentials.

This epistolary tendency first appeared in his father after he suffered his first heart attack and was forced to remain at home all the time. There is no doubt that the complex lives of his other sons which left them no time to spend with him contributed to this new-found devotion to his least favourite son. Maybe the vast distance which separated the two of them was an additional factor behind the rapprochement for absence makes the heart grow fonder and transforms the other into a finer being.

His father's letters contained little beyond trivial details about what was going on in the wider family: the new words his grandson had learnt, the kind of fish they had eaten on Friday and news of relatives who had visited them recently in addition to a few titbits of gossip injected with a sly humour. Abdel could not fail to notice the difference between the father he had left behind and the one, who had begun to write to him, and possibly entertained faint suspicions about who was actually behind the letters. Could this man who appeared so enamoured with marginal details be the father he had known in the past, with his volatile and prickly temperament?

Nevertheless, despite the war which had been waged between them, ever since the incident of the coloured buttons, Abdel felt slightly repulsed by his father's new personality and closer to the father he had known before. It should be said that his father's former haughty behaviour towards members of his family had been allayed by another more lovable characteristic. He was quick to forget the incident that had made him angry in the first place and as soon as he woke up the following morning, would treat the victim of the previous day in a conciliatory manner which implied how repentant he felt. Perhaps it was Abdel's early discovery of this 'weak' spot in his father that had spurred him on in his campaign of covert disobedience and made him find those actions, which his father continued to regard as 'dirty', so alluring.

Reading between the lines of recent letters, Abdel had detected an unstated wish on the part of his father that he should invite him to London, which he continued to imagine as the capital of an empire on which the sun never set, an empire whose glories he had partially lived through, when he was a young man. But Abdel had ignored his father's pleas, using the pretext of the bad weather and the high cost of travel as an excuse for himself even though his father would have been ready to meet the expense.

*   *   *

At home, Abdel began to examine Selim meticulously. He prised open his tiny clenched fists and carefully studied the soft fingers which looked perfectly normal to him; however when he turned his attention to his son's face, he was struck by certain features which up until then, he had barely noticed. For at that instant, by virtue of the light hanging over the cot, he was able to see his son's wide open eyes and his slightly protruding tongue.

Baida was standing about two metres behind him at the time, her face masked by a pale waxy expression, her lips trembling slightly, which made him swallow the hoarse cry which almost exploded out of his mouth. "I've been stabbed in the heart, I've been tricked." He must have realised that any word from him would have brought about the immediate collapse of his wife.

History, it seems, loves to repeat itself. The same events are replayed across generations. We are caught in a vicious circle although the events themselves occur at different places and times. When Abdel's father discovered his son's famous theft of the coloured buttons, he had launched into a furious tirade against the mother which was almost an exact replica of his son's silent outburst at his gentle wife. It was as if the mother and Baida were directly responsible for the aberrations that had affected the son and grandson.

While it had taken his father three whole days to delete

the second half of his son's name, after discovering the secret of the vanishing buttons, it took his son slightly less time. Once he had completed his examination, Abdel instantly wrote off his son's entire existence. If the situations had been reversed, the father and son would have reacted in very different ways: in all likelihood, his father would have happily accepted a mentally handicapped child as a divine test of his patience and would have lavished on him twice the attention he showed towards his other children; Abdel on the other hand, would definitely have been proud of a child who repeated his trick with the coloured buttons.

*   *   *

I think it's possible to sum up Abdel's emotions at this trying time in one word: he felt 'deceived'. Perhaps the dreams he had, which repeated themselves in a variety of guises, were similarly significant: they contained images of featureless animals and people falling into well-devised traps despite the enormous care they took when they moved. The animals assumed various shapes; they were alternately cats, tigers or gazelles; sometimes the dreams took place in the sea, and were accompanied by dolphins and whales. Abdel would wake up in turmoil after every nightmare and start going back over the events of his life, replaying his memories like someone watching a film. It was as if, in this rapid reprise of his past, he was attempting to work out what mistake he had committed; to fix the point where he had gone wrong and which had taken him far away from where he had so meticulously planned to be.

He thought back to his teenage years, when he had suddenly become a prey to new cravings which had catapulted him out of his humdrum existence. He remembered how against his will, he had tried to get his hands on the magazines which classmates had smuggled in and exchanged among themselves. He had poured over the pictures of naked women and in the scenes of explicit sexual intercourse mentally done away with the brawny young men and put himself in their place.

But the thought of paying money for these contraband magazines had plunged him into turmoil. He was caught between two powerful impulses: money and sex. Since the former had been deeply-rooted in him from an early age, he found it difficult to escape it even when confronted by this new temptation, which had begun to disturb his sleep, without any apparent shame. On cold nights, he would wake up, drowning in a pool of sticky liquid which would make him feel mortified. It was as if those naked girls were punishing him, pursuing him deep into his dreams, for failing to buy their pictures.

It was more than likely that his father was behind the proposal that one of his unmarried relatives should take Abdel to the brothel since the series of rapid developments which had occurred over the preceding months had completely exhausted him. Not only had his voice deepened but he had grown noticeably taller and thinner. He suffered from violent mood swings and his pale face sprouted a rash of tiny pimples. His siblings must have felt that they had finally had their revenge, for up till then he had mercilessly exploited and controlled them.

His relative didn't tell him anything about where they were going, beyond saying that he was going to have a nice surprise. They had to take several buses before arriving at their destination, a new district on the outskirts of Baghdad. There they hurried along dirt tracks lined by half completed houses, with piles of building materials strewn around them. It was afternoon, but there was no let up in the blast of summer heat which seared the skin on their faces, forcing them to walk faster and faster and continuously wipe away the copious amounts of sweat which streamed down their foreheads.

His relative had suddenly stopped in front of an isolated house. After glancing quickly around, he pushed open the gate in the high wall, allowing them to slip through the shade cast by the arbour of vine leaves which led to the front door. Despite the heat, Abdel shivered involuntarily at the sound of women's laughter coming from inside.

* * *

Despite his desperate attempts to wipe it from his memory, the image of what his eldest son looked like, the moment the truth dawned on him remained fixed in his mind. The decision to reject the reality of the situation translated itself in a number of ways. He refused to take any photographs of Selim even when he read the entreaty in Baida's eyes that he be included in a passing shot of their other three children. He avoided going anywhere with him outside the house and he did not allow his wife to take him out of his bedroom when guests were present.

This attitude towards his child arose in the first instance from the fact that he had not planned for it. He had mapped out the future with an almost religious care to avoid any unpleasant surprises upsetting his life in the future: whenever Abdel took a decision, he spent ages beforehand considering every aspect of the matter in order to circumvent some unforeseen financial disaster ahead. Even when one of his colleagues offered a generous purchase price, he would content himself by saying: "I'll think about it." But Selim's birth plunged him into a whirlpool of uncertainty of the same kind as had assailed his father after the incident of the coloured buttons and found expression in a single question, which went round and round in their heads. "What went wrong?"

Abdel had been haunted by the same question (though in a less well-defined way) after leaving the brothel. The sun was going down. Above, the deep blue of the sky shot through with the purple hues of eventide stretched into the distance. A welcoming breeze of clean air scented with the fragrance of flowers washed over him replacing the scorching heat of the afternoon. It seemed ages since they had entered the women's house. With every step he took along the dusty ground, he felt as if his body was about to leap into the air and he almost asked his relative whether he had the same sensation of flying. But at the same time, he felt as if he had only spent a few moments in the bawdy house which made him wonder whether the whole incident had really happened. And when he compared his dreams to reality, he found that the former were more intense and arousing than the latter.

He was drinking a glass of coke while his relative talked to the women, then one of them had stretched out her hand and put it on Abdel's rigid arm: "You like me more than the others, don't you?" she'd said, which provoked an outburst of laughter and loud comments among the others and made him shrink further into his shell. The woman must have noticed his extreme confusion for she had got to her feet and given him a slight tug. When he hesitated slightly, his relative shouted at him jokingly. "Go with her, don't be afraid. Hiyam's not going to eat you."

He had been surprised at how easy everything turned out to be: with a couple of movements, the woman was completely naked and with a bit of help from her, Abdel was soon able to get rid of his clothes. The little room was bare except for a mattress on the floor and a pair of purple curtains which were drawn against the burning sun. Even so it was as hot as an oven. The pungent aroma of her scent mixed with the smell of perspiration dripping off her body filled his nostril. When she pulled him to her, he felt their sweat mingle as their bodies rubbed against each other but the pounding sense of lust which he got from those clandestine magazines weakened and then vanished, once she entwined her skinny legs around his back.

He had flung himself to one side of her, utterly exhausted, convinced that something had gone wrong during intercourse, which made it so different from the imaginary pleasures he enjoyed night and day. As he walked silently along beside his relative, he tried to recall some detail of the encounter which had only happened a couple of hours before but his mind was a blank. The only thing he could remember was the smell of the prostitute's body and the state of being awakened, which was difficult to define.

*   *   *

After avoiding Baida for two weeks, Abdel sneaked back into the matrimonial bed. Despite the darkness in the room, there was sufficient light, filtering in from the corridor, for him to see the beautiful contours of her face. The soft patter of rain on the window pane spurred him on to put his arms around her. When she unwillingly turned over on her side, he was able to slip his arms under her neck and send his fingers roaming around the folds of her breasts.

*   *   *

Immediately he reached his decision, he rushed to implement it with his legendary vigour: he would try to have three healthy children to make up for his initial failure and should the congenital defect be repeated, he would return his wife to her family along with her children. In order to achieve his goal, Abdel devoted himself to having sexual congress with his wife at the start of each day, even when Baida was still fast asleep. He performed his task completely ritualistically as if he feared that if he lost his concentration for a second a deformed sperm might be sent to her womb at the moment of ejaculation.

Alongside this rigorous programme of insemination, he also subjected himself and his wife to a special dietary regime, in which taking fish, vitamins and iron became a daily religious duty. When Baida failed to fully implement the programme at every meal, his flint-like eyes would harden with silent anger.

In the weeks before this change in him took place, Abdel had remained in a state of considerable shock, refusing to believe the evidence of his own eyes or what the doctor had said about Selim. Every morning he would get up from where he was sleeping in the sitting room, which he was occupying in the meantime, and go to the bedroom to take a look at his son. When he turned his eyes towards Selim, he entertained a hope that some kind of miracle might have occurred and that the physical irregularities were nothing but marks resulting from a difficult birth. How would Baida have reacted if she had been able to read what was going through his mind? From the bed, where she lay, pretending to be asleep, she watched through half-closed eyes as her husband tiptoed towards the child's cot, leaving a sufficient gap between her eyelids to follow what he was doing. She was filled with an obscure fear whenever her husband put his hand out to Selim.

After he had recovered from the sense of shock, he was filled with repressed rage at what had befallen his son. It was as if the heavens had made his father's curse come true. But the desire for revenge was gradually replaced by depression. For the first time ever, he saw the world as an oppressive and slimy place and found the only way to escape it was by sleeping continuously, either through alcohol or sleeping pill induced stupor.

*　*　*

But suddenly the world shifted on its axis; the layers of ice which over the preceding weeks had built up round his heart were shattered with a single blow. Water bubbled and fizzed through his veins and awoke the rebellious spirit which had always lived inside him. In the heart of the darkness, he was able to make out something that resembled himself. He was like a bow on the point of releasing its arrow, the string pulled back as far as it would go.

But the bow did not represent the present so much as the future. To put it another way: the present was going to be his launch pad for the future. Abdel's plans to acquire wealth remained on target, but he now had an additional objective, to have healthy children.

Was his recovery prompted by a desire for revenge? A wish to avenge himself on those mysterious forces which he had been able to avoid until 'Selim' was born? Throughout his life, Abdel had always felt his father was somewhere out there, contemptuously observing everything he did, which made him in turn more and more defiant. Was he getting his own back on his father now for changing his name or was it instead a persistently frenzied attempt to comply with what his father had foretold for his son?

There is no doubt that his father's death added to Abdel's fragmented state of mind. Along with the sense of guilt and liberation, he became aware of a third emotion: a sense of revulsion at the thought of making money. This was completely unlike his usual semi instinctive propensity for acquiring wealth through discovering new ways of extracting money from others.

When he first met Saleh, he had been totally disinterested in what the other had to say about the theatre in London or the various points of view on the subject put forward by the political press; he had been rather more interested in convincing him that the desk he could make would be far superior to anything Saleh could buy in a shop. Not surprisingly, he had quickly identified Saleh as an ideal customer when he failed to ask how much it would cost even after they had come to an agreement.

Baida appeared to be timidly cautious about the arrangement giving as her excuse that they lived a long way away from each other but Abdel had resolved the dispute with a single sharp look and a terse comment: "He'll pay for transporting it." On the following day, his wife had gone with him to pick up some timber from a scrap yard.

* * *

Abdel had announced that he was going to buy an old car a whole year after the disastrous visit to the brothel. No one in the family had taken the announcement seriously, and when the car appeared beside the house, they were thunderstruck. When his father saw it, he felt sick with anger, for he had not been able to afford a motorcycle despite having spent twenty five years in the same job. He told his son sarcastically: "You must have done a deal with the devil to get it."

At school, Abdel told his astonished friends that his father had given it to him as a present. He did not tell anyone the real reason for buying it. He continued to apply himself to his lessons as before. In the morning he would arrive at school half an hour before the start of classes and would return home at midday when they were over. There he would complete his homework before eating lunch with his family, and sleeping for a few hours.

However when Abdel woke up at nine o'clock in the evening, he was a completely different person to the one he had been during the day, as if an alien spirit had taken possession of his body. Before leaving the house, he would run a charcoal pencil over his flagging moustache then wind a kefiyeh about his head, which added ten years to his age.

He had come up with the idea of buying a car after visiting the al-Safa' night club a couple of times in company with his relative. He was surprised by the number of women there. Sometimes as many as four of them sat round a single table with one or two men and on Friday evenings they were busier with more clients. As he left the nightclub he noticed several of the women making their way along the pavement towards the taxi rank. When he saw the expressions of delight on the drivers faces as the high-spirited beautiful women appeared, he must have asked himself: "I wonder how many of them will get lucky?"

In the months after buying the car, Abdel devoted himself to work, spending the first hours of every night ferrying ordinary passengers about. However, once it was one in the morning, he would head towards al-Safa' club. Among his more regular clients were Julnar, Qut al-Qulub and Jawahir; and with the latter, he went a long way. Before returning home, she would sometimes accompany him to the room he had built on the roof of the family home, which he used for his own enjoyment, and to do his work. Before taking her up to the roof, Abdel would reconnoitre the steps leading upwards, making sure that the whole family and in particular his father were fast asleep. In summer, when everyone retired to the roof at night, they hid out in the basement. The price for all this enjoyment was to take her free of charge from the nightclub to her home.

Abdel was not particularly bothered if Jawahir was reluctant to go with him, for his regular night-time drives had won him the trust of other prostitutes; there was no doubt that his age and self-confidence contributed to his charm. Sometimes, lust got the better of him before he had time to get one or other of them to his bed and he would be compelled to spend the short time he had, clinging to her and abandoning himself to her breasts like a child, while in his mind's eye images of Hollywood blondes and provocative girls from Playboy floated by in the dark.

* * *

His father's death prompted Abdel to add to his range of "rights" In order to increase the amount of state benefits he received, he came to an agreement with a relative who was on a short visit to London that they stage a car accident. The latter ran into the back of his car, crushing it completely. After suffering violent back 'pain', and being shunted from one hospital to another, Abdel was signed off as disabled by his GP. He felt a huge sense of triumph, when he received the piece of paper through the post, stating that he was 'physically impaired', and outlining his new rights and privileges.

This significant success prompted him to draw up similar projects. As he gradually forgot about his father and no longer felt his heavy gaze upon him, his covert goals multiplied and it began to seem as if he was moving towards total conformity with the name his father had almost given him after the incident of the coloured buttons: Abdel Nahāb, Servant of the Looter.

A few years before leaving Iraq, Abdel had been seized with a desire to reclaim his name in its entirety but a feeling of embarrassment at what his father would say coupled with a deep sense of pride prevented him from legally realising his wish. Instead, he had forged another passport under a new name, adding the half of his name that had been dropped to the first part, at the same time as claiming to have lost his first passport. On the eve of his trip he had had two passports in his possession, in two different names: the first, which was forged, bore the name he had carried before his father's wrath had descended upon him and the second, which was legal, bore the truncated version of his name which he had been stuck with since early childhood and which had figured in every subsequent document, like a never ending question mark.

*   *   *

Two months before Baida had the twins Abdel rented a large three storeyed house, as a preliminary step towards buying it. Before they moved in, he had a clear plan in his mind of how the rooms would be arranged.

His children, including the fourth one, who was still just

a possibility in his father's mind, would live on the middle floor. Selim would occupy a secluded room out of sight.

Baida's mother offered to come and spend three months with them. Her presence was an undeniable source of comfort to her daughter, especially as her movements were growing more sluggish and preventing her from carrying out the housework. Her mother must have read the anxiety in her daughter's eyes when she looked at Selim, for she devoted most of her time to him.

* * *

In response to Selim's birth, Abdel also decided to get hold of a million pounds over the next seven years. During the gloomy nights he spent in the sitting room his mind buzzed with get rich quick schemes. He could buy a restaurant or hotel or acquire shares in the nationalised companies, which the government was putting up for sale. Where should he invest? Who could he find to conceal the fortune for him?

He drew up a list of names of every member of his family who was living abroad, but became increasingly convinced that the worst form of jealousy was that, which existed between members of the same family and hesitated to confide in them as a result. When he thought of Raouf, he felt that he had found the person he was looking for.

* * *

Abdel's relationship with Raouf went back to their days at secondary school together. From time to time, he still thought of the first time he had seen him in the middle of a physics lesson. Raouf had appeared at the door to the classroom and stood there waiting for the teacher to notice him while everyone in the class turned to look at him. How tiny the teacher looked in comparison when he stood beside him, prompting one of the inveterate trouble makers to call out jokingly: "It's the inspector." But Raouf's large physical stature was belied by the expression of excessive goodwill, which shone on his face; those thick spectacles gave the impression of extraordinarily weak eyesight and this initially emboldened a couple of pupils to snatch them away from him to find out how little he could see. Raouf did not lose his poise but instead contented himself with taking another pair out of his satchel. However when another pupil tried the same trick, he squeezed his hands ever so slightly. This was enough to make the other pupil squirm in pain and bring home to the others the frightening strength hidden behind the constantly smiling mouth and the slightly protuberant eyes.

A few weeks after moving to the school, Raouf (without knowing it) had come to occupy a place among the students, which was the envy of fathers and teachers. He had become the arbiter of the differences which broke out between the pupils and the depository for their secrets since they asked for his advice even on personal problems.

Abdel's friendship with Raouf was particularly distinctive. He was the first person in whom he confided his innermost secrets; he was happy to boast about his exploits without fear of exposing himself to put downs or competition. The young man who was normally so reserved and silent with other people was transformed. He was like a child with a gentle and loving father, as if Raouf were two decades rather than two years older than him.

For his part, Raouf was much struck by Abdel and his insubordination. In contrast to his friend, he obeyed his father implicitly in everything he did. Perhaps this could be traced back to his Bedouin origins and the position of spiritual leader which his father occupied among the other men in the tribe. When he thought of his childhood, he remembered a large house in the country which was always full of visitors; some of them were there to seek guidance from his father, others to offer gifts or to eat the splendid dinner which was served every evening. But that world had suddenly vanished, when the monarchy came to an end and Raouf had found himself living with his family in a modest house on the outskirts of Baghdad.

When they first met up again after their long separation, Raouf gave an astonishingly accurate account of Abdel's adventures at school which the other man had for the most part forgotten. His admiration of Abdel did not lead him on to disobey his father but rather made him more and more obedient; but Abdel remained an echo of himself. Through him, Raouf realised the dreams which were buried behind the lenses of his thick spectacles.

*　*　*

Abdel asked his younger brother to contact Raouf's family and obtain his address and telephone number in the Emirates. Until then, the only thing he knew about his one and only friend was that he had followed his father's advice and married his cousin despite the wide educational gap between them; for Raouf had completed his MA in electronic engineering before leaving Iraq and would definitely have gone on to work in one of the universities and never thought about leaving Baghdad, had he not been offered a tempting contract with a western company.

At Abdel's insistent urging, Raouf agreed to visit London and stay with him for a week. There were other reasons behind his coming: he needed to buy the latest books in his field of work. On the second day he was there, Abdel started to bombard his friend with complaints. Instead of making a direct approach to him, he talked about the tax system that was imposed on the residents in the country, about how his health had deteriorated after the accident and about the exorbitant cost of looking after Selim, his child; no doubt the stick which he resolutely carried every time they went out together played a definitive role in earning him Raouf's complete sympathy. A day before he returned to the Emirates, he offered to help but Abdel turned him down.

On his second visit, which was to take part in a scientific conference, organised by his employers, Raouf reiterated his offer of help and this time, Abdel accepted 'reluctantly'. Under the agreement, his friend opened an account in his name which Abdel could use whenever he wanted. The next time he visited London, he signed a fake contract to buy the house, which Abdel and his family had moved into.

* * *

I can't find a better word to describe Raouf's behaviour towards other people than 'aristocratic.' For this scion of feudal lords who had failed to free himself from the routine imposed by the choices he had made in his life, found great contentment in offering help to others, whether they were people he didn't know, or friends from his teenage years like Abdel. It is an area, which does not require a great deal of talent apart from the ability to use the single word 'yes' continuously. Raouf had never been able to turn down a request. Even at school when his classmates had asked for things like his slide rule, which he needed for his own work, he would give it to them. As soon as he received a request from a friend or relative in person or by letter, he would rush to carry it out, despite the fact that his behaviour angered his wife and prompted her to complain vociferously about the way he squandered his high salary.

As was customary with Raouf, he didn't tell his wife about the house or shares which Abdel had bought in his name, and he was very careful to hide the contracts and business letters he received from London, in a locked drawer.

* * *

On Raouf's fifth visit to London, his wife and daughter came with him to spend July and August with Abdel's family. At the time, Samia was five years old and apart from a noticeable pallor in her face, was not yet showing signs of kidney failure.

In Abdel's house, Samia threw herself into playing with the twins who competed to gain her affection. How grown up she seemed to them although she was only two months older than they were. The twins loved sneaking into Selim's room whenever Baida's attention was distracted by her youngest child, Lubna. Once in the room, they would behave as if he were their favourite toy. Sometimes they would make him copy the movements of a dog, other times they would ride him like a horse.

Samia was frightened when she first caught a glimpse of Selim. The door to his out-of-the-way room suddenly opened and a small round face with a large nose in the middle of it appeared. His mouth was open and saliva dribbled down his chin. Perhaps her sudden appearance in front of him made him slightly less afraid of stepping outside his room. He took a step forward so that she was able to see his whole body. She was curious and slightly alarmed at the sight of his bow legs, but her fear soon evaporated when she saw the easy way in which the twins controlled him and was replaced instead with a desire to defend him from their tricks. Selim always seemed very happy to see the twins. When they appeared in his room, he would pour out a series of incomprehensible phrases, breathing heavily through his large nose, and cheerfully do whatever they told him to do, occasionally breaking into strangled sobs when they overdid it and hurt him. Throughout her stay in London, Samia continuously kept a zealous eye on Selim and protected him from falling into his brothers' clutches, whenever Baida's back was turned.

*　*　*

Raouf should have arrived in London at the beginning of June for his latest trip, but instead he wrote to Abdel and begged off the visit. He said he had to cancel the trip because his only child, Samia, was ill; she was suffering from fatigue, nausea and weight loss and the doctors had told him that the symptoms all pointed to a serious defect in her kidney. In the last month, Samia had spent most of the time in the hospital.

Abdel needed to meet up with his friend so that he could sign some new documents connected with his shares and the tenancy on his house. Although he could have sent the papers through the post, the fear that they might fall into Raouf's wife's hands prompted him pay for the cost of a ticket to the Emirates from his own pocket. He took an expensive gift for Samia with him to make it appear as if the sole object of his visit was to reassure himself about the state of her health. When Raouf's wife expressed surprise at the extent of Abdel's concern, her husband told her that the two of them were closer than brothers.

* * *

Abdel did not let his wife know when he was coming back from the Emirates. The taxi dropped him off outside his house at a quarter past nine in the evening; as usual, the street, which lay in the suburbs of London, was wreathed in silence. Before inserting his key in the lock, he paused for a little, listening to the clamour of the children coming from inside. When he had traversed the short corridor leading to the sitting room, he was faced with a scene, he had not seen before: the twins were taking it in turns to leap over one of the sofas while Baida sat on the adjacent one with Lubna and Selim on either side of her. Their eyes were glued to the television screen while their mother's fingers were busy with her knitting.

Abdel did not react to the chaos in front of him but his sudden appearance was sufficient to freeze the twins in their tracks. Since he had been away, they had made it their mission to stay up as late as possible and pay no attention to Baida's entreaties that they stop turning everything around them upside down. Abdel rather unexpectedly expressed his surprise at the colour of the wool she was using. When he asked her who the sock was for, she replied hesitantly: "I don't know. It depends on the amount of wool I have." "Make it for Selim," he said firmly as if he had read her wishes.

Abdel did not say another word but the children quickly slunk away to their rooms, since it was more than an hour after their bed time; he didn't want them to go and wished that his spoiled daughter, Lubna in particular would stay downstairs with him a while longer, but that would have meant infringing the laws, he himself had imposed on his house. He was also desperate to have a bath with Baida, a custom, he had established long before he went away. She must have understood the expression on his face, for she pretended to come up with the idea.

*   *   *

When autumn arrived, Abdel received another letter from

Raouf, informing him that what he feared had come to pass: his daughter needed a new kidney and she only had a year to go before she was completely disabled.

He had been turning over this terrible possibility in his mind ever since returning from the Emirates and the letter only acted as sharp reminder that he should proceed with his plan: his initiative would inestimably strengthen the bonds of friendship which joined him to Raouf and put the latter in his debt for the rest of his life.

Part Four
Saleh and His Story

Until he left Baghdad, he was dogged by the soubriquet. It stuck to him, no matter where he went, and he could see it on people's lips and in their eyes even when they avoided talking to him.

While he had loathed the label in Iraq, in London he came to prefer it. It aroused a sense of longing in him that he found difficult to define. Was he missing the scent of perfume, the invisible sound of women's laughter, the rustle of dresses and the whirr of sewing machines that filled the house? Or was he longing for something illusory which memory often fashions from the past?

When he arrived in London, he continued to look over his shoulder for a time as he had done in Baghdad, as if he unconsciously expected to hear someone shouting out behind him: "Dressmaker's son." But as the tremendous sea of strange faces surged around him, his obsession faded and was gradually replaced with a wistful yearning to hear the nickname once again.

Saleh sometimes attributed this nostalgia to another emotion that grew more intense, the longer he stayed in London: a sense of regret.

Regret for the chaste young man he had been back there. Sometimes it seemed to him that the person he now was, was completely unconnected to the person he had been then. The house was always been full of women. From time to time, one of them would steal into his room on some flimsy excuse or other. "I'm looking for my bag. I don't know where I put it," she'd say, or "I'm sorry. I thought it was in your sisters' room."

Some young girls would even be cheeky enough to sit down on his bed and start talking to him. At such times, he would retreat behind the table as if he were violating some sort of taboo by finding any of the women who entered the house attractive, and thereby breaking the pact which existed between himself and the other boys in the neighbourhood that he would not touch their women.

What amazed Saleh now, when he thought back to what he had been like at that time, was the way he had regarded the customers. He thought of them as being under his protection, just as his mother and sisters were. He was the only man in the house. When his mother had taken on the role of breadwinner after his father died, he had assumed responsibility for his family's reputation.

For years the house was like a convent. His mother was permanently swathed in black; when she had removed the wide marriage bed from her room and put a single one in its place, she had eliminated all traces of femininity along with it, the makeup, gaudy night gowns and soft shimmering materials. When his sisters reached adolescence, she tightened her grip on them. He could hear her angrily scolding the youngest of them: "What will the neighbours say if they catch you wearing such a short skirt?"

When Saleh tried to remember his teenage years, he could not recall them. It was as if he had gone straight from being a child to a young man without passing through adolescence: the state when his sensory desires lay dormant. All the while, he and his mother divided up the responsibilities

98

of the house between them like a model married couple. It was up to her to provide for the family while he oversaw his sisters' studies and monitored their behaviour. In order to provide him with the necessary gravitas to carry out his role, he was given his own room and wore a suit and dark tie instead of shorts. It was no longer possible for him to play with the boys in the street.

"You're the man of the house," his mother would say whenever she felt that he was behaving more like a ten year old than a man in his thirties. Her tone was tinged with a fear hidden from the outside world that he would abandon the role of father. "We depend on you for protection."

In the anxious state of siege in which his family lived, Saleh became obsessed about his height. Not a week went by without him measuring himself. He would make a mark on the wall with a pencil against the top of his head.

How happy his mother was when his body put on a sudden spurt of growth and shot above the lines. She marvelled incredulously as he paraded before her, and when she found out he was taller than her, begged him to stand beside her in front of the mirror, crying out in delight as if she had been waiting for this moment all her life. "You're the master of the house now."

But she didn't once think about what was going on inside him. She didn't seem to notice that he had broken out in spots or had fashion magazines in his room.

Faced with this strange fascination with women, which suddenly held him in its sway, his right hand would involuntarily move down to his permanently erect penis and take hold of it. In his dreams he saw a stream of naked young women emerging from the bathroom but before he was able to make out who they were, he would wake up afraid.

The girls from the fashion magazines were the only ones who could quench his thirst. They would stand in front of him and although he didn't know their names, would easily strip off their elegant clothes for him. When he had chosen the one he wanted, she would immediately get into bed with him.

Saleh inhabited a space between two worlds, one filled with genuine women and the other with images of women he didn't know. He slipped into the former in his dreams and was lacerated with feelings of guilt; he slipped into the latter through his imagination and his fingers only to feel deeply frustrated and empty after slaking his desires.

July 17th 1983

As on every Sunday, he spent the morning on his own in bed, waiting for the newspaper to arrive. When heard it thud onto the carpet, he got up immediately and hurried to the front door.

He spread the pages of The Observer out on the bed. He began, as he always did by reading the weather: 'Sunny spells with a few showers. There is an area of low pressure slowly moving over Great Britain.' He looked at the clouds through the window. Yesterday with its beautiful weather seemed like a dream that had no connection with today. He would see the sudden change reflected in the people who lived in the building. The day before his elderly neighbour Janet had said happily: "It's a sunny day. Are you going to the park?"

His ears picked up the intermittent ringing of church bells. As on every Sunday the sound evoked a mixture of emotions in him. A feeling of affection on the one hand for the only sign of life that day; and on the other, another stranger and more inexplicable sensation of total isolation.

He barely remembered Baghdad now except in his dreams, most of which were nightmares and revolved around his returning to the city and being caught by the security forces. Once he had dreamed that he was in a large shop, in which everything appeared to be made out of leather. Bags, belts, trousers, shirts and hats. When he climbed the five flights of stairs leading to the open-plan top floor, the President appeared in front of him. Did he own the shop? What kind of skins were they around him? The only thing he could remember was a sense of complete paralysis and panic. "Don't be afraid, we will forgive you if you are able to cross the desert," The President had told him sternly. The scene changed suddenly and he found himself in a crowd of competitors who were scrambling feverishly to escape a thick cloud of dust that was piling up behind them.

He was curious to see what the latest news was on Neil Kinnock, the main contender in the Labour Party leadership race. The car accident which had almost killed him appeared to have strengthened the feeling among some of the undecided that he was the man to rescue the party from the ruins of the last elections and steer it to a safe shore. His eyes rested on something the politician had said after emerging from the wreckage of his car: "Someone up there likes me." There was an article on another page by Roy Hattersley, a rival contender in the leadership race, entitled, 'Why we lost,' in which he compared the size of the Labour defeat in the election five weeks previously to the one they had suffered in the 1918 elections.

His eyes were drawn to a piece by Patrick Seale: 'Drifting mines in the Gulf threaten oil tankers.' So the newspaper had finally decided to cover the war again; there had been an increase in Iraqi air raids on Iranian oil installations, now that the war had changed direction and Iran had started making incursions into Iraq. The writer put forward conflicting points of view. A statement put out by the World Wildlife Fund stated that sea turtles and species of dolphin, birds and fish were being destroyed, while the League of Gulf States for Protecting the Environment said there was no evidence that it was affecting marine life in the Gulf.

Scheherazade had gone off with Helen the day before to visit her father who now lived in a home for the elderly outside London. As always she had evaded his suggestion that he accompany her. After her previous visit a month ago, he had told her, while they were in bed. "I want to meet him. He knows more than almost anyone else about the modern history of Iraq." She was silent for what seemed like ages. Had he insulted her father in some way by asking the question? Before he could ask her to explain, she whispered.

"Why don't you forget the past and history and enjoy the present? You're still a young man with your whole life in front of you."

"What do you suggest I do?"

"Get married."

"To whom?"

"Why don't you ask your mother to send you a bride?"

As she wrapped her arms about his neck, she softened her serious tone: "Don't you ever think about having children? About a beautiful young woman who will wash your clothes and cook Iraqi food for you?"

He paused at an article by Katherine Whitehorn, entitled "Mr and Mrs?" in which, the journalist explored the reasons behind the reluctance of some couples to get married officially. She could only come up with one reason to justify legalising the relationship. The novelist Kurt Vonnegut and his girlfriend Jill Krementz had decided to get married after going to a funeral service because they had been so shocked at the manner in which Jill Krementz was treated by the deceased's family. He cut out the article for Scheherazade who liked her writing.

February 20th 1969

In his dictionary al-Mawrid, Munir Ba'albeki explains the word 'macabre' rather than giving it a precise equivalent: objectification of death; comprising a personification of death; frightful.

Saleh found another more exact meaning: the dance of death. In his research into the origins of the word, he was struck by an allusion to the Arabic word for graveyard maqbara as a possible source for the word. Maqbara; macabre; maqābir.

According to the Encyclopaedia Britannica, 'macabre' was an allegorical concept which dated back to the Middle Ages. The all-conquering power of death was expressed in every form of creativity, be it drama, poetry, music, or the visual arts. Perhaps the concept derived its momentum from the Black Death which was rife in Europe at the end of the thirteenth century and the Hundred Years' War between England and France.

The creative nature of the work he had witnessed in Baghdad that day had been of a very special kind. Western artists who repeatedly depicted Death as a wily personage preying on the naïve could never have come up with such an idea. Maybe the very fact that there was no equivalent to 'macabre' in the Arabic language had enabled it to come into existence for its creator had forgotten that he was nothing but a tool of Death and that another time, would be the subject of the painting.

He had joined the huge crowd of students walking along the streets from al-'Adhmiyah to Bab al-Sharqi and been swept along with them to al-Tairan Square. Initially, he was only slightly puzzled by the sight of the wooden posts erected around the square. Odd questions such as: When did they finish putting them up? How long did it take? flickered through his confused mind, for the place which he was so fond of had a peculiar atmosphere in it that day.

When he arrived at college, he found that classes had been cancelled for the day to allow students to march to al-Tairan Square. He could have avoided taking part in the demonstration, but was curious to see what death looked like. Throughout his life he had managed to steer clear of anything of that kind. When his father died, he had only been a young boy. His older relatives had kept him away from the actual funeral, and he had merely attended the mourning ceremonies at home.

Was the image he held in his memory a faithful representation of what he had actually seen? There was definitely a chill in the air even when he arrived in the Square, despite the fact that the sun seemed unmoving in the middle of the sky. It was definitely twelve o'clock. He found himself surrounded by a sea of strangers. Workers, peasants, teachers with their pupils. They had come from everywhere. It was a real carnival. He was caught up in the crowds, his body jostled slightly by the tide of people around him, as he involuntarily began to move around the square. Sometimes he drew close to the perimeter, only to be elbowed out of the way at the last minute.

Finally amid the sea of banners and the ringing cheers he caught a glimpse of the spectacle on his right. A row of bodies dangled at the end of thick ropes, each one dressed in a lurid differently coloured tracksuit. Heads lay at various angles: some looked up at the indifferent sky, others hung down as if gazing at the concrete ground.

Had the idea for his novel really come to him then as he processed past the fourteen corpses? He experienced a sickening sense of shock at the macabre, the dance of death. Would its creator have been able to come up with such a scene of horror if the word 'macabre' had entered the Arabic language in the true sense of the word beforehand?

After the ritual ceremonies were over and the President and his deputy had departed, the demonstrators entered the square as it began to empty. He found himself wandering between the wooden posts as the living mixed freely with the dead. In one corner, people started chanting revolutionary slogans and the sound rose up and mingled with the banners hanging in the empty spaces between the corpses. "This is the fate of the enemies of the revolution." "The execution of spies is the first revolutionary step towards national liberation."

17th July 1983

Even when the English are joking, they remain very serious at heart. Perhaps this is what makes it difficult for them to become friendly with foreigners, for they essentially regard the latter's humour as a form of madness which oversteps the boundaries that separate individuals from each other; if they attempt to imitate them their behaviour is classified as Eccentric according to the precise definition given by the Oxford English Dictionary. The closest translation in Arabic to this word is: strangely behaved.

This thought popped into his mind while he was reading an article about the artist and critic, Amanda Fielding. In an attempt to get away from the oppressive life style imposed on her by prevailing social conventions, she had travelled to the Empty Quarter, which was then one of the wildest places in the world, after graduating from Oxford. When she returned to London, she had been converted to a new theory which she had heard about from Bart Hughes, a former medical student from Holland. He advocated trepanation as a way of alleviating depression and stress and achieving a greater degree of self-knowledge and inner enlightenment. Drilling a hole in the head allowed more oxygen and blood to reach the brain as happened with very young babies.

In her flat, overlooking the Thames, in the posh district of Chelsea, Fielding successfully bored a hole in her skull using a small electric drill. She shaved off her hair, and then put on a pair of goggles, taping the edges with sticking plaster to prevent the blood getting into her eyes. After anaesthetising the area, in which she was going to drill, she made an incision with a small scalpel to determine the exact place in which to bore the hole. Her partner Joseph Mellen filmed her during the operation using a camera which Fielding had hired particularly for the occasion. His hands remained steady even when blood spurted out of his girlfriend's head.

Fielding called the film Heartbeat in the Brain. When the drill teeth broke through the outer casing of her skull, she felt her brain pulsate as if it had been released from its prison. She now enjoyed an expanded consciousness without having to resort to LSD; she had more energy and inspiration and was on a permanent high.

Fielding claimed that people who practiced trepanation were less likely to be affected by neurosis and depression and less prone to alcoholism and drug addiction. The procedure also contributed to a permanent sense of well-being. Not content with publicising the benefits of trepanation to the widest audience possible, she also stood as a candidate in the 1978 elections demanding that trepanation be made available on the NHS. She won forty votes.

There was not the slightest trace of humour in any of Fielding's arguments and the counter arguments were similarly serious and rigidly logical. A doctor who was opposed to her said: 'You have to make two holes rather than one to breathe through the head, in exactly the same way as you have to make two holes in the top if a tin, before you can remove liquid from it.'

The art of logical argument is a trait beloved by the English even when the subject under discussion is far-fetched. It requires the complete reining in of any form of emotion, if it is to be done properly. The discussant must be absolutely detached from the subject he or she is defending or criticising.

Saleh eagerly turned to the controversy which had erupted a few months ago over the death penalty. The battle had started in parliament when a few Conservative MPs had tabled a motion calling for the re-introduction of capital punishment. Gradually the battlefield widened and newspapers and radio and television stations entered the fray. The pro- and anti-lobbies unleashed a barrage of new arguments against each other even though both sides knew that it would be impossible to turn the clock back. Those taking part were more concerned with having an enjoyable debate and exercising their intellectual skills, especially as the subject lay outside the emotional life of those involved. They were more interested in the principle of capital punishment than the suffering of the person at the end of the rope.

20th February 1969

Apart from a broadcast recording of parts of their trial in front of a special military court, there was nothing to show that the people who had been hanged had been involved in espionage. The sound of Judge Wutwut sharply reprimanding one of the accused as he choked out an explanation only raised more questions: When and where had the trial taken place? Had the accused sat on benches or been put in cages, which expanded or contract over their chests depending on the answers they gave? Had the trial started by preparing them for the death penalty, since it was broadcast on the night preceding the carnival?

As he watched the market street from his window, he realised that the terror, which still fed his nightmares stemmed from that moment when he heard the accused choking back his rasping breath, in response to a simulated cough from Colonel Wutwut. A 'macabre' sound prepares the way for a 'macabre' sight.

He thought about the title of his last lesson: inert energy. One of his students had asked a question that he thought was rather naïve. "If inert energy equals kinetic energy according to the laws of Newton, then why is the impact of kinetic energy so much more powerful than that of inert energy?" "Can you give me an example?" Saleh asked him. "Uranium can be harmful if someone touches it because of its rays, but a nuclear explosion causes hundreds of thousands of deaths," the student replied, provoking an outburst of laughter from the other students which made him go bright red. Saleh commended the questioner, first of all, and then asked, "Who can explain it?" He passed over a number of answers then paused at a reply which had excited laughter and mocking comments: "Because the inert energy is inert." Should he tell them that Newton's law aimed to disprove the existence of an additional energy source outside the material world? Instead however, he found himself responding as a teacher: "What happens if someone climbs a ladder with a small stone in his hand? While he is holding the object, it won't cause any harm, but immediately he lets it go, the inert energy is released and is transformed into kinetic energy. The higher the person with the stone climbs, the more harmful the stone becomes when it is dropped on someone standing below. Inert energy requires a vacuum about itself to free itself."

At that instant, an image of the fourteen 'sportsmen' flashed through his mind, though this time, with a slight alteration. Each one had a piece of cardboard attached to his chest with his name written on it in bold letters and under it the word 'spy'.

How can we know what a stone's true nature is unless we see it in a vacuum? The larger the vacuum, the better able the stone is to truly express its hidden potential. Would British politicians turn into murderers if the checks on their movements were removed? It had only been six months since the leaders of the latest coup had snatched power, and in that time they had busied themselves taking control of the organs of state security. That day, they had been putting on their first public display, a colourful dance of death, a macabre which spoke to the intestines and paralysed the mind.

Nothing had changed in the little café that adjoined al-Tahrir Square. As usual, its owner was busy concentrating on the tea pots ranged in rows on a hot ceramic top; as soon as the young waiter put down a tray near him, he began to pour a stream of black liquid into the small glasses lined up in an orderly manner on their little saucers. The grains of coarse sugar inside them began to melt as clouds of steam

110

arose from them.

The sweetness vanished on his tongue and was replaced by a strangely acidic taste that blended with the bile rising from his stomach. He looked around the café. Everything seemed normal apart from a picture of the owner of the café, which was missing from its usual place on the wall facing the street. It had been painted by an impoverished artist in exchange for half a dinar and Ibrahim had greatly admired it and hung it in a gold frame. The terrifying events of the morning had no doubt forced him to get rid of his portrait and replace it with a photograph of the President in a splendid military uniform.

He was attracted by the face of the man sitting beside him, who for some reason, reminded him of Ivan Karamazov. Perhaps it was the thick spectacles, the hair parted in the middle and the short buttoned up overcoat. The man was watching him with an odd mixture of disinterest and earnest attention, which made him feel slightly uncomfortable. Despite the curiosity he saw in his guarded eyes, he decided he wasn't a member of the secret police. He seemed to be about the same age as himself or maybe a year or two older and was probably a university student as well.

The man's voice took him by surprise. "Did you see them?" His question seemed to startle the people around them. Some of them remained immersed in a game of dominoes despite the continuing sound of nationalist chants coming from the square; others would go out to take another look at the spectacle then return to the café. "What do you think about going somewhere else?" the man beside him asked in a friendly fashion as if they were old friends.

10th July 1983

The previous Sunday, Scheherazade had suggested that they pass by her cousin's house. They were on their way back home from Hyde Park. The sun had almost set, leaving a glitter of orange sparks on the trees. "Has she left for Baghdad?" he asked. "Yes, but she didn't take Selim with her," she added with suppressed irritation. When she saw the surprise in his eyes, she explained, "You know her father's ill. She didn't want to upset the family." She corrected herself immediately, "At least that's what I think."

When she stopped the car in front of her relative's house, she turned towards him: "I think I'll take Selim home with me till Baida returns. Would anyone in their right mind leave a child with Abdel?" She laughed to conceal her anxiety, and then put her hands to her temples and was silent for a minute:

"That's it, I'll take him now. Helen will love having him. What do you think?"

"It's a great idea. I can help look after him as well. My college is about to start its summer holiday."

"What about your book?"

"I need to study a child like Selim."

When he saw the gleam of curiosity in her eyes, he added: "There's a boy like Selim in my book." She planted a grateful kiss on his cheek. Before getting out of the car, she said hastily: "I'll be back in a minute. There's no need for you to get out." He watched her through the side window as she rang the bell repeatedly. Despite the deepening twilight, he could detect the tension in the way she walked and moved her arms, even from where he was sitting. When she returned, she sat in front of the steering wheel for a time without saying anything. "What do you think Abdel's doing to him?" she finally asked, but before he could answer, she went on in a lighter tone as if trying to ease the worries surging through her mind. "Perhaps he's sold him like they do in fairy stories?" Then she burst out laughing. "I'm exaggerating, aren't I? Abdel's not as wicked as all that, is he?" "No, of course not; perhaps he's taken him to the zoo," he said reassuringly.

20th February 1969

Until the moment they met in the café, his life had been governed by his sense of duty. He assumed that everyone else was like him.

After the voices had faded away behind them, Maher asked, "What made you come today?" The question took his mind off the image, which was still going round and round in his head, of a corpse in a red tracksuit bobbing up and down like a lantern surprised by a sudden gust of wind. "I don't know, perhaps it was out of curiosity," he replied. "What about you?" "Likewise. I've never seen a dead body before."

It was some time before the latter picked up the thread of conversation again. They walked along in silence, the steady sound of their footsteps echoing off the pavement. Now and then they turned to look at the Tigris which was infused with the indigo purple of the setting sun. "Do you know I found out something bizarre and frightening today?" said Maher. "People can watch an atrocity with complete indifference as long as they are part of a large crowd of onlookers. Wouldn't you have been horrified if you had seen these events in a dream?

He was attracted by Maher's manner of talking or more precisely by his expert way of drawing him into conversation. Through apparently innocent school-like questions, he induced him to express his beliefs so that he could start demolishing their foundations, forcing his rival to agree with him at every stage of the conversation until, suddenly, checkmate, he was defeated.

As they were sitting in the Sargon Bar, he discovered a difference between them: while he treated the waiter politely, his companion was very rude to him. Or that's how it seemed at the time. Perhaps Maher's careless attitude towards the outside world and his concentration on some inner ongoing dialogue were what attracted him to him. Now he also felt an inner freedom. As if the customers around them were gelatinous beings who did not have the power to embarrass him. "Do you want to come home with me?" his companion asked, then added when he read the hesitation in his eyes. "Other friends are coming this evening and you may like some of them."

17th July 1983

His eyes took in the news headlines: CND human chain: 10 thousand people opposed to nuclear weapons formed a two mile long human chain across Hyde Park yesterday linking the American and the Soviet embassies; The Battle for Beirut: Heavy fighting flared up on the outskirts of Beirut

114

between the Druze and Christian militias."

A sentence by the famous artist Cezanne came to his mind: "Everything in nature is fashioned from the sphere, the cone and the cylinder. Man must learn to draw in this manner." In his note book he wrote as follows: Everything in nature is fashioned from emotion, instinct and intellect. Man must learn to write in this manner."

He went back to the newspaper: Mrs Thatcher has proposed longer prison sentences for violent criminals to appease Conservative supporters of capital punishment; Nelson Mandela, leader of the banned African National Congress will be 65 tomorrow. He will spend his birthday in his cell in Pollsmoor Prison outside Cape Town."

At the last dinner party she had organised, Scheherazade had intervened when an awkward silence fell between him and her other guest and asked Richard "Do you know that Saleh is writing a novel?" Her voice was loud enough to attract the attention of everyone at the table and increased his discomfort.

"What's it about?" asked the man beside him with what he felt was feigned interest.

"Energy."

"So it's science fiction?"

"Sort of."

"Of course, you're employing the stream of consciousness?"

"I don't think so."

"Can you write a novel in other way today?"

"I think stream of consciousness is an artistic trick to tell a story with fewer mistakes."

"What do you mean?"

"Stream of consciousness is based on the inner voice of the hero. But can we prove that we think this way? Our heads are merely chaotic offices, whose aim is to impose order on what lies outside them."

Scheherazade broke up the conversation between them. "This is a dinner party not a cultural seminar," she said gaily. "Come and serve yourselves before the food is all gone."

20th February 1969

Until the door to the flat opened, Saleh never imagined that a world could exist in Baghdad that was so different to the one he was familiar with. "This is Maha, my wife." said Maher, introducing a young woman who seemed slightly confused to see him. Perhaps she had caught him staring involuntarily at her short skirt, and the well-rounded thighs below. Usually he wouldn't have done such a thing but he was slightly tipsy from the two glasses of araq they had drunk at Sargon's.

Even after all these years, he could still remember his first sight of the sitting room. Was it the picture of Guevara that first drew his attention or that of Guernica? There must have been more than twelve people in the room but as it opened out on to a corridor, some of them were able to sit round its perimeter. He was particularly surprised by the young girls who were there. Some of them sat on the two wooden divans that faced each other while others sprawled on the floor. There was a haze of cigarette smoke and everyone seemed to be slightly drunk. In the midst of all the noise, Sheikh Imam's voice echoed through the emptiness like a mysterious liturgical hum, giving the room an even more bizarre quality.

Maher introduced him to everyone. He began with Samir and his wife, with whom he shared the flat. He noticed the way the atmosphere changed immediately Maher appeared. The men seemed to become more serious. Samir said censoriously: "Where have you been all this time? You knew about our meeting, didn't you?" He sounded upset and his slurred voice was tinged with sharpness. He threw a smouldering glance at Saleh, which further convinced him that something was wrong.

But then Samir returned to the heated conversation he had been having with two other guests and with Maher sitting beside him his tone quietened and became more assured. "I'm saying that our identities are formed after we come into existence. Our choices determine what we become. Isn't that so?" His eyes were fixed on Maher, as if waiting for a word of approval from him. "Where does the unconscious fit into this?" one of the guests asked. Samir's voice rose angrily: "The unconscious is a huge lie which is used to deprive us of responsibility." He suddenly turned on Saleh impatiently: "What do you think?" The crimson hue of his face made the latter react more aggressively. "I agree with you but what about economic factors?" "Forget such nonsense," Samir interrupted him, "Are you a Commie? A follower of the hammer and sickle? Admit it. I won't tell on you." He began to laugh hysterically: "I agree with you!" "Who asked you to agree with me? Hasn't Maher told you it's fun to have ideas but you don't have to believe in them?" His host intervened to protect him. He told Samir mildly but with an undercurrent of sternness, "Why don't you go and wash your face in the bathroom?"

17th July 1983

Before Scheherazade cut into his conversation with Richard, Saleh had been about to draw a comparison between the thought process and the uncertainty principle in physics. We are unable to measure the speed of an electron and its location simultaneously; similarly we cannot think and monitor our thoughts at the same time. The stream of consciousness style of writing is like Bohr's hypothetical model of the atom, elegant but with little basis in reality. When we try to hold on to what is going through our minds, the turbulent waves of ideas, which are moving this way and that suddenly vanish and we are confronted with nothing. The orderly movement of individuals in the street gives no hint of the cacophony of sound swirling through their minds. From the moment it awakes, our consciousness is unfettered. Memories chase each other, ideas mingle, conflicting emotions supplant each other. When we decide to observe this vast outpouring of thought, everything disappears. We think about the world and we disappear ourselves; we think about ourselves and the world disappears.

He paused at an item of news: Terrorist groups in Ulster have reached an agreement on informers: it is believed that Republican and Loyalist terrorist groups in Northern Ireland are working together to 'liquidate' informers who have helped bring about the arrest of eighty people and disclosed details of murders going back over the last ten years.

Why did he like Cezanne's paintings so much? He looked across at the posters on the walls, from where he was lying on the bed. Maybe it was because they seemed incomplete. Or perhaps it was the fact that the faces in the paintings appeared distorted, when looked at on their own but when the painting was taken as a whole, the harmony between its various parts became visible. The sacrifice of the part for the good of the whole. Eliminating difference between the face of a person and the surface of an apple. Everything was governed by the same laws of colour. This was also true of the protagonists in his novel; the differences between them were determined according to the degree and kind of energy, they exercised. In Cezanne's paintings the lineaments of the body were not carefully defined but emerged through the degree of light and shade playing on other surfaces. Similarly the particulars of his hero only appeared when he was put next to the other characters. Mandela and his second wife Winnie Mandela celebrated their silver wedding anniversary this year; the Soviet dissident Yuri Orlov who was on hunger strike in prison died as a result of breathing difficulties.'

His eyes alighted on another painting of Cezanne's, this one of Mont Saint Victoire. Here the artist had composed a landscape using juxtaposed strokes of light and dark colour. When looked at separately, they gave no indication of what the objects were. Only by viewing the shape as a whole, did the spectator discover the details of the attractive scene and his eye had no difficulty in accepting them even though parts of the sky were green.

Were his characters nothing but blocks of colour, possessing light and dark energy? What about emotion? Was it an independent form of energy that had to be added to the other three forms of energy or was it the source of the latter?

20th August 1969

He hadn't seen her when she had first emerged from her room. When he thought back, the only thing he could remember was the way everyone turned to gaze at her, while he remained sitting where he was. He imagined her coming through the door behind him which had been closed up to then. The man beside him whispered jokingly: "Sartre should have said: hell is Selma, not other people."

It must have been half past twelve; some of the guests had left, and now that Samir had gone off to bed, a sudden quietness had fallen on the gathering.

She stopped directly behind him. He only realised when he saw the change in Maher's expression. The latter said: "You've joined us late tonight." "Bushra's only just gone off to sleep," she said apologetically. "Never mind, the evening's only just begun and tomorrow's Friday." There was a brief silence, then she added, "You haven't introduced me to your friend." He stood up to shake hands with her. When he turned to face her, he felt as if he had been struck by lightening.

He was overcome by a feeling that he had seen her before. That he had known her in another time and that life had somehow brought them back together. There was a mysterious invitation in her sparkling eyes which froze the words on his lips and made his heart start to pound. The series of events which had led up to his encounter with Maher suddenly made sense to him. He had been brought to this moment by a succession of blind choices. But the choices had just ended. He was like a sleepwalker, hypnotised by a magnetic force that was totally new to him. Until that moment he had been a dutiful son, doing whatever his family demanded of him, believing that whatever was suitable for them was also suitable for him. His mother had suggested that he marry their neighbour Ilham. "She's like one of my daughters. I've raised her myself," she told him. He saw no reason to refuse since agreeing to the plan would pacify her. It was settled that the engagement would take place when he graduated from university later in the year.

What was it about that instant that made him recall it so clearly? How had he preserved it from the moths of oblivion? Al-Ma'ari says that the word for mankind (insan) is derived from the word for oblivion (nisyan). We walk through the deserts of the past where nothing remains apart from tiny oases which are like energy plants sustaining our souls from death by oblivion.

Selma's sudden appearance injected new life into the party. Most of the guests were about to leave. Three couples began saying their goodbyes to Maher and Maha.

"Where are you going? Only hens sleep at this time of night," Selma said with a laugh. When she saw the couples hesitate, she added firmly: "Well, stay another half hour. We'll have a drink together then you can go."

But they stayed for more than two hours. Selma took the cassette of Sheikh Imam off the player and put on one of Elvis Presley's instead. She commented: "I think you've had enough revolutionary songs for now. It's time to enjoy yourselves."

It was only now that he could come up with a word to describe the look on the men's faces when Selma made her entrance. It was lust. Even when they were dancing with their wives, their eyes stole in her direction from time to time.

Saleh didn't move from his chair, scarcely able to believe what he was seeing. He must be dreaming. Selma's body quivered in time to Don't be Cruel. His eyes caressed her arms and hips as she danced. Ballet, tango, samba. Every cell in her body responded to the fast regular beat while her fingers seemed to talk in mysterious signs. In contrast, the others looked like a herd of elephants with their random clumsy movements.

Maybe she became aware of him as she stopped dancing, when the song reached its conclusion. His eyes were glued to her. It was as if she understood what was going through his mind for she winked at him like a co-conspirator. His heart lurched sideways and his forehead broke out into a sweat.

When the rhythm slowed, and couples formed for One Night With You, she slipped away from the others and stood in front of him, with her hands clasped together. "May I have the pleasure of your hand for this dance?" she begged him with a carefree laugh, which forced him to get up immediately. While they were walking to the middle of the room, he said in a shaky voice, "I've never danced in my life." As she took his hand and led him on to the dance floor, she whispered in his ear: "Don't worry, just follow my instructions and you'll soon learn."

21st February 1969

When Saleh opened his eyes, he wasn't sure where he was at first. The curtains were closed but that did not stop the morning light filtering into the empty room. From where he was lying, he could read the time on the wall clock hanging in front of him The house was bathed in an unearthly silence and there was no sign of life apart from an intermittent rumbling, coming from outside. He turned his eyes towards the shut door, suddenly experiencing a deep sense of longing that made it difficult to breathe. It was not directed at any particular person but was rather more of a desire to melt into his surroundings. For a moment he was filled with a fierce happiness which almost immediately afterwards was replaced by an intense feeling of despair. He found it hard to believe that the door, which was now shut so firmly, had opened to him a few hours previously and allowed him through to join her in her bed.

When all the guests had left, and he was finally getting up to go, he heard Maher say, "Why don't you spend the night here?" When his wife saw him hesitating, she said, "We don't get up early on Friday, anyway." Then she added temptingly, "What do you say? We could all have lunch together."

Even though Selma did not say anything, he presumed she would also press him to stay, but when he looked over at her, her eyes gave nothing away. He thought back to those seemingly endless moments, those seconds in time, when he could have walked away. Instead he had given in to the memory of her pliant body, moving against his on the dance floor. He touches her back with his right hand while the fingers on his left cling to her right hand. She makes his senses swim. He can feel the pulse in her veins as their fingers touch and his blood responds, pulsating in time with hers. The others gradually vanish. They are now together, their bodies a single vessel moving through a calm sea, while their hearts beat as one in the pale flickering light of the candle.

Total darkness settled over the house. His mind went back again to the moment when the song had ended. When he'd dragged himself away from the dream he'd been sharing with her, which had not yet reached its end. When the lights came on and the others began to leave, she disengaged herself from him and went to say goodbye to them.

His eyes were glued to the door to her room, where he could clearly see a streak of pale light shining under the bottom. Was she still awake? The question troubled him. He became aware of guilt seeping into his soul, as if a new spirit had emerged inside him and engaged with the old. For the first time, he felt desire for a real woman, whom he simultaneously regarded as a sister whom he had to protect. He was torn between the two emotions, between total lust and absolute chastity.

He was dozing off when he felt a soft touch on his shoulder. He opened his eyes. He was confronted by an opaque nothingness, in the middle of which was the vague shape of a face. He couldn't see its features, though he could recall them in every detail. Her image was imprinted on his mind. She stretched out a hand towards him, a life boat come to rescue him from the violent tide of passion. Did his body resist the tug of her gentle fingers? He could not now remember. The only thing he could recall was the trance-like state in which he moved as he walked behind her to the square of glowing light coming from her room. Maybe he felt like Armstrong had done when he stepped onto the moon, but unlike the astronaut's, his was a journey from which there was no return.

17th July 1983

His eye was caught by another of Cezanne's paintings: A Kitchen Table. The fruit on its own had no significance and only served to provide a patch of colour which helped create a greater degree of harmony on the two dimensional surface. The third dimension was reflected in the blocks of cold and warm colours which lay adjacent to each other: red next to green; yellow next to blue; proximity next to distance. The artist had completely abandoned a linear perspective. Instead of the size of objects being determined by their proximity to or distance from the person looking at the picture, the artist had painted them bigger or smaller according to their importance in the composition.

In the picture, a ray of light from the open window, illuminated the scene for a moment and was reflected in the painting. His eyes rested on the earthenware jar in the middle. Its interior was clearly visible as if it was being seen from above. As if Cezanne had several different eyes positioned at various places while he painted.

How could he incorporate this principle into his novel? By listing events in non-chronological order? By conflating and separating the voices of the narrator and principle character, so that they came together and separated like two instruments, according to the tempo of the composition?

He opened his notebook and turned to an undated page which was blank expect for a couple of lines he had scribbled in pencil: Impressionism: fixing the principle of transience, the moment which is not repeated. Cezanne: Attempting to capture what is eternal in that moment.

21st February 1969

They assembled round the oblong table in the kitchen. Selma sat in front of him with Samir beside her. He appeared slightly uneasy and eager to placate him. Without looking at Saleh directly, he said, "I don't remember much about yesterday evening. I hope I didn't offend you in any way." Maha interrupted him with a laugh: "Not at all. You were exemplary last night compared to other times. You didn't break any cups or plates." Everyone laughed. Selma continued, directing her remarks at him: "Samir's the nicest of men. Believe me." She lightly touched the thick hair on the back of his head. "But you have to get used to his personality. He's as docile as Jekyll, when he's sober and always ready to help others, but when he's drunk, he's as quarrelsome as Hyde." Maher commented: "Don't forget that Jekyll's angelic nature is due to Hyde's devilry." His wife added with a laugh: "Nevertheless, it's better to avoid Hyde. I'm the only one who knows how to deal with him."

Suddenly he was surprised by the touch of Selma's foot and the voices around him became a blur. Her toes inched their way up the bottom of his trouser legs until they settled on his shins, pulling him into a game of footsie-footsie against his will. Her feet had a life of their own. They were like a couple of unseen kittens, playfully doing whatever they wanted. He glanced across at her for a second and was amazed to see her completely engrossed in a conversation with the others as if she had nothing to do with what was happening under the table.

He recalled the scene he had encountered once he had crossed the threshold into her room. She had closed the door behind them. He stood there bemused, like someone in a dream, light-headedly breathing in the scent of perfume, a blend of jasmine, lemon and damask rose. How mysterious and yet how familiar everything seemed in the pale flickering light of the concealed candle.

His attention was first drawn to the child's cot from where he could hear a faint regular snore. His eyes moved on to where Selma was standing, slightly hidden behind a screen, covered with a piece of yellow material, embroidered with butterflies, flowers and Chinese writing. When she automatically moved towards the low bed, he couldn't believe what he was seeing even as his breath quickened and his heart thudded like a drum. She was completely naked. She whispered jokily after sliding her body between the sheets: "Hurry up! It's almost dawn."

Until that moment, women's bodies had only been abstract entities. They existed in fashion magazines or on the washing line on the roof of the house, where his mother and sisters reluctantly hung out their underwear and the bits of faded rags they used during their periods which were stained with red. As soon as they were dry they took them off the line.

Wasn't it true that at the time, he had a weird belief that outside fashion magazines, real women menstruated all the time and had jelly-like slippery bodies that were nothing like Selma's beautiful one. The reflection of the light burning above him gave him an idea and he stretched out his bewitched index finger towards it to make sure that he really existed, to make sure that the moment was real.

He replayed his faltering footsteps. His mind was gripped by a single image, a volcano erupting, hurling cinders in all directions, and spouting a fountain of lava that streamed unchecked down its sides as if trying to melt the world before it was extinguished.

Before he left her room, she said maliciously: "Are you sorry to have lost your virginity?" "Very," he muttered in confusion and in an attempt to match her tone.

17th July 1983

Why does man become entangled in emotional relationships which by the law of necessity must always come to an end? The question occurred to him while he was reading a leaflet tacked to the trunk of an oak tree. It read:

"Please help us to find Zen, our much loved Burmese cat. He is three years old, with thick white fur and blue eyes."

The moment he left Maher's house he was overtaken by a sense of listlessness which grew more enervating with every step he took towards his home. He heard the sound of his inner voice, talking to a woman other than his mother, be-

128

fore it quickly disappeared. Could it be Selma? She must have read the yearning in his eyes when he announced he was going, but she hadn't even bothered to get up and say goodbye. She merely gave him a meaningless wave of her hand, from where she was sitting and did not suggest meeting again: "Bye." Maher accompanied him to the door and as he was turning to leave, he heard her joining in the conversation.

When he got home, his mother noticed how distracted he was even though he pretended to show particular interest in what she and his sisters were saying. Perhaps she sensed danger but she could find no other means of countering it than reminding him of his future wife. "Ilham was here today," she said. "The poor girl waited for you for more than four hours." Unusually for him, he remained silent. He was struggling against a cloud of depression. Was it because he felt alienated from his family? He had the strange feeling that he would soon be leaving them and this in turn made him feel increasingly tender towards them.

At dawn, he dozed off for a time and had a dream which he could still remember. He and Selma were sitting in a slow-moving bus. From time to time, his body was jolted by a hole in the road, as his eyes peered blindly into the total darkness outside. He had lost all sense of direction and he gripped Selma's arm tightly. He seemed to hear the wind whistling behind him but when he turned round he was surprised to find a number of passengers sitting there. The shrieking sound was coming from the women on the seat directly behind him. He became convinced that they were his mother and sisters, though the meagre light made them look little more than shadows. Suddenly he was conscious of a sharp pain in his right arm. When he looked down, he was taking aback by the sight of blood gushing out. He was also able to see Selma's long fingernails digging deep into his flesh.

But the dream did not stop him thinking about Selma as her image and voice became more and more imbedded in his mind. He rang Maher a week later and could hardly believe his ears when the latter asked him to come and visit them. "Everyone's asking about you here," he said encouragingly. However he was filled with embarrassment, when he tried to ask about Selma and the words stuck to his tongue.

When he entered Maher's house, Saleh was overcome by a strange mix of joy and longing, which made him feast his eyes on every detail in the sitting room. He felt as if he was returning home after being away for a long time. Now and then, he would glance over at the closed door. His heart beat louder, he found it difficult to breathe. A single question swung back and forth in his mind like a pendulum: When would she emerge from her room?

Maha must have read what was going through his mind, for she said reassuringly: "Selma's out visiting some friends and will be back shortly."

Everyone started talking about different subjects. He was distracted for most of the time and unable to concentrate. There were two friends there he hadn't met when he first visited the house. Maher told one of them firmly:

"There is no such thing as human nature, in which we can measure good or evil."

"What criteria do you use for measuring it?" the other man

asked.

"The decisions an individual makes stem from his essential reality."

"Even if such decisions demand the murder of others?"

"Murder is always prompted by noble motives whose objective is to please others or their ideas."

"What forms human identity then?"

"The choices an individual makes."

Before he could expound further on these ideas, Samir eagerly joined the discussion and agreed with what he was saying: "Choices make human nature. Of course this means that if I don't make a choice then I won't have a human nature. There is always more than one choice. Even suicide is a choice, isn't it?

The ringing phone dragged him from one celestial body to another: from the quiet fire of waiting to the hell of despair. Maha lifted up the receiver while he strained to hear what was happening. She came back and announced: "Selma's going to stay the night at her friends." The news didn't excite much reaction apart from a smile between Maher and Samir.

He went back to the poster pinned to the tree: 'If you have any news about our much loved pet, whom we miss a lot, telephone us on the following number, please... Thank you very much.'

He wanted to ask the owners: "Can you describe your feelings of loss?" or "Why don't you buy another one like it? Or do cats have different personalities?"

How long had it been before he heard Selma's voice again?

Maher had spoken first: "I've a friend here who wants to

say hello." Then her voice came on the line: "You seem to forget your friends very quickly," she chided him in reproving tones. There was a silence while he tried to catch his breath, then he replied: "I've been very busy."

Her words echoed in his mind throughout the day. He was wild with joy and immediately forgot the oath he had sworn repeatedly, when he was mad with grief and ill with a fever that had affected him for more than a week: "I will never see her again."

Illness had brought him true relief, extracting him from the whirling fantasies, which had him in their grip; he began by repeating her name in his mind before finding himself compelled to say it out loud. He could see her everywhere he looked, up close and far away at the same time. His memory recalled every single detail of her room, the slightly scented air, the beauty of her skin, her eyes and hair. But he was unable to recapture the moment when they became joined together on the bed. It appeared to have vanished forever. He watched as parts of his body stumbled single-mindedly towards their goal, towards complete union with her. They were now a single being. It was as if he had been moving towards this moment every day of his life, even when he doubted it would ever come. Suddenly the cells of his body started to tremble: he was convulsed by an earthquake; he felt completely at one with the universe.

As he laboured under the fever, other feelings stirred in him: he felt sorry for himself. The instinct to remain, even when it is masked by illness, finds sly ways of preferring life.

After he recovered, he returned to his studies. He threw himself into covering the ground he had lost with the help of a diligent student.

He couldn't remember when the idea came to him to propose to Ilham: Why shouldn't it be now? Perhaps it was while he was ill, when his gentle neighbour visited him every day. His mother once said: "Did you like the soup? Ilham made it." On the day he decided to tell her what he had resolved, the call came from Maher and Selma.

10th April 1969

How much Baida reminded him of Ilham when they first met! Like her, she remained out of the limelight, carefully waiting on others, and rushing to fulfil their every need. Selma and Scheherazade were the complete opposite.

When Abdel came to his house with the table he had made, Baida had come as well. As they were putting it together, he had watched her as she carried out her husband's orders: Give me that board, that screw, this leg..."

She was quiet, accepting of her role in contrast to Abdel who was constantly on the alert, impatient and tense.

What would have happened if Abdel had been betrothed to Selma at an early age, and he to Ilham? Could he imagine Abdel standing in front of him now, grumbling continuously while Selma helped him? While he was watching Abdel and Baida, he came to the conclusion that every woman revealed a particular facet of a man's personality.

What would he be like today if he had married Ilham? What opportunities would have opened up at the expense of others?

The preparations for the wedding were carried out with

astonishing speed. Perhaps this was because their families took no part in it. Selma's parents had divorced a long time ago. Her father, a doctor lived with his young American wife in Los Angeles while her mother lived in Algiers where she taught at the university. Saleh had avoided telling his mother and sisters about his decision.

At that time, he felt as if he was under some kind of hypnotic spell, sleep walking through the days with his feet barely touching the ground.

Maher suggested that they spend a week in London as a short honeymoon. He had a friend who lived there and who was prepared to extend an invitation to them. It didn't take long to obtain their entry visas to Britain. Samir and his wife gave them their tickets as a present.

He spent the night before he was due to leave at home. He slept fitfully. His body tingled slightly as he regained consciousness and he stared out into the impenetrable darkness. Still half-asleep, he groped for the edge of the bed and the wall beside him, stricken by the knowledge that he was close to severing the links which bound him to this place. Soon it would be as if he had never been born here, never crawled across the ground or lain down in its rooms. From somewhere unknown, a sense of regret seeped into him. What did he know about Selma? Who was her first husband? All she had told him was that he was an Egyptian poet, who had been as old as her father. She had got to know him when visiting Cairo a couple of years before. He had dropped the subject when he saw the flicker of annoyance in her eyes. He told his mother that he was going away with some of his university friends. She made her concern plain.

She and his sisters would miss him very much. This was the first time that he had spent such a long time away.

In his mind's eye, he could see a pair of scales. On the right hand side were his mother, sisters and Ilham. Balanced against them on the other were Selma and her child. If he chose his family, he would be putting duty before his feelings; if he chose Selma he would be following that insistent and mysterious wish to go through the locked door into the unknown.

While he was having breakfast with his family, he wondered how his mother would react if she knew the truth? But he quickly dismissed the question from his mind, in his excitement at the thought of going to London with Selma. They had to be at the airport before three o'clock in the afternoon. He had absent-mindedly put their passports and tickets in his jacket pocket instead of in his shoulder bag. Fearful that they would fall into his mother's hands, he wore his jacket even while they were having breakfast.

When he looked back, he remembered how quickly the hands of the clock seemed to move. He felt torn apart, caught in a tug of war between two opposing forces, each side trying to wrest control from the other. One side pressed him to leave immediately, the other to stay and cancel his trip. Just as he was about to leave, he was caught unaware by his youngest sister who came to him with a strange request:" I've got a maths problem I don't understand." Everyone was displeased. Her mother shouted at her: "Leave your brother alone. You'll make him miss the plane."

Where would he be now if he hadn't given in to his sister's plea? Certainly not here on the fourth floor, leisurely watching the pedestrians, cars and clouds go by. He had only spent ten minutes with her but it was enough to change the course of his life completely.

As he set out for Maher's house, everything seemed to be conspiring against him to prevent him from leaving. The bus didn't come as it usually did every half an hour. As he emerged on to the street he saw one just drawing away from the bus stop. When he decided to catch a taxi, they all seemed to have vanished as well.

Finally a private car stopped and offered to take him. It was an old Chevrolet that dated back to the fifties. It only took him a minute or so to agree on a price with the driver. But the traffic was slow. The man commented: "Thursdays are much busier than usual. People leave work early."

His eyes feasted on the city. The river Tigris came into view as they were crossing the Shuhada' Bridge, the blazing sunlight dancing off the shifting surface of the water. Through the faint haze, Tahrir Bridge appeared on the horizon like something in a dream. As they drew closer to al-Sera'i Market, the car slowed down even further. Pedestrians crossed the road unheeding, as they emerged from the covered market. He stared into the cavernous darkness within from where he could hear the cries of street vendors emerging to mingle with the continuous blaring of car horns. The wheels seemed to be turning more smoothly when they reached al-Rusafi Square and he breathed a sigh of relief. The poet's statue grew smaller behind him then vanished completely as they turned left along al-Jumhuria Street.

When they neared Maher's house, he asked the driver to stop a little way away to avoid exciting the curiosity of his conservative neighbours. "I'll only be a few minutes," Saleh told the driver; on the way, it had been agreed that he would take them to the airport as well.

Immediately he passed through the gate into the garden at the front of the house, he had the odd feeling that something had happened there in the time he had been away. Perhaps it was the absolute silence or the sight of Katty the cat standing near the open door and mewing mysteriously.

It didn't take him long to realise what had happened shortly before he arrived. When he entered the sitting room, he was greeted by a particular kind of chaos: the wooden sofas and beds were upturned while books, records and papers lay scattered all over the floor. In Selma's room the scene was even more frightening: there had been a deliberate effort to wreck the way she had arranged it. Bits of underwear lay scattered about the room, ripped into pieces by angry hands.

His heart raced, he found it difficult to breathe. There was only one thought in his mind. He had to get to the airport immediately.

On the way, he was besieged by doubts. Supposing his name was now on the list of those who were forbidden to travel? Supposing they had visited his house and were now waiting for him at the airport? Would his mother have kept quiet? Perhaps they were interrogating her about his whereabouts right now. His fate lay in her hands. Or to be more precise on her tongue.

He told the driver: "Can you go a bit faster? I'll be late for the plane."

But the old car defied his hopes. When the driver put his

foot down on the accelerator, it only resulted in more smoke and noise.

17th July 1983

As was the case with Cezanne's paintings, his novel departed from reality and ended by representing a different version of it. Selma served as the model for the leading character in his novel. Both women had experienced arrest and both had links to important figures in the security services.

Could love grow out of fear?

Until war broke out with Iran, he continued to get news of his country from people coming to London. Sometimes he heard more than one version. One source reported that Maher and Samir had died in Qasr al-Nihāya while he heard elsewhere that they had started working for the secret service. Both versions were possible but he found the former more credible. Death looms on the horizon when the victim has nothing in the way of information to offer his interrogators.

It did not take him long to complete the formalities before boarding the aircraft. The airport staff were about to close the check-in desk assigned to the flight. Through the window beside him, he saw men in plain clothes walking towards the aircraft steps. Had they come to arrest him? For a minute an image of the bodies hanging in al-Tahrir Square came to his mind.

He should have brought a razor with him. It would be the ideal solution. He could cut the arteries at his wrists. But the plane's engines were at full throttle. It was no longer possible to rein in its thunderous departure. When it left the ground, he breathed a sigh of relief.

Baghdad Airport continued to haunt his dreams. He would be off on some journey, when he would find himself landing there for no apparent reason. Immediately he entered the large arrivals hall, he would be surrounded by a group of men who all looked the same. They had finally got their hands on him. He would awake shuddering with fear.

He was the unwitting cause of what happened at Maher's house. The revolutionary organisation, to which he belonged, before the last military coup, had adopted a policy of armed struggle against the new rulers. Saleh had told the party member responsible for him that he wished to resign and had then stopped going to meetings. But it made no difference. When the latter was arrested, he was tortured until he provided names but he was unable to give any details. The secret police must have followed him from his college to Maher's house. Perhaps they thought they had stumbled upon a real treasure trove, a complete party cell.

He didn't hear what had happened to Maher or Samir's wives. But he did hear more than one story about Selma. In one version she had gone back to the house a few weeks after being arrested, accompanied by her child. She had resumed her studies, and was driven back and forth from college in a smart Mercedes car.

After Nazim Kazzar's failed coup attempt, all traces of her vanished.

The sun was finally going down. Scheherazade must be on her way back to London if she had not already arrived. A blackbird broke the icy silence in his flat. It was probably perched on a branch of the oak tree which grew next to the building. It reminded him of the songs the nightingales sang in Baghdad. But there was one difference between them: the blackbirds were free while nightingales were caged.

He recalled his old nickname for a second: "Dressmaker's son." What did his mother look like after all these years? From time to time he received scraps of news from distant relatives.

A man from the security services regularly came to the house with a questionnaire about her fugitive son. "Have you heard from him recently?" "Hasn't he written to you?" They even kept watch on the family phone. He asked "Has he tried to phone you?" or "Why don't you give him a ring and ask him to come home? This is his country."

His mother went on sending him the same commands:" Don't ever come back. We are well."

To fill the vacuum he had left behind, his mother was forced to marry the eldest of his sisters, Nahla, to his cousin, Abbas, even though he was twenty years older than her and not as well-educated as he had left school at an early age. But he had two good qualities which spurred his mother on – he was obedient and a proficient builder. In fact, he had built an annex to the family home to house the couple.

Occasionally he was struck by the paradox that he, who was ready to sacrifice himself for others, had only brought misery to those who were closest to him. The thought aroused a deep sense of guilt in him. Other times, the conditional 'if' entered his train of thought: "What would have happened if I hadn't gone to al-Tahrir Square to see the hangings?" At yet other times, he went back to the point it had all begun:

the moment he had accepted his friend's invitation to join the revolutionary party.

But he was unable to deny that his life had changed radically as a result of accepting the invitation. He had emerged from a lifeless world governed by the whirr of sewing machines into a wider environment. Suddenly he had roots all over Baghdad. He was finally able to meet real workers in the poorer areas and as he read the revolutionary books, churned out by the Beirut presses, he was filled with happiness. Revolution in the Revolution? became his bible and as his maxim, he took the following quotation from Marx: "The philosophers have only interpreted the world in various ways. The important thing is to change it."

Change: everything around him pointed to it. The world was on the verge of a total revolution. Students in the west were setting up roadblocks, the Commune was coming. Sartre had abandoned his ideas on existentialism in favour of Marxism, and was now distributing Maoist newspapers on the streets of Paris.

Spring 1968, Baghdad. There were general strikes across the colleges. Workers from the small number of state factories came out in solidarity. Demonstrations filled al-Rashid and al-Kifah Streets. Good news arrived from the Marshes. Armed struggle had broken out. People from the countryside were about to lay siege to the towns. In his day dreams, Saleh imagined his comrades leading the peasant masses, unafraid of death. They would die with a Cuban cigar between their lips. His dreams went further: Guevara would live again. Instead of going to the Bolivian jungles, he would come to the Marshes. There Saleh would meet him and earn his approval. He would appoint him his assistant, ignoring protests by some of his comrades that he was too young. Che Guevara would not give way. Had not Comrade Castro led the greatest armed revolution this century when he was only twenty-four?

When he entered the arrivals hall at Heathrow Airport he was surprised to see that everything was working normally. There were no strikes, no demonstrations, not even a poster against capitalism; he reassured himself that the situation would be different outside the airport. There he would meet the working class and their allies who were struggling behind the barricades. He would join them immediately just like Marx and Engels had done.

The long peal of the telephone recalled him to the darkness of his room. It must be past ten o'clock. Scraps of light filtered in through the window from the street lamps outside. It was Scheherazade

"How was your trip?"

"Excellent. Helen really enjoyed the place this time."

"How's your father?"

"Good. He's promised to stop smoking. Did Abdel call you?"

"No."

"I am worried about Selim."

Before he put down the receiver, he heard her voice soften slightly, tempting him to go over to her house: "I really missed you."

Part Five
Baida in Her Labyrinth I

When she returned from Baghdad, Abdel appeared extremely affectionate at the airport, which did not accord with the short time she had been away or his taciturn nature. While he was playing with the twins and Lubna, misgivings began to infiltrate her psyche about Selim, and she almost asked him about her son but the words choked in her mouth. Abdel was quick to reassure her that everything was fine with him, though his eyes failed to meet her own.

On the way home, Baida feigned interest in what her husband was saying and the little incidents that had happened since she had been away. He told her that he had taken Selim to see Scheherazade; that Saleh had taken pains to teach him how to count to five, and Helen had lavished attention on him so that he repeated her name over and over for two days afterwards. He was quick to sing the praises of the carer who had looked after Selim while she was away, for in return for the high wage he had paid her, she had taught their son many good habits.

Nevertheless, Baida still felt profoundly regretful that she had agreed to leave Selim in Abdel's care, for although it might have caused difficulties with members of her family, and made her feel more than usually embarrassed in front of them, at least she would not have had to suffer those moments of anxiety now, whenever her eyes met his.

Baida had decided to go to Baghdad after receiving a phone call from her eldest sister telling her that her father was gravely ill and wished to see his favourite daughter. She suddenly found herself faced by a psychological dilemma:

would it be suitable to take Selim with her under such circumstances? Would she be able to protect him from the looks of relatives and friends? How could she explain why she was so attached to him? Strangely enough, Abdel appeared to understand what was going through her mind for he suggested that Selim remain behind with him and that she use the time to prepare her family, so that on subsequent visits, it would be easier for them to accept him.

A few months before she left for Baghdad, her husband's attitude to Selim had undergone a radical change. He had started by making his son less afraid of him by bringing him sweets every day and gone on to take him out with him to the local park. There Selim had played on the slide or in the sandpit with children younger than himself. To reassure his wife that Selim would be properly looked after while she was away, Abdel had suggested that he get a carer who specialised in looking after children with special needs. After the carer had spent a week with Selim, Baida felt that her child was sufficiently familiar with her to allow her to leave him with her completely.

*   *   *

It had been more than eight years since Baida had left the family home and come to London. She was amazed to see how different everyone looked. The children she had left behind had turned into young adults and looked nothing like the way she remembered them, while the adults seemed to have grown very old. Her father was the most affected by the ravages of inner decay; he was now a thin old man, with

146

a very pale face, and eyes that were covered by a fine cloudy film. On the table, next to his bed, were heaped all kinds of medicines. In her first year in London, Baida had been able to follow the details of everyone's lives through the regular letters, her sisters had sent but as the years passed, the snippets of news had gradually dried up as the letters were replaced by greeting cards for special occasions.

On the second day after she arrived, her father summoned her to his room. She sat down on his bed and he took her hand in his as he used to do in days gone by, when he took her walking with him along the banks of the River Tigris. Although they never said very much, they had been in perfect harmony as they listened to the sounds and breathed in the fragrance around them and gazed across at the dense orchards of palm trees on the other bank of the river.

From a very early age, she had felt closer to her father than any other member of her family. Perhaps that was due to the fact that they looked so much alike especially in their facial colour. Baida was the only one of the seven children not to have inherited the pale skin of her grandfather on her mother's side, who was of Turkish origin. She had always felt extremely awkward when other people expressed admiration to her sisters.

She could still remember how shocked she had been when she first found out. She happened to look down at her left arm which was lying next to her mother's right one and was taken aback by the striking difference in colour. She must have been about seven at the time. The strange idea crossed her mind that her mother had painted her skin this colour as a punishment for something she had done as a young child, though, surely, if she had been the tiniest bit fond of her she would have removed the colour by now. Later it occurred to her that perhaps she was not her mother's child at all but the product of a short and secret liaison between her father and another woman, who had left her in a basket in front of the house, after she was born.

After they had been silent for some time, her father asked her how she was getting on in London. "Everything's fine," she replied looking away so she wouldn't have to meet his penetrating gaze, then she turned to him with a sweet smile, prompting tears to well up in his eyes. "I sometimes regret that I agreed to marry you to..." he began, but she quickly interrupted him, "On the contrary, I am very lucky."

*   *   *

While she was putting on her coat, the carer said, "Selim's played a lot today. I don't think he will wake up in the night..." Before she left, she added warningly, "I've left the side light on in his room...Your son is very afraid of the dark." She hurried over to him, her cautious steps, belying the storm of feelings inside which seemed too great for the world to contain; she stopped beside his bed, listening to the regular sound of his breathing and examined his face in the dim light, which was just sufficient to make out his features. She was desperate to give him a cuddle, to spend the night at his side but fear of Abdel's anger froze her to the ground. She crammed her right fist into her mouth to stop the tears that threatened to overwhelm her. She was assailed by an image of the dying father she had left behind but this

148

was not enough to allay her mounting concern about Selim. No one in her family had been able to take her to the airport and they would doubtless not forgive her sudden decision to return to London.

*　*　*

Selim did not recognise her the next day. When he woke up, he was frightened by the steady sound of rain tapping on the window panes. But the sight of Baida, sitting beside him did not calm his fears as it usually did; instead of launching himself into her embrace, he shrank away in terror and raised his hands instinctively as if to shield himself from her. When the twins sneaked into his room, he grew even more scared and started to scream. The noise brought Abdel to the room and when he appeared, Selim rushed over to him, seeking his protection.

But the next day, Selim remembered his mother. He peeped over at her from time to time, from behind his father's shoulder, though it was probably the blue dress she was wearing which reminded him of his ties to her. While he was sitting on her lap, his fingers played with her collar and embroidered sleeves. Suddenly he put out his hand towards her and she flung herself on him covering him in kisses and tears.

*　*　*

In the short time she had spent with her family, she already felt like a spare part. As soon as she got up to do something she found that someone else had beaten her to it. Baida knew this was only natural, but she couldn't accept it.

Her mother was telling the truth when she told her sadly two days after she arrived, "It was not easy to fill the vacuum you left behind you." This had become apparent immediately after she left for London though up till then everyone had always taken her unlimited generosity for granted.

There is no doubt that Baida was hugely influenced by the position she occupied among her six siblings. Her father affectionately called her, "the central stone in the necklace," ignoring the crowning glory of the family, the boy twins who had arrived, only after her mother had born five girls. Baida lay in the middle between the two older sisters and the two younger ones, separated from both sets of girls by an equal number of years. She lived an isolated existence, caught between the older sisters who were absorbed in their secrets and the younger ones who were engrossed in their childish games. The two worlds were closed to her and if ever she tried to join in with one side or the other, her mother would make fun of her. Consequently, she did everything she could to earn everyone's approval. The others were aware of her presence not so much through what she did but rather from the benefits they reaped from the services she was always ready to offer. It was as if her world was governed by ultimate stillness or as if she dwelt in a transparent capsule through which she could see the others interacting with each other. She was shut out from her older sisters' world by the secrets of menstruation, make-up, hair dressing and clandestine love letters and from her younger sisters' by her knowledge.

She took her eldest son into the back garden after Abdel had gone off to the local park with the twins and Lubna. Selim waved at the sun as if in greeting, screwing up his eyes against the bright light. He turned towards a clump of roses repeating joyfully, "Red...red," and tried to escape his mother's hand and run towards the grass, which was still wet from the rain the day before. She grabbed his arms. "The earth's muddy and wet... Dirty." She slowly repeated what she had said but he went on trying to get away from her, saying the final word over and over, "Dirty...dirty." She felt the strength of his body as he struggled against her. The last time she had taken Selim to be examined, the paediatrician had told her, "His brain is a little late developing for his age. He needs to mix with other children and do lots of exercises." She hadn't told Abdel what he had said for fear that he would fly into a rage. When her husband suggested they put their eldest child into a special home, which cared for children like him, she'd said nothing in reply, and he had shouted angrily, "OK, you're responsible for him." She had been meticulous about keeping her son's medical appointments even when she was weighed down by her second pregnancy. Abdel had never gone with her to an appointment, since he believed that she would fall in with what he wanted in the end. He had once accompanied her and Selim to a meeting organised by the Down's Syndrome Association. There had been an exhibition of paintings in the hall where they met and a couple of parents had talked about their experiences with disabled children, explaining how to develop their abilities and looking at some of the difficulties they encountered. While Baida carefully followed everything that was going on in the hall, Abdel remained completely detached, a contemptuous smile pinned to his lips. When the parents clapped and cheered delightedly after some of the children had sung a song, Abdel had sneered, "How are they going to tell their children apart once the performance is over?"

* * *

There was a chilly breeze blowing but despite that, she preferred to stay out in the garden. They sat side by side on a couple of plastic arm chairs. She gently stroked the top of her son's head with the flat of her palm and in time with the slow movement of her hand, asked him the names of things around them. "What's that?" "A tree..." " An apple tree?" "Apple tree" "And those? The clouds? What colour are they?" "Yellow"

Since Selim had been born, she had come to recognise the advantages of doing things slowly. In the first weeks of his life, she had spent long periods of time with him, just feeding him. The health visitor had put him on powdered milk, when it became clear that he was having problems breast feeding, and as the hours ticked by on the clock on the wall, she had transferred him from her lap to her shoulder and back again, burping him after every couple of sips from his feeding bottle.

The discovery of Selim's disability had not changed the way she felt about him. In fact quite the opposite; it had made her increasingly attached to him and perhaps Abdel's attitude had also made her more attentive. From time to time she would wake up in the middle of the night in a cold sweat and rush to his bedside. In the week, following the portentous visit to the specialist, she had become absolutely convinced that she had known about Selim's condition while he was still in her womb and even before that, in the first hours of her marriage, when Abdel had dragged her into a world which she had completely avoided up to then and not even spoken about.

*   *   *

Baida continued to pursue her unhurried way of life, even when the twins were born and despite the many demands they made on her. If they started crying, she would go over to them and put her nipples in their mouths. Each one would suck greedily, pausing only to take noisy breaths. In between feeding times, she would prepare their bottles. She undoubtedly felt proud of having given birth to male twins just as her mother had done after her final pregnancy; in fact the achievement helped her overcome the sense of inadequacy she felt in front of her husband.   In return, the birth of the twins gave her the inner freedom to favour her eldest son more and more.

She spent hours with him, relishing the sight of him attempting to move several feet along his bed on his hands and knees, at a time when the twins were already crawling in and out of the rooms on the second floor.

It was a long time before Selim was able to work out how to get round the obstacles in his way and he would continuously bump his small head against the walls in his room as he attempted to go past them. Baida interpreted his efforts in a curious way. She believed his spirit was attempting to free itself from the constraints imposed on it by his permanent disability; if he hurt himself in the process and whimpered in pain, she read a mysterious protest in his red eyes.

The first sign she had that her son was engaging with the outside world came one day, when Abdel entered the room unexpectedly. Selim stretched out his hand to her sleeve and gripped it hard and when Baida looked down at him, she saw an expression of alarm cross his face, combined with an appeal for help. When his father came up to them, he buried his head in the folds of her dress.

* * *

The ringing of the telephone brought her back to the world around her. She was tiptoeing behind Selim who was lumbering across the concrete in time to her voice, "One, two, three..." She took him into the house with her, afraid that he would dirty himself in the mud, but before she could reach the phone, the ringing stopped. She sat him down behind the kitchen table and put a cup of milk mixed with banana in front of him, praising and encouraging him, as he began to suck through the straw. Then the telephone started ringing again.

She recognised Scheherazade's voice immediately, and felt uncomfortable. To compensate, she became over effusive. Her cousin sounded more affectionate than usual although she still maintained the slight distance between them. Scheherazade avoided asking how her father was or about her sad trip; instead she poured out a stream of questions about the children, asking how they had coped with the weather and the different conditions over there. Before she finished talking, she said she wanted to come and visit them. Baida said over enthusiastically, "You don't work on Saturdays..." But Scheherazade said in a decisive manner, "Next Sunday, if that suits you."

* * *

Ever since Baida had discovered the nature of her cousin's relationship with Saleh, she had regarded her with mixed feelings. After staying in her house that first time, she had decided to avoid repeating the experience again. On the way back home with Abdel, she didn't say a word. They had to take the underground, then a bus and then walk a short distance for the rest of the way. Throughout the journey, her mind was taken up with a single question: "What does Abdel think of Scheherazade?" And since Scheherazade was her cousin, what did he think of her now?

It would not be farfetched to say that Baida equated herself with Scheherazade at that moment. The thought made her break out in a sweat and when Abdel looked over at her, she felt faint with shame. However instead of expressing his disapproval of her cousin, he began to praise her generosity, kindness and good taste. Despite this, she continued to harbour doubts about Abdel's true feelings. He turned to her and asked, "You look pale...Are you feeling ill?" "No, it's just a slight headache. I didn't sleep enough last night."

When they arrived home, she shut herself away in the

bathroom for a long time, overcome by a desire to vomit, and then began to wash every inch of her body. It was as if the fact that she was related to Scheherazade by blood had put her in the same position as her and meant that she would be viewed in the same light by strangers outside the family circle. The idea took tangible shape in her imagination. An image of Saleh came to her mind; once again, she heard the sound of Scheherazade moaning in the night and felt the fluids from their bodies, blending on her own clammy skin.

Baida had continued to expect Abdel to burst into a furious tirade against her family, and when he said nothing, she had interpreted his silence as suppressed anger and believed that he was still fuming inside but on the third day he had suggested inviting Scheherazade and Saleh to dinner.

There was no doubt that the regular meetings between the two couples had gradually allayed her fears and worries, so much so that she began to look forward to Scheherazade's invitations impatiently since, thanks to her, she made direct contact with some British people. When they visited Scheherazade, there were usually other guests there besides them, all of them enjoying the barbeque and wine in her large garden. Now and then, Baida would recall a curious remark made by her cousin in reply to a comment by Abdel on her style of entertaining. "You make your visitors feel as if the house belongs to them," he'd said. She'd interrupted him with a laugh, "That's the best way to do it, because it makes them look after themselves."

* * *

The children's faces were covered in sand and sweat when they arrived back home. Abdel told her reassuringly, "They played on everything." He looked at them directly and added, "You did, didn't you?" The three of them nodded obediently. Baida turned her head towards the window and was surprised to see that dusk had set in. As she stroked Lubna's head, she said, "It's time for your bath now," but instead of protesting noisily, they greeted her suggestion in silence. Her daughter let out a faint scream but one glance from her father was sufficient to quell her. She was filled with a sense of inadequacy. She devoted so much time to her eldest son, she had little left for the rest of them; as she looked at the fear and tiredness in their eyes, she was reminded of a litter of abandoned puppies. She was sure they had not spent an easy time with their father since he gave them little opportunity to express themselves or behave as they wanted to. Abdel believed that children should adapt to the adult world rather than the other way round and if they raised their voices even slightly, he would immediately warn them about doing it again. If they repeated their mistake, he would punish them severely. But they made up for the harsh discipline he imposed on them, by taking advantage of their mother's lenient attitude, immediately he left the house, pushing the boundaries back as far as they would go. At times, they would take their feelings of jealousy out on Selim and gang up against him. They would snatch the toys from his hands or physically harm him. While she was visiting her family, the twins had competed with each other to occupy the place left by her eldest son by imitating the way he moved and spoke.

Selim slept for more than an hour, which made it easier for her to carry out her other tasks. She half-filled the bath with hot water then sat down in the middle. She placed the twins on either side and settled Lubna on her lap. As her daughter watched the soap bubbles floating on the water, she said, "The stars are swimming." One of the twins screamed when Baida splashed water on his head, but he stopped protesting when he heard the sound of his father humming to himself as he walked about the house. For her part, she felt relaxed since it meant she wouldn't have to have a bath with Abdel.

On the evening of her first night in London, her bride-groom had surprised her by running a hot bath for her, liberally scented with lavender. She had closed the door and peacefully undressed before climbing into the bath. The moment her body came into contact with the mauve coloured water, it seemed to revive. She closed her eyes, intoxicated by the sense of tranquillity, which gradually seeped into her being and absorbed the tiredness from her long, wearying journey. When she half opened her eyes, he was standing in front of her, completely naked, his eyes glued to her chest. Her hands stiffened involuntarily around her breasts. She said confusedly trying to make light of her reaction, "I thought you were asleep." He laughed, "How can I sleep with such a beauty here?" He had slipped into the bath and sat down in front of her, pushing his legs towards her then putting his hands on her arms and pulling her to him. Baida felt as if she were watching someone else; as she started to move away from him an idea flashed into her mind, even as her buttocks came to rest in his lap. Without realising exactly what she was doing, she had pulled the loofah off the side of the bath and pretended to be busy soaking it in water. She had rubbed it with a piece of soap and then feverishly starting to scrub her husband's chest and arms.

*　*　*

Baida had not been surprised when he asked to marry her, for her elder sisters had called him her 'fiancé' from an early age, whenever they wanted to make her feel uncomfortable. The blood would rush to her face and she would clap her hands to her cheeks to hide her feelings of intense embarrassment. She was even more distressed by the way her parents indulged their daughters' teasing and seemed to her to be smiling in collusion. She could trace this family conspiracy against her back to the games she and Abdel had played together as children, when his family came to visit them. Niether of them were more than six years old. Doubtless the fact that Abdel had played the doctor in these games was the reason behind her sisters' persistent teasing even though they had long since abandoned those childish roles, but nevertheless, she was convinced from an early age that (like fate) her family had decided to marry her to Abdel.

Her father called her to the guest room. He closed the door behind him then invited her to sit beside him. Abdel's father had come to see them that evening and spent a short time with her father. She was surprised at how soon he had left since he usually slept at their house when he took the trouble to visit them. Her father told her gently, "It's up to you to decide." But she could detect in his tone and the way he was looking at her a mute appeal that she agree to the proposal.

Deep inside, she felt a slight sense of misgiving over her father's uncertain attitude towards his friend's son, but her mother was clearly determined to see the match go ahead. The tone of her voice and the stubborn look on her face, made it impossible for her to even consider refusing.

Baida continued to strive to make her parents pleased with her. If her mother got angry with her she felt a vague sense of injustice, but the slightest suggestion that she had displeased her father was enough to turn her whole world upside down as if she were primarily connected to the rest of her family through him.

After her fiancé left for London and she no longer heard from him, her father asked her if she wanted to annul the engagement. Instead of immediately agreeing, she said, "You decide." But her mother intervened and using a variety of pretexts, persuaded her father not to go back on his decision, "What will people say against them? Wouldn't it be better to give Abdel's father the chance to ring his son first? And more than anything else doesn't the girl's silence mean that she wants to wait a little longer?" Only a couple of days later, her fiancé's family came to call on them. His father beseeched her parents, "Baida is my daughter and Abdel is your son."

Although she had resorted to silence, she fell prey to a series of conflicting emotions that raged inside her like the waves of a turbulent sea. Somewhere deep down a weak but relentless voice urged her to end the engagement and return the ring, necklace and bracelets her fiancé had given her as an engagement present to his family. Elsewhere a chorus of protesting voices, mercilessly berated her for not doing

160

enough to keep her fiancé's attention; she should write to him regularly, let him know how much she loved him and seduce him through gifts and reminders; yet a third group of voices commended her passivity and her resolute commitment to go along with what her father decided for her, and urged her to take no action at all, as had always been her way.

*   *   *

As she approached Selim's room, Baida gestured at the children to be quiet, but encouraged by the fact that their father was sitting a long way away on the ground floor, they started to talk more and more. But no sound came from behind the closed door. For a moment she felt overcome by a mindless fear that Selim had stopped breathing, which made her pray to God to protect him from the devil.

After putting the twins to bed, she carried Lubna to her small room. It only took a couple of minutes for her daughter to drop off to sleep. She very carefully withdrew and tiptoed to Selim's room. The idea that something bad had happened to him grew in intensity with every step she took. From the moment she had seen Abdel at the airport, she had had an inexplicable feeling that something dreadful had occurred while she was away in Baghdad and the more considerate he was to her on the way back home, the more apprehensive she became.

Under the soft glow of the light, she made her way over to Selim's bed. She could clearly hear him snoring and the faint regular sound filled her with a strange sense of unease. She gazed down on his face on which she could clearly see the faint traces of a smile, giving him an expression of happiness, which rarely appeared when he was awake. It was as if in the end, his spirit knew nothing but bliss, absolute bliss..

The air was heavy and the reddening glow of the sunset made her feel even more unsettled so that she hurriedly drew the curtains to shut out the expanse of sky, she could see through the window pane. She stroked Selim's forehead and hair, feeling the warmth coursing through her veins. When she had been away from him in Baghdad, she felt she had lost all sense of place and direction. Sometimes while she was sitting with members of her family, she would suddenly wonder where she was. It was as if she were watching a series of incidents being played out in front of her that had taken place a long time ago and that were totally unconnected to her. In the midst of this overwhelming chaos, the little picture of Selim, which she had carefully hidden in her purse, was like a life line and saved her from complete disintegration. When things got too much for her, she would take the picture to the bathroom, and after carefully shutting the door behind her, would cover it with kisses or talk to it in her mind.

The heat must have made Selim kick away the heavy covers. When she stretched out a hand to draw them back over him, she suddenly noticed the faint trace of a wound on the part of his tummy laid bare by the gap between his pyjama top and bottoms. She ran her fingers along it and shivered at how hard it was. She pushed the clothing back further and further until finally she exposed a long scar, which started at the end of his left thigh.

*　*　*

Unusually for her, Scheherazade was late for the appointment so much so that the others began to doubt that she was coming. This meant that they missed their chance of going to the flea market which took place every Sunday, as Scheherazade always accompanied them if she were visiting. By the time she arrived, it was too late. Most of the traders had gathered up their things by then and left the open square. Perhaps Baida felt afraid that Abdel would be angry at having lost out on an opportunity to go to the Sunday market on such a warm and sunny day, but her tension and upset vanished abruptly when she saw Saleh standing there and she felt surprised and confused instead. Her cousin had come into the house, and she was about to close the door behind her when the other woman put up a hand to stop her, saying with a laugh, "Wait...I want to introduce you to a friend of mine whom I'm sure you will like very much." She drew in her breath sharply. Abdel was only a couple of feet away and must have heard what her cousin had said, but he gave a half laugh instead. This was the first time Saleh had visited them. "I had to drag him out of bed...," Scheherazade added. Baida blushed, immediately remembering the faint cries she had heard Scheherazade make when she and Saleh were making love. When she shook her visitor's hand, the sweat on his palm felt sticky and viscous to her touch.

The sitting room soon rang with the noisy shrieks of the children as they divided themselves up between the guests. The twins rushed over to Scheherazade even though she shrunk away a little from them while Lubna plumped herself down in Saleh's lap. It didn't take long for Selim to

163

emerge. He stood at the door to the sitting room, his right thumb stuck in his mouth, with a faint expression of alarm in his eyes. His brothers and sister seemed to feel his appearance threatened their status with the guests and clung more tightly to them. Baida went over to him and led him to her chair but she looked apologetically round the room as if asking everyone to forgive her son's arrival. Her anxiety only faded when Scheherazade and Saleh seemed to display a genuine interest in him, asking about him and directing questions at him, waiting for his incoherent answers with obvious affection. Even his father appeared to be taking a real interest. Her cousin enquired about his sight and hearing and took care to pose her question in a diffident and neutral fashion. Abdel launched into a confident speech on how well his eldest son was doing; in fact he even started to boast about his ability to learn new words and how much he loved his brothers and sister.

Initially, Baida felt pleased at Abdel's vastly increased interest in his son but then an image flashed through her mind of an incident that had happened a year ago, when Abdel had ranted and raved at her for having allowed Selim to appear in front of some guests. This and the thought of the puckered scar on his lower abdomen which she hadn't been able to stop touching, ever since she had found it, made her feel cold and sick with fear. As he stood there talking, she almost screamed, "What did you do to him while I was away?" But the words stuck in her throat, as if someone had stuffed a thick glove into her mouth and gagged her; instead of speaking she started to stroke her son's head, occasionally wiping away the saliva which dribbled out of the side of his

164

mouth and ran down to his throat.

Gradually she could hear nothing but the sound of Selim's heavy breathing as the voices around her faded and died away. Occasionally she had this feeling of being miraculously swept away to another far away world, where she would find herself alone with her eldest son in the midst of bright, white clouds; perhaps these brief interludes allowed her to escape the sense of inadequacy she always felt when she was in the same place as Scheherazade. Initially, she had breathed a sigh of relief when Abdel expressed a wish to meet her cousin again after they had spent that first night at her house. But as time went by this wish had been translated into an increasing respect for her. In fact Baida could detect a growing admiration for Scheherazade on Abdel's part, which was in marked contrast to the increasingly scornful way in which he treated her.

She went through moments of agony as she thought back over her own very chaste life. As a teenager, she had woken up in horror, after dreaming that she had been with her neighbour's son and spent the remaining hours of the night at the mercy of a cold bath.

Nevertheless, in her heart of hearts, during that time, she persevered in her secret belief that her future husband would reward her for her chastity as a shell is expected to protect its pearl from the elements of destruction. He would reward her not by giving her money or buying her gifts but by putting her above other women and venerating her as her father had done throughout her life. Instead, Scheherazade had begun to occupy a more important place in Abdel's heart. She seemed to have become the source of his

165

self-confidence while all Baida did was shrivel up in front of him. Didn't it matter to him that Scheherazade had a boyfriend whom she was on shamelessly intimate terms with? Or that her bed had been a refuge for a series of strangers who had passed through it before she met her current naive friend?

The voices brought her back to the sitting room again. Doubtless, her moment of abstraction had lent her face a strength and particular allure. She became aware, as she turned slightly to the right that Saleh was staring at her profile with a peculiar yearning; when their eyes met for a second, she felt a jolt of electricity shoot through her body. She entwined her left arm round Selim's neck and began to stroke his chest with her fingers to make him sleepy. Sounding uncharacteristically kind, Abdel said to Selim, "You're tired. Do you want to go to bed?" The guests added murmurs of support. Selim's eyes were more than normally slanted at that moment, which deprived them of any real expression. When his father got up to take him upstairs, she said with a determination that was unusual in her, "I'll take him..."

* * *

Even in the brief time she spent sitting with Saleh, Baida was unable to resist the urge to get up and go to the bathroom. She explained away her absences with a variety of excuses. She had to fetch the tea, or take the plates out to the kitchen or get the fruit or go and take a look at her sleeping children. But she didn't only wash her hands. She also in-

166

spected her face, pushed a lock of hair back into its place or brushed her hands over her chest. When she returned to the sitting room, she avoided his eyes which strayed towards her from time to time, even though she was careful not to sit opposite him.

After supper, they moved out into the garden. Overhead, the sky was still a radiant blue even though the day was nearing its end. Gradually it began to darken until the two giant poplar trees which grew on the other side of the garden fence were no longer visible. Scheherazade suddenly asked, "Do you know that Saleh's writing a novel?" When Abdel and Baida turned to look at him, he became embarrassed. "I haven't written a word yet," he said. "You're exaggerating." Scheherazade teased him, "Don't you believe it! He's very secretive like all Scorpios." Abdel asked, "What's the novel about?" When he didn't reply, Scheherazade turned towards Saleh, "No one's going to steal the idea. Tell us a little about it." Saleh started to stammer, "It's an attempt to re-shape reality without depicting it as it is ... I am trying to approximate Cézanne's style of painting: the view of the subject is not an exact replica as it would be if it were taken by a camera ...aspects of the character emerge through different shades of colours rather than through the pen...." Scheherazade cut in tetchily, "We aren't asking you about your approach or philosophy. That doesn't concern us as readers." She turned away to Abdel and said, "Tell us what you've been doing recently." "Nothing much! I've just made a chess set from bits of oak. The pieces are life-like. The elephant looks like a real elephant with a warrior sitting astride it. There is also a horse..."

"I would love to see it..." Scheherazade said enthusiastically. "Have you thought about selling it?"

Abdel said, "I've made ten sets up to now."

Scheherazade said, "I'll buy one."

Saleh said, "So will I."

Abdel laughed, "You can have them at a reduced price."

* * *

On their way home from Baida and Abdel's house, a strange silence settled between them, each one feeling deeply antagonistic to the other. Scheherazade concentrated on her driving and avoided looking at Saleh while he, for his part, sat holding his small bag close to his chest

He had put part of his novel inside, wanting to surprise Scheherazade with it, when they arrived at her house. But now all he wanted to do was go back to his flat on his own.

Was his sour mood the result of the slighting way in which she had referred to his work in front of Baida and Abdel? Was it brought on by the dark red sky which made the empty expanse in front of them appear to be part of an unending nightmare?

Or was there another reason: something that had stirred inside them simultaneously, a feeling that was common to both of them?

He could see Scheherazade out of the corner of his eye. Her face was a waxen mask. Her hands gripped the steering wheel and her eyes remained glued to the windscreen.

Maybe it could be put this way: they both unexpectedly felt trapped by the other. It was a moment of co-existence, which had come about as a result of a series of choices and coincidences.

Things seem to happen independently of each other and Saleh was only now discovering how hard at work the Fates had been, spinning the threads of the present moment, without him being aware of what they were doing.

In contrast, his spirit longed to experience other possibilities, choices which he had ignored up till now. What if I had refused my friends proposal to join the revolutionary organisation? What if I had not gone to al-Tahrir Square to see the hangings? What if...?" But if he had made some other choice, it would have broken the chain of events, which had brought him to this present moment, to his sitting beside Scheherazade one evening, in a city that he had never thought he would live in.

Is it possible to say that the present is a prison which has been constructed by the past?

Or that this sudden sense of suffocation was a form of protest by the other spirits which remain imprisoned inside him like possible things, which had not been given the chance to realise themselves because of the choices he had made.

Perhaps Scheherazade was feeling the same.

Once in an intimate moment, he had told her, "We're like the Tigris and Euphrates. We sprang from the same lake then separated before coming together again after travelling many miles. "When it was too late," she had added with a laugh.

But now for reasons that were unclear they were more like two identical magnetic poles, each of them trying to escape the other.

She must have guessed what he wanted; she drove to the block of flats where he lived and stopped in front of it. Before she kissed him on the cheek, she said quietly, "I'll give you a ring soon."

Saleh breathed a sigh of relief as he watched her tail lights gradually disappear even as he experienced a pang of desire for her. He passed his hands over his shoulder bag. The pages of his novel were still unread, virginal; his characters still had the power to alter their fates.

How difficult it would have been for them to do that if he had shown them to Scheherazade?

Before opening the door to his building, the first words of his novel came to his tongue, and he mumbled it under his breath.

"When the doorbell rang, she thought it was the Jehovah's Witnesses. Instead, she was surprised to see a short well-built man with broad shoulders waiting outside..."

Part Six
The Artist I

When the doorbell rang, she thought it was the Jehovah's Witnesses. Instead, she was surprised to see a short well-built man with broad shoulders waiting outside. He had a prominent forehead, which made his eyes appear sunken; even when he smiled reassuringly, his piercing gaze bore into her, exciting a sense of unease.

"Mrs Haya?" he asked in a friendly voice. She nodded her head in reply.

"I've got a letter for you."

"Who from?"

"From someone dear to you."

"Why didn't he send it by post?"

"Because ... he has passed away."

"Who is he?"

He could see an expression of bewilderment cross her face, as if she knew who the dead person was.

"Can I come in?"

Before she could answer, he had walked past her into the flat then proceeded down the short corridor to the doorway at the other end, as if he were familiar with the layout of the house. Without hesitating, he pushed open the yellow-painted door which led to the sitting room.

The stranger showed no sign of embarrassment about sitting down on the small sofa without her permission. Morning light streamed through from the window above his head, making it difficult for her to make out his features. As she feigned composure, she felt as if she was back in that same place, she had often visited in her dreams. Whenever she woke up from the nightmare, she would tell herself, "You're perfectly safe. It was only a dream. You're thousands of miles away from him. There are mountains and oceans and deserts and countries between you." She almost asked her guest: "Are you real or just a ghost?" since she was unable to see how else he could have crossed those natural and artificial barriers so easily and emerged without any advance warning. "Mrs Haya?" What extraordinary politeness! She should not have opened the door to a stranger without a prior appointment and she would not have done so in her first two years in London. But as time passed, she had grown more comfortable, and gradually began to forget what she had been through over there. In fact on certain occasions, she even doubted that her past had really happened; she felt sometimes that she had been reborn the moment she arrived on this island, that she had been given a new soul. She thought back to those first minutes in Heathrow Airport, and how apprehensive she had felt, even after going through the controls, because of the security guards standing behind her.

The visitor's sharp but faltering voice that seemed at odds with his appearance penetrated her thoughts. "The Artist sent me. You knew him of course?" He must have noticed the shock on Haya's face, even though there was little to show for it apart from an increasing pallor about her mouth. He added, "I know that he died a long time ago but he entrusted me with something for you." When she still didn't react, he hurried out his excuses, "These have been difficult years for me. I've been working on my business.

174

I've had to keep my head down as I am also a refugee. But I've always remained loyal to him and I've come to fulfil my commission." He opened the black diplomatic bag and took out a box wrapped in flowery paper which had lost some of its sheen because of its age. "The Artist left this for you. His deputy gave it to me himself a day before the coup attempt took place."

"I live in London with my family," the visitor said before leaving. "You must come and visit us one day. I've got two children. We are almost neighbours." At the door to the flat, he stopped for an instant. From the inner pocket of his jacket, he took out a business card and gave it to her. It read Salam Salman. Contractor. As he stepped out into the darkness, he added: "If you need any repairs done to your flat, then I will be pleased to help. I have workers who are skilled builders, electricians and plumbers. I will never forget what the Artist did for me. Without his help, I would never have earned a penny."

*   *   *

When she was alone again, the atmosphere seemed stuffy and oppressive, as if the visitor had sucked out all the clean air and exhaled stale air in its place. She opened the windows to the flat and let in a stream of cold air, which set the chain of bells jangling on the back of the front door. But the smell of putrefaction remained as if the molecules of air were coated in something rotten. She took out a bottle of Chanel Coco perfume, which Thomas had once given her and sprinkled it over the bed and chairs and carpets but it was no use. Was the smell coming from her? She tried to remember if she had shaken hands with the stranger before he left. She smelled the palms of her hands. The smell was there, lodged between her nails and on her skin.

She got into the bath and immersed herself in the warm water, which she had drenched with scented oil. She tried to think back to the last intimate moment she had spent with her friend, the painter, and recall parts of the film they had watched together in a local cinema. She tried to remember what her child had said that morning, before she left him with the nursery teacher but it was no good. "Mrs Haya?" His voice filled her mind. It cut through her like a sharp blade and when the sound vanished, his predatory eyes stared back at her instead, filling her with a strange and incomprehensible feeling that she could only vaguely understand. It was as if she were naked, as if her body had been X-rayed and the rays had pierced through her clothing and exposed the bones, viscera and fluids within, confirming a single truth, that man was essentially bestial.

The question remained locked inside her, even though she was unable to put it into words. Where had she seen this man before? How else could she explain away the feeling of nausea that had flooded through her the moment she set eyes on him? Mrs Haya? No, Mrs Haya had died a long time ago. Why hadn't she changed her name when she arrived in London as other women did when they were escaping the violence of abusive husbands? It would have been better. She should have told the immigration clerk exactly what had happened to her in her country instead of claiming that she had come to Britain to study. If she had done so she would have been given protection and benefits. Human rights organisations would have contacted her and offered various forms of assistance. Do you need a psychiatrist to help you get rid of the nightmares? Does the flat you're living in help you forget them? Do you want a disabled parking permit so that you can put your car wherever you want? Can you show us the marks the torture left on your body?

Haya could imagine herself exposing her naked body as she had done in the Fortress. But this time they would not be trying to extract a confession from her, or taking pleasure in her body. She would be doing it for herself to help her get as many benefits as possible, a permanent decent salary, comfortable accommodation, security and special medical care. If she slightly exaggerated the effects of the torture and ill-treatment she had suffered, she would get an even better allowance and benefits. But the humanitarian organisations had one thing in common with her torturers: they both wanted her to undress, to appear naked in front of them; to be something that could be analysed into its primary components. In both cases she would have had to submit willingly and accept the penetrating way they looked at her.

Instead she preferred to work as a model at a private art school, when she arrived in London. She posed naked in front of the students for hours on end each day, and found nothing disgraceful in the job since as far as the students were concerned, she was just a being without a personality. Perhaps the fact that she was pregnant emboldened her somewhat in her work. As the days passed, the changes taking place in her body provided additional visual material for the students. The only thing she could remember now about the experience was that she had been affectionately known as 'The Young Mother,' instead of being called by her real name.

In addition to the low wage, she earned, Haya had also enjoyed the strange sense of anonymity she got from the job: as she stood completely naked in front of a group of strangers, she could observe the angles of her body from a technical point of view and look at the way they were transformed into curves, shades, perspective and colour. It was as if her body had assumed a life of its own, which she could only watch as an outsider through observing the students' painting. As they applied their brushes to the canvases, it gradually emerged in front of her from a variety of perspectives. It assumed many different positions, depending on the angle from which it was being viewed. She discovered the nature of sight itself and watched the way their eyes looked at her, engaged with her body and then transformed it according to what they saw in their imagination.

She learnt about her body for the first time, through those brush strokes; rather she came to see it through an ever changing aesthetic perspective, fashioned according to what those young artists saw. In the curving lines, she could make out the distinctive contour of her thigh, elegantly tapering away at the edges to reveal her gleaming legs.

Haya pushed away thoughts of her visitor as she busied herself drying and combing her hair and putting on light clothes to fetch her child from the nursery. She still had half an hour before she had to leave the house. She went into the sitting room and was surprised to see the packet sitting silently on the low coffee table. A strange feeling stirred inside her and for a few minutes she was incapable of moving a muscle in her body.

She put out her hand to the box and felt a jolt of electricity run through her, as if her fingers had come into contact with those of the Artist across the divide which separates life from death.

The Artist wouldn't have wrapped the parcel himself. He had an army of servants, spies and murderers at his disposal to do things like that. All he had to do was raise his little finger and his deputy would understand what he wanted and hurriedly carry out his orders. Even if the box contained a present, he wouldn't have chosen it himself. He might have seen it and nodded his agreement. For a second she had an overwhelming desire to take the box and throw it down the rubbish chute but as her fingers touched the edges, she felt faint. She would have to put on her washing up gloves before she could pick it up, but as she went to the kitchen to fetch them, she was seized with curiosity to find out what the Artist had sent her. Especially as he was no longer alive.

A muddled thought came to her mind: When people die, we have unlimited time to remember them in the way we want to, without them being able to trouble our lives in any way. Perhaps that's why we feel they are better than we are and what makes us feel guilty about them deep down.

But this was not how she felt about the Artist. She had only ever asked herself one question about him, even after she had heard of his hideous death and that was whether she would have killed him if she had had the opportunity.

When news of his death reached her, she had felt an indefinable sense of relief at first. While he was still alive, she

179

had felt like a fly caught in a proverbial spider's web, seemingly unable to deny the ties of love that had bound her to him inside the Fortress, or the way that her body had trembled as he ejaculated into her even after it became clear that she was pregnant.

She was surprised when she opened the package. It contained a shell-shaped container and underneath, lying at the bottom of the thick cardboard box, a notebook with thick crimson covers. She opened the ivory lid of the container. A blaze of light danced in front of her eyes as the rays were caught and reflected off the diamond necklace within. Haya did not doubt that the stones adorning the central body of the necklace were genuine. When she put it around her neck, she was dazzled by the shaft of light emitted by the large pear-shaped stone, which settled above the mound of her breasts.

She took off her pullover. The necklace surmounted her cleavage like an upside down crown. An image came to her mind: she was standing in front of the Artist wearing nothing but the necklace. His sweaty fingers ran over her, like they used to do, moving between her breasts, and squeezing them until her hand came up to push them away. She pictured her face, devoid of any expression of pain or maybe with a smile of pleasure hovering about the lips, encouraging him to explore other parts of her body. During those heavy moments, Haya had been haunted by a particular kind of fear, which made her touch her face and pulse while screaming soundlessly, "I'm alive. The Artist is my protector," as she envisaged the faces of the other prisoners. Whenever she recoiled from him with a sense of rebellion, she would think of the graveyard that the Artist had taken her to see or those moments in the Fortress when she had stood naked in front of the guards, and her fingers would soften as they touched his naked body. In the end he had been her deliverer. And now he was continuing to pay the price of the pleasure he had got from her by sending her a diamond necklace from beyond the grave, as if keeping her alive or sending her to Britain with envelopes stuffed with dollars, had been insufficient recompense. She had had no choice but to use the money. She had become a prostitute through fate rather than through personal choice. She could have used her body to gain the sympathy of charities here by exposing what had been done to her but she had preferred to leave the profession. Now she had received another inducement from the Artist to take up this line of work again.

* * *

She woke up in the night filled with dismay at what she had done. How could she have thrown the necklace away? She could have sold it and put the money into a special account for her son. After all, he was the Artist's son, wasn't he? She suddenly thought of how he occasionally blinked his eyes rapidly and realised he'd inherited the trait from his father. The Artist had hidden this involuntary mannerism behind his dark glasses but it was clearly visible in her son. Suddenly she leaped out of bed and went to his room, spurred on by a thought, which had just that minute, come into her mind. Did he look like the Artist? Ever since he was born she had always convinced herself that he took after her completely. But now as she leaned over his face in the middle of the darkness, and studied the narrow forehead, thick eyebrows and sharp nose, she saw the features of the person who had turned her life upside down.

She returned to the box which was still lying where she had left it, and cautiously drew out the notebook and opened the first page. The words struck her like a blow on the face, and heightened the sense of being caught in a long unending nightmare, "To Haya, my sunshine… I hope that we will soon be together again." As she clutched the book, she felt his fingers brush the back of her hand; her head swam and for a moment the world spun round her. She didn't let go. She threw herself down onto the sofa and repeated determinedly, "Don't be afraid. He's dead and buried. Who knows? The Leader might have dissolved his body in nitric acid."

She ran her fingers over the pages, as she turned them unconsciously. She was torn between wanting to tear up the book and get rid of her past forever and to keep it to exorcise the devils within her. She and the Artist had shared the same past, after all, and unless she opened the notebook, it would haunt her forever.

Shortly after she arrived in London, her father had come on a visit and told her about the rumours, which had started circulating immediately after the Artist's mysterious death. According to these stories, the senior officials who had gathered at the international airport to welcome the Leader back, on his return from Europe, were unaware of the frightening series of events that would take place, when his plane landed.

Apparently, the control tower had been taken over by members of a faction belonging to the Artist, who were hiding out there with mortars and sniper rifles. However, elsewhere in the airport, another group of men was preparing to bomb the tower, immediately the plane exploded.

People said that the Artist had managed to stop the various units of the army communicating with each other, early on the day the Leader was due back, and had then imprisoned the ministers of defence and the interior. He had also prepared a statement that would be broadcast after the Leader was assassinated, which would claim that the conspiracy had been organised by the two ministers, who were hoping to restore reactionary leaders in the army to power and remove the 'Organisation.'

* * *

She woke up again for no reason at all thinking wrongly that she had slept sufficiently although in fact she had only dozed off for half an hour. She looked up at the low ceiling, spotted with faint patches of light which filtered in from the small light in the corridor. The faint rumble of a freight train passing close to the kitchen came clearly to her ears and as it rattled by she suddenly pictured her guest in another place, somewhere she thought she had forgotten forever. She saw him three floors below ground, watching the prisoners as they lined up in front of the guards. He was short in stature and in his tracksuit and sandals, did not appear to pose much of a threat even though he was carrying a long whip.

When she first passed through the gate into the Fortress,

she had heard the sound of something vibrating through the thick walls that seemed to be coming from light years away. Initially she thought it was a hallucination caused somehow by the two men who were accompanying her, but as she moved forwards, the buzzing grew louder. For the first time, she became aware of the dim lighting in the building. There were no windows opening to the outside and it was impossible to tell whether it was night or day. As she drew near to the spiral staircase, she was uncertain about what she was seeing and could not work out if it was real or a dream. In front of her was a huge copy of Edvard Munch's painting, The Scream and above it picked out in pale yellow light bulbs, which flashed on and off, continuously, was the maxim, "Abandon Hope All Ye Who Enter Here"

She opened the Artist's notebook unwillingly and saw several sentences, written in a fine and elegant hand. They were arranged with infinite care despite the absence of lines on the page. "I have just learned that the Leader wants to kill me. What angers me more than anything else is that he is accusing me of being solely responsible for what has happened in the Fortress and is going to put me on trial. I wouldn't be so angry with him if he had come and told me, "I want to kill you for the good of the country." On the contrary, I would have cheered him on while I faced the firing squad. But now he has condemned me to another fate. I am to be humiliated and made the scapegoat."

She tried to go back to sleep. She turned off the light in the corridor, assuming that there was little likelihood that her child would wake up in the middle of the night; she firmly closed the door to her room to prevent the rumble of trains getting through and squeezed her eyes shut. But she couldn't shut out the distinctive sound of people screaming. It grew louder making her press the palms of her hands against her ears. She felt herself sinking, heard herself being sworn at by the guards who pushed her this way and that. "You whore! We'll make up for the custom you've lost from your comrade clients." When she faltered slightly due to a sudden attack of dizziness, one of the two men had grabbed her by the hair until her legs had given way under her. As she slid to the ground, somewhere jumbled up with the pain in her scalp, she had heard them say, "You haven't seen anything yet."

She thought of her immaculately groomed guest. Yes. She remembered him. His colleagues had called him, Abu Harb, the warmonger. He hadn't become Salam Selman then. On the third day after she had been arrested, she had discovered why the other prisoners were so afraid of him and had seen for herself the irrational madness, which could turn him into a real monster. He had suddenly exploded with anger at a number of prisoners who were lined up outside the toilets. She was unable to do anything except watch as he advanced towards them, lashing their frail bodies with his whip. From inside the cubicle, he dragged out a prisoner who had not yet finished emptying his bowels. Naked from the waist down and walking on all fours, the man began to beg, "Forgive me, I won't take such a long time again, I swear to you… "Then, in the middle of the small yard, her guest had started to kick him, striking him harder and harder with his right foot until he grew tired. He had turned to one of the other prisoners and ordered him to take the slop bucket from the toilet and pour it over his victim's head. At that point, the guard who was escorting her had turned and screamed, "Turn your face to the wall."

* * *

With Thomas, Haya had taken another step forward in discovering her body. When he first invited her for a coffee, she had never imagined that she would get involved with him almost immediately. He was an art teacher at the college which she attended twice a week. She had heard some of the students make silly jokes about his clumsiness. Maybe she had accepted his invitation out of pity, feeling sorry for him because of his thick glasses, old suit and unfastened tie or perhaps it was because he was so much older than her. She had learnt from conversations among the students that he was the same age as her father and she had therefore assumed that his feelings towards her were paternal especially as she was close to her due date.

He must have sensed her slight nervousness for he started to reassure her only minutes after they had sat down together in a cafe near the college. "My daughter had a baby only two months ago," he said in a friendly manner. "She was terrified at the thought of going into labour. But everything turned out fine. Have you had any pain yet?" Haya interpreted his words as an attempt to dissuade her from going on with her work as a model. "No. I still have more than a month to go. I hate staying at home." She was very surprised that Thomas showed no interest in the baby's father as if it were normal that he was nowhere to be seen. "How many

186

children do you have?" she asked him. He paused for a second, and then said, his cheeks reddening slightly, "I've just got the one daughter. I've been divorced for a long time." He hurried on lightly with his pointless confession, and joked, "I am not cut out for marriage. I think I am better at being a single father."

At their second meeting, Thomas asked her if she would model for him in his private studio, and she could think of no reason to refuse.

The studio turned out to be nothing more than a room in his small flat. Haya was surprised and depressed at the sight of the paintings and array of junk metal, bits of old cars, different kinds of pots and pieces of iron and copper, that lay strewn about the place. She said with a laugh: "Do you work as a scrap merchant?" But Thomas took her remarks seriously. He took her into his bedroom and showed her a large glass fronted cabinet through which she could see abstract sculptures made out of different materials. She wanted to ask him what was in the wardrobe beside it. But then, as if he could read what was going through her mind, he pointed towards it and said: "I put all the clothes and small secrets I own in that. Do you want to see inside?" Instead of replying, she left the room. She had just noticed the tangle of covers piled up on the bed.

He asked her if she would like tea or coffee. When he went off to the kitchen to make the drinks, she followed him without thinking. Perhaps she wanted to make sure that she got a clean mug. The sight of a sink filled with dirty crockery confirmed her fears. "The kitchen is the only place I don't bring my work into," Thomas said in confusion, when he saw her standing behind him. "It's just for eating in." She told him gently but firmly, "Go and tidy your studio and I'll make the tea."

But she didn't stop there. She cleaned all the areas that had been used, and then tidied up the tins which were lying around and arranged them neatly on the three shelves. She was astonished at the number of cans of baked beans she found and almost asked Thomas about them when he came back to the kitchen to find out what was taking her so long. "You didn't have to do all that," he said apologetically, his face going an even darker shade of red. Whenever they felt embarrassed, their colour intensified, differing in its hue, according to the state they were in.

When she saw the chaos in his studio, she wanted to ask if he had ever had a woman model there for him before. Instead she put the palm of her hand on the edge of her back and said, "I feel tired. I need to lie down." He said in confusion as if he had been caught doing something strange, "Do you want to lie down on my bed or on the sofa?" "I'd prefer to go home." "Could you call me a taxi?" After a couple of moments of silence, he muttered, "Would you like me to come with you?" before adding in slightly louder voice, "I'll worry about you if you go on your own."

* * *

Driven by a keen sense of curiosity, she returned to the crimson notebook. "You might ask what made me adopt such a path in life. Would you believe me if I said it was art? Yes, art. When I was at secondary school, I was passion-

188

ately interested in painting. A new art teacher had joined the school who fired the students with enthusiasm for the subject and my interest almost certainly can be traced back to him. He organised a large exhibition which became an annual event and was attended by officials and written up in the press.

"I still wonder if he was right to reject my paintings and refuse to let them be included in the school exhibition. He always said the same things when I submitted a piece of my work, "You are using all the wrong colours." Or "You haven't mastered how to draw yet...." When I joined the Organisation, I resented him even more when I heard it rumoured that he was a communist; some of my classmates even went so far as to say that he used the exhibition as a way of getting students to join his party.

"I'll tell you what happened. You are like a voice speaking inside my head, enabling me to understand myself and the mysterious changes that have taken place within me. My first act of sabotage was prompted by envy. I was jealous of the students who were taking part in the exhibition and angry because I had not been given the chance to have my work admired by the visitors or to see my name in the newspaper. While I was painting, I used to dream about how the art teacher would recognise my talent one day. Can you believe it? And not only that. Not content with giving me the chance to show off my work at school, he would enter my paintings in national exhibitions as well. I used to imagine myself visiting major exhibitions with him and holding long discussions about art. But instead he ignored me; he ignored my efforts and behaved as if I didn't exist. You know, if he had shown any interest in me, I wouldn't have joined the Organisation or fallen under the Leader's spell. I might even have become a communist.

"And so to my first act of sabotage. When the students entered the sports hall and looked at the paintings hanging on the wall, they found to their horror that their works of art had been disfigured. Someone had plunged a sharp knife into them and made deep geometrical incisions in the shape of circles, triangles and squares.

"The Leader did little to show his appreciation beyond giving me a slight nod of his head. He put his hand on my shoulder, and looked down at me, "This is the first small step on the way to achieving something greater, which will raise you to the skies." When I asked him what I had to do, he told me sharply, "You know what I'm talking about."

"I was terrified after I had slashed the paintings. For the next week, I thought every policeman I saw was going to arrest me. Everyone knew I was to blame. When I asked the Leader who was two classes above me what I should do, he said coldly, "You'd better stay with me during the break; that way, people will see you've been carrying out orders from the Organisation."

That incident made me realise that although he was still a young man, the Leader was enormously farsighted. The headmaster merely announced that the annual exhibition had been cancelled and explained away his decision by saying that occasions such as this had a negative effect on students preparing for exams. The art teacher, for his part, turned pale whenever our eyes met. I sensed that he regretted the way he had humiliated me but it was too late now.

"In fact, the sight of his pale face only made me more determined to carry out my next task and do what the Leader had asked. I had to make sure it stayed pale forever. It was as if his face predicted his end, as if its expression signified a fate that had been etched out for him long ago, before he ignored my paintings or joined the school. Before he was born.

I must stress that what happened after the art master disappeared utterly convinced me that the Leader's prophecies would come true. When he told a number of students, "In thirteen years' time, I will be Leader of the republic," I believed him completely, though the others didn't take him seriously. When the teachers and students looked at me, I could see them thinking, "You're the one who killed him." But none of them dared go to the police, because they were afraid of the Leader. Although he always pretended to be very polite to them, they recognised that there was a volcano lurking behind his calm exterior, which would wipe them out of existence if it erupted. The headmaster decided to get rid of the art class and use the room for sport instead. Can you believe it? He justified the decision by quoting the maxim 'a healthy mind in a healthy body.'

"As you can see, the Leader has shaped my course in life or perhaps it would be more correct to say: he has given my life perfect meaning. When I carried out the deed, he told me, "You will always be my right-hand man."

But he hasn't kept his word even though I have never done anything that he hasn't first agreed to, or that doesn't represent his point of view. He has been my guiding light ever since the art master died. Now he rewards me by making me responsible for all the 'ugly' deeds that have taken place since the Organisation came to power, as if he were some kind of angel and evil people like me were abusing his kindness and doing damage to the country and its people."

*   *   *

For a moment, she saw the Artist's eyes in front of her then they vanished and were replaced by those of Thomas. How similar their eyelids looked when they aren't wearing glasses.

Immediately they arrived at the flat, Thomas had wanted to leave. "You must need to rest," he said. But she replied in a friendly tone, "If you want to have a cup of tea, then I'll join you." When she got up to go to the kitchen, he muttered quickly, "I can do it. Why don't you lie down on the bed and I'll bring it you." She felt embarrassed as she made her way to the bedroom. She imagined him standing and watching her as she waddled off like a penguin. Wouldn't it have been better to let him leave immediately?

He sat down on the chair beside her bed as she started to touch her undulating belly.   As he watched the expression change on her face, he asked: "Is something wrong?" "The baby's kicking. Do you want to feel it?" He moved forward cautiously without believing what she was saying. He said delightedly. "It's very strong. You must expect him to arrive at any minute." "You seem to have gone through a similar experience," She teased him and maybe this emboldened him to go one step further: "Can I listen to his heart beat?" His stumbling footsteps and the lines on his face didn't repel her. "Take off your glasses first," she ordered.

She suppressed a laugh when she saw the colour of his eyes. His thick glasses had obscured the blue pupils. But when he took them off, she could see how the heavy eyelids together with the funereal eyes and scanty eyelashes made him look exactly like a frog.

The Artist's face loomed up in front of her again. The only difference between his eyes and those of Thomas was the way they looked at her. The Director of General Security's eyes concealed a cynical smile while those of Thomas presented a secret childish wish to be taken care of. Perhaps that was why she had run her fingers through his greying hair as he placed his head on her bare belly.

She immediately regretted the involuntary gesture but he didn't try to take things further. Instead he said in a steady voice, as he stood beside the bed, "I'll leave you now so you can have a rest." Before she could nod her head even slightly, which would have been sufficient to send him off to the front door, she was overwhelmed with a sense of loneliness. It was as if Thomas' imminent departure had awoken an instinctive fear in her which she had become increasingly aware of the further her pregnancy advanced and which was made worse by her complete inability to tell her family about it. When her father visited her, she had held her stomach in with a wide belt and when he asked her one day: "What was it like in prison?" she had told him, "I promise you nothing bad happened to me." This was enough to make him look up from the ground. She had invented another lie to restore his sense of pride: "I came to London because of pressure from Amnesty International. I wasn't the only one."

She said in a neutral tone to hide her eagerness that Thomas should remain: "Why don't you stay here today?" Perhaps the proposal surprised him a little. The colour rose in his cheeks. He said pretending to joke with her, "I'm not used to sleeping in the sitting room." "You can sleep here." She thumped the empty space beside her with the palm of her right hand.

* * *

Whenever Haya wondered how she could have fallen in love with such a clumsy man as Thomas, she remembered the first night she had spent with him.

He lay prostrate beside her, taking every care not to touch her body as her breathing quickened under the strain of her pregnancy. All the same, she felt a kind of relief that she was unable to define. For the first time in her life, she was aware of the contours of her body as they must look to another person. It was as if Thomas' sudden appearance in her life had extracted her from the thick layers of loneliness that engulfed her and put her back in contact with a family that was larger than her own.

In the months before her baby was born, she had been continuously afraid that one or other of her relatives would turn up. When her elder brother announced that he wanted to come and visit her, she had told him curtly, "I'm busy studying at the moment. I'll be completely free in nine months' time."

She fell into a dream in which there were no images at all. It consisted of nothing but snarling voices which made her think that she was still in the Fortress and she woke up afraid. For a second she seemed to see the Artist, lying beside her and she recoiled in fear but the particles of light filtering through from the corridor were enough to bring her back to reality. Had she put her hand out involuntarily, meaning to grab hold of him? She shrank back, until she was lying on the very edge of the bed while Thomas went on pretending to be asleep.

She became aware of an odd sobbing sound coming from somewhere in the darkness. When she put her fingers up to her eyes, she found they were streaming with tears even though at that moment her whole being was suffused with an intense sense of happiness, as if she had just discovered signs of human life on a completely deserted planet. She was aware of her existence for the first time. She was no longer part of the furniture around her. When Thomas' fingers touched her shoulder, she found her body instantly gravitating towards him.

She buried her face in his half naked chest, her body wracked with searing sobs. She could do nothing but scream at the pain of everything she had endured in the Fortress, while Thomas patted her back harder and harder to comfort her.

Since coming to London, she had done her utmost to repress her memories. She pretended that everything she had been through had happened to some unknown stranger, even when her body was awakened by traces of the old pain. As her breathing grew more sluggish she could clearly visualise the hall she had been pushed into when she first arrived at the Fortress.

She had blinked in surprise at the bright neon lights as she walked slowly forwards, unable to work out exactly what she had to do. Her mind was more than usually turned in on itself, leaving her on her own. Someone in the line of men sitting in front of her called out, "Come here, don't be frightened." Perhaps the laughter, which greeted this remark, had somehow transferred itself to her facial muscles for she appeared to be joining in the joke. The earth shook under her and she found her body gradually advancing in front of her. When someone slapped her, she didn't notice the pain until the guard screamed, "You're still being stubborn, you bitch, even though our chief's here."

The slap restored her to her senses for a couple of seconds and she realised she was completely naked. Since arriving at the Fortress, she had become used to the guard constantly fondling her hips. Now she had only one thought in her mind to the exclusion of all else and that was to conceal her breasts. Perhaps that was why they were laughing. By covering her breasts with her hands, she left what lay between her legs completely exposed.

Obeying an order from her guard she got down on her knees. She crossed her arms firmly across her chest and glanced down in satisfaction at her pubic hair, which would stop their eagle eyes penetrating any further. She was unaware of the blood dripping from her nose. As she knelt there, alert and waiting for the next order from the guards, she heard someone say in a quiet voice that was quite unlike anything she had heard in the Fortress up till then, "Leave her alone." When the room was completely silent, he had added: "Go and get her a blanket."

"What do you do with your relatives when they turn into a never-ending nightmare? Do you flee from the country or get rid of them?

My family didn't dare lift a finger against me. In fact they were only too ready to do what I asked. But their presence was a constant reminder me of the miserable childhood I had suffered. Imagine what it was like for a child like me. He has begun to be aware of the world around him and started to ask his mother for explanations. "Where's my father?" he says. His mother replies: "He's gone to Paradise." "Who's that other man who visits us from time to time?" "That's your uncle. He's the one who looks after you."

"I didn't find out the truth till I was ten years old. My uncle wasn't my uncle. He was actually my father's cousin. He would come and see us every two or three weeks and bring us presents. Every year, before Eid my mother and I would go to the massive house in which he lived. She would busy herself with domestic chores while I spent my time serving his children. I never got irritated by their contemptuous glances or their insults or abuse. I knew my place.

"I discovered the truth later. I was ten years old at the time. I had come back home early from school because the teacher was ill. When I went into the house, I heard the sound of vulgar laughter coming from my mother's bedroom. Did we have guests?

Who do you think was in the house? Was it really my pitiful mother and timorous, pious uncle?

Once the Organisation assumed power, I began to feel oppressed by the thought that there were people out there who could show me up in front of the men who worshipped me. While I had such relatives, how could I maintain my standing in their eyes? How could I guarantee that they would not revile me or betray me to the enemies of the Organisation?

"I was very lucky in my assistant who was not only keen to carry out my orders but also willing to fulfil those desires that I was too scared to admit to myself. I breathed a sigh of relief, I tell you, when I learned my relatives had completely disappeared without my having been a party to the business."

* * *

She followed the progress of the freight train through the kitchen window. From where she was standing on the fourth floor, it looked like a phantom body submerged in a cloud of pale light. The rumbling filtered through to her like vibrations caught in the walls of the building.

How normal the Artist's world seemed, when seen through his papers, now that the years had passed and its distinguishing marks been erased. Her father had told her that the Fortress had been bulldozed and a public park put in its place. "What about the graveyard?" she had asked him.

"What graveyard? No one mentioned one. Are you sure?"

"No, there were only rumours."

The Artist had called it 'the garden.' "Do you want to see my favourite creation?" he asked her a week after he had moved her from her cell to his palace. Everything was different there; she had a hairdresser, masseuse and nurse and tens of servants who did her bidding round the clock.

She thought he was going to take her to his studio as he had constantly told her he was an artist during the nights she spent with him. Weighed down by a mix of dull fear and absolute gratitude, she nodded her head and agreed to everything he said. A white apparently circular wall loomed up in front of her. She followed him through the wooden door, which was engraved with Kufic inscriptions and lines and stepped inside.

The Artist wore a strange expression on his face, a mix of utter repose and tenderness, which made him look as if he were about to enter a place of worship. He led her along narrow alleyways lined with cypress saplings behind which were a row of glass-domed marble cells, each one painted a different colour. Around each cell, cloves, damask roses and lilies were planted in a variety of geometric patterns.

Each cell had a different number fixed to its door. Behind the small windows she could see the flickering of concealed lights, which she presumed to be candles. It was only then that she realised she was in a graveyard. She felt a shrill scream rising from somewhere deep inside her, which calcified when it reached her throat. When she looked at the Artist, she saw that he was entranced with joy, which frightened her even more. She watched him pause in front of each cell and greet the occupants with great politeness and piety.

After leaving the 'garden', she gradually began to recover, although she was still trembling all over. She crossed her arms over her breasts to keep them from his gaze. He looked at her thinking she wanted to ask him who the dead were.

"They were guests of the Fortress… Only the bravest of them are buried here."

She took the open notebook from her bed. "I had to get rid of my assistant. He knew too many secrets. It wasn't difficult to find a reason. All I had to do was ask, "Who told you to get rid of my family? I might have complained about them a bit but that didn't mean I wanted to harm them. What would you have said if I'd started treating your family in the same way?"

"I had learnt this particular nugget of wisdom from the Leader. People are only tools; use them to accomplish a particular goal and once you've achieved your purpose, get rid of them. I never imagined he would apply it to me as well. We were closer than brothers."

After they had returned from the garden, and were in bed, the Artist had suddenly turned towards her, with a frown. She had been scared at the sight of the three deep creases on his brow. Was it her turn to be taken to the graveyard? She twisted her face into a grimace and planted a dazzling smile on her lips but perhaps he read what was really going through her mind.

"Do you know that I first saw the garden in a dream?"

"What do you mean?"

"I would dream about it every day. It would wake me up. One day, I thought: Why not turn it into reality and adorn it with beautiful flowers and plants? Immediately I'd finished making the graveyard, the dream stopped."

"What about the numbers?"

"Do you mean the numbers on the tombs? They belong to those fraternal enemies of ours who refused to give in; we couldn't use them for our own purposes and had to neutralise them. It's my way of honouring them. You believe me, don't you when I say that they are my only friends?"

He had lapsed into a solemn silence. His eyes were half closed; as his right hand began to move through the air, he seemed to her to be conjuring up that specific group of victims, and running his fingers over their stiffened bodies. He spoke again and his voice sounded sad, "You know, the minister of health has asked me to supply more body parts but I've had to turn down his request. I will not disfigure a single one of those brave men."

Part Seven
Baida in Her Labyrinth II

She woke up feeling scared, weighed down by a nightmare that had returned in many different forms. It was pitch black in the room and for a moment she didn't know where she was but the rhythmic sound of Abdel's snores and the smell of sex splashed on her body and nightdress brought her bemusedly back to the present. Images from the nightmare danced in front of her eyes as she stared upwards at the darkened ceiling. Chess pieces as large as human beings were ranged against each other in a game that seemed to be taking place in a hall that dated back to the Middle Ages. Baida was ensconced on a black throne at one end of the room while at the other on a brown throne, sat Scheherazade. She could see two horsemen among the combatants, one dressed in black and mounted on a black horse and the other riding a pale horse and wearing light coloured attire. When she scrutinised them more closely, she was able to make out that they were Abdel and Saleh, despite the fact that they were wearing masks. At the far end of the hall, Scheherazade looked angrily across at her and shook her hand menacingly.

Someone must have been killed. That was what had made her scream out loud, but before she could get up from her throne, British policemen had appeared and started making their way towards her. When she tried to run away, she realised she was trapped and the only way to escape their clutches was by waking up. Unconsciously, she found herself wondering over and over again who had been killed.

She was pretty convinced that Abdel had split open the other knight's skull, but then another thought occurred to her and that was that the chess game was only a pretext. It was no longer a game but a battle in which the two horsemen competed for her. In contrast they were totally disinterested in her cousin.

She suddenly had the feeling that Abdel was prey to her innermost secrets, which she herself was only occasionally aware of. The thought exploded in her mind like a sharp pain in her side. Nothing had changed since Scheherazade and Saleh's last visit. Every day Abdel diligently practiced his favourite form of bathing and had sex with her in the subdued glow of red light cast by a red table lamp. For her part, Baida maintained her own way of making love: she stood a few metres back from the spectacle and watched impassively as it took place in front of her. First he stripped her of her underwear, carefully removing the garments he had personally bought in line with the diktats of leading fashion magazines, then he slowly, relentlessly proceeded to force his way into her. At the beginning, she remained as rigid as a corpse as she waited for the torture session to end but while colouring with embarrassment, she had raised the subject with her elder sister, the latter had told her with a wink: "Just pretend..." Following her instructions, she had started to wriggle her body as Abdel lay on top of her. This gave him an additional satisfaction and pleasure which made him desist from criticising and ridiculing her. Little by little Baida had learnt how to withdraw from her body, leaving it behind to practise its insane rituals; as she closed her eyes, she imagined herself draped in white looking

206

down from the ceiling on the strange scene that was taking place a short distance away.

Ever since Scheherazade and Saleh had left the house two weeks before, she had been unwillingly consumed by a single feeling. Can we say that she was in a state of enlightenment, that she had been transported from a place of chronic darkness to one that was permanently luminescent even in the furthest reaches of the night? Watch her as she walks through the dark, listening to the violent beating of her heart, touching her heated skin with her cold finger tips, as a current of sweet sensation courses through her. An image comes to her mind conjured up by the feeling, a picture of rain falling on parched earth. From far away, she sees Saleh's eyes again or to be more precise the stolen loving glance he directed at her that had lasted for less than a second.

That same night she had feverishly moved about the house, long after Abdel had gone to sleep. Her body felt as light as a feather and for an insane moment she seemed to be walking on air, her feet barely touching the ground then she was assailed by feelings of guilt as she thought of her father: How would he look at her now if he could see the state she was in? Would he think her feeble-minded? Debased? What would happen to her if she destroyed the beautiful image he had of her that he would take with him to the grave? She went to the bathroom and turned on the cold shower, letting the water flow over her head and body; she vomited up the acid yellow contents of her stomach then took another shower, but when she crept back to bed those thieving loving eyes appeared once more, taking her back to the spot where time and place converged, or to put it more correctly at the point of light, at the point where the four directions meet, at the point of existence.

*   *   *

But this mixture of intoxication and shame vanished when her elder sister phoned one evening to tell her that her father had died. When she first heard the news, she was not much affected, since she had been expecting it daily ever since returning from Baghdad; in fact she sometimes doubted whether her father was still alive after all this time. Her sister added: "He didn't suffer and he was still smiling in his usual way even after he died."

Baida carried out her commitments to her family even going so far as to remind Abdel of his daily bathing ritual after the children had gone to their rooms. But in the middle of the night, she woke up for no reason, gripped by a sudden feeling of terror. She had the impression which sometimes came to her while she was asleep that she was about to fall off the side of a very high mountain only to discover that she was on the edge of the bed, but this time she was in a safe place and when she closed her eyes she saw an image of her father holding her hand before she had returned to London. Had he wanted her to remain with him? Had he been apologising for letting her down? As they exchanged looks, she had sensed that fellow feeling in her father that set them completely apart from the rest of the family, not so much because of their ideas but because of their temperament. Her sisters and brothers had the same blunt nature as their mother. She was inordinately proud of this side of herself and described it as a 'strength'. This quality was accompanied by other complementary characteristics, irascibility, extreme inconstancy, coarseness and a tendency to keep things for herself. Baida and her father were the total opposite. If Baida sometimes saw a look of regret in her father's eyes over his choice of wife, she was also aware, that deep down in his heart he believed that all the torment he suffered from his wife had been worth it because it had brought him Baida, who was like a mirror image of himself.

Nevertheless the two of them had not had much time together for immediately she opened her homework book to show him what she had done and the teacher's encouraging comments, one or other of her siblings would break up the session and forcibly drag her father's attention away. He would say with a laugh, "You're just like your mother." And if his words reached her mother's ears, she would protest from where she was sitting, "What's wrong with her mother?" at which point her father would reply humbly, "It was a complement, of course."

Baida always believed that it was only her mother's influence that had made her father agree to her remaining engaged to Abdel after he had broken off contact with her. Throughout his life, he had always given in to his wife, abandoning what he had determined to do if she opposed it, in order to avoid the hell that she was capable of creating for everyone. Immediately he retreated from his proposed course of action, her expression would change dramatically and the rest of them would breathe a sigh of relief once more.

She was convinced at the time that her mother's continued determination to marry her to Abdel, despite the fact that they hadn't heard from him for a long time, stemmed from a desire on her part to get Baida away from her father especially now that her four other sisters had left the house and the twins had gone off to Basra to study at the university. She was afraid that if she were left alone with the two of them, they might form an alliance against her, based on a shared silence and mutual agreement.

She dozed off for a second only for her father to appear to her, this time wearing a pure white suit; he was sitting on his rocking chair under a trellis of vine leaves which looked similar to the one in their house but smaller somehow. It was surrounded by high walls. All that could be seen of the sky was a narrow blue strip. How healthy he looked. His eyes were radiant with happiness. She wondered for a second if it were a dream, if she had dozed off into a light sleep as dawn approached but the solidity of things around her convinced her that it was real. She took several steps forward until she was standing in the shade of the vine; a bunch of ripe grapes, hanging down from above, scraped the top of her head; she could taste the berries on her tongue and her mouth filled with a delicate sweetness tinged with a slight lemony tang. Before her father emerged from the door in the wall opposite, he opened his hand and showed her a white perfectly formed cylindrical shell. "This is for you." He paused in the middle of the gap that separated the trellis from the wall and looked at her; "Don't lock the door. I'll be back tonight." She asked him to wait so that she could go with him, but her voice faded and when she tried screaming, she failed to make herself heard.

She woke up to the sound of Abdel's heavy breathing. The

patch of dark sky, visible through the gap in the curtains had lightened and turned dark blue. She was suddenly overcome with a peculiar loathing for Selim, which ran parallel to her regret at having abandoned her dying father and left him in alien hands rather than remaining beside him to the end, as she should have done. But this sudden surge of feeling against her eldest son quickly evaporated, and a sense of absolute devotion to him flooded through her in its place: he was like a true mirror image of her. When she looked at him, she saw her weaknesses reflected back, which made her become even more resigned to them or to put it another way, made her refrain from taking any action at all. For what more did she want other than her passionate love for her son and her compulsive need to protect him? Nevertheless, she hadn't seen anything wrong in leaving him with Abdel for a month so as to avoid giving her family a sudden shock.

*   *   *

She finally summoned up enough courage to ask her husband about Selim's scar. He was sawing up planks of wood in readiness for a couple of wardrobes he was making for the children's rooms when he felt her standing behind him. He shot her a fleeting glance out of the corner of his eye then returned to his electric saw and carried on with what he was doing. She went on standing in the gap between him and the door of the workshop, looking at him with a strange expression on her face that he had not seen before. Abdel said: "This wardrobe's for Selim. I'm making it larger and

211

nicer than the ones for his brothers and sister." Baida remained silent and unusually for her did not reply. "It's going to be sunny for the rest of the day... Perhaps we could take the children to the park this evening... Selim would really enjoy that..."

Suddenly her voice rose in a strangulated cry, as if she were struggling against someone, who was trying to stop her from speaking. "What happened to Selim while I was away?" Abdel gave a short laugh then hurriedly delivered the answer he had prepared, "It was only a small accident, which I'll tell you about when I've finished this job." He bent over the workbench again, positioning the saw carefully over the plank. He stopped abruptly, a mocking smile in his eyes: "I was expecting you to ask me about the scar immediately you got back from Baghdad, rather than waiting for three whole months.... Have you only just noticed it?"

Baida shrunk away from him as if she had been caught committing an unforgivable offence; at that moment, a feeling sprang up in her which ran counter to her doubts and made her a prey to two conflicting ideas, that the father was behind what had happened to their son or that Selim himself had caused the harm to his body as a result of Abdel's or the carer's negligence when they were looking after him.

* * *

She dismissed the scar in Selim's side from her mind, after Abdel had reassured her, until she saw it in a dream. She and her son were alone in an abandoned castle. The high-ceilinged rooms were connected to each other by a series

212

of doors, with each one leading into the next: it was like a real-life labyrinth. Selim seemed to float between the rooms with light graceful steps that were at odds with the way he normally moved; on the other hand, she felt weighed down by tiredness and was unable to keep up with him. He would emerge in front of her but immediately she approached, would rush away to the room next door, leaving behind a trail of raucous laughter that made him sound like a full-grown man. Suddenly wisps of smoke began to filter into the room. She was certain the castle was about to go up in flames. She had to get hold of Selim and leave immediately. Where was he? She raised her voice and called him but he went on with his game of hide and seek. "I'm here… Look behind you." She was filled with an odd sense of joy mingled with terror for, although he didn't look any different, her son was cunning and seemed highly intelligence. She redoubled her efforts to find him before it was too late. The smoke thickened. The room got hotter making the sweat pour down her face. One question went round and round in her mind. Was she going to lose him now he was cured? Would her entreaties to the Lord be frustrated at the very moment he granted her only request? Flames suddenly billowed out of the dense smoke, making it virtually impossible to move. She could do nothing but scream. The noise of her cries rang out, mingling with Selim's maniacal laughter.

She woke up terrified and without knowing what she was doing ran to Selim's room. When she touched his forehead, she was surprised to find that he had a temperature, and was reminded of the dream she had just had, whose details she had almost forgotten.

She softly stroked Abdel's shoulder until he regained consciousness. She told him what had happened but when she said they should take Selim to hospital, he got angrily out of bed. "If he's feverish, then it means he's got a cold. Give him a cold compress and some Calpol…That'll fix it." But as she stood there, unmoving at his head, his tone grew harsher, "I sometimes think you don't even know you've got three other children. If he isn't any better tomorrow, I'll take him to a friend of mine who's a pharmacist and understands these things better than any doctor… Don't worry."

* * *

The next day, the fever had disappeared. In fact Selim was well enough to go downstairs by himself and sit in the kitchen with his brothers and sister. However he adamantly refused to eat anything though this could have been his way of attracting his mother's attention. Baida expected all traces of the cold to be gone by the following day but at midday Selim had still not emerged from his room.

As she stood outside his door, she heard the faint sound of sobbing coming from inside and when she reached him she was surprised to see that his eyes were swollen with tears. She ran her fingers over his cheeks; they touched his right ear, and he immediately screwed up his face in pain and let out a choked cry.

Abdel was not at home. She waited for an hour, hesitating over whether to take Selim to the doctor without her husband's agreement but as she saw the agony on her son's face, she grew more and more worried. His eyes insistently begged her for help, pleaded with her to come to his rescue.

The taxi ride to the surgery took only ten minutes, but it seemed an age; once they were there, they had to wait for another hour. When they finally saw the doctor, he said impatiently, "You should have brought him in this morning... I might have left by now."

When the doctor shone a small torch into Selim's ears, Baida was able to see the gluey fluid which had accumulated there. After he had completed his examination and gone back to Selim's notes, he said sternly, "I see he was supposed to have seen the specialists more than three months ago. You know he needs to have regular ear, thyroid and eye examinations but you don't appear to have attended any of them."

She didn't say a word. She remembered that the appointments had been scheduled to take place while she was away. She had been on the verge of cancelling her trip to Baghdad but Abdel had promised faithfully to keep them. Instead, he had let Selim injure himself. The doctor added, "He's suffering from acute inflammation of the middle ear due to a long term blockage in the Eustachian tube." She was filled with a sense of unease suddenly desperate to know what had happened to Selim while she had been away. As he was getting up from the bed, she said: "Can you examine his tummy? He cut himself."

*   *   *

Baida remained locked away in a world of her own. Suspicions gnawed away at her continuously: What had happened to Selim while she was away? Where had his father taken him and what exactly had he done to him? She was terrified of leaving him alone with his father when she had to go out. She took him with her sometimes but she kept feeling mortified by the curious stares of other people, which she was unable to ignore. She berated herself for her weakness. Was it not this over sensitivity to other people's reactions that had made her leave Selim behind with Abdel when she went to visit her family? She increasingly began to take him out with her when she went to the shopping centre near where they lived. She bought a pair of dark glasses to hide behind so that passers-by couldn't see how she was feeling when they looked at Selim. Anger coursed through her when she saw a woman gazing at him in astonishment and she would say to herself, "Your son might look nicer than mine now but wait till he turns into a devil like all the others."

Their joint trips to the local shopping centre became something of a ritual. Every three days she would take Selim to the mall, and let him run about at will until he became tired. She would point things out, endlessly repeating their names until her son could say them properly. Gradually her immersion in Selim's 'slow' world eased the tension within her and replaced it with a mysterious contentment and acceptance. They grew closer as they continued to visit the mall together, until they were like a couple of young lovers, oblivious to everyone but themselves.

Baida had pushed the memory of her last visit to the doctor to the back of her mind, when a letter had arrived from him addressed to Selim's parents. The few lines did not contain any details but asked that they bring their son to see him. For a moment she recalled the sight of the doctor examining the scar on Selim's flank and his words came back to her. "It seems to be a scar from a kidney operation and not something he got from playing with a knife as you've just said." He covered Selim up again and turned him over carefully. "He's shown no previous symptoms of kidney disease. Has he been operated on abroad?" When she still said nothing, he said grimly, "I must see the father as well. Make an appointment with the secretary to see me in the near future." Instead of telling Abdel about her visit to the doctor, she had resorted to silence.

While she was re-reading the letter, several images flashed in front of her eyes, Abdel grimacing angrily, Raouf and his pale daughter and the sullen face of his disgruntled wife. A vague suspicion crossed her mind, but she pushed it away immediately, reassured by the picture of her husband's friend's kind and comforting face which appeared in front of her, instantly dispelling the unknown fears which had shaken her for a couple of seconds. She had felt such a warm regard towards Raouf during his last visit. Her husband's image replaced that of his friend, in her mind. She imagined him for a second, grinding his teeth with annoyance, when he found the letter, and the way he would hurl a series of questions at her in which abuse would be mixed with blind fury, "Why didn't you wait for me to return so that we could have gone to my friend the pharmacist? Don't you know that the doctors here are illiterate and exaggerate everything? What did you tell him? Tell me…"

The scene filled her with conflicting emotions. On the one hand, she felt a sense of revenge at the thought of Abdel trapped in a corner, which made her laugh hysterically. On the other, she was gripped by a feeling of terror which made her limbs quake and her body shiver with cold. The air stuck in her throat and made it difficult to breathe.

She heard the key rattle in the front door and her heart started to race. Before Abdel entered the house, she pushed the letter into the dressing table drawer and pretended to be combing her hair in front of the mirror.

Baida had almost forgotten this incident when the post arrived and a handful of letters dropped through the letter box; her pulse immediately quickened. She rushed into the corridor and before Abdel emerged from his workshop, slid the medical letter in its distinctive brown envelope out of the pile and pushed it under the sofa.

After her husband left the house, she picked up the envelope and carefully opened it. It was from the health worker and requested that they fix up an appointment for their son so that certain necessary tests could be carried out on Selim and they could discuss what he required with his parents.

* * *

It was an unusually bright autumn morning and a few blackbirds were singing determinedly in the garden. Sunlight streamed across the bed as if nature had decided to apologise for the wretched week of storms and pouring rain that had just passed. The sky was surprisingly free of clouds and its blueness seemed to go on forever. There was no doubt that the weather was behind Abdel's relaxed demeanour when he suggested taking the children to the park. In response, Baida said, "I'll take Selim to the shops to buy some winter clothes for the kids.

Her son galloped off along the wide walkways, smiling at all the children he passed, shouting out "What's your name?" then saying excitedly, before any of them could answer, "I'm Selim." Baida was infected by his gaiety. Light-hearted, she ran after him without a care in the world. When she finally caught up with him, his heart was racing.

When she emerged from the covered mall she was surprised to see that the sky had clouded over and for a moment, she wondered if the radiant morning had been a dream. It was not yet three o'clock in the afternoon but the gloomy sky made her feel as if a long time had passed since they had left home.

On the way back to the house, Selim began to show signs of tiredness but he went on watching the other passengers on the bus with interest; from time to time his eyes slid sideways to the pavement outside when his attention was caught by something he didn't recognise and he would ask, "What's that?" Whenever he sank back into himself and stuck his thumb in his mouth she would hurry to deflect him from what he was trying to do. "What did you eat in the restaurant?" "What colour are your new shoes" As she did this, she would continually wipe the dribble away from the corner of his mouth and run the tips of her fingers through his wispy hair.

*　*　*

Immediately she turned the key in the lock of the outside door, she was struck by a sudden sense of foreboding. A few minutes before, she had experienced a moment of pure joy when her son who was walking several paces ahead of her recognised the gate to their front garden. In fact she was even thinking of telling Abdel about Selim's latest achievement.

When she entered the hallway, she thought the others must still be at the park because it was so quiet but when she went into the sitting room, she noticed the back of Abdel's head and shoulders, outlined against the glass wall separating the garden from the dining room. He must have heard their voices for he turned towards them. Baida thought he looked strange. He had an apprehensive expression on his face that she hadn't seen before, which was exacerbated by the cloudy glass which separated them. Her heart beats quickened under the weight of some nameless fear.

Abdel said coldly, completely ignoring his eldest son who stood there waiting for his father to pat him on the head: "Leave Selim with the other children. I've got something to say to you."

When she came back down, she saw Abdel seated on a chair in the sitting room, with a couple of sheets of paper in his hand. Baida knew what the matter was, before he even opened his mouth. They were the letters from the doctor which she had hidden away in a drawer. Just the day before, she had been on the point of taking them out and finally getting rid of them but one of the twins had come and complained about his brother and she had forgotten what she had resolved to do and only remembered later when she had left the house to go to the shopping centre. She had considered going back home again and tearing them up but been reassured at the thought that the children and their father were spending the day outside. Abdel said, "Lubna took the letters out. I didn't go near your dressing table."

Then he launched into a long and irate tirade, peppered with furious questions: "Did you take him to the doctor without my knowledge? Is that how a loyal wife treats her husband? Stabs him in the back? How could you go to the doctor's surgery on your own? What did you tell him? What can I do now so long after the letters have come?"

She maintained her silence. The sound of her husband's voice reached her intermittently, and in time with it, tears welled up in her eyes and gradually washed away the terror that had filled her at the start and made her tremble involuntarily. From some unknown point, deep inside her, she rallied. Her strength grew and transformed itself into words, which she flung into her incoherent interjections, even in the midst of her defeat, "The doctor said it was an operation… Where did you take him while I was away?.. What did you do to him?"

She felt utterly defeated. It was as if those few moments had liberally repaid her for the choices she had made in her life or to put it more precisely, had failed to make. When she went to the bathroom, the image she drew comfort from was an image of Selim rather than her father- Selim shouting out his mysterious expressions to the people shopping in the mall.

* * *

Maybe it is not enough to say that Selim was like a mirror

in which Baida saw her weaknesses reflected. The opposite was also true. She saw her strengths reflected in him as well. Since she had been a young girl she had been trained in the art of self-sacrifice. But the other had to be weaker than her in order to have a rightful claim on her. When she had been a teenager she had daydreamed that she worked in the leper colony her father had talked about one day. She was the nurse-in-charge and instead of neglecting the patients like the health workers, her father had talked about, she had taken great pains over their welfare and devoted the utmost care and attention to them. She had earned a great reputation, but on the day she was due to meet the president to receive an award, she was struck down with the disease. She had got the disease by ignoring the health guidelines and having direct contact with the patients through refusing to wear gloves or a mask. Before she emerged from the daydream, she saw herself lying in a quarantine room.

After Selim's birth and when she received news of her father's first heart attack, she occasionally indulged in a fantasy that she was living in a small flat in London with Selim and her father. At such intense moments, she would experience a sense of ecstasy. But when the twins and Lubna were born, her dreams became tinged with bitterness as she realised she would never be able to fulfil them and gradually she relinquished them.

* * *

As she watched Abdel restlessly move from one floor of the house to another or from his workshop to the garden, she longed to take Selim and flee to Baghdad but the thought of her mother's frowning face, and the scolding she would receive for having left her family behind made her cringe. She would say that she had come for a visit; she wouldn't tell her that she was going to stay for a month until the crisis had safely passed and she could return home. As she became more convinced by the idea, other problems occurred to her, sowing themselves in her mind like harmful weeds. She imagined her sisters, with their children in tow, standing round her son with expressions of disbelief and mockery on their faces as if they could see Baida's long expected failure which they had never stated openly, clearly written in Selim's eyes.

She was surprised when the bread, meat and milk ran out for Abdel was usually meticulous in filling the house with food before the old supplies were exhausted. He had always been responsible for doing the shopping because he knew the cheapest places to shop in. When she went to the workshop to ask him to buy what she needed for lunch, she found him sitting in his rocking chair. He had two large screws in his hands which he was unconsciously turning over and over between his fingers. His face was noticeably pale and that, coupled with an odd presentiment of danger, made her draw back from what she had been meaning to ask him. She said instead, "I'm going to the supermarket for a bit."

She went to fetch Selim from his room but found him sunk in a deep sleep. When she put her hand on his chest to wake him, she felt as if her other hand was reaching out to prevent her disturbing his sleep. She thought she would wait another hour before getting him up but when she looked at the clock, she saw it was close to midday and decided to leave him behind.

She hastily grabbed the bare essentials and joined the long queue at the cashier's desk. It was Saturday. With the all the tension at home, she had forgotten that it would be crowded because of the weekend. She almost thought of leaving the basket and giving up her place in the queue but troubled by an image of her children crying with hunger, she remained where she was.

When she got near the house, she saw an ambulance standing in the road. At first she thought it had come to take away their elderly neighbour who had been in and out of hospital the past couple of months. But her mouth went dry when she saw Abdel standing beside it. He waved at her, as he was getting into the car, "Stay with the children... It's just a little accident. Don't worry about him."

* * *

Once the ambulance had driven away, the street resumed its usual calm and the small crowd of people, who had been passing at the time, broke up. Before they left, a few of them looked at her sympathetically but apart from that there was nothing to indicate the nature of the disaster that had taken place behind the walls of her house.

Part Eight
The Artist II

She didn't tell Thomas what had happened to her in prison and he never asked her about the past. Perhaps he assumed that she had left her country for reasons of the heart and it was up to him to treat her and her pregnancy as if they were one and the same. He was at the hospital while she was in labour, and when the pain got too much for her, she clung onto his hand to stop herself screaming despite being encouraged to do so by the midwife.

Thomas stayed with her for three months after the birth. In the morning he would wake her up with a cooked English breakfast and remind her of the baby, if she demurred. "Fatty dishes help produce milk, my gentle cow," he would say.

Haya still had the piece of paper on which Thomas had written down his list of housewifely chores. "You're a good father," she told him with a laugh before he left the flat, and then added, "or a good mother." On the paper, which was still stuck to the kitchen wall, Thomas had listed his tasks in numerical order, beginning with bathing her and the baby, and ending with doing the shopping and the cooking.

He had never really gone back to his house. He visited her two or three times a week and sometimes would take her out driving at the weekend to towns along the south coast.

At the start, she had been reluctant even to take a short trip outside London because she was breastfeeding the baby. But Thomas had persuaded her to change her mind, "I'll take complete responsibility. Country air is good for children, you know."

Through Thomas, Haya discovered the timeless quality of the English landscape. No matter what the season, the green covered hills never lost their extraordinarily vivid colouring. Wherever she went, she saw immaculately pruned trees and thorny hedges that looked as if unseen hands had worked their way over every inch of the enormous fields and moulded them aesthetically into one seamless whole. Time seemed to stand still. Maybe it was the soft rain falling throughout the year that contributed to the pervasive sense that there was no past. The present was all that existed. Yesterday, today and tomorrow. Could she deny that she was beginning to escape her nightmares? That these tranquil colours that shifted from grey to green in line with the seasons were having a calming effect on her?

Or maybe their encounters in her flat had something to do with it. She felt as if she were taking part in a non-stop carnival of joyful pleasure. Thomas was enormously exact and diligent in everything he did, his actions spiced with a dry wit, which none of his students or colleagues would ever have suspected. In contrast, his clumsy behaviour and the absorbed expression of spurious solemnity on his face provided her with plenty of ammunition with which to tease him constantly. As her English gradually improved, she began to emerge from her chrysalis and discover another woman in herself, one bold enough to ask for anything she wanted.

After bathing her baby and putting him to bed, Thomas would turn his attention to her. He would fill the bathtub with hot water, adding a mix of natural fragrances and shampoo and then call her when the bubbles foamed. Although he got into the bath with her, he did not let up on his work, but continued to carry out his duties with a seriousness that made her laugh. His fingers massaged every part of her body with cool detachment until her breasts and thighs tingled with excitement. She felt relaxed in her movements because deep down she was persuaded that he was unable to see the details of her body without his thick glasses. As she gazed at his heavy lids and weak eyes, she would ask, "How come you're so experienced, my elderly frog?" and he would pant heavily in reply, "Relax completely, my foolish dove; talking will only damage your health."

At first she didn't understand why Thomas was so intent on buying a huge wardrobe for her. When he had finished installing it, she found herself confronted by a mirror, which ran the length of the wall parallel to her bed. Initially she thought he wanted to make the small bedroom appear larger and it was only later, after she had finished having her bath that she discovered what he was really aiming at. She watched him in the mirror as he shaped her body, touching the edge of her thighs, running his hands along her calves and down to her feet, like a skilled sculptor who was absorbed in the primary material he was working in: his clay.

Once when Thomas was trying to reach his glasses, which he had put on the bedside table, she pushed them away from him so they fell on the floor. "All I have is the picture," she choked out, suddenly aware of a violent current sweeping through the length of her body. "You own the reality."

Her eyes greedily followed what was happening in the mirror while her trembling fingers clung to his arms locked around her back.

But Thomas had other reasons for installing the mirror. Very often, after they made love, he would eagerly draw the outline of her image as it was reflected on the white wardrobe door and occasionally put tropical fruit in her lap or hang a necklace of grapes, cherries or strawberries about her neck.

Haya was not ashamed to indulge Thomas' whims. On the contrary, she was fascinated by them despite the ridicule she heaped upon him whenever he suggested doing something new. His only reply was to insist determinedly, the blood mounting in his cheeks, "We are creating something extraordinary together, my bewitching doll."

She had been surprised by the pictures she had seen in Thomas's flat. They were vibrant with colour; the outlines she had sneered at were here transformed into exciting images. She ran her fingers over the surface of the painting hanging on the wall, feeling the softness of her naked body stretched out on the bed, which contrasted with the solidity of the fruit protruding in relief.

Despite her many unkind comments, she was deeply content with what Thomas had done. For the warmth that suffused the colours seemed to confirm her ever more rooted belief that she and her baby and Thomas were a single unbreakable unit. Every day, she witnessed new evidence of this in her friend's face. How exuberant he seemed; how attentive he was to his clothes now; how much more self-confident he had become. Once while he was putting a bunch of chrysanthemums in the vase beside her bed, he said,

"You have made me feel like a new man."

Thomas' exhibition 'The Fruits of Paradise' did not excite

much interest.

He only sold three of the forty paintings on display. But as far as he was concerned, something much more significant happened while the exhibition was on. He got to know Christine.

Rubbing the palms of his hands together, he told her, "My exhibition is transferring to Manhattan. Christine owns a gallery there and she's excited about the paintings. She wants to meet you."

For the first time since she had got to know him, she felt Thomas distancing himself from her in the three hours she spent with the two of them in the restaurant. He was completely engrossed in his conversation with the American tourist. They talked about famous artists, poets and singers from the fifties and sixties, a time, when she had been nothing but a child living in a city thousands of miles away from the west. But she didn't feel her relationship with Thomas was threatened. In spite of her short dyed blond hair and the skilfully applied make up which concealed many of the lines below her eyes, Christine looked as old as her mother.

Thomas suddenly turned towards her, "Christine is talking about bringing out a book in which the paintings will be set beside erotic recipes using tropical fruits and brandy. What do you think about helping to write it? It's a surrealist work of an unusual kind."

When he returned from New York, he avoided meeting up with her, explaining each time he phoned, that he was busy at work. When he finally came to her flat, she realised from the first that something inside him had changed. He avoided meeting her eyes even when she was sitting in his lap. And instead of picking her up in his arms and carrying her off to the bedroom, as he usually did, saying on the way, "What do you think if I take you now, my ungrateful virgin?" he stared steadily out of the small window. When she took off his glasses, she was surprised to see that his eyes were bloodshot.

After a silence that seemed to Haya to last for ages, Thomas finally said, "I haven't slept since coming back. I have to decide between staying in London and moving to New York. I've got nothing here apart from you. But I'll always regret it if I don't go to New York."

"What's stopping you from going? Whatever happens, we'll still remain lovers, won't we?"

"Do you know that my exhibition is going to some of the bigger cities in the west of America?"

"It's an opportunity for you. You must take it."

"But Christine's imposed a condition; she says we must get married."

She was about to ask him to repeat what he had just said, but the air tightened in her chest and she was unable to get the words out. However any doubts she might have had vanished when she saw the resolute lines on Thomas' face.

How long did it take to put on her old mask again, to disregard the rage that welled up inside her and say in a quiet, reassuring tone:

"If I was in your position, I would agree immediately. It's the chance of a lifetime. It won't come again."

* * *

She would never forget the days following their separation. After Thomas had left, she escaped to the nearby park, where the sight of falling leaves made her long to disappear into nothingness. Her body which had brought her happiness with Thomas once again became a source of misery. They had been like hermits when they met in her house. There they had rushed to divest themselves of anything that tied them to the outside world. There was no past, present, or future. Instead, their only concern was to wear their naked bodies. Every time they met they were joined together like twins who had just that moment come down from their mother's womb. "The body is the dome of the soul." Where had she read that? When their bodies were joined in love, she felt dizzy; her air passages were constricted; her blood failed to circulate; words rattled in her throat. But there at that mysterious point, the miracle had happened: it was simultaneously fusion and creation; a surging flood, which passed in the blinking of an eye, and pushed the scattered atoms of her body into unity with the absolute.

How long had it been before he surprised her with a telephone call? "Do you know who it is?" he asked her. "Not really." "It's Thomas. You seem to have forgotten me." After taking several deep breaths, she said, "Are you talking from New York?" "No, I'm in London. In fact, I'm calling from a phone box near your house."

Haya was amazed at how easy it was to substitute 'I'm busy today,' for the 'Come over immediately,' that was on the tip of her tongue. Thomas asked regretfully, "Tomorrow?" "No, the day after."

Thomas seemed embarrassed when they met although

he kept up his jokey manner with her. When he tried to embark on the stammering apology he had prepared, Haya gently put her hand over his mouth, and instead of the icy barrier he had expected, she buried her head in his chest.

They made love silently on the cold leather sofa. She never once lifted her gaze from his face and arms and he thought she was trying to convince herself he was really there.

But, in fact, she wanted to allay her doubts on another score altogether. She wanted to assure herself he was dead.

He had died a week after they separated. As the screams of her hungry child echoed through the flat, she sat waiting for a miracle to happen that would take her out the cocoon of utter misery in which she found herself.

A short note arrived from her brother. It said simply, "I am sorry to tell you Father is dead."

This new source of grief was like a layer of lava spewed out by a fresh volcano to bury the old. With it grew a sick feeling of guilt. How else could she explain the fact that her father had cut all contact with her for over a year but that he had heard what had happened to her inside the Fortress? Did he know that the Artist had planted his seed inside his daughter's womb? Was it this that had made him shut himself away inside his house and shrink in shame from other people? Her mother didn't tell her much on the phone, worried perhaps that it might be tapped. The only thing she learned was that there had been a sudden rise in her father's blood pressure, which had led to a brain haemorrhage.

She remembered how on hearing the news, she had been struck by the contrast between the two men. Although they were of the same age, her father had died, weighed down by grief at the thought of what had happened to his daughter, while Thomas had taken only a few hours to decide to abandon his lover and marry someone else. The former had gone to his grave, dragged down by the laws of gravity, while the latter had risen to the top, pushed there by the law of weightlessness. The former had belonged to a world governed by absolute values; the latter to a world of relative values, which were fashioned like clothes, according to individual preferences.

She locked herself away in her flat as she mourned for her father. The moving trains were her only link to the outside world, an incessant reminder of its presence beyond the kitchen window. But an instinct for survival stirred within her, much to her surprise and she lavished care on her child.

Suddenly a crack opened up at the very core of her despair and amid the layers of depression, there appeared a violent beauty. One afternoon, she awoke to find the leather sofa on which she had lain down in the final hours of the night, bathed in sunlight. She felt herself washed clean of grief, as light as a butterfly; from the heart of darkness, light had sprung; from the abyss of death, life had been reborn.

She realised at that moment that her father had been the umbilical cord, which attached her to her country and kept her constantly turning around it. Now she felt like a star that has broken loose from its orbit, and is free to move unfettered towards its extinction.

Ever since she was a child, the two of them had formed a secret alliance. His unspoken requirement was that she would out do her four brothers and be more masculine than they were.

To earn his absolute approval, she had joined the Revolutionary Army.

* * *

The telephone rang. It was Thomas on the line again. "Do you fancy meeting this evening?" "I am busy today." "With whom?" "That's none of your business," she said. There was a moment's silence, as if he was surprised at her reply, then he asked, "What about tomorrow?" "The day after tomorrow would be better. Friday evening is more suitable for a mother like me."

She regretted that she had agreed to meet him. She should have said, "No," even though not in her nature.

Haya had always been keen to conceal her weakness from other people. With her slender build and broad shoulders she had involuntarily become a source of strength to those around her. At home, she had been the centre of equilibrium within the family. When squabbles broke out between various members of the household, they had turned to her to seek a solution. She was like a candle, her father said. Her radiance lit up the home. It never occurred to him to ask whether she had any problems of her own.

Would she have told him what was going through her mind if he had talked to her before it was too late? Before one of her classmates dragged her off to join the Revolutionary Army? He had only become a member in the first place, after failing to win her love. Maybe he thought he would be able to get her to become a member in the future so at least

236

they could be together. Once she was close to him, he would win her admiration with his heroic deeds. To this end, he had smuggled out secret leaflets to her, which would have been enough to get her executed if they had been found on her person.

She flicked through the crimson notebook, her eyes drawn to a paragraph that was set apart from the rest of the text. It was as if the Artist were speaking to her directly. "I miss you terribly," he had written. "Do you believe me when I say I've only ever been attached to one other person in my life apart from you and that's the Leader? I've always thought that it's a sign of weakness to be attached to a woman. I don't know how you managed to win me over. I think I lost my head the moment I saw you kneeling before me. You reminded me of a palm tree that still clings to the soil, even though its roots have been splintered by an axe."

She recalled a scene, she had watched through a peephole and which the Artist had no doubt prepared for her, thinking that she and her class mate were more than friends. The two men were sitting face to face: the Artist behind the table and her fellow student in front of it.

"You advocate armed struggle against us, don't you?" the Artist had asked while the other man remained silent. "Here, take this." The Director of Security pushed a gun towards him. It slid across the table and stopped at the edge.

"What do you want me to do with it?"

"First, make sure it is loaded."

Her classmate carried out the order; the pallor on his face was more marked and she could see his knees shaking. Suddenly the Artist raised his voice. "Now's your chance to kill the second most important person in the land. What are you waiting for?" Deep inside, she could hear herself calling out. "Come on, do what he's asking you. I'll serve you for the rest of my life. I'll always be true to you." Her silent pleas grew more urgent when the Artist tempted him even further." Do you see that door?" he asked. "You can escape through it as soon as you've got rid of me. It leads outside."

*   *   *

She locked the door of the bathroom behind her and turned on the hot tap. The sound of water gushing into the bath broke the heavy silence but she remained on tenterhooks, her ears pricked for any noise coming from outside. She was inhabited by a single desire that made the seconds freeze in their tracks: she wanted Thomas and his student to leave her flat immediately.

She didn't know how much time passed before the miracle happened; suddenly she became aware of the patter of feet on the wooden floor in the corridor then the brief click as the front door closed slowly behind them, as if her guests were trying to disappear from her world with as little sound as possible.

She wandered aimlessly round the small flat. Maybe she wanted to make sure that she had regained possession of it, that she was its sole mistress. Her eyes fell on the bouquet of lilies that Thomas had bought. She hesitated slightly after taking them out of the vase, as if unsure what to do with them, and then opened the kitchen window and threw them out into the dark vacant lot beside the station.

She started at the sight of the white sheets and covers on the bed. They were like bits of debris, poking up here and there, a memento of a recent bombardment that had left nothing behind except the acrid smell of gunpowder. She opened the window wide. The dry, frosty air flowed in. She took repeated deep breaths while her eyes tracked the specks of light scattered over the slate roofs.

When her feet touched the water in the tub, the skin on her legs crawled from the unaccustomed heat. But she eagerly submerged herself, letting the water envelop her in its folds. The steam rose steadily narrowing her field of vision until her reflection in the large wall mirror vanished from her gaze. She touched her damp hair. For a moment she was back there. She feels the rhythmic touch of fingers running through her locks. Her body throbs in time with them. Desire is a bottomless pit. When she closes her eyes an image rises in front of her, an octopus, brimming with vitality.

Were they Thomas' fingers?

Before he arrived at the flat, she had convinced herself that he would not stay long. She had prepared a white lie that would put an end to any hopes he might have of renewing their relationship, without having to reopen the wounds of the past. She would tell him, "My former fiancé will shortly be arriving in London." If he asked her why she had never mentioned him before, she would reply, "He's my child's father. He was in prison for political reasons and released a couple of months ago."

But he had surprised her by bringing a handsome young man with him. "This is Ian," he had said. "You must remember him. He was one of my best students. He says he knows you."

She felt embarrassed at his last words, which evoked a world submerged in the distant past. She looked brazenly at the young man, masking the confusion she felt inside. "Did I pose for you?" Her sudden question brought an added blush to Ian's cheeks. He said, after overcoming his shyness," I sat a long way away from you in the back row." She felt like flirting with the bashful man as her eyes took in his blonde innocence. "I can make up for that if you want," she said, winking at Thomas. Looking at him now, he seemed to her like an old clown. "I'm jealous," he said. "It hasn't taken you long to find favour with her. I should have thought twice about bringing you with me."

Why had Thomas brought Ian with him? Was he hoping to avoid an outright rejection from her or trying to escape the question she hadn't asked the first time he had seen her. "Why have you come back?" Perhaps he thought that by having his young friend with him, he would be able to answer the question without putting himself in the position of the accused.

"I didn't think my exhibition would be so vilified. Everyone attacked me, women's organisations, religious organisations, even the anti-abortionists." Thomas lowered his voice, as if he were trying to sound dryly ironic rather than aggrieved, while all the time his eyes ranged round the room (which he had once known so well), taking in every detail.

When they had finished the first bottle of Bordeaux, she had asked him about life in New York. Instead of answering directly, Thomas launched into a stream of complaints about how far his flat had been from Manhattan. "It was no-where near New York. It was in the middle of boring subur-bia. Christine didn't tell me that. Even her gallery was miles away from the centre of New York."

Thomas seemed to have aged considerably in the three years he had been away. Perhaps his constant whinging and Ian's presence made her more aware than ever of the wide age gap between them.

A strange feeling of curiosity towards her young guest stirred inside her. "Where do you live?" Before he could re-ply, Thomas rushed to answer, in a manner quite unlike his normal self. "I am currently staying with him. Of course, it's only temporary. His house is full of paintings. You should see his work. You would really like it."

Prompted no doubt by a sense of loneliness, Thomas gulped back his glass of wine even faster than before.

Even though she and Ian had said nothing to each oth-er, she was very much aware of him. Everything apart from him reminded her of the past: Salam Salman, the Artist's memoirs, her father's photograph and her former lover whom she wished would leave. Only Ian symbolised the present for he embodied that instant which had brought the two of them together in her sitting room. Everything about him suggested a world untouched by the fingers of decay. "Where are you from originally?" she asked. "From a village about thirty miles from Glasgow. Have you been to Scotland?" She could hear the brassy tones of Nina Simone coming from the music player but was unable to make out what she was singing. Ian was her single point of focus.

Thomas suddenly got up from his chair and without giving

his student time to catch up with him, or her a chance to say goodbye, announced, "I'm leaving." She had never seen him so annoyed before. She was pulled this way and that by a series of conflicting emotions: relief that he had gone and guilt for having neglected him. Joy at being left alone with Ian and despair at having lost him again, this time maybe forever.

They had sat for a long time in silence, and then Thomas' student had risen apologetically: "I think I should go now," he said. But as he was leaving the room, she stretched out her hand to his right shoulder. It was as if his body were waiting for just that moment, for he wheeled round and embraced her. She turned out the lamp in the short corridor, plunging them into darkness, which was alleviated only by a faint light coming from the sitting room. She led him to her bedroom; immediately the door closed behind them, the darkness fell again punctuated only by fragments of pale light filtering in from the outside through the narrow gap in the curtains, which were enough to guide them towards the wide bed.

The relentless sound of a bell gradually penetrated her consciousness. Where was it coming from? How long had it been ringing? She had been wrapped up in her own world, hungrily teasing out the secrets of the young man's body. In her mind's eye, she could see the clothes she had scattered all over the place, in her wild desire to fuse with the other.

What had been going through her mind as she felt his whole body tremble under the penetrating touch of her bold fingers? Had she thought for a second that she was satisfying a desire buried deep within her father that she should really

242

have been a boy? Was Ian not her virginal girl?

She hurriedly put on her dressing gown and rushed to the front door, worried lest her child be awakened by the incessant peal of noise.

Thomas loomed up in front of her. He was standing in the darkness on the landing, which separated the two opposite flats. At first she could make out nothing except the pale ray of light reflected in the lenses on his glasses. "I'm sorry to wake you up," he said. "I forgot that Ian has the keys to the flat. Has he gone?"

She was silent for a few seconds, filled with childish embarrassment as if she'd been caught red handed by her father, doing something he disapproved of. A counter emotion surged through her, a sense of rebellion from deep inside at the guilt she was feeling. She almost replied with an uncharacteristic "yes," but instead found herself telling him to come in. When she reached the bedroom, she turned towards him. He appeared completely resigned. When she said, "Go in and I'll join you in a minute," he initially looked around as if not quite believing what he was hearing. She opened the door a little, then pushed him gently inside before closing it behind him.

The steam cleared. She glanced over at the mirror. A strange face loomed up in front of her. It would look much better if the hair were cut short. She grabbed handfuls of her tresses and piled them on top of her head. She would go to the hairdresser's tomorrow and ask him to take it all off. She would look like Joan of Arc as she had once seen her in the cinema, the only difference being that the latter had had her hair shaved off in preparation for immolation. For baptism by fire. She had finally won her release from her man-made prison. She too would like to be baptized by fire. But she would do it with her own hands.

She is in bed with the two of them. She's no longer haunted by the sense of shame she felt, when she saw Thomas standing at the front door. They are all equal now. They lie side by side in silence; now that she has pulled the curtains tight across the windows, a rich darkness fills the room, in which the outline of their bodies only appears as an even darker shade.

When she had first entered the room, she was scared that Thomas might react angrily at finding himself placed in this strange position. Would she attribute it to his jealousy? To his love for her? What would she do if that happened? Maybe it would make her forget how he had let her down. She'd throw Ian out of the flat and ask Thomas to forgive her for the hateful crime she had committed in despair at his leaving her.

But instead, she heard them talking amicably, laughing quietly. For a moment she suspected they were gay lovers. The idea made her feel strangely jealous of Ian so that she quickly hung her robe on the back of the door. Once it was shut, she slipped lightly into the tiny space between them, laughing, "Make way for me"

When did she hear the loud wails coming from her child's room? He must have been crying quietly for some time before starting to scream. During those moments, she had lost all sense of place and time.

What violent forces was she prey to at the time? She was inhabited by two beings that were alien to her but in harmony with each other: unruly, male and female.

She hastily got out of bed and stumbled off to her child.

How long had she rocked him before he fell asleep again? The scraps of light filtering in from the corridor were sufficient to make out his face.

Something she had always denied now struck her with the force of lightening: he looked just like his father 'the Artist'. Before she left his little room, something else pierced her memory. For a moment she recalled the incident in dazzling clarity. She had always refused to accept that it had really happened, assuming that the images were no more than a passing nightmare.

She was standing behind a pane of dark glass, through which she could see the two of them. There must have been a guard nearby who was giving them orders but she was unable to see him. At first, she found it hard to believe that one of the men was her colleague from university. Where was that sense of pride which had been his distinguishing mark in college? She could hardly believe that this was the same man whom she had seen only two days before. What had happened to him since he had last met the Artist?

She didn't know who the other person was. He was most probably a fellow student. The two men were completely naked and walking on all fours. Although the pane of glass was sound proof, she guessed that they were barking at each other. From time to time, they would glance sideways at the guard as if to make sure that he was pleased with the way they were behaving. Then they paused for a second. They must have received a strange order that required them to think about how to carry it out. Who was the other prisoner, now advancing on her classmate? He stayed where he was, his backside turned submissively and made no move, even when the other man suddenly mounted him from behind.

She felt overcome with nausea. She groped her way to the bathroom, knelt down in front of the toilet bowl and clasped her hands to her stomach.

How long did she spend there? She was shaken by regular bouts of sickness. Each time the retching died away in her throat, she spewed out another image from the Fortress which had been buried inside her without her knowing. She relived the moments, the pleading sound of prisoners' voices, the blood-clotting terror, the graveyard, and the Artist's innocent comments. As the bitter taste of alcohol clung to her mouth she noticed it had the saltiness of blood. When she opened her eyes, she noticed bits of red swimming in the toilet bowl. In contrast, with each contraction and bout of vomiting she gradually felt herself becoming lighter as if she were stripping away bit by bit the warts of despair, which had attached themselves to her stomach lining.

When she went through the door into the bedroom, she felt as if she were moving from one planet to another, stepping from one geological age to the next. Her nostrils were filled with a sharp acrid smell that conflicted with the quiet in the room. She was caught between two worlds, governed by opposing forces; before her lay subtlety, minimum sincerity, self-worship, romantic fornication, and false innocence; behind cruelty, unbridled emotions, madness, absolute truths and self-denial.

A feeling of anger mounted inside her at the sight of her

slumbering lovers. They were like a couple of innocent children who appeared to have no connection with what they had just taken part in. Should she wake them up, tell them what had happened to her classmate, who had dreamed of realising an earthly paradise for the poor? She remembered how eagerly he had followed every titbit of news about the revolutions and coups taking place in the world. And she had known, as she watched him walk naked on all fours, that the thing that grieved him most was that his guard had come from a deprived family, something that was totally at odds with everything he believed in.

How would Ian and Thomas react if they had to suffer the same experience? Would they commit suicide like her classmate had done?

The question echoed in her confused and heavy head. In the darkness a snowball rolled down an icy slope, grew larger and larger, moved faster and faster. Voices sneaked into her throat. Whispered in her ears. "Mrs Haya?" "No I am the mother of the Artist. Do you want to see him? He's been reborn and will soon be back in the fortress." "Why are you carrying that stick in your hand?" "Don't be frightened. It's just a broom handle, a hollow pipe."

She must have gone mad. She only had a vague memory of what happened next. Details came and went haphazardly. The huge ceiling light ablaze. Sitting on a chair coldly watching what was happening out of the corner of her eye. An octopus squirming greedily, wriggling its arms in all directions.

Then another image returned: She is swooping down on her victims and pulling the covering away from them. They are filled with panic when they see the thick stick raised above them. In the blinding light, they look like microscopic naked creatures when she turns her magnifying glass on them. In a harsh voice that is completely alien to her, she shouts, "Come on now, it's your turn to do it together. You must put on a good show for me."

Part Nine
Baida in Her Labyrinth III

Immediately she closed the door behind her, the noise of the street rose up to greet her, cutting her off simultaneously from the pungent mix of perfume and hair dye within. The beauty parlour, which she could see through the plate glass window now seemed like a distant world; hours rather than seconds seemed to have passed since she had been inside, seated in front of the young hair dresser as he murmured his approval of her soft hair, or with her hands stretched out before the manicurist, who had coolly worked on her nails, removing traces of the previous varnish and applying another more vivid in its place.

She had only decided to get rid of her long hair when the hair dresser finished washing it. A pale woman with damp straggly locks loomed up in front of her as she peered at herself in the looking glass. It was the first time Baida had examined herself in a mirror since the accident happened but the image that looked back at her bore no relationship to what she was feeling at that moment. The face appeared expressionless and unmarked by her journey into hell; there was little to show that this was the first day she had ventured outside. The hairdresser asked: "How do you want me to cut it?" Before she could say as she normally did, "I'll just have a trim," she noticed a black and white photograph of a girl in her twenties, wearing a white shirt with a raised collar, and short hair, cut above her ears; she pointed to it.

Abdel said, "Scheherazade's coming today." For the first time since Selim's death, the words meant something to her.

"When's she coming?" she asked. He replied, "At six o'clock." Her cousin had visited her regularly while she had been ill. Doubtless, it had been her who had asked Abdel to take his wife to hospital when a week had gone by and she hadn't eaten a thing. There she had been put on a drip, which fed liquid nourishment into her arteries. Baida had meekly obeyed the doctors and nurses' instructions: "Sit on this chair," "Open your mouth," "Pull up your shirt sleeve a bit." She behaved like a robot, carrying out their orders without evincing any sign of the emotion within. She would break into fits of laughter or strangled sobs at what was happening around her as if the series of external scenes had lost all kind of meaning. The sight of her three children standing vacantly in front of her, one behind the other, would invoke an image of customers queuing in a shop; she would laugh at the picture they presented but the next minute, think of herself lining up in the supermarket, hours before the accident happened and begin to beg the imaginary shoppers to let her through. "Please let me pay before you... My son's going to fall through the window...I forgot to close it." At such times, Abdel would merely drag the crying children out of the room.

Even at the funeral, Baida had surprised some of those present by her seeming lack of grief. Her face was a pale mask, exhibiting none of the signs of sorrow that were apparent on Abdel's. But it was like she was sleepwalking. She kept up a neutral conversation with Scheherazade who never left her side, but when she suddenly asked if it would rain the next day, the latter had looked at her before holding her close. But Baida's mind was on other things at that moment.

She was really worrying about who was at home looking after Selim. He should have been fed an hour ago and must need to go to the toilet. Now and then, however, she had an inkling that everything that was going on around her, had something to do with her eldest son. At such moments, she was reassured by the limpid sky and the green tree tops in the graveyard, which inspired her with the feeling that Selim's total innocence would attract the protection of angels.

She was initially shocked by her reflection in the mirror. As she peered at herself through the droplets of water and the clouds of heady perfume, she felt as if she were watching a strange being forcing its way through an iron wall until finally taking shape in front of her. She stared at the other woman curiously, noting her roguish eyes with their spark of fun and duplicity and the slight smile playing about her lips as if she were suppressing a laugh. Then a puff of steam rose up from the kettle near her chair and partially blotted out the image. She glanced over at the picture of the model and noticed that the top two buttons of her shirt lay open, exposing the topmost shadow of her cleavage; when the hair dresser turned away to get a different pair of scissors from the nearby trolley, her fingers slid over to her shirt and quickly unfastened her own top button.

On arriving home from the cemetery, she had searched the whole house for Selim; she had gone from room to room, and looked under the blankets, in the wardrobes and under the beds, calling out his name monotonously from time to time, "Selim." Abdel had taken her to their room and shut the door, but Baida had begun to talk to her son as if he were

253

sitting beside her, only stopping when the sleeping pills took effect and she dozed off.

In the days that followed, she busied herself with his toys. She spent hours in his room, alone with them, arranging them in the same way he had, placing the tiger next to the lamb, the train next to the car and Superman next to the Barbie doll; when one or other of her children poked their heads through the door, she would hold up her hand, palm outwards to stop them coming in, saying, "Leave your brother alone… Don't disturb him."

But this shocked disbelief gradually gave way to a feeling of remorse. What if she'd taken her courage in both hands and asked Abdel to go to the supermarket instead, or had remained at home and cooked the small amount of macaroni she still had in the house for the children; what if she had woken up Selim and taken him with her? He would have enjoyed being among the crowds and looking at the things in the shops.

She was caught in an unending loop in which the echoes of the conditional, the what ifs, gnawed away at her soul. She completely lost the will to eat and speak until she was taken off to hospital.

There Baida had gradually learnt how to avoid walking over the minefield of memory, which only returned her to the circle of misery, she had been in before; she learnt how to avoid mentioning Selim's name by steering clear of words beginning with the letter 's' and how to pile images of her other children on top of him whenever he came to her mind. The transformation did not come about immediately. It happened one dark and overcast morning when

254

she turned and caught sight of the children, who had been brought in to see her, and took in the details of their appearance. They looked like lost little lambs, with their bedraggled hair, damp clothes and wandering eyes. For the first time, she asked the nurse for something to eat.

As her remorse abated, her feelings of rage towards her husband mounted despite her efforts to avoid thinking about her dead son. It was as if she now placed the entire responsibility for what had happened on to Abdel. It was possible after all, wasn't it, she asked herself, that he had opened the window on purpose and encouraged his disabled son to throw himself out. Any doubts she might have harboured about how true this assumption was, only made her more determined to cling on to it. Maybe it was because of this emotion, which she hadn't experienced before, that she was able to pick up the pieces of her splintered self and start eating again, which allowed her in a short time, to regain all the weight she had lost. But now, as she looks at the refection in the mirror, it is as if she has come face to face with another woman, who appears to be totally unrelated to her; she looms up in front of her like an image from a dream that has been haunting her for ages, a dream about someone who shares the same body as her but has avoided declaring herself openly until now.

It would only be half true if I said that Baida's emotional world was dominated by rage at this time. On the contrary, when she saw how devoted Abdel was to the children, she occasionally felt grateful. There is no doubt that the moment we are living in has the power to obliterate the past of which nothing remains except the pulses of light coming

255

from a dead star.

She tried to recall memories of her father to comfort her while she was in hospital but her mind was too feeble to probe beyond the events of the past minute. The noises seeping in from the corridor outside her room, the colour of a bunch of wilted roses, which the cleaner had just that minute tossed into the rubbish bin and the pungent smell of food. All the objects and activities in the hospital merged into one and formed a wall that separated her from the outside world; her attempts to imagine herself on the other side only brought her closer to the minutiae of the hospital.

As the hairdresser put the final touches to her hair, he said: "That new style makes you look just like Audrey Hepburn." When she didn't respond but merely continued to stare at him impassively in the mirror, he added, "Ask anyone, they'll tell you the same thing." Perhaps it was the flattery, which made her agree to have her nails done.

Before going home, she stopped at the local park. She was surprised to see how much the trees had altered since the accident happened. The leaves had changed. They were no longer green but yellow and red and all the colours in-between. Now that they had shed most of their foliage, the trees were almost completely bare, while the leaves lay on the ground, ornamenting the green of the grass with their pastel shades. It appeared to Baida as if they were solemnly gearing themselves up for winter, which would soon be upon them: for death. She passed by the playground. There were a number of children there, some of whom were going down the slide, while their parents looked on. She felt hemmed in and hurried to the exit along the cement path which ran through the green grass and was meant especially for walkers and joggers. The unusual clearness of the day had left the yellow leaves dry and they crackled underfoot as she walked.

*   *   *

The sun had almost set when she arrived home. She noticed Scheherazade's car parked in front and felt slightly giddy. "Has Saleh come as well?" The question surfaced somewhere deep within her then as quickly disappeared, leaving little trace behind apart from a slight disturbance in her breathing. Once inside, she was taken aback by the unexpected racket. Her children had divided themselves up among the three guests, Scheherazade, Saleh and Helen, with each one competing to get the most amount of attention. Abdel looked at her in surprise. After casting a quick glance at her cousin's hair, he said in a voice filled with sarcasm: "You look more like Scheherazade than ever." Glimpsing the look of discomfiture in Baida's eyes, Scheherazade intervened to soften the impact of his words. "Oh, how I wish that were true!" Saleh added casually: "That suits you better," and she caught a faint look of admiration cross his face, a slight smile and crinkling of the eyes which seemed to whisper soundlessly in her ears, "I've dreamed that you would look like this."

There was no doubt about how surprised everyone was at the enormous improvement that had taken place in her since Scheherazade's last visit four days previously. Then Baida had refused to leave her room although Abdel had knocked repeatedly on the door, which she had locked behind her, to tell her, her relative had arrived. At the time, she had been in a frenzy of violent rage, directing its barbs first at herself, then at her husband then back at herself again. Without knowing what she was doing, she had begun to tear her underwear into little pieces, using her teeth and fingers. When Abdel finally came to bed late, after Scheherazade had left and the children were asleep, she had felt like a deflated balloon. As she hovered between sleep and wakefulness, she had stretched out her hand towards him, her fingertips grazing his back. It was like a wall, cutting him off from her and protecting him from the torrential flood of hatred, which poured out of her with every breath. But Abdel had interpreted her gesture as an invitation to sex and a sign that she was completely cured. When he turned over, she had drawn him towards her with the fingers of both hands. They were back at their old long-interrupted game of pull and push but now Baida had taken charge for the first time, just as Joanna had done in past, intensifying his excitement. Despite the total darkness, she had slid her right hand down to his engorged penis and drawn him determinedly towards her, then left him to penetrate her swiftly and completely.

In that moment, Baida had been caught between two violent emotions, an all-consuming pleasure of a kind, she had never experienced before, and a grief that pierced her to the quick, like an imaginary dagger. Feelings surged through her, tossing her back and forth, settling in her heart for less than a second before slipping away to be replaced by other sensations that came on the wings of everyday images that she had lately encountered.

The hum of adults talking and children interjecting filled her mind. For a second, she saw an image of pale trees and leaves, juxtaposed against a sea of light shining down from overhead or dappling the edges of the large park. When she had first seen it, it had evoked an emotion in her that she had been unable to define but which she now recognised as a profound longing for death mingled with an intense hunger for life, or rather a hunger for a new life that would take place in another time and place, that was totally unconnected to her current one. For a second, she recalled those brief moments of intense lovemaking that had taken place only four days previously not in detail but rather as unadulterated emotion. How easy that previously unknown sense of absolute hatred had made her search for a pleasure, which she had read and heard so much about without ever experiencing it before. For the first time, Baida had not found it necessary to observe proceedings from the ceiling as she had always done in the past, leaving her body in Abdel's hands to turn about as he wished. Instead she and her body had been plunged into the search for orgasm. The convulsive journey had led, little by little and with persistence and determination, through the cleft of a narrow tunnel to a door, which opened out on to a place where the sun shone and the forces of gravity were banished. It was as if her hatred at that moment had become a shield with which to protect herself from the other and at the same time make him a neutral tool that could simultaneously provide intense pleasure and inflict violent pain.

When the guests left, Baida went back to the sitting room. She threw herself down onto the sofa, on the spot where Saleh had been sitting. Abdel asked her if she wanted to go to sleep but his words passed over her. She felt as if she were under the influence of some opiate which had seeped into her veins and made her cells numb. She touched her prominent dimples but could feel nothing beyond the glow coming off her cheeks. She stroked the edge of the sofa where Saleh had leant his elbow, her mind replaying the scene that had just occurred. She wasn't sure whether it had really happened. Perhaps she had dozed off for a second and had a short dream. Her mind went back to it again. After having kissed Scheherazade and Helen goodbye, she had stretched out her hand to Saleh, as she usually did, to bid him a formal farewell. When their fingers touched, she had felt an unknown power forcing her to squeeze his fingers momentarily. She had been instantly overcome with embarrassment and tried to withdraw her hand but found he was still holding on to it. He had then squeezed her hand three times, causing a sensation like an electric shock to course through her. She had almost fainted and had stared at him beseechingly until he had loosened his grip, repeating as he left the house, with his eyes on Abdel: "We'll see you soon."

* * *

However Saleh did not make any other move towards her, and she began to wonder if she had imagined his response to her indiscreet fingers. How could a man who enjoyed an emancipated relationship with an exceptional woman like Scheherazade be attracted to a nobody like her? Even if she were prettier and younger than her cousin, wasn't the fact that she was married to Abdel enough to make him shun her? She had often noticed the amused smiles he secretly exchanged with Scheherazade whenever her husband started boring them with his boasts about some commercial project or other, which made her shrink back in her chair in embarrassment or excuse herself from the room on the grounds that she had to go upstairs to see the children. After their last visit, however, she had begun to look in the mirror much more frequently than before. Using her knowledge of Scheherazade, she had carried out an inventory of her own and the other's body, comparing details such as how slender they both were, the shapeliness of their legs, the curve of their buttocks and the size of their hips. The balance seemed to be weighted in her favour, if she excluded the unique charm that only Scheherazade possessed from the equation. Even when she was silent, everyone vied for her attention so that she became the centre of any group she was in and stimulated others to take part in the conversation. Baida wondered how the shy reticent girl, which was how she vaguely remembered her cousin from their days in Baghdad, had turned into such a woman. How she wished she could find out what Scheherazade had done since leaving her country of birth. Before the accident, her feelings towards Scheherazade had wavered between unrestrained admiration and deep revulsion but the latter's unexpected support for her after Selim's death had removed this sense of repugnance. Gradually she had begun to imitate her cousin.

In fact, even when she was in hospital, she had occasionally found herself adopting Scheherazade's manner of talking.

Nevertheless, the latter had not lowered her guard but maintained the barrier between them, which doctors, in particular, are adept at erecting between themselves and their patients. Unconsciously, Baida came to regard it as a barrier between strength and weakness, which could only be overcome by adopting the character of the other in its entirety and then entering into competition with her. And so it was that Scheherazade, who had surrounded Baida with particular care and warmth during this period, involuntarily played a part in transforming her cousin into her stubborn rival.

When the hairdresser had finished fixing her hair and showering her with compliments, Baida had felt an obscure sense of achievement, as she looked in the mirror, at having finally surmounted the barrier between them. But two weeks after that emotional contact with Saleh, she began to be haunted by doubts of another kind: she sees Saleh lying beside Scheherazade in post-coital bliss. Driven by a desire to make her laugh, he begins to tell her what her cousin has done. Scheherazade looks at him disbelievingly at first but his unwavering gaze and air of conviction convinces her and she bursts out laughing. She turns to him, after a short while, as if to make amends, and pretends to be sorry for her cousin. "Don't forget, she's been ill," she says. "Of course, you didn't see her in hospital." Baida was haunted by the idea that Scheherazade would call Abdel and tell him what had happened and began unconsciously to dread the sound of the phone. It was as if she were suspended between two pulleys: the desperate fear of hearing her cousin's voice was counterbalanced by her despairing hope of hearing Saleh's.

But one morning she woke up, having suddenly arrived at a strange decision. The idea came to her like a bolt of lightening and made the blood surge through her veins. She would erase the past, which only existed in the detritus it left behind. She took out the old photographs and pile of letters from her father, and then pulled out the secret album, which contained snapshots of herself and Selim, which she had taken in photo booths at odd intervals. She looked at one or two of them but they left her unmoved, as if they were signs from another planet. When she tore up the first one, her heart stopped for a second. But then she gathered up the various bits and pieces and took them out into the garden, where she began to throw them one after another onto a fire, she had lit on the barbeque.

When she had finished, she felt strangely light as if her body was floating free in the void. She hurried to Selim's room, which had remained locked since his death. The walls looked different somehow, as if their colour had changed since then. The pale blue seemed darker, but the bed was as rumpled as ever, as if her son had only got up a couple of minutes before. His paintings too were little more than lines and splashes of colour on the walls, which looked like some mysterious sign that had nothing to do with her son, but which left her, nonetheless, with an indefinable yearning. She phoned a shop that specialised in selling second hand furniture and offered to give the owner Selim's bed and wardrobe for nothing. She collected all his toys and clothes and put them in two large suitcases and three plastic bags, which she took by minicab to a nearby charity shop. When night fell, there was nothing left in his room except the paintings. Abdel didn't say a word when Baida told him, "I'll sleep in the other room." She took nothing with her except the duvet they kept for guests and a single pillow, content to sleep on the thick carpet in the room.

Her first night was filled with a succession of fragmentary dreams that seemed to merge into one another. Now and then she was woken by the sound of a child crying, but when she looked in on her children, they always seemed to be sleeping soundly. Once as she lay in the impenetrable darkness, she was able to recall a short dream she had had a couple of minutes before. She was walking through a large green field with Scheherazade, who was carrying an umbrella, which was large enough to cover the two of them. She was surprised at her cousin because the sky was completely clear. "Wait and see," Scheherazade said, as if she could read what was going through her mind. Suddenly the scene changed. She was no longer walking through the field, but was perched on top of a towering cliff, as the rain poured down around her, and struggling to stop herself from falling by clutching at a stone that jutted out from the ground. Scheherazade ignored her screams for help and carried on walking beneath her umbrella. But then she had felt two strong hands reaching out to help her and resolutely beginning to pull her up. She had peered through the mist and the gloom, in an effort to make out the face of the unknown man, but when she saw he looked like Saleh, she had woken up in a panic.

She was not completely able to rid herself of the vacuum, which Selim's absence had left inside her. Or perhaps it was more than that. She was mercilessly driven by a mercurial mix of heartache, confusion and remorse, which kept her on the move, and made her run up and down between the various floors of the house even after she had managed to halt the flow of memories. In her empty state she gravitated towards others who arouse a mass of conflicting feelings in her. She thought of Saleh and her body relived the warmth that had coursed between them the moment their fingers touched. Shame overcame her and she wanted to die. Her mind darted off to Scheherazade but the thought of her cousin filled her with terror and a vague feeling of failure. She turned to Abdel, and found herself once again consumed by rage.

But once she was installed in Selim's room, she gradually came to feel that she was colluding with Abdel: he might have been responsible for Selim's fall from the window, but she was the one who had erased all traces of him from the house. As she looked around, she could find nothing to show that he had lived there for the last seven years. Even the children seemed to be in cahoots with her; they never mentioned his name, though they still kept up their stream of exaggerated complaints about each other in order to gain her sympathy and get her to side with one or other of them. For a second, an image of Selim rose up in front of her; she remembered how fond he had been of his siblings though they had often hurt him. Immediately one or other of them said he wanted to play a game with him, Selim would jubilantly rush to do whatever his brother wanted, forgetting the slaps, the other had meted out to him only minutes before. A strange idea flashed through Baida's mind. Absolute goodness is kneaded out of idiocy and absolute evil is the primary fruit of intelligence.

* * *

She awoke to the shrill sound of the phone. From her bed, she could hear the rumble of Abdel's voice as he murmured a greeting. "Welcome…How are you? We'll expect you for supper tomorrow." She presumed it was Scheherazade on the line and was amazed when Abdel told her it had been Saleh. She looked at his face, searching for some hint of surprise at the call but could see nothing but satisfaction at the thought of the meeting ahead. Scheherazade was the one who always phoned so why the change this time? Was Saleh expecting Abdel to be out? The hands on the ornate clock pointed to half past ten. Her husband was usually busy in his work shop at this time or out at some second hand tool shop but today he had been exceptionally late leaving the house.

If Abdel hadn't been here, she would have picked up the phone. The thought filled her with consternation. What would Saleh have said? Maybe Scheherazade would have been standing behind him as he made the call to find out whether his claims about her were true. Baida remembered the snatched glances they had exchanged at the last meeting, the bold way in which he had watched her as she walked. For a moment, he seemed to have been comparing

266

her with Scheherazade. Was he wishing that he could put her in her cousin's place? She looked in the mirror, running her fingers gently over her breast and down to her hips. She moved her fingers up to her short hair, which now seemed softer and thicker than Scheherazade's even though it was cut in the same style. Her mind went back to Saleh, and she thought of his hands running through Scheherazade's hair. When they were in the throes of passion, did he like to clutch at the hair on the back of her head? Even though her cousin only came up to his shoulder when they were walking beside each other, once they were in bed she'd make up for that by laying her head next to his. She could see their images in the mirror, absorbed in each other as they made love behind her. Scheherazade, poised and assured, compensating for her slight stature by playing the combined role of petulant young man and officious doctor: Stop, push, put your hand here, there, hold me tighter…She slipped in and out of a series of strange day dreams before the children returned from school and monopolised her attention. In one of them, she saw herself and Scheherazade sitting on her cousin's large bed. The latter turned and whispered cheerfully: "Saleh's told me everything." When she saw how embarrassed and defeated Baida was, she squeezed her clasped hands, very sweetly, saying: "This happens all the time …" Then, she called out something to her boyfriend who was standing behind the door, before adding in a whisper:" I'm sure you're going to enjoy this game."

* * *

She woke up in the middle of the night with a vague sense of melancholy; she must have had a bad dream. The nightmare had forcibly extracted her from her gentle sleep and the remnants of sticky sensory passion left behind by her sequence of daydreams. Through the window, she could see the bare poplar tree, wreathed in gauzy red-tinted mist. It looked like something from an imaginary world, which had no connection to the reality, which had begun to crumble around her. She touched the walls of the room and the blue curtains at the window trying to remember where she was. She threw herself on the floor then covered her body and head with the duvet. Spheres of coloured light rose up in front of her, floating freely through an imaginary sky and filling her with a savage sense of ecstasy, then the room began to spin around her in time with the moving balls. To prevent herself slipping away, she stuck out her hand instinctively to find something solid to hold onto and found herself gripping Abdel's arm. He had popped into Selim's room, a short time before while she was still dozing. "Hold me tight," she muttered deliriously.

Her body gradually gravitated towards his, tempted by his fingers and kisses, but as she veered between wakefulness and sleep, between imagination and reality, she did not recognise him, even as he started to strip off her clothes. She heard Scheherazade moaning, just as she had that first night she had spent in her house, but this time she seemed to have penetrated her room in order to follow the scene more closely. The further Abdel went, the more her cousin's features came to resemble her own. She began to imitate the wild sound, which back then, had made its way so determinedly through the wall between their rooms, and which now transported her to a world, whose existence she had never dreamed of before, so that she ended up by merging completely with the other woman on her snug bed. When Abdel left Selim's room, pleased with the night's outcome, Baida was still embracing her pillow.

*   *   *

Scheherazade and Saleh arrived in the evening. The hands on the clock on the wall in the kitchen pointed to five past six. It seemed much later, the darkness made more intense by the thick cloud, which had persisted throughout the day. Nevertheless it was extremely mild for the beginning of December. "We're going to have an Indian winter this year." Abdel said, when he met them at the front door, after Scheherazade had said that she hoped it would snow in time for Christmas. Saleh said: "Don't jump to conclusions. You can never count on British weather."

After welcoming her guests and accompanying them to the sitting room, Baida went to the kitchen to make tea. She felt unable to breathe, as if her lungs had contracted and something was blocking her air passages. She thought it might be the thick pullover she was wearing and took it off but it made no difference. She opened the window. She was drawn to the dark shadows of the trees in the heavy air. The air felt oppressive as if a storm were about to break, awaking in her an obscure yearning. Suddenly she heard a voice say: "Can you give me a glass of water?" When she turned round, she was unable to believe her eyes. Saleh was standing near the door, in the gap that separated the kitchen from the corridor, the darkness of the latter, making his face glow brightly. For a second, he looked like a stranger, not the same person she had seen a couple of minutes before with Scheherazade. Taken by surprise, she hurriedly began to search the small cupboards for glasses, blind to the fact that they were there in front of her, lined up on the table. Saleh must have seen how confused Baida was by his arrival, for he made a move towards the glasses, and said: "Here they are."

They stood face to face with only a couple of feet between them. From the other room they could hear the intermittent sound of voices. As Saleh held out an empty glass towards her, she noticed, in his laughing eyes, his relish at her confusion. She clamped her teeth on the edge of her lower lip. She was suddenly afraid that he would take hold of her hand so she tried to hide it, busying herself filling the glass with mineral water.

Saleh said jokingly: "It's real water. How do you make it?" She replied in a tone that was unusual for her: "That's a secret." The latter added cheerfully before returning to the sitting room: "I hope you'll tell me some day."

She moved drunkenly through the emptiness, as she sought to hold on to the waves of air that had carried Saleh's voice. Without knowing what she was doing, she went to the table and picked up his glass and drained the remaining drops of water, even as her eyes sought the spot where he had placed his lips on the rim.

*   *   *

270

During dinner, she continued to steal glances at Saleh, but he appeared to be engrossed in his food. Scheherazade commented on her cooking, "This reminds me of food my mother used to make." Then the three of them began a disjointed conversation that Baida heard little of beyond the rhythm of voices. Only when Saleh spoke, did her senses respond, but she was unable to understand much of what he was saying because she was listening too hard. Instead she sucked in the sound of his voice. Everything in her reverberated to her involuntary proximity to him. The air became trapped in her bronchial tubes and when she was finally able to exhale, the outpouring of breath left a burning sensation in her lungs that filled her with a sweet numbness. Baida was sitting beside Abdel and opposite Scheherazade and Saleh. Pretending that she needed to look after her guests and husband, she continuously piled food on their plates, serving a series of salty, sour or sweet dishes. When one or other of them turned and asked her why she wasn't eating, she unwillingly pushed a morsel of food into her mouth but a short time later made some excuse like she had to go and look at her children so that she could escape to the bathroom and get rid of it.

The incident didn't happen until after she had served tea and sweets and cleared the plates and remains of food from the table. Saleh helped her carry out the task. When his shirt sleeve touched hers for a second, while they were putting the plates in the sink, she was forced to hold on to the edge to prevent herself from falling as she was overcome by a sudden attack of giddiness.

All the same, she was constantly aware of the huge gulf,

which separated her from Saleh. He felt sorry for her. That was all. All the smiles and charming comments he paid her, were merely prompted by pity. Once she was convinced of this, she felt alienated from him and Scheherazade. She was sure they discussed her in bed; had she got over her illness? Was she still ill? She became aware that her cousin was watching her curiously, searching for signs of derangement.

She took out the best china cups she had in the house and laid gold coloured teaspoons beside them. "Shall we light the candles?" Abdel asked. The idea met with enthusiastic approval from everyone. Despite the lateness of the hour, they could hear the intermittent song of a blackbird, coming through the window. Perhaps the unusual mildness and the radiant terracotta colour of the clouds had made it believe that dawn was approaching.

Everything around them seemed to be summoning them away from the small kitchen and out into the street. But they remained where they were, continuing to chat in the pale flickering light of the candles. An image of the local park with its bare trees and shadows came to her mind and she almost suggested going there but bit back the words for fear that the others might interpret them as a sign of madness. She effortlessly slipped into a daydream. She saw herself running through a big field surrounded by cedar trees, with Saleh racing along behind her. They were making for a hillock, dense with evergreen oak and beech, where they had left a small tent, which would hold them close throughout the night.

The others resumed their light hearted conversation. She pretended to listen, sharing in the laughter whenever she saw Scheherazade's eyes sparkle and light up in a smile. She offered them another cup of tea and before they could agree, rose from her place to prepare it. When she pushed back her chair, she avoided looking at Saleh, who was sitting opposite, as she had done throughout the meal, despite having a strong impression that his eyes were fixed intently upon her. She had to circumvent his gaze for fear of exposing her feelings to Scheherazade and Abdel. For a moment she had an odd idea that they were aware of what was happening inside her. She was terrified at the thought and rushed out to the kitchen, pretending that she had to take a look at her sleeping children. When she returned to her seat, she saw they were drinking another cup of tea. Scheherazade glanced over at Saleh, intimating that it was time to leave, and then turned to her. "Baida must be feeling tired after all her work." At that moment, and without her imagining for a single second, that Saleh might ever touch her deliberately, she felt a slight pressure on her shoe. At first, she thought it was merely an unintentional slip but the light and playful pressure continued as the strange sneaky foot started to roam along the edge of her right shoe before creeping under it and climbing over it; when she initially looked over at Saleh to find out what happening under the table, his face was a blank. She began to feel ticklish. As the game of footsie-footsie continued and their shoes became more passionately involved with each other, she imagined removing them, so as to leave their naked feet free to indulge in a game that only a couple of playful kittens could better.

*　*　*

The following morning, the telephone rang but before she could get it to, it fell silent. She walked away but it began ringing again a short time later. She thought it might be Saleh but when she put the receiver to her ear, she was unable to recognise the voice at the other end of the line. The caller must have sensed her coolness. "Is this a bad time?" he asked. She hurried to correct herself. "No, of course not... You sound different..." Saleh said jokingly: "We may sound different on the phone, but we feel the same... Don't forget it's the first time..." Baida didn't understand what he meant by this last remark but replied nevertheless, "That's true." Abdel had left the house a couple of minutes before and most probably wouldn't return before noon. The thought made her tighten her grip on the receiver despite the turmoil she was in. Her eyes followed the telephone wire down to where it was plugged into the point, low on the wall, which connected it to the network and imagined it extending as far as Saleh's mouth. The thought made her touch the top of the receiver with the fingers of her free hand as if trying to catch every last bit of sound from the other's voice. However, her terse replies had the opposite effect on Saleh. "I seem to have made you uncomfortable by what I'm saying," he said. There was a long silence and he would have ended the conversation there and then had it not been for her cry of entreaty. "No, not at all..." Saleh said, "Will you take my home telephone number now?"

* * *

Three days later, she summoned up the courage to phone him but when she heard his voice, she was struck with a violent sense of remorse at what she had done; rather than being pleased at fulfilling the desire that had been burning inside her for days, she found herself racked with shame and perturbation. She unsuccessfully attempted to recall how much she had longed to meet up with him, but instead only felt a sense of degradation. It was as if by lifting the receiver, she had revealed the true essence of her body which until then she had kept hidden and which was unlike anything that Abdel engaged with. To put it another way, in lifting the receiver she had exposed the torrent of emotion inside her, which had shaken her to her core. She struggled to drag out meaningless expressions, which had little to do with how she was feeling: "How are you?" "I… I'm fine… And you?"

Since Scheherazade and Saleh's last visit, Baida had been living on another planet where the laws of gravity did not so strictly apply. It now took her seconds to mount the stairs to the first floor and when she climbed the steps to the park, her legs rushed ahead of her as if freed from the weight of her body.

There was no doubt that her mood owed something to the latter days of autumn in London. The heavy clouds whose colours fluctuated between red and white, and which the British merely regarded as a precursor of bad weather, had become a pleasure to her, augmenting her passion without subsuming it. She felt compelled to go out into the still, moisture laden air, even when there was the clap and crack of thunder and lightening about; only a short time previously she had been morbidly terrified by such conditions but they now gave expression to what was going on inside her.

Saleh's voice broke the protracted silence. "Wouldn't it be possible for us to meet?" "We see each other all the time, don't we?" she said, naively, and almost told him the secrets that lay buried inside her: how he was always with her; how, it was him she addressed her words to, even when there were other people present, and how, at times of silence, she would pick up his voice in her imagination and engage him in wistful conversation, with each one confiding in the other, the intensely private thoughts that were going through their minds. Once she imagined him asking her if she felt annoyed by his relationship with Scheherazade and she had shaken her head in denial in the same way her cousin did, when she rejected some idea or other.

* * *

She finally agreed to meet, after a series of compulsive phone calls, which nevertheless only left her feeling frustrated and facing new doubts. Once they exchanged greetings, she would find herself unable to confide the thoughts and feelings, which only moments before she had been determined to tell him about but which now crumbled into nothingness. Instead she would begin to imagine Saleh on the other end of the line, with a sarcastic and bored expression on his face, which would put her on her guard and make her start to stammer. As soon as she put the receiver down, the storm clouds would gather again, compelling her back to the phone. When Saleh wasn't at home, she would relax, experiencing a momentary sense of freedom, but then in her mind's eye, she would pursue him to Scheherazade's flat, assuming her cousin's persona so that she could follow their stormy encounter in detail.

Baida had a strange dream, which she only partially remembered when she woke up. She was in a small and very dark windowless room which made her unable to work out where she was. She began to run her hands over the smooth walls to find a way out and by chance stumbled across a round aperture, whose cover fell away as soon as she pushed against it. In front of her, she could see an expanse of calm sea. Dawn was breaking or maybe it was sunset. Suddenly she noticed an unusual flurry of movement on the shore. A crowd of people came hurrying down to the sea as if they were running away from some kind of danger. They hastily began to push the line of boats, drawn up on the sand, out into the water. Was it a sudden sense of panic or the sound of approaching footsteps that made her try to escape her prison cell? She put her head through the small window, as she heard the rattle of keys behind the door, and then forced her shoulders through. Only then, with half her body outside, did she discover how high off the ground she was. Footsteps sounded behind her and she woke up. When she opened her eyes in terror, she found Abdel beside her, snoring deeply and she clung to him.

It was easier to meet up with Saleh than she imagined it would be. She picked up the receiver after her husband had left and heard his voice, raised enquiringly. Immediately he realised who it was, his tone softened. "It's sunny today," he amended. After a long silence, she asked: "Do you think it will stay like this till Saturday?" "Probably." She could barely recognise her voice which seemed to be coming from the other side of a thick wall. "What do you think about going out if..." Saleh quickly replied: "Even if the weather's bad, there are other places we can go to."

* * *

By 'other places' he could only mean his flat. Before she left for the appointment, she told Abdel: "I'm going to Oxford Street to do some shopping." When he wanted to protest at her leaving the children with him, fear that it might bring about a relapse in her mental condition kept him silent. She had only been walking for a couple of minutes when Saleh's car appeared at the time they had agreed upon.

As soon as she got in the car, she began to worry that Abdel might have followed her and was about to put out a hand to Saleh as if to seek his protection but managed to restrain herself. Her heart pounded within her, making her tighten her arms instinctively across her chest. She felt she was about to die and the thought of being discovered with Saleh filled her with terror so that she could think of nothing else. She wanted to ask him to stop the car and let her out, for they were still near enough to her house for her to walk back. And then, she murmured to herself determinedly, I'll stop this madness forever. I'll live for my children. There will be no more phone calls, no more glances, no...Saleh braked hard as if he could read what was going through her mind. Suddenly it was possible. She could go back now; all she had to do was get out of the car. But her heartbeats slowed when she put her hand out to the door handle, and instead she was filled with a strange anxiety, which made her unable to breathe. She realised he was following her every move with intense interest, despite pretending to be unconcerned. Therefore, she would not be able to change her mind about leaving without him immediately trying to prevent her. Time seemed to stand still. During those long, heavy moments, she thought back to the shapeless years of her life, to the bleak nightmarish times, which continued to haunt her dreams, and to her suppressed anger at Abdel, which still gnawed away at her soul. When Saleh put out his hand to her, the gesture doubtless seemed like a miracle. Perhaps the steadily falling rain, now drumming on the windscreen also helped her decide and made her submit to the gentle tug of his hand. He had sneaked his right arm behind her and now cupped the back of her head with his right hand, drawing her face close to his. But she resisted his efforts to kiss her on the mouth as a wave of giddiness passed over her, making her fear that her heart would stop beating. Maybe it was the thought of what would happen to Saleh if she was found dead in his arms that stopped her: how would he explain it away to the police? What would other people say? Baida pushed Saleh's head away and put her hands up to his temples. She looked into his eyes, which were filled with an ardent longing, seeking to reassure herself that his feelings were genuine. But having convinced herself, she was then beset by doubts. Was this really happening? She listened to the drumming of the rain on the car windows intermingled with the jerky sound of their breathing, then buried her head in his chest, like someone who has finally

279

reached a safe haven after having been lost for a long time. In her mind's eye, she saw herself as a young child, burrowing under the thick coverlets of her parents large bed, as if she were setting out on an imaginary swim that would take her to the ends of the earth.

Saleh's flat seemed larger than when she had last been there over seven years ago. She had only come that time to help Abdel bring the bits of the book case. She looked at it out of the corner of her eye and felt confused. She remembered how keen her husband had been to act the professional at the time and behave as if he hadn't met his client before. When Saleh handed over the money, she had wanted the earth to open and swallow her up. On her previous visit to the flat, she had given no thought to Saleh's bedroom, which led off the sitting room, but now after several minutes had gone by and as she sat on the black sofa, her mind was on fire with a single question: did it have a double bed? She imagined her cousin laughing as she pushed Saleh towards the room. She probably came to his flat in her time off, with her white coat and stethoscope. Scheherazade had told her that the hospital, where she worked, was only about ten minutes' walk away. Baida remembered how she and Saleh had smiled slightly when she'd recounted the fact to her cousin.

Saleh came back from the kitchen with a tray on which there was a teapot and a couple of mugs. As he put it down on the table set in the middle of the room, he said, "A cup of green tea will soon warm you up." But instead, she felt the cold creeping into her limbs as she watched him sit on a rocking chair on the opposite side of the room. The distance that separated them seemed larger than it really was;

in fact the room seemed larger than it had been before. Was this due to the pastel shade of the new carpet or something else? When she had come here with her husband, she had felt sorry for Saleh. How awkward he looked as he moved clumsily around and made various suggestions, while she and Abdel had assembled the book case! "Would you like some coffee now?" he had asked, and when neither of them had answered, had added earnestly. "Then what about some fresh orange juice." "Don't put yourself out," Baida had said, as she picked up one end of a wooden shelf. Saleh had looked over at her husband: "You've got a talented wife... I don't even know how to bang a nail into the wall." But when she looked at him now, he seemed far removed from the person she had seen on that first visit. In her eyes, he was better looking, quieter, taller, more elegant, wickeder and funnier than before, and the more determined he appeared to remain at a distance from her, the more she ached for him. He took a sip of the tea, which she hadn't tasted before and which only left a strange bitter taste in her mouth. "Do you think the room's changed much?" Saleh asked. Before she answered, she looked about her: "A great deal... It's much nicer." Baida felt Scheherazade's presence in the atmosphere although there were no visible traces of her. She must have been responsible for the severe scheme of decoration which governed every aspect of the room.

She was consumed with a single desperate wish. That Saleh would come and sit beside her instead of remaining on the other side of the room, from where he watched her with burning eyes. It had seemed to take ages to get from the car park to his front door, the distance appearing much greater than it really was. Saleh walked a little way ahead of her. He opened the heavy door to the flats then banged it shut behind them. In the lift, the atmosphere between them was strained. She was so scared that she had almost asked him to stop and take her back to where she had come from but the words dried up in her mouth. The one thing that reassured her was that Saleh was tall enough to protect her from any attack, should someone decide to assault her in the dark building. As Saleh was about to open the door to his flat, the blood froze in her limbs: Supposing Scheherazade were there! It was a trap…She ran her fingers through her hair trying to drive away her fears. When he said jokingly: "I bet they have fewer keys in prison," she only heard the last word he uttered. Nevertheless, she nodded in agreement then forced herself to give a brief smile, which quickly disappeared, as she walked slowly into the dark entrance hall.

When she sat down on the sofa after he had gone into the kitchen, she found herself wondering whether Saleh had all along planned to bring her to his flat. She shrank back against the sofa, as her eyes fell upon the shut door to the bedroom. She wanted to slip away, to get out of the flat before he reappeared and took her off to bed as Abdel had done. Was he even now in the bathroom getting ready? But Saleh's re-emergence with a tray of tea dispelled this sense of deep unease as did the fact that he sat down on the other side of the room. Gradually she felt a strange sense of inner peace steal over her, which was in stark contrast to the sound of the heavy rain, drumming against the window panes.

It was not quite five o'clock when she arrived home, but it was nevertheless completely dark. She expected Abdel to explode with anger the instant she appeared but instead found him relaxing with the children in front of the television. With their clean clothes and shining faces they looked as if they had just that minute emerged from the bathroom. Had their father not been present, they would definitely have thrown themselves at her, but ever since her last illness he had constantly warned them against annoying her. Abdel asked her indifferently if she had bought anything. "No." Baida said. "It was very crowded...Saturday's not a good day for shopping." Suppressing an involuntary laugh, she added, "The children need some winter clothes. I'll buy them the day after tomorrow." Abdel nodded, without looking up from the television, where they were showing an old western. The lights in the sitting room seemed very bright and it was some time before she was able to see her surroundings properly. Everything seemed to glow and shimmer. It seemed ages since she had gone out that morning. Her eyes eagerly alighted on the pattern of little flowers on the armchair. She wanted to go and sit on the big sofa, and envelop them all even Abdel in a hug. When Saleh offered to drive her home, she had refused. She felt she needed some time on her own before returning to her familiar world. While she was waiting for the underground train to arrive, her feet had moved unsteadily over the platform. The air was like alcohol, almost tangible, but liable to evaporate between her fingers, once touched. Her memory seemed to stand still for long moments. She could not work out where she was and only regained her bearings when the train had gone several stops and she realised she was travelling in the wrong direction. Her senses were heightened. The world around her seemed newly minted as if it had come into being only a couple of seconds before. She was aware of her body for the very first time. She eagerly touched the skin on her face, running the tips of her fingers of her right hand down her neck and over her bosom. Her memory raced, lurching drunkenly over the few hours she had spent with Saleh, but the more she tried to recall the time in detail, the more her head hurt, the pain leaching into her brain little by little.

"You seem tired," Abdel said.

"It's nothing… Just a slight migraine."

"A bath will relax you."

She nodded. Before she left the room, she almost touched his hair, without any of the distaste she usually felt. Was it pity that prompted the gesture or the sense of guilt that was even now seeping into her, making her headache progressively worse, each time she tried to recapture a glimpse of the strange hours of that day?

When she emerged from the bathroom, she found that the children had left the sitting room. She felt disappointed and at the same time, grateful to Abdel for having sent them away. She was torn in two. On the one hand she wanted to be with them to make up for the fact that she had been absent since morning and on the other, to be alone with Abdel, to assuage the sense of guilt, which was still making her head pound.

* * *

When she woke up in the middle of the night, she had the illusion that she had slept for a long time. She thought dawn was breaking when she glimpsed the glowering red sky in the vertical gap between the curtains but Abdel's loud snores made her realise she was mistaken. She thought his heavy sleep might be a sign of his pleasure at her having returned to their marital bed. After leaving the bathroom, she had slipped off to their bedroom without telling him and put on nothing but her short satin nightdress. She had decided to turn off the small table light with its red lamp shade. In the pitch dark, spots of gleaming light danced in front of her eyes, leaping about in all directions. As Abdel took off his clothes, she gestured to him to hurry up, though in her mind she was already rejecting him and putting Saleh in his place. But his clumsy haste at times extricated her from her fantasies and made her feel irritated with him. She was like a Christmas light, flickering on and off in turn.

She drew back one of the curtains and was surprised to see the sky had turned a pale white. Her eyes were suddenly drawn to the slate roofs of the houses, which were thickly covered with snow. She transferred her gaze from the white expanse of garden to the trees, where white clumps of snow dotted the dry blackish branches. As she raised her head to the sky, she realised that the snow was still falling; the flurry of soft rich flakes, floating steadily through the air, reminded her of the moment when she and Saleh had become one, their bodies pulsating violently as they moved in time to a wild rhythm, which made them cling fiercely together and go further and further towards the impossible.

The sight of the heavily falling snow overwhelmed her with emotion. She felt completely at one with the unending whiteness that covered everything before her; it was as if the dancing snowflakes were passing through her network of cells as they made their way down to the roots of the trees. She found herself suspended between earth and sky. A series of conflicting feelings overcame her. Part of her was desperate to die, but another part longed to go outside without her clothes on and bury her body in the pure, unsullied snow. She turned round and found herself facing the dark room. For a moment she wondered whether it was all a dream but the smell of sex from the bed and the clamour of Abdel's snores brought her back to reality.

*　*　*

She woke up late to the sound of her children coming from the landing, where they were hovering, mindful of their father's strictures about not going inside. When she called out her daughter's name, the three of them peered in at her, their small heads, poking up one on top of the other and eyed her with fear and curiosity. She patted the bed, invitingly and they raced over to her, each one shoving the other out of the way in order to be the first to climb on to the bed. The twins landed up on either side of their mother, leaving Lubna behind on the floor. She began to cry in protest and Baida had to get out of bed and pick her up.

She pulled back the curtains and was enchanted by the view: the dazzling white and the silence were so extraordinary that even the children looked up for a second from the game they were playing, before returning to their hiding places under the bedclothes. She ran her eyes over the scene in front of her, moving from the top of the sky, to the roofs and the trees and down to the small garden of the house. Everything was shrouded in brilliant white. She wished she could capture the moment, the coldness and whiteness outside and the warmth and noise within, and set it in stone so that it would never disappear. Abdel appeared and the children's eyes moved apprehensively back and forth between him and their mother. Baida said quickly: "Let them play here if they want." For a moment, the family was gathered together in an instant of rare accord, against that backdrop of extraordinary whiteness. Her husband sat on the edge of the bed, while she remained under the covers. Around her, the children started to quarrel over who should sit next to their father. It was as if they had all been here since the beginning of time and Selim had never been part of them. When she had sat opposite Saleh in his flat the day before, she had been reminded of her dead son. Perhaps it was the look of entreaty on his face, which made him resemble Selim, and made it so easy for her to say, as she used to say to her son, "Come here" as she patted the surface of the sofa with her right palm.

As she ran her fingers through her children's hair, she swore to herself repeatedly that she would not see Saleh again. Abdel said with mock severity: "Come on, everyone get up. It's breakfast time."

*   *   *

In the evening she felt in low spirits. The trees, roofs and clouds seemed closed in on themselves. She rushed out into the garden and touched the snow, earth and grass with her finger tips and when it left no impression on her, she began to pick up little balls and push them into her mouth. She could hear the sound of Saleh's voice in her mind and began to mutter to herself to make him go away. She would not meet him the next day as they had previously agreed.

In bed, she replayed the incidents of the day before. Initially, she was filled with a sense of disbelief. Had Saleh really laid his head in her lap while his legs protruded over the edge of the sofa? How much time had elapsed before his lips found their way to the rounded part of her dress, which lay above his head? The fingers of her right hand had been busy playing with his hair as she used to do with Selim when he had surprised her by putting his arms round the lower part of her back.

She had not been able to believe what was happening; everything seemed to be taking place in slow motion; the sounds around her became magnified; as their panting bodies bore down on the sofa, the whisper it made, sounded more like a high pitched roar, causing her to breathe in sharply and cling tighter to Saleh. She remembered now how she had nodded off for a moment and dreamt briefly that she was walking along a rope stretched between two mountain peaks. The sea raged beneath and she was suddenly aware that she didn't know how to swim. She had woken in a panic to find herself in the pale darkness of Saleh's bedroom, where the ribbon of light coming through

288

the half-closed door, was sufficient to allow her to see the lineaments of his face. He had sneaked his left arm behind her neck and with his right hand, begun playing with her short hair. His eyes were fixed on her face. She had felt confused when their eyes met and buried her head in his chest, as if practising some necessary ritual which would drive her, against her will, further and further down a long endless tunnel. Suddenly, the face of her relative had loomed up in front of her, maybe because at that instant she had happened to glance over to where she could see a woman's dressing gown, hanging on the back of the door. It obviously belonged to her cousin. She no doubt kept it especially for the times after they had been making love. She could hear her brazen voice. Imagine her lightly, gaily moving around the flat. Without her clothes on, perhaps; teasing Saleh and keeping him tormented until the cold stung her. For a moment she had been ashamed of her relative and was about to apologise on her behalf, when she discovered that she was naked as well. Saleh, who had appeared so incapacitated, must have taken her clothes off when she fell asleep. Then another thought startled her: What if Scheherazade were to come in now? She no doubt had a spare key to the flat and could come and go as she pleased. She seemed to hear the sound of a key turning in the lock and the blood froze in her veins. But then she had been filled with a strength she never imagined she possessed. She had got up from the bed and while Saleh watched her bemusedly, had made her way towards the purple robe and put it on. Without looking at him, she had nevertheless been able to imagine the look of astonishment in his eyes.

* * *

The alarm clock rang, the shrill sound only lasting for a second, but seeming to go on for hours. She had been half-awake for a long time but the strident noise reminded her that she was meeting Saleh at twelve o'clock as they had agreed to go to Regent's Park to look at the snow and the black swans. She was transfixed with a vivid image of the two of them, she in her black coat and he in his brown mackintosh, as they walked side by side through the white expanse and he slid his arm around her shoulders. She turned over on to her stomach and pushed her head under the pillow, holding down the edges to block out the sound. In the pitch black, an image came to her mind of a girl floating on the surface of a narrow river, dressed in the pure white gown of a bride and surrounded by a cloud of petals that drifted along beside her. When she took a closer look at the drowning girl, she was reminded of herself twenty years ago though her own face had never had the extreme pallor of this one.

She was filled with remorse as she mentally followed the minute hands of the clock, ticking by as the time of her appointment came and went. She should have seen Saleh today if only to tell him what she had decided. It is better to stop, she would have told him. I've got three children and a husband and Scheherazade's my cousin. She imagined a smile, lighting up his eyes and suddenly felt embarrassed. Maybe he wouldn't want to be reminded of what had happened the day before? As you like, he would reply quietly. I'm joking, she would say, her lungs contracting. You're the air, I breathe. She pulled the pillow even tighter over her head, while her ears separated out the noises coming from the street, until the only sound that was audible was the roar of Saleh's car as he drove away from the spot they had agreed upon.

*   *   *

Abdel gently woke her up: "Do you want a bowl of soup?" She said apologetically, "Later... I'm thirsty." After she had drunk half a glass of water, her husband continued, "Scheherazade's visiting us today." Her heart beat violently; she turned her face towards the window. "Do you want me to put her off?" "No, we haven't seen her for ages." She bit off the question that was on the tip of her tongue. "Is she coming on her own?"

*   *   *

When the guests arrived, she was half asleep. But the ringing of the doorbell and the sound of various people talking woke her up. She could make out the cheerful voices of her children and Helen. She was torn between hoping that Saleh had come and that he had not. It seemed ages since she had seen him, three months rather than three days. She had spent the time alternating between sleep and wakefulness, between the first floor and the ground floor, between the garden and the house. She would watch herself as she moved about but her apparent sense of freedom belied the tension within her as she struggled to hold back the scream she could feel at the back of her throat, which threatened to explode out of her at any minute. Sometimes she would give in to an agreeable stillness and throw herself on the bed in exhaustion, hoping to fall into a deep sleep but when she was finally about to drop off, the soft sound of Saleh's name, coming from she knew not where, would ring in her ears and grow louder and louder until it restored her to wakefulness again.

She was astonished when she opened the window. The snow had completely disappeared and instead of the whiteness, dark clouds hung low over the trees. Everything seemed frighteningly still. The air, the dry tree, the grass, and the lights coming from the windows of the houses behind, heightened her sense that the last couple of days had been nothing but an illusion. It was as if the snow had never fallen, she had never met Saleh out there and there had been no white nights.

Abdel knocked at the door to the room. "Where are you? Everyone's waiting for you." "I'm coming; I'll be there in a minute." Baida remained seated in front of the mirror where she began to apply a layer of foundation to her face to conceal the round black circles under her eyes and the pallor of her skin. Suddenly a question loomed up in her mind, causing her to feel perturbed. Had Saleh told Scheherazade about the relationship? When she managed to push the idea out of her mind, another took its place: Would she realise he'd betrayed her? She couldn't remember where she had read that women were equipped with special antennae, which they used to unearth their husbands' secrets. She thought about her own powers of detection: she could tell what Abdel had been up to, the moment he walked into the house and whenever her relative and her boyfriend came to visit, she was able to work out what they had been doing together that day, which often made her feel depressed and agitated, especially when she guessed that they had been making love shortly before arriving at her house.

There was a brief silence when she entered the sitting room. It seemed smaller than usual and the bright lights made her feel as if she were swimming freely through a sea of emptiness. She was surprised at the welcome she received from the guests. Scheherazade embraced her with a warmth that was unusual in her and her daughter, Helen, kissed her on both cheeks with unfeigned enthusiasm; when it was Saleh's turn to shake hands with her, she shrank back slightly, searching his face for signs of irritation, but she could only detect the artificial detachment, which the two of them were used to showing whenever they found themselves among other people.

The telephone rang in the hall and Abdel got up to answer it. His voice drifted back to them, murmuring words of welcome: "You mustn't be late. We'll expect you for supper." When he returned to the sitting room, he said, "That was Hussein… He asked if we would like to see them!"

*   *   *

They picked up the conversation about the war between Iran and Iraq, from where they had left it before supper. "It'll be the longest war in history… It'll last for twenty or thirty years at least," said Hussein. "You're a pessimist. Saddam won't be able to continue fighting for more than six months," Saleh said, and Scheherazade asked him jokingly, exchanging a conspiratorial smile with Hussein: "How do you work that out?" "Everyone inside the country is against him including members of his own party. He's killed its most prominent leaders," Saleh replied heatedly. Abdel hurriedly interjected, "Would anyone like some tea?" Hussein seized on the idea with enthusiasm. Baida got up from her arm chair in the corner, and said: "I'll make it."

She was busy setting out the cups and saucers when she heard him asking: "Do you want any help?" She turned towards him. He was standing beside the kitchen door and about to climb the stairs to the bathroom. She was thrown into total confusion. She thought this would be the last time she would see him. Her hands began to shake. Against her will, her feet rushed her over to him, her fingers drew him into the kitchen and she shut the door behind them. She could still hear scraps of conversation from the room next door, which was only about two metres away from where they were standing, and the sound made her more reckless. She linked her arms behind his head and pushed her body up close to his as if she wanted to erase the gap between them. There was nothing the other could do except grab her waist with his hands, which in turn enabled her to hold on to him even tighter, to the point where she lifted her feet off the ground, the moment they embraced.

Saleh looked embarrassed, which she explained away instantly as a sign of his distaste of her. He must have read the trace of shock on her face for he whispered with a reassuring smile: "They're waiting for tea." She came back down to earth. For the last time, she planted a deep kiss on Saleh's lips, at the same time as an image of her cousin rose in front of her. She was filled for a moment with a strange sense of equality with her but it disappeared and was replaced with an urgent fear that someone from next door might come in. She pushed herself away from him and went to the table to finish getting the cups ready while Saleh slipped out of the kitchen.

*　　*　　*

Before Hussein and his family left, he remarked to Scheherazade: "Yesterday they brought a woman into the hospital who had been run over by the underground." He paused for a second at the signs of astonishment, which swept across the faces of the people in the room and then added casually, "She was only in the resuscitation unit for a couple of minutes before she died." Scheherazade asked: "What was the matter with her?" Hussein replied, "I didn't see her myself but those who did, said her death was a blessing." Saleh asked how the accident had happened. "It seems she threw herself in front of a train or was pushed off the platform as the train was coming," Hussein said, and then went on, "Perhaps she fell after losing her balance or because there were too many people... There could be thousands of reasons, as you know." Abdel asked at which station the accident had happened. The others seemed surprised by his question and Baida recoiled from the astonishment she could see on their faces. "I don't know," said Hussein. Before accompanying them to the front door, Abdel launched into a tirade against the awfulness of the public services in

London. "The underground here doesn't compare with any metro in Europe. It really is like a third world country," he added sharply, his tone unsuited to the time, and the other guests made haste to leave.

* * *

Baida remained in the sitting room. She told Abdel that she wanted to wash the dishes before going to bed but she found herself instead, drawn to the seat which Saleh had occupied throughout the evening. The air in the room was heavy with the smell of smoke and she could still hear the echoes of chatter and laughter, the guests had left behind, with the occasional screech from one of the children filtering down from upstairs where they had been holed up in Selim's empty room. She had remained silent throughout the evening apart from occasionally exchanging polite remarks with Barbara. Now and then Hussein had deigned to translate for his Scottish wife but his enthusiasm had not been able to keep him away from the discussion for long and he had soon plunged back into the debate. When she had heard her daughter crying, Baida had made her way up to the second floor. One of the twins had stolen her doll, but as she seemed ready to go to bed, she picked her up and took her to her room. The twins and Hussein's young son had gone on playing hide and seek, while Helen and Nadine, Hussein's daughter, had sat in Selim's quiet room overseeing the game and finding new places for the three young boys to hide. From the darkness in which she had been standing, Baida had been able to make out the voice of Scheherazade, who had come up to the bathroom, asking her daughter if she wanted to go home. Then she had heard her husband's snicker. A second later, he had opened the door to his daughter's room, but hadn't said anything and quickly returned to his guests. Suddenly she had heard the tread of feet on the stair carpet and blood rushed through her veins. She had leapt off her daughter's bed as if she had been waiting impatiently for this moment to arrive. For once, the landing next to the banisters had been free of children, and when Saleh appeared, she had stretched out her hand towards him quickly and drawn him into the darkness of the room and shut the door behind her.

*　*　*

She woke to a dream: she was on the underground, which was moving very slowly; Selim was sitting beside her. He seemed completely healthy and was enthusiastically chanting a song, while she ran her fingers through his fine hair. When he tried to get up and run about, she grabbed hold of him, afraid that he would disappear. The train stopped and immediately the sliding doors opened, several people got on, bringing a cloud of fog with them into the carriage. Within only a few seconds, it was difficult to see. She glanced at the child in the seat beside her. At first she thought it was Selim but when she looked more closely she realised it was some other boy. She leaped up distractedly to search for her son, her eyes, trying unsuccessfully to pierce the veil of fog, and then she heard the automatic doors close. As the train started to move the sound of Selim crying on the platform

297

reached her ears and she woke up in terror.

She felt a strange sense of regret that she hadn't got out of the train, as if Selim were still waiting for her there on the platform. A real cry came from outside and when she listened again; she made out her daughter's voice and hurried to her room. Lubna had wet the bed and was afraid that her father would come in. He was always warning his children about how he would punish them if they did such a thing. "It's the rain," the little girl kept on repeating as she sobbed brokenly. Baida hugged her close to her breast telling her reassuringly that her father wasn't coming and then hastily changed the sheets before he appeared.

Suddenly, she recalled her dream about the underground and Hussein's story came back to her. She remembered how she had almost asked a question, while he was talking, but had held back at the last moment for fear that the others, and in particular Abdel, would make fun of her. She had wanted to ask, "What was the woman called?" The agony of the unknown woman transferred itself to her although Hussein had avoided going into detail about what had actually happened. In her mind's eye, she could see the brittle body, mangled by the cold iron girders and the spurts of blood it had left behind. By the time, she said goodbye to her guests, an excruciating pain had transferred itself to her legs and arms and she was barely able to stand.

After Lubna had gone back to sleep, she returned to bed, treading cautiously to avoid waking Abdel. When she lay down on her back, the image from her dream came back to her. Once again, she saw Selim standing on the platform watching as the train moved away, while she, her face glued to the carriage window, stared sorrowfully back at him. At that instant she was filled with a strange sense of resignation, as if the train were a living being, which had the power to decide what should and shouldn't happen.

There must be someone up in heaven who befriends each child, she told herself; an angel, perhaps in the guise of their mother, who allows them to feel secured. How would Selim cope? He was kept apart from other children while he was alive. Who would play with him? Who would respond to his special needs? Then she had another idea which struck her like lightening. Up there, her son would be liberated from his body so that he would break free from his disability, like a butterfly bursting forth from its chrysalis.

Sleep stole over her like a white screen passing across her eyes. She saw herself walking free through spacious rooms flooded with startling white light; through the uncurtained windows, she watched a myriad of snowflakes, drift ever so slowly down to earth. But then darkness came and occupied the emptiness, suddenly returning her to wakefulness and the rhythmic sound of Abdel's snores. She escaped from the present, going back in her mind to those other moments which now seemed like some kind of illusion. "Do you want to play hide and seek?" she had whispered to Saleh. Before he could answer, she had taken his hand and drawn him towards her daughter's bed, perching on the edge so that he was forced to sit beside her. Outside the room, the children's voices grew louder, as if one or other of them were about to push the door open at any minute. Reading the fear in Saleh's sudden intake of breath, she had pushed her body into the space between the bed and the carpet without letting go of his hand, which had compelled him to squeeze his long thin body in after her so that he could lie beside her under Lubna's bed.

There had only been enough room for them to lie on their sides, facing each other. When she heard the door creak, she had drawn her legs up as far as they would go and Saleh had done the same. She had heard the muffled sound of Helen's voice telling Hussein's son to hide while the twin, who was counting in the next door room, stopped and set out to search for the others. "Go under the bed," Helen had whispered and before he was able to conceal himself, she had left the room and shut the door. The young guest had not been fazed by the sight of two adults, hiding in the same place. Perhaps he thought that everyone, young and old, was taking part in the game. A question had crossed Baida's mind at that minute: "Will he tell his parents what he has seen?" But she had dismissed it immediately, telling herself: "Who believes what children say?"

*   *   *

She woke up late the next morning. On hearing her children's voices, she realised it must be Saturday. When she turned over she saw that Abdel's side of the bed was empty. She presumed he had gone to the weekly second hand market and was suddenly overcome by a desperate desire to get up and ring Saleh. Before she could get out of bed, she remembered that he normally spent the weekend at Scheherazade's. She shrank back under the blankets. Her chest constricted, she was unable to breathe and whenever she

300

did exhale, the breath felt warm on her hands.

Nevertheless, she was filled with conflicting emotions; a mix of regret and yearning, desire and fear, ecstasy and suicidal depression surged through her, followed by a profound sense of guilt. But she no longer had a headache. It was the first day she had woken up without being haunted by the last, in the shape of a migraine, or rather an open wound, that demanded that she go further and further into the past, leaving a continuous thread of blood behind her, like the woman who had been crushed by the train. Then she was struck by another image. She imagined herself in a theme park riding in an open carriage, which was slowly ascending a steep railway. Immediately it reached the top, it hurtled downwards towards the bottom. At that instant she was terrified. She wished she had never chosen to come on this ride but at the same time, running parallel with that, she was filled with a sense of wild elation.

There had certainly been a sense that she was complying with the rules of the game, when Saleh left her daughter's room: after he had gone down two or three steps, she had cautiously emerged onto the landing. He had almost reached the sitting room, when she heard Helen's voice somewhere in the darkness, saying aggressively, "Got you." Somehow, she was imbued with a sense of strength or perhaps it was a sense of weakness arising out of her complete inability to change the course of the train as it hurtled along the rails suspended high up in space. She turned towards the voice coming from Selim's room. The door was slightly ajar and, through the small vertical gap between the edge of the wall and the door, shadowy faces appeared, whose features were masked by the overwhelming darkness inside the room. Helen and Nadine had turned off the lights and were keeping a very close watch on the corridor. After she had turned on the light, Baida said jokingly: "Darkness will wear out the nosey." But the laughing girls stayed silent. In fact when Baida looked at them, she saw they were shocked and almost frightened by her sudden appearance.

*　*　*

Her heart jumped when the phone rang; ten days had passed since their guests had visited them, during which time she had dialled Saleh's number continuously, whenever Abdel left the house and had even taken advantage of his time in the workshop to try again, each time without success.

She lifted up the receiver, longing to hear his voice and almost said his name out loud before knowing who was calling. It was a woman. She couldn't work out who it was until after she had been told. "It's Scheherazade. Have you forgotten what I sound like?" Instead of rushing in with excuses as she normally did, Baida found her voice taking on the self-assurance of the other woman and her teasing manner: "No, but your voice sounds sweeter than before." Instead of prompting a laugh from Scheherazade as she had expected, a heavy silence settled between them, which seemed to last for ages. Suddenly, her cousin started talking again: "Is Abdel at home?" Before she could tell her that he wasn't, Scheherazade explained, "I've got a friend who needs a skilled carpenter."

Baida was sitting with her children watching television when her relative rang a second time. This time Abdel was closer to the phone than she was. She raised her head to look at the clock on the wall. The hands pointed to half past six. In the gap between the curtains, she could see the pitch black hue of the sky. Her husband's voice filtered in from the corridor. At first he sounded loud and jovial but then unusually for him his voice grew quieter until as the conversation continued, it evolved to the point where he was reduced to murmuring obscure words of enquiry: Really? Impossible? Are you sure? Then he became silent, only repeating a word now and then, which signalled his agreement with whatever Scheherazade was telling him. Yes…OK…fine.

At that instant, she realised they were talking about her. For a second, the sound of Helen's voice flitted across her mind, the moment Saleh had slipped out of her daughter's room, and she cowered back, overwhelmed by a profound sense of unease.

I see her in front of me lying on the sofa. She has folded her arms across her chest and pulled up her legs as far as they will go, as if hoping to bring about a miracle that will enable her to return to the World of Possibilities, and let her hide away from a reality that she temporarily lost the codes of its movement; and when she got them back, it was too late.

Part Ten
The Divine Names I

The World of Possibilities:

A belated return to the 'possibilities of existence.'

While Sultan al-Kamel was laying siege to Damascus, Mu-hyiddin bin Arabi was completely immersed in a problem that had been haunting him for days, namely, whether animals were resurrected in the afterlife?

Maybe this is what made him so impervious to what was taking place outside the house, as the soldiers made ready to defend the city, for the air was constantly full of their shouts and the clatter of weapons and the neighing of horses. From far away the muezzin could be faintly heard, after every call to prayer, calling on God to make King al-Nasr victorious and summoning the people to wage a holy war again Sultan al-Kamel who had handed over Jerusalem to the Franks without a fight.

I imagine him sitting in an iwan, like the one in my grandmother's house in Baghdad, behind a thick, yellowish gold curtain made of broadcloth, which is suspended between the two parallel walls, and which separates him from the courtyard. When the violent tide of sound from outside recedes and the house is enveloped in absolute silence, the trickle of water, from the fountain in the middle of the courtyard, filters through to his ears, and distracts him slightly from the world he is in: the world of imagination, in which the righteous servant meets his Lord through fantasy and dream. In this magical city, the human and divine, which make up the essence of man, converge, though this can only be achieved through a variety of endeavours, everything from continuous fasting and prayer to silence and sleeplessness and the internal repetition of the sacred names of Allah.

The year is April, 1129 AD. Spring had come to Damascus with a flourish and the whole house was fragrant with the sweet scent of orange blossom, which wafted across the courtyard from the tree in the middle and seeped through the narrow space under the broad curtain, to remind Muhyiddin of his home.

He had been applying himself assiduously to his prayers for more than four hours and when he finally emerged from his nightly tarawih prayer, everyone in the large family was fast asleep. His thoughts turned to a conversation he had had with his students that morning. They were disgruntled with what al-Kamel was doing. Twenty five years after Saladin had liberated Jerusalem, his nephew had handed the city over to the Frankish leader, Frederick II, even though he posed no threat to his kingdom. In so doing, he was disregarding the sacrifices Moslems had made under his uncle's leadership, which had brought about victory in the battle of Hattin, and resulted in the liberation of Jerusalem and many other towns. Not satisfied with handing over Jerusalem to the Franks, Al-Kamel had now come to wrest control of Damascus from his nephew, al-Nasr, who had taken the place of his dead father, known as 'al-Muaddham.'

Muhyiddin did not say a word during the discussion. Instead he thought about all the struggles he had seen, no matter whether they were between brothers or strangers, or between members of one or different factions. He remembered the devastation, fires and slaughter, he had seen on his way from Seville to Damascus, which had gradually made him conclude that such wars would last forever. Even when peace broke out, it appeared as pestilential as the plague. His mind went back to the brutal scenes he had witnessed in Cairo where the air had been filled with the cries of the sick and the roads piled high with the corpses of the dead. At night, he had seen people searching for their loved ones by torch light, so that they could lay them to rest, according to the religious rites, before the Sultan's labourers arrived to pick them up, from where they had been tossed in the road, and bury them in the big freshly dug ditches.

The thing that had most surprised him in Cairo was that life went on as normal. The merchants carried on trading, people went on shopping, sometimes even going to the market directly after burying a member of their family. It was as if there were two forces moving in parallel: one leading to death and the other to life. It was then that he came up with the theory of the Divine Names, which even eight hundred years after his death, would be of interest to notable academics. How else could one explain why some people were abundantly protected from harm while others were ruined, without either group doing anything to influence the outcome, were it not for the Divine Names of God, al-Mumit and al-Muhiy, the Slayer, and the Life Giver. The names competed with each other to impose their authority over the alleyways and neighbourhoods of Cairo, one summoning its victims to death, the other to life. Once someone had fallen under one or other of their sway, the other name left him to his fate and stopped intervening.

Were the internecine wars between the Ayyubids in any

way different from those that had taken place between the Muslims and Christians in Andalusia, or between the Seljuks and Byzantines in Anatolia? Were these wars any different to the wars the Crusaders had fought against the Muslims, the Almohades against the Marabouts, the Franks against the Byzantines, or the Ayyubids against the Fatimids?

And now the story was being repeated all over again.

*   *   *

He woke up late the next day. Instead of returning to the urgent question that had been occupying him the day before, his mind now dwelt on an old vision which he thought he had forgotten about entirely. Initially it came as a sound. He heard a woman's voice, reading a few lines of poetry to him. Then he found himself pacing around the Kaaba. It was dark, except for the gauzy light of a full moon, which flooded every corner of that Holy Place, and which had induced many people from Mecca to come and perform the rite with him, despite the lateness of the hour. He found his feet veering off the paved surface on to the sand, and began to recite some verses of poetry, which had just that minute come to his mind:

Ah, if only I knew if they knew whose heart they have taken
I wish my heart knew what mountain track they have followed.
Did they survive their journey or did they die?
Lovers are always bewildered in love and confused.

310

Suddenly, he felt silken fingers softly brush against his shoulder. Who did they belong to? When he turned his head, he saw a young girl behind him, her wide eyes lit up by a shaft of moonlight. "What were you saying, my Lord?" she asked, in a tone that was both playful and serious, sweet and severe. He repeated the first line with difficulty, unsure whether she was really human or not. "I am amazed at you," she said, in astonishment. "How can you, the greatest mystic of our time, say something like that? Is not the person who steals one's heart known to the lover? Is it not true to say that love holds sway only after a person has become acquainted with their beloved and the longing for feeling has made its presence known by being absent? What did you say next?" When he stumblingly recited the next line: "I wish my heart knew what mountain track they have followed," she shouted with mock displeasure: "Oh, my Lord, since the heart is not allowed to know about the paths that lie hidden between the heart and the subtle membrane that envelops it, how can someone such as you desire to know what he cannot attain? What did you say next?" Before he could utter another word, he heard a woman calling out:

"Come on, Nizam, let's go!"

How long was it since that conversation had taken place? Twenty years or maybe more? Despite that, he could still recall the incident as clearly as if it had happened the day before. After returning home from the Kaaba, he had performed the evening prayer, and gone to bed early. Before falling asleep, he started to recite the litany of God's Holy Names, but paused when he came to The Beautiful. An image of a pair of glittering kohl-lined eyes appeared to him, which seemed to grow evermore beautiful, the more he repeated the Divine Name. Her name slipped into his mind and he began to repeat it to himself quietly: Nizam. What a name! It contained the beauty and order of the universe.

In the morning, he felt he had sinned. How could he have allowed the name of a human being to become jumbled up with the divine? Since it was his custom, when he was in Andalusia to tell his sheikh and companions, not only what sins he had committed but what sinful thoughts had passed through his mind, he now set off for Abu Shuja'a al-Asfahani. He was astonished at what he found there.

Struggling to hide a smile, the sheikh told him: "You've done nothing except repeat a particular trait of the beautiful name. The only way for each name to fulfil its essence is through the way it is made manifest among God's creations." He barely gave him pause for thought, before asking: "What's her name?"

"Nizam."

"Her real name is al-Nizam."

"How do you know, my Lord?"

"Because she's my daughter... Her aunt calls her 'Ain ash-Shams."

* * *

That night he had a dream which opened up the path of knowledge before him: huge beings gleamed with light. On the back of each one, a Divine Name was engraved, glittering with a light that was illuminated with the colours of the rainbow. From far away, a gelatinous throng of beings advanced, which was as dark as the void around it. When they were several metres away from the Divine Names, the beings stopped, the dread in their souls making them even more shadowy than before. Muhyiddin heard one of the Divine Names, asking: "Who are they?" Another name replied almost inaudibly: "They are some of the entities of possibility." The entities approached timorously. A Divine Name shouted: "What do you want?" From their midst, a voice, which was as faint as an echo of an echo, could be heard saying: "Non-existence has blinded us, so we are unable to perceive one another or to know what God requires you to do with us." A particular Divine Name, who was unrecognisable because it was surrounded by other illuminated beings, persisted: "So what?" There was an almost imperceptible cry. "If you were to make manifest our entities and clothe them in the robes of existence, you would be doing us a great favour and we would undertake the appropriate veneration and reverence," murmured the entities feebly. "Your sovereignty will only become genuine when we become manifest in actuality. Today you only possess sovereignty over us potentially and virtually. What we are asking you is more in your interest than in ours."

At first the Divine Names were silent, then they began to whisper angrily to each other: "It's true! We're almost choking to death."

The scene in front of him changed. Now he saw a group of Divine Names entering a large courtyard, where a radiant man was seated on a throne. Above his throne, the word, Powerful, flashed on and off. They held a muffled conversation with him, in which they doubtless asked him to breathe

313

existence into the entities of possibility, the specifications of which, each of them were carrying in themselves in a state of suppressed passivity. Powerful said: "I am under the aegis of the name, Desiring, so I cannot bring any of you into identified existence without it specifying that it should be so. The possible thing itself does not enable me of itself unless the command of the Commander must come first from its Lord. For when it commands the thing to enter into existence, saying to it, 'Be', then it gives me the ability of itself and I undertake to bring it into existence and immediately give it engendered existence. So my advice is the following: Go to the name, Desiring. Perhaps it will give preponderance to and specify the side of existence over the side of non-existence... Then, I, Commander and Speaker will join together and give you existence."

Next he saw the delegation moving to another area where the word, Desiring, was written up over the door. Its answer was no different to that of Powerful: "Knower is the one who knows what has been decided for you... If it knows about your being brought into existence then it will be possible for us to specify an existence for you... You must go to Knower because I am under its aegis..."

But Knower's reply was also disappointing: "Desiring has spoken the truth. And I have precedent knowledge that you will be given existence, but courtesy must be observed... We are all under the authority of the name of Allah. We must all be present with it for it is the Presence of All-comprehensiveness."

When Allah saw the delegation of Divine Names surrounding him, he asked: "What's the matter?" After a heavy silence, the voice of Knower stated clearly: "The possible things have requested that we give them existence."

They waited for a bit, then the name of Allah said, "I will enter into the presence of the Essence to tell him about the matter."

Part Eleven
Parallel Lines

He was about to leave the sitting room, when the final item of local news on the 10 o'clock bulletin, brought him to a stop.

As he listened to the details, Abdel remembered the story Hussein had told about a woman being run over by an underground train. The report accompanying the item which lasted no more than a few minutes, contained brief statements from a couple of men who had been working at the station, where the accident happened. One of them said that the victim had been Asian. Judging by her face which had been left untouched by the wheels of the train, she looked to have been in her thirties. Was this the same accident Dr Hussein had been talking about?

The news item did not leave much of an impression upon him apart from further convincing him that the public services in the 'Old Empire,' as he liked to call Britain, were backward, and giving him the added pleasure of being proved right yet again. Nevertheless, without wanting to, he put his hand out to the scrunched up piece of paper on the coffee table that he had been about to throw into the waste paper basket. Instead of tossing it away, he spread it out on top of the table and smoothed out the creases.

The wrinkles, caused by screwing the paper into a ball, made the words appear fragmented and hesitant. Or as if the person, who had written them, had been heavily drugged. My dear husband…I am going to visit my family…I am very ill… I am sorry… I hope to come back soon...

There were a couple of barely discernible words on the last line, which had been repeatedly crossed out. However when he turned the paper over, he was just able to make out the letters though they appeared back to front: Forgive me.

He thought about phoning Hussein to ask if the accident, he had just seen on television, was the one he had been talking about but angrily dismissed the idea: She's in Baghdad now, he told himself. He would call her without delay and urge her to come back. There's really no reason for you to have left. You're the best mother in the world... We all need you back... Let's start afresh. We won't see your cousin again and that's all there is to it.... London's a huge city... No one bothers about anyone else's business...

Abdel had not understood why Scheherazade was so angry with Baida, for he had never once questioned how strong her relationship with Saleh was. The disparity in their ages had been the only thing that had continued to concern him, so much so that at one time, he had considered advising Saleh to think about starting a family. His relatives in Baghdad would be able to send him a bride once the war with Iran was over and Iraqis were able to travel again.

He pushed aside these initial doubts as thoughts of a more troubling kind crowded into his mind. For over a week now, he had unsuccessfully been trying to withdraw money from the account he had set up in Raouf's name. The cashier at the NatWest bank had told him that it had been closed a short time previously. He had been on the verge of asking him about his deposits. His friend had given Abdel the cheque book he had received from the bank after signing all the documents, to enable him to withdraw what he wished. He thought about the money that had gone into the account to pay for the monthly rent on the house, which was in Raouf's name, and felt afraid. Could his childhood friend have undergone a transformation and turned into a cheat?

He had been trying to reach him by phone for several days without success. Whenever he rang, all he got was a continuous high pitched noise that indicated that the line had been cut off.

He had thought about going to the Emirates to find out what was happening and had intended to leave the day after next but now Baida had taken it into her head to visit her family, a decision that seemed both strange and unjustifiable to him. Why couldn't she have waited until after he returned from his trip? Wasn't the account as much for her as it was for him?

He deeply regretted not having told her what had happened with Raouf. Maybe if he had, she would have postponed her trip or perhaps cancelled it altogether. And he could have shown her how unconcerned he was about what Scheherazade had told him on the phone, and thereby allayed her sense of guilt and put an end to whatever else was troubling her. They could have taken the family to Italy or Spain. Perhaps a holiday would have lifted her spirits and reconciled her to her life with him and the children.

When Scheherazade had spoken to him on the phone, she had not been her normal self. She had been furious and her voice had lost the sardonic wit, which was her distinguishing feature and which made other people find her so unsettling. Instead, she had unleashed a torrent of coarse and angry abuse: "Do you know what Baida's done?" Before he could say anything, she had shouted with a hysterical laugh: "Of course you don't… They say the husband's always the last person to know."

Abdel hadn't said a single word to Baida about what Scheherazade had told him. But nevertheless he could feel her watching him, her jaw and cheeks propped up in the palms of her hands as she followed his every move from where she was sitting in the kitchen or sitting room. His blood boiled as he passed back and forth in front of her. Surely she was aware that something momentous had happened. Would she really continue to look as calm as she did, if she knew that he knew about what had happened between her and Saleh? Her distinctive pallor reminded him of how she had looked after Selim had died, but apart from that there was little that was different. It was as if her features lay hidden behind a mask.

Once, when he had seen her sitting beside the table in the kitchen, he had almost hit her. But before he could give in to this urge, an even stronger emotion had taken its place and filled him with a desire to embrace her. The mere thought of how she might respond was enough to arouse him, despite the intense sense of isolation he was feeling, which was heightened by the sound of rain tapping on the window pane.

Abdel was caught between two opposing forces, which made him incapable of making a move towards his wife. One minute, he would be thinking one thing, which would make him feel closer to her, the next he would be thinking the complete opposite. In all the time they had lived together, he had always been amazed by Baida's extraordinary compliance. He couldn't remember a single occasion when she had opposed a decision that concerned her life as well as his or remonstrated against the bouts of rage, which would shake him from time to time.

He could not imagine her abandoning the values, her family had instilled in her. In this respect, she was completely different to Scheherazade, as unalike her as the earth is to the sky. It was this contrast between them which made him find her cousin so attractive. How he enjoyed his encounters with Scheherazade, for with all her liberated talk and almost masculine physical gestures she reminded him of a world that was based on freedom. In such a world, he could pretend that everything was possible and do whatever he wanted. He often imagined himself taking Saleh's place in her bed but, when he thought of Baida with her exaggerated femininity, his fantasy would come to an abrupt halt. Instead of pitting himself against the dominant authoritative woman, he would choose the one who was entirely submissive to his unrestrained virility

Maybe it was all the figment of an adolescent imagination, he thought. Scheherazade had often said how jealous Helen was of Saleh, and how her daughter talked about him maliciously even when other guests were present. He made his way cautiously to his daughter's room and peered into the darkness. The even sound of Lubna's breathing reached him, checked for a moment then resuming with a choked intake of air. He left the door to the room slightly open. He sat down on the carpet beside the small bed and put his hand out to the gap between the base and the floor in order to measure the distance between them. When he had asked Scheherazade where Saleh and his wife could have hidden in a place that was crowded with children, she had replied in a voice that bore more than a hint of sarcasm. "They were under your daughter's bed... Playing hide and seek." He tried unsuccessfully to squeeze under the bed. Going on the evidence, it seemed impossible that one person, let alone two could have crammed themselves into the space.

He would phone Scheherazade and tell her she was wrong. It's just your daughter's imagination, he would say. Nothing more.

But as he turned over the creased letter, he was beset by other doubts. Was Baida the victim of some conspiracy that Saleh had engineered against him? He had often noticed how jealous the latter was of him. Whenever Scheherazade noticed some improvement or other he had carried out in the house, she would make fun of Saleh's ineptitude. Hadn't she once said, mockingly: "I should find a husband, who is good at three things: plumbing, electricity and carpentry." She had turned to him and asked with a laugh: "Do you know anyone fitting that description? It doesn't matter if he is illiterate."

Abdel did not let the children watch television. In fact, he ordered them up to bed before it was seven o'clock. Lubna was the only one to ask where her mother was and he interrupted her sharply: "I'll punish you if you ask for your mother again."

Now and then he listened at the doors to his children's rooms to make sure they were observing the strict rule, he had instilled into them even before they could talk: that there was to be no talking, laughing or crying, after they had gone to bed. He was always criticizing Baida for the lax manner, she had with the children and the way she gave in to whatever they wanted. Now he had ample opportunity to make them more self-reliant.

Beginning tomorrow, he would start training them.

He paced back and forth between the sitting room and kitchen. The walls looked very faded. He had been intending to paint the whole house, he recalled, but Selim's sudden death had made him put off the task. The job would be a great way of keeping the children occupied during the coming week's holiday and starting their education. Hadn't he begun to learn carpentry, when he was only a bit older than the twins?

He scrunched the paper into a ball and threw it into the dustbin. He put his hands under the tap on the sink and began to soap them thoroughly before rinsing them under the hot water. It would be nice to have a bath. As he was about to get into the water, it suddenly occurred to him to wonder for the first time how Baida would pay for her ticket if she really intended to go back to her family. Had Saleh given her the money? Or had she forged his signature on the cheque and withdrawn the sum from his account? Abdel had sometimes asked her to pay bills with a cheque. Falsifying his signature wouldn't present any difficulties to someone who knew Arabic. It was the name he had originally been given before his father irrevocably changed it: Abdel Wahab.

*   *   *

But Baida had not thought about how she was going to pay for her ticket until after she had shut the door behind her. She only had sufficient money in her purse to pay for the weekly groceries. Apart from that, she just had a rucksack in which she had put various disparate objects: two pairs of knickers, a toy dog belonging to Selim, two sticks of red lipstick, a toothbrush, a towel and her passport.

Immediately, she shut the door behind her, she realized she had left the key inside. This, along with the letter she had left for Abdel, severed the last of the ties that bound her to her husband. He'd be back soon, After he'd taken the children to school. She ran her fingers over the door as if trying to touch the children she was abandoning into his strict care. How would they accept the fact that she was no longer there? She began retracing her footsteps. She ran her hand over the myrtle hedge which Abdel had pruned only a couple of days before. She snapped off a twig and rubbed its leaves between her fingers.

Above, the ashen sky seemed to press down upon her. The rain fell softly. It was so fine that she only became aware of it when it touched her face. She ploughed through the last remaining dry leaves. On the pavement opposite, she noticed a leafless beech tree, which only a short time before had been resplendent in its crimson robe. As she stood before it, wiping away the drops of fine rain from her eyelashes, did she feel they shared a common fate?

An image of Abdel loomed up in front of her, as he had been when he had spoken to Scheherazade that last time. She had been watching him from the kitchen. Before it actually happened, she had often played out the scene in her mind. Ever since she had heard Helen's voice proclaiming that she had caught her and Saleh, she had been resignedly waiting for the sentence, which had been passed on her, to be carried out.

In the ten days leading up Scheherazade's last call, she had had a series of dreams, which seemed to be the same dream in different guises: in one of them she had been standing beside the parapet of an old stone bridge. At first, she thought it spanned both banks of a river but when she looked down she had seen a bottomless chasm, plunging into the depths below. It grew darker but when she wanted to leave, she found they had locked the gates at either end of the bridge.

She began to walk more quickly, afraid that Abdel might arrive. How would he react if she told him she had left her key inside? First he would scowl, and then he would sigh. Finally he would say in that cold voice, that always brought on a bad migraine: Well, that doesn't surprise me.

In another variant of the original dream, she was walking through a large park, rimmed with thickets and ponds. A short distance behind, came Saleh, walking very slowly. The snow fell steadily, while the gloom was tinged with a yellowy-reddish light. Everything seemed extraordinarily sublime to her and infused with a mysterious beauty. What was it that the scene inspired in her? What conflicting emotions? A sense of utter despair, of uncertain and violent turmoil. She seemed to be someone else; to be more intrepid, more at ease with herself. When she turned round, she noticed Saleh had fallen far behind. She was about to call out to him to hurry up, when she realised that someone else had taken his place. Was it Abdel? He had something over his head which made him look inhuman. As if he were a robot charged with carrying out some task or other. Was he going to kill her? She forced herself to walk faster and faster. But despite her efforts, he gained on her, until she woke up in a fright and heard Abdel snoring beside her.

Now she was going into the underground station. The distinctive rumble of trains reached her ears. Like the violent thudding of a heart. Simultaneously, the sound of voices faded around her. People rushed about in all directions and when a crowd of them moved towards her, she thought they would crush her underfoot and pressed back against the wall.

As soon as she squeezed into the last carriage, she wanted to get off the train again and go back home, but the doors shut before she could make up her mind. As the train took her further and further away from Abdel, she pictured him reading her faltering words, and his image loomed ever larger in her mind.

She lost her train of thought, distracted by the faces of passengers around her. People sat immersed in what they were reading, so as to avoid catching the eye of the person next to them. Those, who were standing, stared fixedly at their reflections in the window. A young man and his girlfriend got into the carriage, attracting her attention. Despite the crowd of people, they continued to embrace each other. She couldn't take her eyes off them as they engaged in a lingering kiss, completely ignoring the passengers around them. Prompted by the sight and the rocking of the train, another scene flashed into her mind. It seemed to have taken place a long time ago to someone else entirely. She was back in

Lubna's bedroom, in the dark space under her small bed as Saleh's hands touched the most secret parts of her body, and sought to prise open the cramped passages into her soul. Her fingers clung to his clothes, as if she were unconsciously trying to make the moment last forever; the moment when they melted into one another, amidst the children's cries on the other side of the bedroom door.

What is it that keeps a particular moment in our memory, making it as vivid as if it has just happened, while whole years can pass by without leaving a trace behind them?

It would not be surprising if Baida wasn't asking herself such a question when she got off the train. Why else did she choose to get out at this particular station, other than that it was close to Saleh's flat? Immediately she emerged into the pale morning light, she was assailed by doubts and fears. What if Scheherazade were there? What would she do if Saleh rebuffed her?

When she was in sight of Saleh's block, she almost turned round and went back to the station, but then she had an idea. She would say: I've come to ask if I can borrow some money for my plane ticket. I'll send it back to you immediately I get to Baghdad. She repeated the words to herself in various configurations, as she ran her hand up and down the wall of the four-storeyed building. I've decided to go back to my family... Can you lend me the money for the plane ticket? It seemed different to the way she had pictured it. The bricks were more yellowy than red as she remembered them.

What would she say if he suggested she stay with him? I've got three children. It doesn't matter. I'll be like a father to them, even more so. You deserve to live your life without responsibility for others. I love you. What about Scheherazade? You're everything to me. I want you even though you have a relationship with Scheherazade. She said this in a loud voice, which made her laugh. What would Saleh look like on his own? Without the reflected glory of her cousin? She had another idea. She would phone Scheherazade and apologise. A different image loomed up in her mind: this time it was of Scheherazade as a supremely self-confident and liberated woman, who paid no heed to traditions. I apologise. I did it because I was ill. I wasn't completely cured. But the image of her cousin revived her fears. She was enormous, with penetrating eyes that seemed to pierce right through her, heightening her sense of frailty and awkwardness. She had often detected a certain disdain mixed with pity, behind her cousin's sympathetic expression and kind words, which had shaken her self-confidence and driven her to silence and self-effacement.

She carefully studied the list of names beside the entrance. When she came to Saleh's name, she was assailed by a sense of unreality. Has she really severed all links with her previous life, cut herself off from the world, which up to that morning had cocooned her completely? Now she was about to take another step that would lead her into the unknown. Invisible hands pulled her away from the door as others drew her towards it.

She pressed the bell for a second, her heart thudding. After taking a couple of deep breaths, she raised her thumb cautiously but with determination. He can't have heard the bell. You must stand firm, even if it is for the first time in your life. But no one answered. Is he still asleep? I'll ring longer and he'll wake up. She began to ring the bell repeatedly. Suddenly the door opened to reveal an old man with his dog. He looked at her in surprise and asked: "Madam, do you want to come in?" Instead of saying no, she remained silent, adding to the expression of surprise on his face and tingeing it with alarm. He hurried away, talking to his dog. She looked up at the window of Saleh's flat. The curtains were closed. Is he hiding behind them? Or maybe he's with Scheherazade? Perhaps the two of them are spying on her and having a laugh at her expense. Involuntarily she put her hand up to her face. As if by so doing she could ward off any evil done to her by their malicious glances.

* * *

But Saleh really was out. At the very moment when Baida was leaving the underground station and turning right, he was locking the door of the building behind him. He was at a loss for a moment: Should he turn right and go to the Italian cafe next to the station or left towards the park? In a departure from his normal routine of having his morning coffee near the station, he went with his second choice.

He thought back to the chaos he had left behind. Bits of paper littered the flat. Pages from his novel lay torn and scattered over the sofa, the sitting room floor, and between the covers of his bed. Shredded pages from his diary blocked the bath and the toilet bowl. Black ink seeped out of the cistern, surprising him when he pulled the chain, before it too gradually drained away along with the torn scraps of paper.

The top of the coffee table was the only place in the room,

which was still in order. On it, there was a piece of white paper, folded in two, its neat appearance, in sharp contrast to the disarray elsewhere in the room. "Through all this, I hope to rid you of any illusions you might have about your-self. You will never be a writer until you learn how to be truthful…Put the keys to my house in the post. Don't ever try to contact me again…"

Saleh guessed that Scheherazade had carried out the attack shortly before he arrived home the day before; if he hadn't agreed to go for a drink after work in a nearby pub with a couple of colleagues, he would have got back before she had had sufficient time to mess up the flat. When he first opened the door, he thought that burglars had paid him an early visit. Caught by surprise, he was about to phone the police, when his nose picked up the smell of a scent that Scheherazade had bought him. She had told him at the time with a laugh: "Don't forget to bathe in it before we meet… It's my favourite perfume." He had wanted to ask her how she had discovered it, but preferred to keep quiet. Now as he stumbled from room to room, like someone in a dream, he was astonished to find the whole flat smelt of lemon flowers. When he came across the scent bottle, lying in the sitting room, amidst a mess of cooking vessels and scattered cush-ions, he guessed who the perpetrator was.

Had Scheherazade found out about his affair with Baida?

Over the last week, he had noticed a sudden change in her attitude towards him; when he had gone to her house at the weekend, she had asked him to sleep in the sitting room. For her part Helen had also seemed unusually aloof and correct and had only emerged from her room two or three times.

He had woken up in the middle of that night to hear the sound of rain. A band of pale light filtered into the room from the door, which was not properly closed. He felt terribly alone as if he were stranded on an abandoned planet, far away from any sign of human life.

Had Scheherazade started another relationship? Was she gradually cutting him out of her life? At that moment, he was acutely aware of the difference between his adjoining worlds: her house and his.

When he was in Scheherazade's world, everything was warmth and a total coming together. She brought her patients and colleagues to life with the funny and detailed stories she told about them; she united past and present, although she had only spent her childhood in Baghdad. It was as if their relationship provided them with a bridge, which transported them back to a hypothetical past, snatches of which could be heard in the old Baghdad songs, that were playing on the cassette player each time he came to the house, or tasted in the local dishes, she had begun to learn how to cook and which she only made when he came.

His own world was marked by its solitude. But it was a particular form of solitude, dominated by a covert desire that he had had ever since he was a teenager, to experiment in secret and try his hand at whatever he wanted. In this world, he could write whatever he wished, about whomever he liked, and on whatever subject he wanted. He could invite a colleague or student to spend the night with him if he found her attractive or shut himself away; if he wanted he could throw open his flat to a group of colleagues. In this

333

world, it was not so important to carry out his desires as to create possibilities, which could be realised. It was a world of possibilities rather than one of applications.

As he turned over on the narrow sofa, a thought occurred to him. When he was with her he was completely at one with the universe. She was the umbilical cord, which attached him to the womb. When he was on his own, he was disconnected from the world around him, so that he was able to break it up into its primary elements. On his small desk, he had written a sentence from Socrates, which had remained hidden from everyone until the day before, when Scheherazade had come and flushed the paper down the toilet. The unexamined life is not worth living

But as he lay there in Scheherazade's house, feeling utterly abandoned, with the ceiling seeming to press down on him in the darkness, and with the wind moaning and the rain spattering against the window pane, he had been more than ready to relinquish his second world. Should he go to Scheherazade's room and ask her to marry him?

He was consumed by a single wish, which he would have given his eye teeth to have fulfilled. He wanted Scheherazade to come and put out her hand to him; to take him to her bed and rock him to sleep again.

Until that moment on the sofa, Saleh had never thought about making love to Scheherazade in this way. When he reached orgasm with her, it was not merely like the moment when a snake sloughs off its skin, as he told her occasionally while they were having a cigarette together or a glass of champagne after their passion had abated; rather it was a moment, which gave him an imaginary power and made him feel much greater than he really was. At such times, as he looked at Scheherazade through half-closed eyes, he imagined her to be much younger and prettier than she was. The sound of her words and sighs urging him on, would reassure him that she was still there beside him with her noble lineage, her achievements and her complete self-confidence, for it was as if she injected this mixture into his veins in return for his merging with her.

The park appeared bare although the cypress and cedar trees had lost none of their greenness. The pond looked like it always did. It was as if the glowing colours, he had seen when he had last been there, had derived from his relationship with Scheherazade. Over the years they had been together, Scheherazade had always been keen to keep their relationship light hearted and playful. Even when he excused himself from going to stay with her for the weekend, she had never asked him for a reason.

He returned to his flat and encountered a scene of depressing chaos. He was torn between wanting to put things back where they belonged and leaving everything as it was. He paused for a second in his bedroom, in front of the mirror on the wardrobe door and touched the scratch marks on his face and the red love bites on his neck.

Two days after rejecting him, Scheherazade had paid him a visit. "Helen's going to sleep over at Nadine's," she said, smiling broadly. "Will you let me stay the night with you or have you other plans?" He was so astonished that he could barely speak. "Even if you don't want me to, I'll stay the night here… It'll be my final attack," she joked.

As was his custom on such occasions, he had done

everything he could to make up for the fact that his flat had none of the luxuries of hers. He bought the finest champagne he could find and lit candles, instead of the table lamps, which were scented with basil, jasmine and damask rose, and whose fragrance permeated every corner of the flat. The house was completely quiet, save for the soft melody of Satti's piano sonata which filtered through from the sitting room, the notes sounding like the splash of water from an imaginary fountain.

In the middle of the night, he had woken up to hear a suppressed sob. He turned towards her. He asked her warily: "Is something hurting you?" "Go to sleep," she choked. "It's nothing. Just a stomach ache." When he woke up in the morning, he found her getting ready to leave. "I've made a huge amount of coffee. Do you want a cup in bed?" Before he could answer her, she had looked at him closely, and then put her right palm up her mouth for a second before breaking into a snort of laughter. "Don't look in the mirror before I've left the house," she warned him. When she saw the alarm on his face, she mumbled teasingly: "It's nothing dangerous. You won't be able to sue me. I've merely put my signature to a painting, I've just completed."

* * *

When Scheherazade left Saleh's flat, she felt happy and at peace, a mood, which was completely at variance with the nightmare she had been living in, ever since Helen had told her what she had seen in Abdel's house. On her way to the hospital, she went over the details of their passionate encounter. Saleh had seemed so loving. When he woke up and found her ready to leave, she had glimpsed a look of distress cross his face as if he were about to lose the one thing on which his life depended. "Don't be afraid… We'll see each other soon," she told him reassuringly. At that moment as she looked at his face, she half expected him to surprise her and ask: "What do you think about getting married?" Instead, adopting the fatherly tone of voice, he unconsciously liked to use when he found himself constrained by his weakness, and taking advantage of his superior height, he said: "Don't tire yourself out today." Then he further boosted his self-confidence by adding: "You worked very hard last night and you deserve a holiday." When his words failed to evoke the good humoured response he was expecting, he put his arms around her and kissed the top of her head. "Don't mess up my hair," she teased and scolded simultaneously. "My patients will get angry with you. You must get a hair dryer… At least, for my sake…" But he pretended not to have heard. "Do you want to meet at the weekend?" he had asked instead, keeping his voice neutral. She had shaken her head decisively: "No, not this one…" "the one after?" "I'll see…OK?"

Once she reached the hospital, she did her rounds quickly; maybe her sense of inner peace was reflected in the way she talked to her patients. She could see the gratitude on their faces becoming more and more pronounced, with every word of encouragement or reassurance she gave them.

Between appointments, she hid herself away in the toilet to escape the prying eyes of those around her. There she scrutinised her face. After seeing her second patient, the three

337

faint lines on her forehead seemed slighter deeper than they had been the day before. She ran her fingers over them, gently smoothing them out. When she smiled the lines across her forehead almost disappeared but the skin around her eyes became wrinkled instead.

She still felt calm, when she arrived home. After supper, she asked her daughter if there had been any phone calls for her. When she said there hadn't, she felt her spirits sink. Was she hoping for a phone call that would help relieve her of the burden of knowing a secret that she wished had never been brought out into the open? Wished had remained nothing but a subject of conjecture? Helen had stuck to her story about what she seen. "Ask Nadine if you don't believe me," she said. She felt even more alarmed at the thought of someone like Nadine being a party to her humiliation. How could she face her old friend and countryman, Hussein, again, if she were to continue her relationship with Saleh? She had always been open with him about her relationships with men, even though she knew him to be slightly traditional in his attitudes. Despite that, he had always treated her with a respect that had at times bordered on adulation. Now she was placed in the impossible position of trying to explain the incomprehensible: that her own cousin had gone off with her longstanding boyfriend.

She glanced across at the red phone and murmured to herself: "What are you waiting for? At least phone and ask whether I enjoyed last night... Yes, I enjoyed it very much..." "Shall I come over now?" "I'll make an exception this time." Let them all go to hell... She was accustomed to breaking taboos and enjoying the shocked expressions on other people's faces. So Abdel and Hussein would be witnesses at the wedding and Baida a maid of honour. She'd arrange a huge wedding to which she would invite all her previous lovers. She'd celebrate the years she had spent with them. And then to crown it all, she'd marry someone, from back home, who had ridden over from her birthplace on a coal black charger.

She suddenly thought of Saleh as she had said goodbye to him that morning. He had been brimming over with power and self-confidence, in complete contrast to what he had been like when she had first got to know him. How confused he had been then in his dealings with the outside world! When they had first gone to a hotel together, he had cringed as he handed over their passports to the clerk at the reception desk. Once they were in their room, she had burst out: "Why do you hang your head like that? You look as if you're expecting someone to hit you. Why are you so terrified of other people? Have you committed a crime?" He had sat in the armchair furthest away from the bed and folded his arms across his chest. But it had not taken him long to earn her approval again: "I'm sorry… You'll have to accept me as I am… If you can't, then you had better leave immediately."

It suddenly dawned on her that she was attracted to men who were weak and ineffective; by the time she broke up with them however, they had become strong and successful. It was as if she infused them with her strength and then had to accept their hatred of her in return. Was she destined to repeat this game interminably? Maybe she was attracted to such men because they enabled her to extend the limits of her power. They stirred up such a rage in her that she was determined to persevere and challenge the boundaries, which stood in their way, and goad them on until they had become like her: frank, direct and resolute.

She slept fitfully, waking each time she had a dream. She frequently saw her father lying on his sick bed, his face no longer marked by the anger he had shown when she told him she was going to marry Stephen. "How can my daughter, the doctor, marry a penniless tramp?" he had demanded at the time. She had replied coldly, without a hint of tenderness in her voice. "That's my problem." "What about my political opponents? What will they say?" "Why are you so concerned about what your enemies will think? They'll be against you whatever happens." "And what about me? What I think about your ridiculous decision?" "That's your problem," she'd replied after a short silence. Her father had risen from his chair without saying another word and left the cafe. She hadn't seen him again for another ten years until after Stephen had died.

When she got up, Helen had left the house. How much more mature and eager to please she had seemed in the last week! She would quietly appear when Scheherazade was at her desk, or in the sitting room or in bed and ask: "Would you like a drink? Do you want any help?" It was as if she were trying to tell her: We're much better off without a man like Saleh.

She rang her secretary: "Can you cancel my appointments. I'm ill myself today."

She wanted to give Saleh a ring. She started to dial the number which she knew by heart, but changed her mind before she had finished. She put down the receiver and went to the kitchen. A cup of coffee would clear her head. She must avoid going anywhere near the phone. It would be a backwards step, if she called Saleh first.

She returned to the sitting room and sat on the chair, which was furthest away from the phone. But this only made her want to call him more. She turned to look at a black and white photograph, which had been among the ones Baida had brought from Baghdad when she first visited her. It was propped up behind the glass of a cupboard containing antiques. She opened the door and slowly reached out towards it. Her eyes lingered on it, taking in the details. It showed her standing among a group of relatives in Baghdad. It must have been taken shortly before her last trip to London. She could just detect a gleam of exasperation in her eyes as if she were irritated by the family gathering. But despite all Baida's attempts to remind her of who was with her in the picture, she had been unable to recall the exact moment it was taken. "Where are you?" Scheherazade had asked, surprising a reply from her cousin that was tinged with disappointment and astonishment. "Can't you see me? That's me beside you. You're holding my hand."

She dug out the magnifying glass that she occasionally used to examine X-rays. She put the photo down on the coffee table. She lit the light on the magnifier then placed it over the exact spot, where she and Baida were standing. As she looked at the figures, she became aware of the frighteningly large age gap between them. Baida was just a beautiful child who couldn't have been more than six years old when the picture was taken, while she was a miserable teenager of about seventeen. What kind of impression had this photo left on Saleh? He must have realised the difference in their ages, which she had managed to conceal up to then by wearing elegant clothes, never appearing without make up and cutting her hair in a boyish fashion.

Without realising what she was doing, she took off the top of her lipstick and began to smear it over the spot where Baida appeared. The end result was bizarre. The red struck an ugly discordant note against the black and white tones of the photograph, which dated back to the end of the fifties. She thought about tearing it up but in the end decided against doing such a thing. Although she had forgotten everything about its origins, she still wanted to keep it.

She put a little bleach on a small plate. Then she soaked one of the cotton buds she used for cleaning her ears in the liquid and brushed it across the red mark. After repeating the process several times, she left the photograph to dry. When she returned to the room, she found that Baida had disappeared and left nothing behind but a splodge of white.

As she looked at the photo, it crossed her mind that Baida had died. The pale spot which had taken her place seemed to resemble a little ghost. The two of them stood side by side among the assortment of relatives, staring straight ahead, challenging the layers of time and the power of forgetfulness. She wondered how old the people in the photograph were now. That young man would be in his mid-thirties if he was still alive. That sixty-year old woman must be dead. She was probably Baida's grandmother. An idea came to Scheherazade, which she was unable to put into words, but which remained trapped inside her like a question mark. Vast changes had taken place between the moment when the photograph was taken and the present moment. What was a possibility then was now an unchangeable reality. This reality which had come into being was, however, only one of several realities, several possibilities, which could have been realised when the shutter clicked on the old box camera. The people in the photo were lined up side by side in front of the high parapet on the roof of the house. She could tell it was winter from what they were wearing and, by looking at the direction of the slanting shadows, stretching out behind them, she guessed it was about four o'clock in the afternoon. Thanks to the magnifying glass, she was able to track down the tiny shadow left behind by Baida's body. She asked herself: what would have happened if Baida had not appeared in the photo for some reason. She obviously wouldn't have brought it with her from Baghdad and Saleh wouldn't have discovered the difference in their ages, which in turn would not have made him prefer her cousin. Did this photograph lie behind his betrayal?

Scheherazade pushed the persistent thoughts out of her mind by turning on the cassette player. The sound of Louis Armstrong's big optimistic voice stole over her, as he repeated the refrain: "And I think to myself what a wonderful day."

She felt ashamed of having erased Baida from the photograph like that and started to tear it up. But as she looked at the little bits of card, scattered over the coffee table, she was filled with a sharp sense of remorse. It was as if her action had been prompted by a desire to escape a path, which had been unalterably mapped out for her years before she came to London.

She spent hours assembling the fragments of paper. This

head didn't go with that arm. That skirt didn't match this shirt. When she finally picked up the fragment with the white spot on it, she was surprised to find that it was intact. On one side, she could see her left hand, holding the remnants of a tiny hand.

The smell of chlorine, which still hung over the bits of photograph, she had arranged on the table, filled her nostrils, reminding her of the dressing gown, she had left in Saleh's flat. She liked to put it on, before they went to bed and made love. She would wander round his flat, savouring the smell their previous encounter had left on the Japanese robe, which Saleh had bought her for her birthday. But when they had last met, it had smelt of nothing. "Have you washed my dressing gown?" she asked, a sudden picture of Baida, wearing nothing but the short robe, looming up in front of her. He avoided looking at her directly: "I took it to the dry cleaners," he said. "But I liked it as it was," she asserted. He laughed: "It needed to be cleaned… If I hadn't cleaned it, you would have accused me of living in squalor, as you've done in the past." As she turned over on the bed, she put her bare hands on the pillow and buried her head beneath it: "I wanted that dirt. I liked that dirt. That was the one thing in your flat you should have left as it was."

* * *

At the beginning, Helen felt a sense of relief. Was it really true, she wondered? Did this mean that Saleh wouldn't come to their house any longer or occupy the place he used to? When she told her mother what she had seen at Abdel's, she had never imagined that she would get so angry. In fact she thought she would laugh uproariously at the story and pat her on the shoulder and say: "You were right to constantly dismiss him. I was mistaken in him."

But the days that followed revealed a fact that that she had been unaware of previously. Her mother's relationship with Saleh was unlike the short-lived relationships, she had had before he arrived on the scene. She was like a bird with a broken wing without him, despite all her attempts to hide her suffering. She abandoned her morning routine of getting up early, doing her exercises, having a shower and then preparing an English breakfast. Instead, Helen had to wake her in the morning and she would have nothing before going to the hospital except a cup of milky coffee.

Her face looked older, the lines deeper than before. She no longer listened to the jazz and blues music, she used to love but sat in silence. Deep inside, Helen began to fear that her mother might die.

Scheherazade had only told her about her father's death, two years after it happened. He hadn't lived with them. Nevertheless, at Christmas and Easter, he had occasionally taken her to her grandparents' house in Somerset, where she would spend a couple of days with the two of them on her own. When had she made that momentous discovery? Was it before or after her fourth birthday? She was sitting with her father on the train on their way to Somerset. It must have been summer since her mother had dressed her in a short sleeved shirt just like the one her father was wearing. "Look," she said, as she studied her hand lying on top of his big one. But he didn't think it important and merely nodded his head before going back to his book. For her part, she was blinded by the contrasting colours of their skin, his white, hers brown, as they lay next to each other. Once at her grandparents' house, she retreated into herself, as she observed the striking differences in colour between them. Was this why she had been sent to bed early? She spent ages in the overreaching darkness, listening to the voices of the adults, talking behind the closed door.

Now Helen remembered how safe she had felt with the three men who had preceded Saleh even when they ignored her. She was always very polite to them and whenever one or other of them went out with her and her mother, their skin colour always made her feel much stronger. They enabled her to challenge the other kids at school, who were forever reminding her what colour she was, with comments like: "Where's your father from?" They helped her stand up to the teachers who would look at her in astonishment, when she told them what she was called. "What's your name?" "Helen Clark." "Clark?" Then suddenly Saleh had appeared.

"Do you know that my father was very handsome?" she asked him one day when her mother had gone out to buy the Sunday paper for him. "I know," Saleh replied. He was lying under the duvet, which covered the whole of his body. "Do you know that all my mother's boyfriends have been good looking?" She went on sharply. "I don't know what my mother's doing with you." "What's wrong with me?" Saleh asked her with a laugh. "You've got a neck like an ostrich and your skin's…" Before she could finish the sentence, her mother had entered the room and heard her last words. She shouted furiously at her: "Apologise to Saleh and then go to

346

your room immediately and shut the door behind you."

While she was supervising the game of hide and seek, Ramsi, Nadine's younger brother, had come and complained: "There are demons in that room. I'm never going in there again." His sister had shouted: "You're imagining things. You only get demons in cartoons." He dug his heels in and Nadine said: "I'll hide with you, OK?" but Helen stopped her: "Take him upstairs. There are lots of places to hide there." An image of Baida flashed through her mind. Had she really gone downstairs after rocking Lubna to sleep or was she ill again? "What about if we stay where we are and don't say a word for ten minutes?" she suggested to Nadine. "Perhaps we'll see the demons."

She had barely been able to believe her eyes when she saw the tall, thin figure of Saleh, tip toeing towards the stairs. She had no reason to suspect he had been with Baida. She was about to shout, 'boo', when the door to Lubna's room creaked open again and the word stuck in her throat. She and Nadine were standing in the dark, their eyes pressed against the narrow crack in the door, looking out onto the corridor, which was slightly lighter than where they were positioned. As soon as Saleh disappeared, Baida appeared in front of her. She looked like a real ghost, as she moved past, with her feet barely touching the ground. "Got you!" Helen shouted involuntarily from where she was standing.

* * *

Even though she had her own key and he was always telling her to use the flat whenever she wanted, Scheherazade still

347

felt uncomfortable, when she let herself into Saleh's flat. It was as if she were going into a forbidden world that she was not allowed to enter unless he were present.

Although it was only five days since she had last been there, it felt much longer. She wished she hadn't turned down Saleh's offer to spend the previous weekend with her. She had tried to meet up with some of her old friends and been surprised to find they had other things to do. She could have visited Hussein and his wife Barbara but didn't feel like seeing them.

She would like to have met up with one or other of her old lovers. But their admiring glances would have been insufficient to distract her from the anger, which still seethed inside her like a boiling cauldron whenever an image of Baida popped into her mind. It was as if she held her cousin solely responsible for the despair and loneliness she felt. Nonetheless, she fought back against the depression, which threatened to overwhelm her. This is London, she told herself. When you need your friends, they're nowhere to be found but when you no longer need them, they're at your beck and call.

She felt a strange aversion to the place that had formerly been such an oasis, and allowed her to escape the routine of her daily life. In the past , it had made her feel as if she were back at university, with no ties or obligations. Sometimes, she even forgot she had a child when she was surrounded by the fantasies Saleh regularly wove around her through his candles and music. When they met, it was as if they didn't have a past; they were happy to speak the vernacular of the city in which they had been born on different sides of the river, she in al-Rusafa and he in al-Karkh. Together they created a fantasia of the past. Saleh would tell her about the nightingales, he had taught to sing so beautifully that the radio station had recorded them to start its early morning broadcasts. For her part, she would tell him about the three lotus trees in the garden of the large family home, she had learnt to climb at an early age. The seeds of the lotus fruit were so large, she said, they were the size of water melons.

But now this flat was the domain of her beautiful cousin. How many times had she come here with Saleh? What did they say about her? Was she as quiet as ever? Scheherazade thought of Baida as she had seen her in the past, her eyes fearfully following Abdel as she watched his face contract in a frown, only recovering her normal demeanour when he relaxed. She was forever slipping away from their gatherings; when she stayed she had eyes only for her children and would watch their every move. Sometimes hours would go by without any one being aware of her presence. Suddenly someone would turn towards her but even while she was talking to them, she would keep an eye on Abdel to see whether he approved or not. Once she had asked Saleh what he thought of her. After a short silence, he'd said, "She epitomises motherhood." "And what else?" she'd asked. He had turned to her with a laugh: "She's your cousin, isn't she!"

In the bedroom, she opened the door to the wardrobe which she had always thought was where he kept his old things. She was surprised by its contents, which were nothing like she had imagined. Hundreds of files were neatly stacked on the three shelves. She drew one out and looked at the title on the front. It read Animals and plants of the Kalahari desert. Inside were articles and photos cut out from newspapers and magazines. The second file had a strange title: The hundred worst plagues in history. Another was entitled: Characteristics of a Piscean.

She couldn't see what was written on the files at the bottom of the wardrobe and had to squat down to reach them. She picked one out at random and was surprised to see the name Baida written on the cover.

She hesitated a little before opening it. She sat on the bed. She ran her fingers over the title. Should she open it or return it to its place? Would she be shocked by what it contained or relieved? Her curiosity intensified. Maybe it was just like all the others? An image of a large spider moving around in its thickly threaded web flitted through her mind. She drew out a number of other files, some of which had the names of people she knew on the front. But her suspicions weren't misplaced; she found a slightly larger file with her name on the cover.

She decided to open Baida's file first. She had an obscure feeling that its contents would have a decisive impact on everything around her. The world seemed like a labyrinth; the files, tools, which would enable her to make sense of it after it was broken down into its primary components, without their maker imagining that what he was holding were no more than fragments which were barely connected to the whole.

'What distinguishes Baida from Scheherazade is the way she relates to the outer world.' Her breath stuck in her throat as she read the lines. 'Baida's relationship is characterised by a total denial of the self, while Scheherazade's is the com-

350

plete opposite: she denies the world when it stops her pursuing her desires.'

In another passage, he had written: 'After saying goodbye to her, I found I was going in totally the wrong direction. It was as if I had become intoxicated by that kiss, which she so shyly gave me. Her moist lips were like the petals of a Damask rose.'

She turned to another page and glanced down at the final paragraph. 'Baida in her fragility, reminds me of an oyster. When she is with Abdel, she is stripped of her protective shell. Now, for the first time, she is with a man who recognises her right to keep on her armour; at our every meeting, she gives me a magical seed pearl from her mysterious secret world.'

She calmly tore out the pages from the file, and tossed them into the air, Inside, however, she was seething with anger.

A hope of a different kind stirred within her: She would forgive him if he had written something flattering about her body. She opened her own file. She felt as if it belonged to one of her patients.

'Our relationship is like a dervish dance. The dancer turns in the same way every time, expecting a miracle to happen though it never does. How can I explain this longing to her? When I am with her for more that twenty-four hours, I start to feel stifled. Is there something wrong with her or..'

Scheherazade did not take the trouble to read the next line. She was overcome by a deep depression, which made her feel as if she were watching someone, afflicted with an imaginary illness. Someone, talking about a woman who had nothing to do with her. The thought made her start to tear up the contents into little pieces.

Frightened that anything of the file should remain, she threw every scrap of paper she could find into the toilet bowl and pulled the chain. She noticed the ink run on some of the bits of paper before they were flushed away.

She felt relieved. As if she had managed to rid herself of a loathsome nightmare. Curiosity propelled her back to the wardrobe. Whenever she had teased him about what it contained, Saleh had always told her the same thing: "You're looking at Pandora's box."

A huge blue folder, equipped with an additional surround, fastened by two buttons, excited her interest. On the front page, she read the words, The Artist, written in large letters.

She remembered how Saleh had sometimes talked about his plan for a novel. These pages must form part of his treasure. How self-assured and animated he had seemed when he was asked about it.

She was gripped by a sudden feeling of powerful satisfaction. This book belonged to her as much as it did to Saleh. Whether he liked it or not, she had been the source of its inspiration. "Let him write something else, now that he's with..." but she was unable to utter her cousin's name, so great was the torment raging inside her.

She sat down on the floor and with as much care as if she were performing a religious rite, began to tear up the draft, page by page. Apart from the faint rasp of paper as she ripped the pages in two, there was no other sound.

Her desire to obliterate the years she had spent with Saleh was so strong that she was not even worried by the thought of him returning: I'll force him to do it in front of me, she thought.

She opened the drawer to the table beside Saleh's bed. She ran her fingers through the papers, photos and bits of foreign money. She paused at a small blue notebook. She opened the first page and saw a neatly written phrase: The Artist: Final Chapter. Underneath he had written in red ink: A possible ending.

She put the notebook on the bed and started to tear up all the photos she could find. She began with a photograph of herself, which Saleh had taken. As she looked at it, she was struck with the feeling that she was nothing but a naked organism placed under a huge microscope. She moved on to his other photographs, which for the most part had been taken in Iraq. Now she was filled with a desire to put an end to any thoughts Saleh might have about writing again. It was as if by tearing up these photographs of faraway places, she was cutting the umbilical chord, which fed his memories and imagination. "You'll have to remain a teacher," she said, and then added in a louder voice. "That's what you've been created for."

Before she left the flat, she went from room to room and overturned the furniture and broke the cups and plates by throwing them on to the wooden floor.

Before opening the front door, she looked back. When she saw the chaos, she was filled with a strange feeling of exultation. The room looked as if it had been struck by an earthquake. As she was closing the door behind her, she remembered the blue notebook. She went back to fetch it and put it in her handbag.

She would read it on the train home and then tear it up.

The sun seemed to have stopped moving. It had been beating down on the Artist's head for ages, making him feel as if the moment were frozen in an endless labyrinth of time. Through the car window, his eyes followed the line of the horizon sketched neatly above the flat land. Over there, not far away, he could make out a peasant astride a donkey, moving very slowly across the landscape. The rippling band of the glittering mirage only served to lighten the image. It was like something in a dream, interrupted only by the drone of helicopters, which ceaselessly circled over the long convoy of Mercedes cars.

He felt completely at ease with himself. Even now as he was perched on the edge of the abyss, his followers stood submissively beside him, awaiting his command. Everything was completely in order. In front of him, sat his driver; he sat behind, smoking one of the Leader's favourite brand of cigarettes. From his position in the middle of the convoy, he could direct his men in the other cars, using the wireless beside him. He pressed a button on the small control mechanism, which he held in his hands and heard a voice answer immediately:

"Yes, Sir."

"How are the negotiations going?"

"Excellently, Sir. I've conveyed everything you ordered me to say,"

"What did they say?"

"They asked us to wait while they informed the Leader."

"Did you tell them about our hostage?"

"Yes, Sir."

He turned to his right. Beside him was a small submachine gun. On the other side, a short distance away, sat a grossly obese man with a double chin, whose eyes were tightly bound by a strip of white cloth. "Do you want to smoke?" the Artist asked, without looking in his direction. After a brief silence, the other man asked, his voice shaking slightly: "How can I smoke when I'm tied up like this?" As he examined the strait jacket, which prevented him from moving, the Artist said: "I can loosen it a bit, if you want. It does seem very tight." The other man seemed to suspect he was joking for he merely sighed. The Artist said reassuringly: "There's no need to be frightened... You're a highly successful minister of defence; the country needs you. I never betray my friends." The other man paled. His jaw trembled slightly before he regained sufficient control of himself to speak. "I swear I didn't know what the Leader was planning for you. Where are we now?"

"We're near the border."

"Which border?"

"Guess!"

"You want to kill me... I've treated you like a son. I've always spoken highly of you."

"Don't worry. You're with me. I hate killing and loathe the sight of blood. I'm sure you're red-blooded."

Silence settled between them. The lower lip of the other man trembled and he started to sweat, beads of perspiration breaking out on his forehead, despite the air-conditioned coolness of the car.

Once again, the Artist asked himself the question that had been going round and round in his head ever since he realised that his plot to assassinate the Leader had failed. What other life would have given him as much pleasure as the one he had led inside the Fortress that he'd built with his own bare hands? Sometimes when the night was quiet and a pleasant breeze stirred the air, he would become frightened lest the people outside forget the terror that lurked behind its walls. He would give orders for loud speakers to broadcast the recorded screams of prisoners from the roof and the wind would carry the howls and entreaties across the land. People believed, or so his agents told him later, that the cries were made by prisoners who were already dead, prisoners who had lost their lives in the prison and were buried under its floors.

The all pervasive climate of fear meant that the Leader and his ministers enjoyed absolute security. In fact, even the people had benefited hugely from his efforts. As long as they didn't step out of line, they were also able to live without anxiety. He had co-opted the criminals who now played a useful role in society. The country was completely stable. There were no burglaries, murders, road accidents or fraud. The police and courts were almost superfluous. It was an Utopia, governed by fear. The fear acted like a virus. It penetrated the body's cells, but rather than harming them, protected them from its ills. The cost had been tiny, when the benefits to the population were taken into consideration. A mere two or three hundred lives…members of the opposition, who had chosen to resist the authorities. And he hadn't treated them like cattle, or left them to rot in the wilderness and be torn apart by birds of prey. No, every one of them had been given his own marble tombstone, a grave, planted about with flowers. In another ten years, the poplar, willow and pine saplings would have grown into proper trees, which would shade them from the harsh summer sun and thrushes and nightingales would serenade them with beautiful airs.

The Artist turned to his guest and studied his jowls, which seemed even heavier close up than in the documentaries he had seen. He was also surprised at the fiery colour of his face and the slightly flattened nose. Maybe he should have checked his origins before appointing him minister. He was probably descended from one of the Mongol hordes that had once invaded the homeland. Suddenly a bomb exploded, making the Minister of Defence's body jerk involuntarily.

"What's that?" he asked.

"It's nothing. Don't worry... Just a show of strength... They won't be able to break us."

"What's stopping them? The Leader won't lose any sleep over me."

"We've got someone who's much more important to him."

"Who? The Minister of the Interior?"

"No... We took him prisoner to stop the police moving."

"Then the Minister of Justice?"

"We wouldn't have considered an idiot like that. We've got the Mother of the People."

Silence fell, interrupted only by the faint, continuous drone of the helicopters, which they could still hear through the armour plating of the car, though it helped to deaden the sound.

"Do you know her?" the Artist asked him.

"No. But I've heard a lot about her. They say she's the only person who can stand up to the Leader."

"She's a great woman. She's been like a mother to me."

"Why don't you persuade her to mediate between the two of you?"

"It's too late for that."

Some of his aides had told him that she was responsible for the change in her son's attitude towards him. They said she had become infuriated after meeting the mother of one of his prisoners and learning what went on in the Fortress. She had summoned her son and given him a slap for letting his deputy, the Artist, do whatever he wanted with God's creatures.

He didn't believe the story; after all he had ringed her house with guards and did not allow anyone in to see her without his prior approval. It was a trick by his old friend. He realised he needed someone to blame as he tried to improve his image at home and abroad. There was no one better placed for the role than his deputy. The Artist's responsible for all this wickedness, he would say. I didn't know anything about his crimes.

Maybe he had spread the story about his mother in order to make him react in a certain way. The Leader didn't like things to end quietly. He liked high drama. Well, he was certainly giving him what he wanted. Had he ever imagined that his right hand man would kidnap his own mother? Especially as he was like her own son. You made me carry out this crime, he silently addressed the Leader. She was now in the second car to last with his deputy sitting beside her. He clicked the button on the control panel and heard a composed voice say:

"Yes, Sir."

"How's the Mother of the People?"

"She's very well, sir."

"Take good care of her and tell her that the crisis will soon be over."

He wanted to talk to her but was suddenly filled with a sense of unease, which made him sever the connection. The mere sound of her voice would be enough to upset him at a time when he needed all his wits about him. It was different with the Leader. He brought out the tiger in him. Made him long to tear the world apart to please him. But his mother made him feel like a child, who wanted nothing more than to be rocked to sleep. How many times had she done just that when he had hidden in her house, while working in the underground? He would never forget the hours she had spent beside him, when he had been suffering from a deadly fever. At regular intervals, she would dip a piece of cloth into a saucer filled with cold water, and then place it over his forehead, as her fingers stroked his curly hair with incomparable gentleness.

"What would you do if you were in my place?" he asked the Minister of Defence. "Can you take the blindfold off? I feel dizzy, the latter replied as if he could read what was going through his mind. Without commenting, the Artist reached out with his slender fingers and undid the two pins fastening the bandage.

His guest's eyes were bloodshot where the sweat had soaked into them through the blindfold, and he had some small scratches near his enormous ears. He wiped his eyes with the edge of the strait jacket, and then turned to the Artist and asked: "Do you want me to mediate between you and the Leader?" When the Artist said nothing, he tried again.

"Let's face it, you've been friends since childhood."

"How can you mediate?" the Artist asked in a tone of false naivety.

"Set me at liberty and you will see, your Excellency."

But the Artist ignored his suggestion. He raised the machine gun in his right hand, while keeping his eyes fastened on his guest. With his other hand, he pressed the switch operating the automatic window.

The hot air scorched him. The sun had moved a little way towards the west and its rays now fell directly on his stomach and lap. He moved the window up and down repeatedly. From his seat in front, the driver watched his boss in the mirror with a sense of trepidation as he tried to work out what was going on. Something 'exceptional' was about to happen, but he didn't know what.

"Can you play cassette number three, please," the Artist asked his driver, very politely. Two long, silent minutes passed before he located the cassette in the small compartment on the right.

An isolated burst of music as someone played the qanun for a couple of minutes was followed by another silence. : "Are you enjoying the music?" the Artist asked his guest pleasantly.

"Very much."

"I've got something for you now, which you'll enjoy even more."

But instead of music, the sound of men's voices, interspersed with the clatter of cups and glasses, filtered into the air. "The most effective way of starting afresh is by trying the Head of Security, Sir." The voice sounded loud and clear. After a short silence, another voice said, very drily: "Of course... But he has done a lot for the revolution."

The Artist shouted at his driver: "Stop the cassette." As he turned to his guest, the muscles of his face twitched involuntarily.

"Were you able to work out which voice was yours and which the Leader's? Is this how you reward me for raising you to the position of Defence Minister?"

"Sir, the Leader was playing a trick on me. Everything I said at that meeting had been agreed by him beforehand."

"Get out of the car."

The Minister of Defence fumbled with the door handle, like someone in a trance. It was as if he were unable to believe what was happening to him. "It was a trick, sir," he kept on repeating with trembling lips until three bullets pierced his skull, when his body was half out of the car, and caused the blood to spurt out in all directions.

The Artist shut the car door, and slapped his hands against each other as was his custom when he had completed some project or other to his liking. But satisfaction gave way to anger when he found two spots of blood on his carefully ironed white suit. One was on his left thigh and the other on the hem of the right sleeve of his jacket.

The red light on the control panel lit up; when he pressed the receiver button, he heard the voice of the man who was responsible for carrying out the negotiations. "Sir, the Leader wants to talk to you."

* * *

The urgent peal of the phone echoed through the flat, but Saleh ignored it, preferring instead to concentrate on the task in hand: he had gathered up the various bits of paper from his novel and after matching them with each other was now trying to glue the fragmented pages together. It had been relatively easy to sort out which pages belonged to the novel because he had chosen to write it on yellow paper in order to keep it distinct from his other jottings. But he soon encountered another problem which left him feel dismayed and hopeless. When he had finished arranging each page, he realised that there were still bits missing from the middle which meant that all he had to show for his efforts was a piece of paper that was full of holes and devoid of meaning. Had Scheherazade torn out the pages first and then carefully chosen which parts to destroy? There was no doubt that she had been absolutely determined to make it impossible for him to reconstruct the work, which had taken him ten years to put together. He was back where he started. If only she had left him a tiny fragment it might have allowed him to pick up the threads again.

He waded into the ghastly sea of papers searching for something that might be of use to him. When the phone rang again, he felt so numb that he was unable to get up from the floor to answer it.

He looked around him. He took in the chaos Scheherazade had left behind her and was struck by a peculiar sense of fear. A fear of going mad that had stalked him in the past in the guise of a clown. It would urge him to take leave of his senses. As he stood on the underground platform, waiting for a train to arrive, he would hear the clown calling out to him: "What are you waiting for? Throw yourself off. Nothing will happen to you. I'm with you." But he would quickly move far away from the platform edge. Now he wondered whether that moment when he had squeezed under Lubna's bed beside Baida had not in fact been a summons from the clown? He had only now discovered what dangers were lurking there among the children and felt alarmed. Had the hand that had drawn him there come from the rational world?

He was overcome with a deep sense of guilt: Had Baida been in her right mind when she squeezed his hand? Had he taken advantage of her in some way when he responded to her in the way he did?

He thought back to the one time they had come together on his bed. There had been a look of embarrassment in her defeated eyes, which had made her act contradictorily. While she abandoned herself to him physically, she mentally withdrew from him. He was captivated by her femininity, even more attracted to the fragile creature who had been compelled by the harsher hands of others to retreat deep into her shell. He should have left her longer to gather her thoughts. But when she put out her hand to him, he felt as if she were begging him to help her extract herself from the quagmire of her own weakness

She had given him the impression, with her stammering and lack of knowledge, that this was the first time she had made love in her life.

For his part, he had discovered a world, he had never

known before. When he was with her, the pulse beat of the world slowed and its elements dissolved until it was nothing but primordial matter in which objects had not yet been defined and made specific. Scheherazade nurtured a sense of power and mastery in him, but Baida, without meaning to, gave him a paradise of a different kind, one that could be described in a single word, solitude. It was as if her very presence provided him with a bridge that connected him to the far distant stars.

In the few hours, he had spent with Baida, he had been overwhelmed by a mysterious emotion. Was it fatherliness? When he was with Selma, he had been driven by childish impulses, which had made him flee from his weak and obsessively controlling mother to another woman who was also powerful and dominant. In London, he had met Scheherazade; she had also been a mother figure but one who was strong and compassionate. The child in him had been able to continue with his games, but had been free. In his relationship with Scheherazade, he had had his first experience of what it was like to be loved with generosity but without having to give up his inner freedom in return. But the child in him had wanted to grow up and become a father, with consequences that were now all too apparent. The chaos, which Scheherazade had left behind her, served as a reminder that the world of exile, which had been given a solidity through his relationship with her, was about to vanish as the morning mists vanish when the sun appears. But the clarity of everything about him only gave him a feeling of hopelessness. It was as if all those small secret pleasures, which had awoken inside him during the years they had spent together had now lost their meaning. Now he faced a reality, with which he had no connection at all.

As Saleh lay on the leather sofa, he was caught between two opposing forces that, like magnetic poles, were trying to exert their influence upon him; he was caught between Baida's weakness and Scheherazade's strength, between the abyss and the mountain top, between being a son and a father. When the telephone rang the next time, he thought it might be someone calling to ask him out.

The sound stopped, the moment he picked up the receiver. He waited, eagerly for it to ring again. He moved aimlessly round the flat. He went back to the phone. Involuntarily, he began to dial Scheherazade's number. The ringing tone evoked a contrary emotion in him. He replaced the receiver. Then he dialled Baida's number but put the phone down when he heard Abdel's voice on the other end of the line.

Ibn Arabi says that the word 'al-qalb' ('heart') is derived from the root taqallub meaning 'flux'. According to his version of things, the heart is in a constant state of flux, every moment different from the one before and the one after. In order to support his argument, he cites a sacred saying of the Prophet, which states: The hearts of all the children of Adam are like a single heart between two fingers of the All-Merciful. In contrast to al-'aql or reason, which is derived from al-'aqal meaning the cord hobbling or fettering a camel's feet, the heart belongs to a world, which responds according to how much pressure is applied to it by the Lord's fingers. In Saleh's case, this pressure is embodied in his fingers as they move between the two telephone numbers. They are like two incompatible magnetic poles, alternately and from one minute to the next, competing to gain possession of his heart.

He frantically started to clear up the mess in his flat by putting everything back where it belonged. He put the bits of broken glass in a heavy duty bag. In another, he put all the papers he had found scattered around the bedroom, sitting room, toilet and kitchen. Completely despairing of ever being able to write his novel again, he picked up the pages and pushed them into the bag.

While he was hoovering the sitting room floor, he noticed a piece of paper under the coffee table. As he carefully drew it out, his heart leaped. It was the final page of his novel which had somehow escaped Scheherazade's notice. Or maybe she had left it behind as a memento. Saleh clung to it as if it were made of gold. He would now be able to follow in the Artist's footsteps. Scheherazade was his Ariadne. This piece of paper provided him with the end of his piece of thread; now all he had to do was follow in the Minotaur's footsteps without fear of getting lost in the labyrinth.

* * *

Immediately he stepped outside the Mercedes, he knew he was embarking on an experience, which would end in death.

He was engulfed in the roar of the helicopters. About a hundred metres away, he could see one stirring up a storm of dust as it landed. Was the Leader on board? A thought occurred to him and he smiled: even now at the moment of surrender, he could still strike terror into his enemies. As he took a couple of steps forward, the soldiers hung back, too afraid to come forward. It was still blistering hot even though the sun was well down on the left and a searing wind stung his face. It was afternoon. He could tell by the length of his shadow, which stretched out beside him.

As the Artist expected, the Leader had been as hard as steel.

"All you can do is surrender," he had told him in a sharp voice over the wireless.

"What about your mother?"

"Kill her if you want. She's not only my mother."

"You're playing with my emotions."

"You've only got five minutes."

"What will you do after that?"

"Wipe your convoy out of existence."

His driver had observed the course of the negotiations with a remarkable indifference, though he had remained alert to his master's orders throughout the conversation. The Artist thought about killing himself. He would take the revolver and stick it into his mouth then press the trigger. Boom! It would all be over. But the idea filled him with distaste. The mere thought of how his driver would react were he to see his idol doing such a thing made him put the tempting thought out of his mind. Maybe he should ask him to get out of the car, instead, so that he could quickly put a bullet through that weak spot in his brain - his blind loyalty to the Leader and absolute trust in him?

A number of soldiers appeared, half hidden behind a small thicket. Should he walk towards them? Another helicopter landed at the other end of the field. He and the Leader had agreed on only the one point. After giving himself up, he would telephone his deputy and ask him to convey the following order to the rest of his men: Get out of your cars without your weapons. The Artist has concluded a deal with the Leader over your safety.

Once again, the question flashed through his mind: what had really made him get out of the car? He could have stayed inside until the Leader ordered the convoy to be bombed. Bullets and bombs were relatively painless ways to go. He would be dead before he felt anything. Now he had no cards left to play. He had left his machine gun on the car seat and as he walked forward, his men fell further and further behind. The Leader would be watching his progress with huge enjoyment, from where he was sitting in the big aeroplane. He thought about why he had changed his mind: why he had decided to wait to negotiate, instead of crossing the border quickly before the forces arrived. Had he been hoping to reach a deal over how he would die? He had an intimate knowledge of how the Leader's mind worked. He knew he would exact a terrible revenge on him, which would be more dreadful than anything he had done before. But it would have been worse to go to another country, where he would have been humiliated by the people in power. That was why he had immediately dismissed the idea. He should have made a stand in the capital and fought alongside his men to the last. That way he would have gone down in the history books as a tenacious fighter. He had told the Leader over the wireless, "I hope you will forgive my men. They were only carrying out my orders." After a short silence, his lifelong friend had said, "We'll think about it." Perhaps the

Leader had been surprised by the compassion he was showing to his former victims: "Will you promise to keep the
graveyard, I built in the Fortress and bury me in it?" he'd
asked politely. This time, the Leader's response had been
just as vague: "Everything's possible."

Overhead, the noise of helicopters grew louder. The soldiers began to advance cautiously on all sides. He suppressed a laugh at the sight of their battle helmets. He understood now why he had laid down his cards and accepted
every one of the Leader's conditions. He wanted to be tortured just like his prisoners had been tortured. The thought
overwhelmed him. How much pain would his body be able
to endure? Certainly more than the Leader who has never lived an experience like this. His men had tortured for
the sake of extracting information, but the Leader would be
torturing him for the sake of revenge: he was the embodi-
ment of revenge. There was no one like him in the whole
world. Would he cut off his arms and legs and disembow-
el him while he watched? Anything was possible with the
Leader. Overcoming the limitations of the body was the way
to sainthood; to the devil; to the divine. A final thought echoed through his mind. Keep the Fortress, he would tell the
Leader. It will be your talisman and protect your rule. I will
continue to serve you even when I lie surrounded by my
victims. We will all support you. The Fortress and graveyard
will send shivers of fear down your subjects' spines. I will
not tell him the truth: that in my graveyard I will be fighting
alongside its inhabitants to build another world, which will
be protected by other laws: and in which the sheep and the
wolves will live side by side.

The number of guards increases. They become more daring; press in on him on all sides; their faces become blurred as sweat drips into his eyes and his dark glasses fall to the ground. An image of Haya flashes through his mind and he is filled with a strange rush of joy. He finds himself laughing hysterically as strong hands take hold of his elegant body and prevent him from turning one more time to see the last vestiges of his power, the unmoving convoy of Mercedes cars drawn up only a few metres away.

* * *

When she emerged from the underground station, she was surprised to find how quickly darkness had fallen. The hands on her watch pointed to five past four. The sky seemed to hang more heavily than when she had last seen it. Maybe it was the thick clouds and the light steadily falling drizzle, which she could only make out with difficulty that made it seem like that.

Where should she go now? She had spent the day moving from train to train and from station to station. She'd followed the recorded announcements, as she waited on the platforms, and stepped back to avoid the gap between herself and the carriage doors. Hands seemed to push her towards the electrified rails and she had drawn back as far as she could go till she was left clinging to the tunnel wall. She remembered the story Hussein, the surgeon, had told about the woman who was killed by an underground train. She felt unable to breathe and left the station in search of fresh air.

It seemed ages since she had left the house and locked the door behind her. What were her children doing? They must be home by now. She could imagine what was happening. Their father would have just fetched them from school and they would be looking around for their mother. Where's Mama? Lubna would ask. Abdel would quell her with an angry glance, making her cower away in fear. The twins would be perfectly quiet as they waited for their mother to return and their father to leave the house for a little. Why hadn't she taken her children with her? The thought filled her with remorse. Why had she written that letter of supplication. She could have told him: I'm going to Baghdad with the children. Would he have agreed? She ought to have stood up to him if only the one time.

Instead, she got out at the underground station that was closest to the house and caught the bus, which passed near by the house. When it reached the stop where she should have got off, she was unable to move and the bus drove on. Everything seemed near and far away at the same time. Could she have lived in that house for all these years and then completely severed her ties with it by shutting the door behind her? When the bus returned along the same route, she summoned up her courage: "I'll get down and go home," she told herself, rehearsing what she would say. "I want to buy plane tickets for me and the children. Can you pay for them?" No, she'd put it another way. "Can you lend me the money?" Or maybe one word would be enough: "Divorce. I want a divorce." When she spoke the word out loud, her body trembled. She could imagine her mother and sisters crowding round her: "Have you thought what this will do to the reputation of the family? Have you thought about us?" If only her father were alive to support her. She would have drawn strength from the look of sympathy in his eyes and been able to face the others. The bus passed her house. It doesn't matter, I'll come back in a while, she said to herself. I'll be stronger next time.

She went to a telephone box. She dialled Saleh's number. The phone rang repeatedly without a reply. This was the seventh time she had phoned him. He must have gone to Scheherazade's. Should she phone him there? Her face broke into a wide smile which she could see reflected in the glass side of the telephone booth. It was as if she were saying to her cousin: I'm like you. Immediately afterwards, she was seized by a contrary emotion. She would ring and ask her forgiveness. "I need a small sum of money and I will send it to you immediately once I arrive in Baghdad." Or she would begin by saying: "I'm sorry…It was because I was ill. You're a doctor. You'll understand."

As she meandered bemusedly around the city, she twice found herself near Scheherazade's house, but on both occasions, her heartbeats quickened and she felt unable to breathe when she tried to cross the road towards it. She only recovered when she removed herself from the vicinity. At that instant, she suddenly she remembered the first time she had met Saleh at Scheherazade's.

He had seemed very introverted. From time to time, Scheherazade said something to bring him out of himself. "Do you know that Baida and Abdel come from al-Karkh as well?" "Is that true? Whereabouts?" His face brightened when her husband said: "We were living near by. Perhaps we went to the same school." Her cousin hurriedly turned towards her. "Baida's family left the district when she was seven." "I was five," she corrected her, her voice faltering slightly. "Oh, that's a big difference," Scheherazade said, with barely concealed amusement. "I remember the last time I went to visit them there with my mother before they moved. We took a photo on the roof, didn't we?" "Yes, a large number of relatives came to say goodbye to us," Baida said. Saleh said, "Many of those alleyways no longer exist." "That's what always happens," said Scheherazade in an attempt to stop the conversation from getting too serious and keep it light hearted. "Life in the alleyways belongs to the middle ages. We're in the twentieth century now."

Her eye was caught by the huge illuminated advertisements. She was in Piccadilly Circus surrounded by a group of French tourists. She could go one of three ways: south to Scheherazade's, north to Saleh's, or west to her home. No, to Abdel's house. She didn't have a home; or money or a family. She thought of the beggar she had seen sitting outside King's Cross station.

He had had a dog curled up beside him, whose face bore the same expression as its master's, pathos mingled with a touch of pride. It was as if he were saying to the passers-by: I will make you feel better in yourselves by letting you leave a coin in this plastic saucer. He repeated monotonously: "Any spare change."

Selim loved dogs. His eyes would light up with surprise whenever he saw the boxer that lived next door. Maybe their neighbour's kindly way with children had something to do with her pet's good nature. The species seemed to have

373

been created for its interest in children. If only her husband had agreed to her request for a dog! She had phrased it as a question: "What do you think about getting a dog like our neighbours' for the children? Selim would really love it." But Abdel had snapped with that cutting edge to his tone, which made her blood boil. "Have you any idea how much vet's bills are, and that's without counting the cost of the food? You know, we're not millionaires."

If there had been a dog like a boxer with Selim, then he would not have fallen out of the window. But who had opened it and dared him to jump? He had never once put his hand on the window catch. Was it the twins? Or Abdel? What was the use of knowing the truth? Guilt at having abandoned her son weighed down on her. He had felt frightened enough of his father and the twins to continue to cling on to her. Despite that, she had not seen anything wrong in leaving him with them and going shopping.

A question flashed across her mind: Had Abdel sold Selim's organs before throwing him out of the window? But she thrust the thought out of her mind immediately. Instead she conjured up an image of Rocky, the neighbours' dog. Whenever it saw Selim, it would run over to him and start to lick his face. Despite its huge mouth and nostrils, her son had not been scared of him.

She turned on her heel and started to walk back to the underground station. Before descending the stairs, she took out the rubber boxer dog from her bag, which emitted a funny squeak whenever it was pressed. It had been Selim's favourite toy. His lopsided eyes would gleam at the noise and he would imitate the funny bark. If they let him have a dog like Rocky in Paradise, it would help to calm him. Do animals have their own Paradise? They only act the way they do because they've been made that way. They play tricks just to satisfy their stomachs. When they've fulfilled that objective, they return to being their friendly selves. They bear no evil, no revenge, no hatred. There is nothing unpredictable about them. If it weren't for hunger, the monkey, the sheep and the wolf would live peacefully side by side. Maybe there is a special Paradise for them, she concluded. But she would still ask God to allow Selim to have a Boxer.

She was drawn by the rapid, rhythmic beat of a drum. In a short passage, she glimpsed a black musician bent over his instrument. Her feet moved towards the platform and she began to drag herself through the crowds of passengers. The noise reached her clearly after dissolving into its primary elements, transforming itself into sonic vibrations, which faded and grew louder around her.

Before the train moved away, she noticed an old man and young child, through the window. They were standing on the platform. The old man was holding the child gently by its hand. For a second, she had the strange idea that they were pointing at her. As she looked at their images, caught between the reflections of light in the glass, and the jumble of other faces, they seemed to resemble her father and son. In contrast to the other passengers, they looked blissfully happy, their faces exuding a radiant joy. She emerged from her reverie as the train plunged into a dark tunnel and saw nothing but her own face, reflected in the window opposite. To her surprise, no one was sitting in the seat beside her, although the carriage was crammed full of passengers. She noticed some of them glancing in her direction. From time to time, they would lift their eyes towards her then once more bury themselves in what they were reading. She got to her feet again, stepped off the train. She walked along several tunnels before reaching another platform. She found that she'd left her bag somewhere and had nothing in her hand except Selim's toy dog.

Before she left the hospital, the psychiatrist had told her: Don't hold back. Learn to say what you want. He had really been saying something else, which she hadn't understood until now. If you want to contact me secretly then I can arrange that. I want you. But she had chosen to keep silent. He had corrected himself in a half playful tone, as if realising that he had revealed more than he should have done: You must avoid going through anything too emotional. She had wanted to ask him how she could do that, but instead had merely nodded her head.

She was overcome with a storm of longing to see her three children again. Her feet carried her out of the station. Instead of the familiar streets, she found herself surrounded by desolate houses and roads, she had never seen before. The street lamps threw a ghostly yellow light onto the pavements, heightening her sense of loneliness. Was it a nightmare? But the tall, bare London trees, and the heavily falling rain convinced her it was real.

She felt warm once she entered the station again. She noticed several people looking at her in astonishment, and became aware that her hair and clothes were drenched. Scheherazade and Abdel might agree to send her back to hospital. The doctor would gloat. She had rejected him be-

376

fore. This time would be different though. She'd be naked. They would all see her. Maybe Saleh would say that he had only been humouring her in case her illness returned. Why was everyone staring at her? Were her wet clothes transparent? Could they read what was going through her mind?

As she went down the escalator, she was invaded by two contradictory emotions. She longed for Selim and felt an aversion to her other children. Hadn't they continuously tormented him when he was alive? Her dream would come true: she would see Selim on the platform from her place on the train. This time however, she would get off and grab him.

When the train set off, she scrutinised each station carefully before it moved on. Then she came back down to earth. This time she was overcome with a rush of love for Lubna and the twins, and hurriedly got off the train.

Baida continued to move through her endless labyrinth, flitting between her three children and her dead son, between a world deep under the surface of the earth and another above it, between dark and light, between cold and warmth, between reality and fantasy.

Even as the muscles of her body began to sag, she still kept a firm hold on Selim's toy, squeezing it from time to time so as to hear the sound it made, which had always made Selim break out into peals of laughter.

Part Twelve
The Divine Names II

More than a week went by as he waited for an answer to the question that had been troubling him for the last seven days, namely whether animals were resurrected in the afterlife. Instead, he was haunted by images of Nizam, who had died in Baghdad the previous year. She would take shape before him, as modestly dressed as she had always been,, her head covered by the same silk shawl she had worn in the past, which left her face exposed. Despite the darkness in the iwan, he could still make out the dimples in her glowing cheeks. It was as if time had stood still since that first time he had met her after their conversation in the Kaaba. She had appeared before him when Sheikh al-Asfahani had taken him, as he always did, to the little orchard, which was right beside his house. She was reading a book among the Damask roses, pacing slowly back and forth along the short path, hedged with myrtle bushes. When she became aware of them, she stopped. Her father asked with a laugh: "Is this the woman who debated with you at the Kaaba?" Her face flushed crimson red. "She does that with everyone... Her aunt, my friends, the sheikhs, me. If anyone ever says anything, she starts arguing with them immediately and leaves them speechless." She shrank back without a word, biting her lower lip, like a naughty child, and looked away from him, while her fingers gently caressed each other over the leather cover of her book. She seemed much younger than the woman he had seen as he circumambulated the Kaaba, and he felt almost fatherly towards her. She retreated even further into silence, when her father said proudly: "She's reading Diwan al- Hammasah. She has memorised more than half of it by heart… She has a formidable memory."

And now here she was before him once again. For a moment, he believed that she was really there. They would sip from love's chalice and engage in sweet revivifying conversation, as they had done once a week in the past. She would recite Arabic and Persian poetry, she had learned by heart, while he would resort to the old odes about lovers standing beside abandoned encampments, which were all he could remember. The matchless poem by Malik bin al-Rib came to his mind with its famous opening:

Oh how I wish I could spend the night…

He recalled how they had taken it in turns to extemporise verses, using the same meter and rhyme as the ode. Sometimes she would recite the sadr, the first hemstitch of the line, which he would follow with the 'ajz, the second, or they would reverse the roles. For example, she would say, "You doves, of Arak and Ban" and he would reply, "Be kind to me and don't aggravate my sadness with your cooing." When it was his turn to set out the first hemstitch, he would say, looking meaningfully at her, while a nightingale serenaded the stream behind him, "Oh what a wonderful thing is a veiled gazelle," she would reply joyfully, looking boldly into his eyes, as she tried to read what images were going through his mind: "hinting with a jujube fruit and winking with an eyelid."

Only now did he realise how illusory the experienced moment was. We are nothing but the unadulterated shadows of the Divine Essence: The entities of possibilities are clad in the vestments of existence and put into the world of visible things for a while but they leave no trace behind them.

During his time in Damascus, Muhyiddin Ibn 'Arabi had been given the ability to attract souls to him, by clothing them in imaginary images: all he had to do was concentrate on the name of the person he was seeking and wish for them; then the other would materialise and meet him in the barzakh, the isthmus between the world of spirits and the world of man. Similarly he could conjure up minute particulars from the far distant past, although he was unable to recapture the feelings they had once aroused in him. It was as if they were lost forever. This was what made his longing for Sheikh al-Asfahani's house seem like a bottomless well.

When he left Mecca for Anatolia, he thought that everything would remain unchanged while he was away. But on returning from his travels, he learned that Sheikh al-Asfahani had died and that Nizam and her aunt had gone to Baghdad. Later he heard that after the latter's death, her niece had joined a house for pious women, who had decided to remain celibate.

When he went to Baghdad, he longed to visit the house, which was in al-Halba district. But his steps faltered, as he drew near it, as if it had been ordained by a divine decree that he should avoid meeting her.

*　*　*

A number of his students visited him afternoon prayer. They sat in front of him on the thick Persian carpet, propping their backs against the wall. Some of them talked about the situation in Damascus: the spread of hunger, the rise in prices and the growing number of people, who were being killed while defending the city walls. "This is the worst siege Damascus has ever been through," one of them said. Another fixed his eyes on Muhyiddin as if seeking an explanation. "How is it possible for an uncle to wage war on his nephew while at the same time handing Jerusalem over to the Franks without a struggle?" he asked. "How can al-Kamel have changed so much? He was once a stubborn warrior, who fought to defend the honour of Islam. Now he has betrayed the most sacred thing the Moslems possess?"

Muhyiddin said nothing. His eyes acquired a fixed smile which convinced some of his guests that he was in the throes of ecstasy. Was he about to utter a new illumination? They became impatient to hear what he would say next. In fact, he was trying to recall a dream, he had had the night before that had burst upon him like a flash of lightening.

"All these disputes are caused by rivalries among the Divine Names," he said, in a brittle voice as if reading from an open book. "What is the Avenger, the Harsh Punisher and the Conqueror when compared with the Merciful, the Forgiving and the Gentle, for the Avenger seeks revenge against the person, who is being avenged, while the Merciful seeks forgiveness from his avengers. Each one views the matter in accordance with his own true nature. If there is to be authority, there will certainly be controversy. Whoever looks at the Divine Names will believe in Divine Strife. Conflict in the world comes about as the various names compete over created beings and pull them in different directions."

He thought of the vision he had had the day before when

he had gone into a total trance: The Knower, the Speaker, the One Who Wills and the Powerful had all appeared in front of him. They were holding a dark gelatinous being that looked like one of the possibilities. All of a sudden, it slipped out of their grasp and escaped to the stars, whose glittering light poured forth in all directions. Gradually, as the heavy clouds began to glow and fill with thunder and lightening, fighting broke out in the newly born world of sensory perception that was worse than anything the Divine Names had seen before. A voice arose from a group of bodies, which had split away from the others because of the conflict between them. "We will return to non-existence if you continue fighting with each other like this. Is there no one among you who can draw up a boundary between us, which will allow us to maintain our existence, and allow you to continue to impress us?" From far away, two beings gleaming with sapphire light, approached, saying in an assured tone: "We may be able to do that." One of them said, "I am the Arranger and this is the Applier. We are under the Lord's command. He has appointed us as his ministers and it is our job to put such principles in place as will protect and develop the kingdom."

*   *   *

At first he'd thought it was Nizam again. But his guest emitted such a great light that he began to think that he was in the presence of another extraordinary being.

He sat in front of him, clothed in golden raiment that looked like nothing Muhyiddin had ever seen before. The light reflected from the courtyard dissolved in front of his eyes, and created a space between him and his visitor, which was filled with striking colours. He tried to steal a brief glance at him but his eyes were veiled as if by a gleaming cloud. He covered them and tried to recall the image through his imagination. A young man appeared before him, soaked through with beauty. The radiant smile, which lit up his face, filled him with a sense of peace, the like of which he had never experienced before.

His son, Sa'ad ed-Din, came in carrying a plate of food. He moved forward cautiously, as was his custom, and placed it in front of his father before leaving the iwan. When Muhyiddin was about to eat, the guest spoke for the first time in a voice that carried a hint of reproof: "Are you going to eat while I'm here?"

He knew that this being, whom he had never seen before in his life, had assumed an image created for it through his imagination. In a flash, he recalled the sacred saying: On the Day of Judgement, Allah manifests himself to creation in an undefinable image, for He says, "I am your Lord, the most high", and they say, "we seek God's protection from you," and He manifests himself according to what they believe in so they prostrate themselves in worship."

He found himself irresistibly drawn towards him: it was as if a magnetic force were pulling him towards the other until he fused with him completely. He was overcome by a violent sense of joy, as if he had been rewarded for everything he had ever worked for in his life. The Beloved was present for the first time in a most resplendent image. His voice reverberated around him. "Do you still think about her?"

"My Lord, I have no other beloved but you."

The guest whispered: "I sent Nizam to you so that she could initiate you into the ways of love. She was a stage on your journey to me."

"But I am not free of her."

* * *

He spent the next three days, pondering a puzzle of another kind. If the Lord hadn't wanted his servant to fall in love with another human being, why had he planted the seeds of love in his soul?

But Muhyiddin believed that every aspect of the Divine Names found form in man's nature. The world was like a mirror, in which the Lord could see his attributes reflected, and man was its polisher. Without the Lord, man would have no existence, and without man, the Lord would be unable to view himself through the world, which he had created.

Does this lead to the Divine Jealousy of loving anyone except Him? Or is the beloved, God himself, concealed within such famous beauties as Zeinab, Layla, Suad and Hind? once man falls into the trap, he discovers that the imaginary image of the beloved, which he carries within himself, is much greater than the beloved really is. He immediately starts to feel restless. He begins searching for someone else who will match the image of the beloved. But it is a world of mirages; every time we draw near the illusive water, we find we have further to go before we reach it.

Was not his situation with Nizam like that of Qais and

Layla? He thought of Qais, lying on his back and calling out: "Layla, Layla!" as he put handfuls of ice on his chest to be melted by his burning heart. Suddenly Layla appeared: "I'm here, I'm the one, you've been asking for, I am your beloved; I am the delight of your eye; I am Layla." But he pushed her away: "Get away from me! You're distracting me from thinking about you with your declarations of love."

He recalled something that Sheikh al-'Uraybi in Andalusia, had said to him: "Oh God, give me a lust for love, rather than love." When a man yearns for he knows not what, when he loses his appetite, cannot sleep and becomes emaciated and upset then he is suffering from the affliction, which Muhyiddin describes in a single verse, which he wrote after returning to Mecca from Anatolia: My love for you has wasted me. I am as wraith-like as an imaginary dot.

That day his first revelation came to him: the breath of creation lay hidden in womankind. During the difficult days that followed, he had frequent recourse to a saying of the Prophet, which he had scarcely attended to before then: "two things of your world were made lovely to me, perfume and women; and the coolness of my eyes is in prayer."

Compelled by his unquenched ardour for Nizam, he agreed to marry the young widow of his Sheikh. At the beginning, Muhyiddin asked for her hand reluctantly, only doing so to carry out Sheikh Sudkin's wish that his young son, Sadruddin, would have someone to take care of him. With Zainab, however, he discovered that love making could become a spiritual act; when lust permeates all parts of the body, so man aspires to be totally annihilated by his partner, without realising that the motive behind that the longing of the part to be annihilated in the whole, and the longing of of the whole to reclaim the part.

In Mecca, he received that revelation despite his age – he was forty five at the time – completely changed the way he thought about relationships between men and women. Love is a divine stage. In the act of making love, when body is joined to body, the hidden power of existence is made manifest and the Lord's love is made known: " I was a hidden treasure and I wanted to be known so I created the world and through it I was known." In the two opposing roles of male and female (the actor and the one who is acted upon), the knowing servant discovers the secret of creation. It is like the way the Lord opens up images in the natural world.

* * *

Immediately he opened his eyes, the following morning, he knew that something had changed. The house was silent apart from the trickle of water coming from the fountain; the brusque voices, which had sounded continuously over the last couple of weeks, had disappeared. Even his students had a more relaxed air about them when they came to see him. "The siege is over," one of them said. "Al-Nasr has surrendered to his uncle." He seemed to be waiting for his sheikh to say something, but Muhyiddin remained silent. A curious smile played about his lips, which made the others look at his pale face expectantly. "Al-Kamel did not avenge himself on his nephew. In fact I've heard that he's given him a princedom in Jordan." There were gasps of surprise as he recounted how the new ruler had given gifts to the poor and taken the wounded to the hospitals, instead of treating the members of his family, who had rebelled against him, as enemies.

Muhyiddin thought of what he'd seen when Antakia was conquered. When he entered the city with the Seljuk king, Kaikawas, there had been dead and wounded Byzantines lying in the streets. As smoke billowed out on all sides, he could hear the weeping and wailing of women and children. Prisoners were led away by the victorious soldiers, shackled together in chains.

The Divine Names were manifesting themselves throughout the city: the Humiliator and the Bestower of Honour, the Creator of the Harmful and The Creator of Good; the Taker of Life and the Giver of Life.

A sheikh, who had escaped the English king after the fall of Acre, told him how they had tied the women and children together with ropes, before Richard ordered his soldiers to put them to the sword.

As if he could read what was going through his mind, one of the assembly called out in a loud voice: How do you explain the holy verse of the Qur'an from Surat Sad, which says: "I had no knowledge of the High Council when they were disputing?"

But Muhyiddin had sunk into an even deeper silence, which infected those around him, so that they too fell silent. He mulled over whether to answer the murid's question or not. Should he spoil this splendid day by giving him an answer now or leave it till later? And what should he tell him? That the peace that had only just descended on Damascus was only transitory and would not last? That the dispute between the Divine Names, which lay behind it all, not only affected the visible world but the invisible one as well? The highest throng, the world of the angels was governed by the same principle, though to a lesser extent since blood, darkness, punishments, pain and oppression did not exist there as they did in our world. What would he say if one of his other students asked him what lay behind the dispute? Would he tell him that the whole problem was caused by rivalry between the Divine Names and that this lay at the root of all other problems in existence. So how far is The Creator of The Harmful from The Creator of Good, The Bestower of Honours from The Humiliator, The Constrictor from The Reliever, How different is light from darkness, non-existence from existence, fire from water, bile from phlegm, movement from stillness, servitude from divinity?

When he opened his eyes, he could see five planes in front of him, ranked one on top of the other. Written on the front of the highest were the words: The realm of the Divine Essence; this was followed by the realm of Reason, then the realm of the Spirits, then the realm of Ideals. The lowest plane was engraved with the following: The world of the Senses. He could hear a loud noise coming from there, which gradually faded away completely as it reached the highest plane, notably, the realm of the Essence.

The room took shape again. He smiled at the aspirants who were waiting for a word from him: "Conflict in the world comes about as the various names compete over created beings and pull them in different directions," he said. When he was met by a profound silence, he hurriedly lightened the atmosphere: "Let's go to the Ummayad Mosque."

* * *

The good news finally reached him. He saw the Prophet in his white robe, his face, radiant with light, coming to him when he was half asleep. Without Muhyiddin saying a word, the other answered the question that had been plaguing him ever since the start of the siege of Damascus.

When he woke up from his sleep he could recall the exact words the Prophet had spoken, without uttering a sound: Animals have no other life apart from this.

But he immediately regretted that he had not asked him about the children who had been killed. Were they to be considered possibilities that had been given existence which was then taken away from them before their minds matured and their personalities shaped up? Was there a special Paradise for them and another for the insane? Where was the logic in all that, when man was the manifestation of the only mirror in the world in which the Lord could see his own image?

Do these two categories (namely the children and the insane) exemplify a regression of the Possibilities of Existing and a return to the world of forms from which they had come, whereas the Divine Names keep realising their substances through man, generation after generation? It was as if all humankind's continuing creativities a continuing revelation of some attributes of the Real; on the other hand the growing of harm, oppression and cruelty generation after generation reveals the gradual realisation of other Divine Names.

A question flashed through his mind like a bolt of lightening, for which he immediately sought forgiveness from the bottom of his heart. If the Possibilities had known in advance how Divine Names would be determined in them, when they were transported to the visible world, would they have urged the latter to alter them from a potential existence to real one; in other words, applications rather than hypotheses.

And now I find myself asking if I would have allowed these possibilities, namely Abdel and Baida and the rest, to come into existence if I had known in advance what would happen to them?

I can see the child Selim standing at the window in his room. He is watching a cat, cautiously make its way along the garden fence towards a thrush. The bird is too busy singing to notice it. Should he jump out of the window and catch it? When he tries to speak, the words disintegrate and he lets out a strangled screech instead. It is really this that makes him leap out of the window.

His brothers, the twins stand behind him and watch what he is doing. I don't know for sure whether they have previously agreed to take the catch off the window. Or whether it was his father, Abdel? May be it was Baida? But she forgot all about it after the accident happened.